5w

BEAST MASTER'S PLANET

TOR BOOKS BY ANDRE NORTON

BEAST MASTER'S PLANET

A Beast Master Omnibus

Andre Norton

A TOM DOHERTY ASSOCIATES BOOK

New York

TOR®

This is a work of fiction. All the characters and events portrayed in these novels are either fictitious or are used fictitiously.

BEAST MASTER'S PLANET

Omnibus copyright © 2005 by Andre Norton

The Beast Master copyright © 1959 by Andre Norton
Lord of Thunder copyright © 1962 by Andre Norton

All rights reserved, including the right to reproduce this book, or portions thereof, in any form.

This book is printed on acid-free paper.

Edited by James Frenkel

A Tor Book
Published by Tom Doherty Associates, LLC
175 Fifth Avenue
New York, NY 10010

www.tor.com

Tor® is a registered trademark of Tom Doherty Associates, LLC.

Library of Congress Cataloging-in-Publication Data

Norton, Andre.
    [Beast master]
    Beast master's planet : an omnibus of Beast master and Lord of Thunder / Andre Norton.—1st ed.
       p. cm.
    "A Tom Doherty Associates book."
    Contents: The beast master—Lord of Thunder.
    ISBN 0-765-31327-8
    EAN 978-0765-31327-0

    1. Storm, Hosteen (Fictitious character)—Fiction. 2. Human-animal communication—Fiction. 3. Life on other planets—fiction. 4. Circus performers—Fiction. 5. Space colonies—Fiction. I. Norton, Andre. Lord of Thunder. II. Title.

PS3527.O632B4 2005
813'.52—dc22

2004065930

First Edition: May 2005

Printed in the United States of America

0 9 8 7 6 5 4 3 2 1

For

OTIS LOUIS ERNST

Soldier

Engineer

Collector of Indian Lore

1914–1958

CONTENTS

PUBLISHER'S NOTE

The Beast Master was first published in 1959. Miss Norton, having already established a reputation for exciting science fiction adventure in dozens of novels, was known to readers of all ages as one of the most dependably entertaining authors in the field.

Hosteen Storm, the Navajo hero of *The Beast Master*, was immediately a popular hero. The combination of military experience and Native American traditions gave him a background virtually unique in the annals of SF. Combined with Storm's special ability to communicate telepathically with the animals of his beast master team, he remains, more than forty years later, a most appealing and intriguing character.

Living on the colonized but still largely untamed and mysterious planet Arzor, Storm has his hands full with issues that most adventure novels don't often treat. He brings with him the pain and anguish of having experienced a war that ultimately destroyed his home—Terra, the longtime science-fictional name for Earth. And he bears the emotional scars of personal tragedy, a burden passed down from his family. His adventure and his emotional baggage are inextricably entwined, their mutual resolution essential to the successful conclusion of the story. He also has plenty of flat-out action—on horseback, like a range-rider in the American West, but also involving more sophisticated vehicles and equipment appropriate to a frontier light-years from Earth.

This is vintage Andre Norton—straightforward on the surface, but with hidden layers of meaning and theme that enrich the novel without slowing it down.

Lord of Thunder, first published in 1962, continues Storm's story, allowing readers to learn more about the mysteries of Arzor and the aliens who, uncounted ages before, created mysterious machineries that confound both the human colonists and their native aboriginal allies.

New adventures have, in the past few years, been written by Miss Norton and Lyn McConchie, about Hosteen Storm and his unique animal cohort. These two original novels are the rock on which those newer novels are based. Rich in alien color and the sense of wonder of all good science fiction, these first two novels of Hosteen Storm are published together for the first time in this omnibus edition.

They have stood the test of time, and remain as exciting and fresh as when first published. Welcome to the excitement of the future!

THE BEAST MASTER

CHAPTER ONE

S ir, there is a transport leaving for that sector tomorrow. My papers are in order, are they not? I think I have all the necessary permits and endorsements—"

The young man who wore the green of a Galactic Commando, with the striking addition of a snarling lion's mask on the breast of his tunic, smiled with gentle detachment at the Commander.

That officer sighed inwardly. Why did they always dump these cases on *his* desk? He was a conscientious man, and now he was a troubled one. A fourth-generation Sirian colonist and a cosmopolite of mixed races by birth, he secretly believed that no one had fathomed this youngster—not even the psych-medics who had given the boy clearance. The Commander shuffled the papers and glanced down again at the top one, though he did not have to read the information on it, knowing it all by heart.

"Hosteen Storm. Rank: Beast Master. Race: Amerindian. Native planet: Terra of Sol—"

It was that concluding entry that made all the difference. The last desperate thrust of the Xik invaders had left Terra, the mother planet of the Confederacy, a deadly blue, radioactive cinder, and those here at the Separation Center had to deal with veterans of the forces now homeless—

All the land grants on other worlds, the assistance of every other planet in the Confederacy, would not wipe from the minds of these men the memory of a murdered people, the reality of their own broken lives. Some had gone mad here at the Center, turning in frantic rage on their allies from the colonial worlds. Or they had used their own deadly weapons on themselves and their fellows. Finally every

Terran outfit had been forcibly disarmed. The Commander had witnessed some terrible and some heartbreaking sights here during the past months.

Of course Storm was a special case—as if they weren't *all* special cases. There had been only a handful of his kind. Less than fifty, the Commander understood, had qualified for the duty this young man had performed. And of that fifty very few had survived. That combination of unusual traits of mind that produced a true Beast Master was rare, and they had been expendable men in the last frenzied months before the spectacular collapse of the Xik invaders.

"My papers, sir." Again that reminder, delivered in the same gentle voice.

But the Commander dared not let himself be rushed. Storm had never shown any signs of violence—even when they had taken the chance, as a test, of giving him the package from Terra that had been delivered too late at his base after he had departed for his last mission. In fact, the youngster had cooperated in every way with the personnel of the Center, helping with others the medics believed could be saved. He had insisted upon retaining his animals. But that had caused no difficulty. The staff had watched him closely for months, prepared for some paralyzing stroke of delayed shock—for the outburst they were sure *must* come. But now the medics had reluctantly agreed they could not deny Storm's release.

Amerindian, pure blood. Maybe they *were* different, better able to stand up to such a blow. But in the Commander's mind a nagging little doubt festered. The boy was too controlled. Suppose they did let him go and there was a bad smash, involving others, later? Suppose—suppose—

"You have chosen to be repatriated on Arzor, I see." He made conversation, not wanting to dismiss the other.

"Survey records, sir, state that Arzor possesses a climate similar to my native country. The principal occupation is frawn herding. I have been assured by settlement officers that, as a qualified Beast Master, I may safely count on employment there—"

A simple, logical, and satisfactory answer. Why didn't he like it? The Commander sighed again. A hunch—he couldn't refuse this

Terran his papers just on a hunch. But his hand moved slowly as he pushed the travel permit into the stamper before him. Storm took the slip from him and stood up, smiling aloofly—a smile the Commander was certain neither reached nor warmed his dark eyes.

"Thank you for your assistance, sir. I assure you it is appreciated." The Terran sketched a salute and left. And the Commander shook his head, still unconvinced that he had done the right thing.

Storm did not pause outside the building. He had been very confident of getting that exit stamp, so confident he had made his preparations in advance. His kit was already in the loading area of the transport. There remained his team, his true companions who did not probe, with the kindest of motives, or try to analyze his actions. It was enough that he was with them, and with them only was he able to feel normal again, not a specimen under clinical observation.

Hosteen Storm of the Dineh—the People, though men of a lighter shade of skin had given another name to his kinsmen, Navajo. They had been horsemen, artists in metal and wool, singers and desert dwellers, with a strong bond tying them to the barren but brightly colored land in which they had once roamed as nomad hunters, herders, and raiders.

The Terran exile shut away that memory as he came into the storehouse that had been assigned to him for his small, odd command. Storm closed the door, and there was a new alertness in his face.

"Saaaa—" That hiss, which was also a summons, was answered eagerly.

A flapping of wings and talons, which could tear flesh into bloody ribbons, closed on his padded left shoulder as the African Black Eagle that was scouting "eyes" for Sabotage Group Number Four came to rest, sleek head lowered to draw its beak in swift, slight caress along Storm's brown cheek.

Paws caught at his breeches as a snorting pair of small warm bodies swarmed up him, treating his body like a tree. Those claws, which uncovered and disrupted enemy installations, caught in the tough fabric of his uniform as he clasped the meerkats in his arms.

Baku, Ho, and Hing—and last of all—Surra. The eagle was majesty and winged might, great-hearted and regal as her falcon tendencies dictated. The meerkats were merry clowns, good-humored thieves who loved company. But Surra—Surra was an empress who drew homage as her due.

Generations before, her breed had been small, yellow-furred sprites in the sandy wastes of the big deserts. Shy cats, with hairy paws, which kept them from sinking into the soft sand of their hunting grounds, with pricked fox ears and fox-sharp faces, possessing the abnormal hearing that was their greatest gift, almost unknown to mankind, they had lived their hidden lives.

But when the Beast Service had been created—first to provide exploration teams for newly discovered worlds, where the instincts of once wild creatures were a greater aid to mankind than any machine of his own devising—Surra's ancestors had been studied, crossbred with other types, developed into something far different from their desert roving kin. Surra's color was still sand-yellow, her muzzle and ears foxlike, her paws fur sand-shoes. But she was four times the size of her remote fore-fathers, as large as a puma, and her intelligence was higher even than those who had bred her guessed. Now Storm laid his hand on her head, a caress she graciously permitted.

To the spectator the ex-Commando might be standing impassively, the meerkats clinging to him, his hand resting lightly on Surra's round skull, the eagle quiet on his shoulder. But an awareness, which was unuttered, unheard speech, linked him with animals and bird. The breadth of that communication could not be assessed outside a "team," but it forged them into a harmonious whole, which was a weapon if need be, a companionship always.

Baku raised her wide wings, moved restlessly to utter a small croak of protest. She disliked a cage and submitted to such confinement only when it was forced upon her. The thought Storm had given them of more ship travel displeased her. He hastened to supply a mental picture of the world awaiting them—mountains and valleys filled with the freedom of the true wilderness—all he had learned from the records here.

Baku's wings folded neatly once again. The meerkats chirruped happily to one another. As long as they were with the others, they did not care. Surra took longer to consider. *She* must wear collar and leash, restraints that could bring her to stubborn resistance. But perhaps

Storm's mind-picture promised even more to her than it had to Baku. She padded across the room, to return holding the hated collar in her mouth, dragging its chain behind her.

"Yat-ta-hay—" Storm spoke softly as always, the sound of the old speech hardly more than a whisper. "Yat-ta-hay—very, very good!"

The troop ferry on which they shipped out was returning regiments, outfits, squads to several different home planets. That war, which had ended in defeat for the Xik invaders, had exhausted the Confederacy to a kind of weary emptiness, and men were on their way back to worlds that lay under yellow, blue, and red suns firm in the determination to court peace.

As Storm strapped himself down on his bunk for the take-off, awaiting the familiar squeeze, he heard Surra growl softly from her pad and turned his head to meet her yellow gaze. His mouth relaxed in a smile that this time did reach and warm his eyes.

"Not yet, runner on the sand!" He used again that tongue that now and forever hereafter must be a dead language. "We shall once more point the arrow, set up the prayer sticks, call upon the Old Ones and the Faraway Gods—not yet do we leave the war trail!"

Deep in his eyes, naked now that there was no one but the big cat to see, was the thing the Sirian Commander had sensed in him. The galaxy might lie at peace, but Hosteen Storm moved on to combat once again.

There was a company of Arzoran men on board, third- and fourth-generation descendants of off-world settlers. And Storm listened to the babble of their excited talk, filing away all the information that might be useful in the future. They were frontiersmen, these fighters from a three-quarter wilderness world. Their planet produced one product for export—frawns. Frawn meat and frawn-skin fabric, which had the sheen of fine silk and the water-repellent quality of ancient vegetable rubber, were making modest fortunes for the Arzor men.

The frawns moved in herds across the plains; their shimmering blue, heavily wooled foreparts and curving horned heads sloping sharply back to slender, almost naked hindquarters gave them a top-heavy look, which was deceitful since the frawn was well able to protect itself. There was no meat elsewhere in the galaxy to compare with frawn steak, no fabric to match that woven from their hair.

"I've two hundred squares cut out down on the Vakind—running straight back to the hills. Get me a crew of riders and we'll—" The fair-haired man Storm knew as Ransford held forth eagerly.

His bunk mate nodded. "Get Norbies. You don't lose any young stock with them riding herd. They'll take their pay in horses. Quade uses Norbies whenever he can get them—"

"Don't know about that," cut in a third of the Arzoran veterans. "I'd rather have regular riders. Norbies aren't like us—"

But Storm lost the thread of the conversation in the sudden excitement of his own thoughts. Quade was not a common name. In all his life he had only heard it once.

"Don't tell me you believe that blather about Norbies being hostile!" The second speaker had challenged the third sharply. "Me and m' brother always sign Norbies for the roundup, and we run the tightest outfit near the Peaks! Two of 'em are better at roundin' herd than any dozen riders I can sign up at the Crossin'. And I'll name names right out if you want me to—"

Ransford grinned. "Climb down off your spoutin' post, Dort. We all know how you Lancins feel about Norbies. And I'll agree with you about their bein' good trackers. But there has been trouble with stock disappearin'—as well you know."

"Sure. But nobody ever proved that Norbies made them disappear. Push anyone around and he'll try to loosen your teeth for you! Treat a Norbie decent and square, and he's the best backin' you can get in the outcountry. The Mountain Butchers aren't Norbies—"

"Mountain Butchers are herd thieves, aren't they?" Storm asked, hoping to steer the conversation back to Quade.

"That they are," Ransford returned pleasantly. "Say, you're the Beast Master who's signed up for settlement, aren't you? Well, if all the stories we've heard about your kind of trainin' are the straight goods, you'll be able to light and tie right off. Mountain Butchers are a problem in the back country. Start a stampede in the right stretch of land, and they can peel off enough young stock durin' it to set up in business. A man and his crew can't cover every bit of the range. That is why it pays to hire Norbies, they know the trails and the broken lands—"

"Where do the Mountain Butchers sell their stolen goods?" Storm asked.

Ransford frowned. "That's something every owner and rider, every frawn-protection man on the planet would like to know. There's just one space port, and nothin' passes through that without being checked double, sidewise and across. Unless there's some hidden port out in the hills and a freebooter runnin' cargo out— why, you've as good a guess as I have as to what they want the animals for. But they raid—"

"Or Norbies raid and then yell about outlaws when we ask pointed questions," the third Arzoran commented sourly.

Lancin bristled. "That isn't so, Balvin! Don't Quade hire Norbies—and the Basin country swings along by Brad Quade. He and his folks has held that district since First Ship time and they *know* Norbies! It'd take an eruption of the Limpiro Range to make Quade change his mind—"

Storm's gaze dropped to his own hands resting on the mess table— those brown, thin hands with the thread of an old scar across the back of the left one. They had not moved, nor could any of the three men sitting with him see that sudden change in his eyes. He had the answer he wanted. Brad Quade—this man of importance—whom he had come so far to meet. Brad Quade who had a blood debt to pay to other men on a world where life did not and could not exist, a debt Storm had come to collect. He had sworn an oath as a small and wondering boy, standing before a man of power and knowledge beyond that of other races calling themselves "civilized." A war had intervened, he had fought in it, and then he had journeyed halfway across the galaxy—

"Yat-ta-hay—" But he did not say that aloud. "Very, very good."

Immigration and custom inspection were only a formality for one with Storm's papers, though the Terran was an object of interest to the officers at the space port as he loosed his animals and Baku. Beast Team tales had been so exaggerated across deep space that Storm believed none of the port personnel would have been surprised if Surra had answered in human speech or Baku waved a stun ray in one taloned foot.

Men on Arzor went armed, though the lethal blaster and the needler were both outlawed. A stun ray rod hung from all adult male belts and private differences were settled speedily with those, or with one's fists—a custom Storm could understand. But the straggle of plasta-crete buildings about the space port was not the Arzor he wanted. The arch of sky overhead, with the tinge of mauve to give it an un-Terran shade, and the wind that swept down from the distant rust-red ripples of mountains hinted of the freedom he desired.

Surra held her head into that wind, her eyes slitted, and Baku's wings lifted a little at its promise. Then Storm halted, his head snapped around, his nostrils dilated as Surra's could. The scent borne on that wind—he was pulled by it, so strongly that he did not try to resist.

Frawn herds ranged widely, and men, who perhaps on the other worlds of their first origin had depended upon machines for transportation, found that the herder here must be otherwise equipped. Machines required expert tending, supply parts that had to be imported at astronomical prices from off-world. But there remained a self-perpetuating piece of equipment that the emigrants to the stars had long known at home, used, discarded for daily service, but preserved because of sentiment and love for sheer grace and beauty—the horse. And horses, imported experimentally, found the plains of Arzor a natural home. In three generations of man-time, they had spread wide, changing the whole economy of both settler and native.

The Dineh had lived by the horse and with the horse for centuries, back into the dim past. Love and need for the horse was bred into them. And the smell of horse now drew Storm as it had when as a child of three he had been tossed onto the back of a steady old mare to take his first riding lesson.

The mounts he found milling about in the space port corral were not like the small tough pony of his native desert land. These were larger, oddly marked in color—either spotted regularly with red or black spots on white or gray coats and with contrasting dark manes, or in solid dark colors with light manes and tails—strikingly different from the animals he had ridden in the past.

At the shrug of the Terran's shoulder Baku took wing, to perch on the limb of a tree, a black blot amid the yellow foliage, while Surra and the meerkats settled down at the foot of the bulbous trunk, allowing Storm to reach the corral fence alone.

"Nice bunch, eh?" The man standing there pushed up his wide-brimmed, low-crowned hat, plaited from native reed straw, and grinned in open friendliness at the Terran. "Brought 'em in from Cardol four-five days ago. Got their land legs back now and I can road 'em on tomorrow. They ought to make fellas set up and take notice at the auction—"

"Auction?" Storm's attention was more than three-quarters claimed by a young stallion trotting around, his tail flicking, his dancing hoofs signaling his delight in his freedom to move. His sleek coat was a light gray, spotted with rich red dots coin-sized and coin-round, bright on the hindquarters, fading toward the barrel and chest, with his mane and tail copying that same warm color.

The Terran did not, in his absorption with the horse, note the long glance with which the settler measured him in return. Storm's green uniform might not be known on Arzor—Commandos furnished a very minor portion of the Confed forces—and he probably wore the only lion mask badge in this part of the galaxy. But that searching examination assessed more than his clothing.

"This is breeding stock, stranger. We have to import new strains from other planets where they shipped horses earlier. There won't be any more of the pure Terran breed to buy now. So this bunch will be driven down to Irrawady Crossin' for the big spring auction—"

"Irrawady Crossing? That's in the Basin country, isn't it?"

"You hit it, stranger. Plannin' to light and tie on some range, or take up your own squares?"

"Light and tie, I guess. Any chance of a herd job?"

"You must be a veteran, come in on that troopship, eh? But I'd say you're off-world, too. Can you ride?"

"I'm Terran." Storm's answer fell into a sudden silence. In the corral a horse squealed and reared, and the ex-Commando continued to watch the red and gray stallion. "Yes, I can ride. My people raised horses. And I am a Beast Master—"

"That so?" drawled the other. "Prove you can ride, boy, and you've signed yourself on with my outfit. I'm Put Larkin; this here's my own string. You take your pay in mounts and get your workin' horse into the bargain."

Storm was already climbing the rail wall of the corral. He was more eager than he had been for over a year. Larkin caught at his arm.

"Hey, those aren't gentled any—"

Storm laughed. "No? But I must prove I'm worth my pay." He swung around to watch the stallion he had marked in his heart for his own.

CHAPTER TWO

Reaching down, Storm jerked at the fastening of the corral gate just as the young horse approached that point. The red and gray mount came trotting out without realizing for an important second or two that he was now free.

With a speed that left Larkin blinking, the Terran leaped down beside the hesitant horse. His hands were fast in the red mane, drawing the startled animal's head down and around toward him. Then he breathed into the stallion's expanded nostrils, keeping his grip in spite of an attempted rear.

The horse stood shivering when Storm loosed his first hold, to run his hands slowly along the arching neck, up the broad nose, cupping them over the wide eyes for an instant, coming down again to smooth body, legs, barrel. So that at last every inch of the young horse had experienced that steady stroking pressure of the gentling brown hands.

"Got a length of rope?" Storm asked quietly. Larkin was not his sole audience now, and the horse trader took a coil of stout hide twist from one of the other spectators, tossed it to the Beast Master.

The Terran looped it about the horse just behind the front legs. Then in what looked like a single, swift movement he was mounted, his knees braced under the loop, his hands resting lightly on the mane. The stallion shivered again under the grip of the rider's legs, neighed a protest.

"Look out!" At Storm's warning the stallion whirled, plunged away into the open with a bound that did not dislodge his rider. The Terran leaned forward so that the coarse hairs of the mane whipped into his face. He was crooning the old, old words that had tied horses and his race together for the countless years of the past, letting the mount race out his fear and surprise.

At last, when the space port lay behind as a scattering of white beads on the red-yellow earth of this land, the Terran used pressure of his knee, the calm authority of his mind, the gentle touch of hand, the encouragement of voice, to slacken the pace, to turn the now trotting horse back to the corral.

But Storm did not halt by the knot of waiting men, heading instead for the globular trunked tree where his team lazed. The stallion, catching the alien and frightening scent of cat, tried to shy. But Storm spoke soothingly. Surra got to her feet and strolled forward, her leash trailing across the beaten earth. When the stallion would have attacked, the Terran applied knee pressure, the murmur of voice, the weight of mental command, as he had learned to control the team.

So it was the cat that raised forepaws from the ground, sitting well up on her haunches so that those yellow slits of eyes were not far below the level of the foam-flecked muzzle. The stallion's head tossed restlessly and then he quieted. Storm laughed.

"Do you hire me?" he called to Larkin.

The horse trader stared his wonder. "Boy, you can sign on as breaker any time you've a mind to stack your saddle in my camp! If I hadn't seen this with my own eyes I'd have said some harsh things about double-tongued liars! That there animal's your trail horse, if you want to fork him all the way to the Crossin'. And what are these here?"

"Baku, African Black Eagle." The bird mantled at the sound of her name, her proud fierce eyes on Larkin. "Ho and Hing—meerkats—" That clownish pair sniffed high with their pointed noses. "And Surra—a dune cat—all Terran."

"Cats and horses don't rightly mix—"

"So? Yet you have seen these two meet," countered Storm. "Surra is no wild hunter, she is well trained, and as a scout also."

"All right," Larkin was grinning. "You're the Beast Master, son, I'll take your word for it. We hit the trail this afternoon. Got your kit?"

"I'll have it." Storm rode the stallion back to the corral to turn him in with the rest of the herd.

The trail herd was compactly organized by a man who knew his business. Storm had high standards, but he approved of what he saw some two hours later when he joined the party. Ransford and Lancin accompanied him from the veterans' muster-out, willing to hire on as riders for the sheer pleasure of plunging at once into their normal routine of life. Joining with the Terran they bought a small two-wheeled cart for their kit, one that could be hooked on to the herd supply wagon. And when that was packed the meerkats climbed to the top for a ride, while Baku and Surra could be carried or range as they wished.

Storm accepted Lancin's advice in shopping for his own trail equipment, following the veteran's purchases at the space port stores. At the last he changed into the yoris-hide breeches, lined with frawn fabric, tough as metal on the outside and almost as durable as steel, worn with high boots of the same stuff in double thickness. A frawn shirt of undyed silver-blue took the place of his snug green tunic, and he left the lacings on the breast untied in imitation of his companions' informal fashion, enjoying the freedom of the new soft wear.

Before he left the Center he had obediently exchanged the deadly blaster of service issue for a permitted stun ray rod and the hunting knife of the frontiersman. And now as he settled the broad-brimmed hat of local vintage on his thick black hair and looked into the mirror of the dressing room, Storm was startled at the transformation clothes alone could make. He had further proof of that a short time later when he joined Larkin unrecognized.

Storm smiled. "I'm your breaker—remember?"

Larkin chuckled. "Boy, you look like you were born center-square down in the Basin! This all your kit? No saddle?"

"No saddle." The light pad he had contrived, the simple headstall, were his own devices. And no one who had watched his taming of the stallion questioned his choices when he again bestrode the red and gray horse for the ride out.

On Arzor, galactic civilization was an oasis built around the space port. As they left that cluster of structures behind and moved south into the haze of the late afternoon, Storm filled his lungs thankfully, his eyes on that range of mountains beyond. There was a flap of wings and Baku spiraled up into the mauve sky, tasting in her turn the freedom of the new world, while Surra lay at ease on the cart and yawned, lazing away the hours before the coming of night, her own special time for exploring.

The road swiftly became a track of earth-beaten hard stone, but Storm knew that Larkin intended to cut across the open lands, making use of the quickly growing wet-season grass for the herd. This was spring and the tough yellow-green vegetation was still tender and thick. In three months more or less the mountain-born rivers would dry up, the lush grass carpet would wither, and trail herds must cease to move until the coming of fall produced a second wet period to revive the land for another short space of a few weeks.

When they camped that night Larkin appointed guards, with a changing schedule, in four-hour shifts.

"Why guards?" Storm questioned Ransford.

"Might not be needed this close to where the law runs," the veteran agreed. "But Put wants to get his schedule working before we do hit the wilds. This herd's good stock, worth a lot in the Basin. Let the Butchers stampede us and they could gather up a lot of the loose runners. And, in spite of what Dort Lancin says, there're a lot of Norbie clans who don't care too much about *working* for their pay in horses. Outer fringe tribes raid to get fresh blood to build up their studs. Breeding stock such as this will bring them sniffing around in a hurry. Then there are yoris—horse is tasty meat as far as those brutes are concerned and a yoris kills more than just its dinner when it gets excited. Let that big lizard stink reach a horse and he high tails it as fast as he can pick up those hoofs and set 'em down!"

Surra aroused from her nap, stretched cat fashion, and then came to Storm. He hunkered down to meet her eye to eye, in his mind outlining the dangers to be watched for. She was already familiar, he knew, with the scent of every man in the herding crew, and with every horse, either ridden or running free. Whatever or whoever did not belong about camp during the hours of the night would have Surra's curiosity to reckon with. Ransford watched her pad away after her briefing.

"You put her on patrol too?"

"Yes. I don't think any yoris can beat Surra. Saaaa—" He hissed the rallying call and Ho and Hing tumbled into the firelight, climbing over his legs to rear against his chest and pat him lovingly.

"What are they good for?" Ransford asked. "They wear pretty big claws, but they're small to be fighters—"

Storm fondled the gray heads with their bandit masks of black about the alert eyes. "These were our saboteurs," he replied. "They dig with those claws and uncover things other people would like to keep buried. Brought a lot of interesting trophies back to base, too. They're born thieves, drag all sorts of loot to their dens. You can imagine what they did to delicate enemy installations in the field—"

Ransford whistled. "So that's what happened when the power for those posts on Saltair failed and our boys were able to cut their way in! Say—you ought to take them up to the Sealed Caves. Maybe they could get you in there and you'd be able to claim the government reward—"

"Sealed Caves?" At the Center, Storm had learned what he could of Arzor, but this was something that had not appeared on the Emigrant Agency's record tapes.

"They're one of the tall tales of the mountains," Ransford supplied. "You ought to hear Quade talk about them. He knows a lot about the Norbies, went through the drink-blood ceremony with one of their big chiefs. So they told him about the caves. Seems that either the Norbies were more civilized once—or else we weren't the first off-worlders to find Arzor. The natives say there are cities, or what used to be cities, back in the mountains. And that the 'old people' who built them went inside these caves and walled up the doors behind them. The big brains down at Galwadi got excited about it one year—sent in some expeditions. But the water is scarce up there, and then the war blew up and stopped all that sort of thing. But they posted a reward for the fella who finds them. Forty full squares of land and four years import privileges free." Ransford wriggled down into his blankets and pillowed his head on his saddle. "Dream about it, kid, while you're riding herd circle."

Storm deposited the meerkats on his own blanket roll where they crept under cover. Baku, one leg drawn up into her under-feathers in the bird of prey's favorite sleeping position, was perched on the rim of the baggage cart. He knew that both the animals and the bird would remain quiet unless he summoned them to action.

The stallion that he had named Rain-On-Dust because of its markings was too untried for night herding. So the Terran pad-saddled a well-broken mount Larkin had assigned him as second string. He rode into the dark without any uneasiness. For the past years the night had provided him with a protective shield too many times for him to worry now.

Storm was close to the end of his tour of guard duty when he caught Surra's silent alarm—that swift mind flicker, cutting as keenly as her claws. There was trouble shaping to the northeast. But what—or who—?

He turned his mount in that direction, to hear a squall of cat rage. Surra was giving tongue in open warning now, and Storm caught an answering shout from the camp. He snatched his night beam from the loops on his belt, flashed it on full strength ahead of him, and caught in its path a glimpse of a serpentine scaled head poised to strike. A yoris!

The horse under him plunged, fought against his control, screaming in terror as the musky scent of the giant lizard reached them and the harsh hissing of the yoris hurt their ears. Storm gave attention to his own coming battle, having little fear for Surra. The dune cat was a good and wary fighter, used to strange surprises on alien worlds.

But with all his skill Storm could not force the horse to approach the scaled menace. So he jumped free, into the taint of reptile reek, borne downwind, wafting on to the herd beyond, where hoofs pounded hard on the earth. The loose horses were stampeding.

That part of Storm's mind that was not occupied with the action at hand, speculated on the oddity of this attack. From all accounts the yoris was a wary stalker, a clever wily hunter. Why had the creature headed in tonight with the wind to carry its scent ahead to frighten the meat it hungered for? There was no yoris hatched that could match speed with a panic-stricken horse, and the lizard had to depend upon a surprise attack to kill.

Now, cornered and furious, the scaled creature squatted back upon its haunches, its fearsomely taloned forelegs pumping like machine pistons in its efforts to seize Surra. If the enraged eight-foot reptile was brute strength at bay, the cat was fluid attack, teasing, tempting, always just a fraction out of reach. Storm whistled an urgent call to pierce the hissing of the lizard.

He did not have long to wait. Baku must already have been roused by the clamor. Though the night was not the eagle's favorite hunting time, she came now to deliver the "kill" stroke of her breed. Talons, which were sickle-shaped, needle-sharp daggers, struck at scales while wings beat about the eyes of the yoris. The lizard flung up its head trying to snap at the eagle, exposing for just the needed instant the soft underthroat. Storm fired a full charge of his stun rod at that target. Meant to shock the nerves and render the victim momentarily unconscious, the impact of a full clip on the throat of the yoris was like the swift sure jerk of a hangman's noose. It choked, beat the air with struggling forefeet, and collapsed.

Storm, knife in hand, leaped forward, moved by the battle reflexes drilled into him. Viscid blood spurted across his hand as he made certain that particular yoris would never hunt again.

Though the yoris was dead, it had lived long enough to bring the orderly herd close to disaster. Had the attack occurred when they were deeper into the wastes, Larkin would have had little chance of retrieving many of the horses. But, though the stampede carried the animals into the wilderness, the mounts were fresh off the space transports and not yet wholly acclimated, so the riders had hopes of rounding them up, though to do so they must now lose valuable days of travel time.

It was almost noon on the morning after the stampede that Larkin rode up to the supply wagon, his face gaunt, his eyes very tired.

"Dort!" He hailed the veteran who had come in just before him. "I've heard there's a Norbie hunting camp down on the Talarp. Some of their trackers could give us twice as much range now." He slid down from his overridden mount and stalked stiff-legged to the wagon to eat. "You talk finger-speech. Suppose you ride over and locate them. Tell the clan chief I'll pay a stud out of the bunch for his help—or a couple of yearling mares." He sighed and drank thirstily from the mug the cook handed him.

"How many did you boys bring in this morning?" he added.

Storm gestured toward the improvised corral they had thrown up to hold the strays as they were driven back.

"Seven. And maybe we'll have to break a few of them for riding if the rest don't find more of the regular stock. The few we have can't take all this work—"

"I know!" Larkin snapped irritably. "You wouldn't believe those four-footed idiots could run so fast and so far, would you?"

"I could—if they were deliberately driven." The Terran awaited the results of that verbal bomb.

While both men stared at him, he continued. "That yoris attacked with the wind at its back—"

Dort Lancin expelled his breath in an affirmative grunt. "The kid's got a point there, Put! You could almost believe that lizard *wanted* to mess us up like this."

Larkin's eyes were hard, his mouth a thin, unsmiling line. "If I believed that—!" His hand went to the grip of his stun rod.

Dort laughed angrily. "Who you goin' to put to sleep, Put? If some guy planned this deal, he's out there combing the breaks for strays right now, not standing around to wait for you to catch up with him. You'd never set eye on his trail—"

"No, but the Norbies could. Storm, you're green and from off-world, but you've a head on your shoulders. You ride with Dort. If you find any more strays, pick 'em up. Maybe that educated cat of yours can hold 'em for you in some cutback. If there was any funny stuff behind that yoris attack, I want a Norbie scout nosin' around to uncover it."

Surra could match the pace of the tired horses as they headed toward the distant river bottoms. And Baku rode the air currents above, a fourth and far-searching pair of eyes. By all rights the eagle should locate the native camp first. Storm knew that was true when the black wings spread in a glide and Baku perched on a rock outcrop, her dark plumage very visible against the red of the stone. Having so attracted the Terran's attention, she took off again, leading them more to the southeast.

The horses, scenting water, quickened pace, winding through a thicket of pallid "puff" bushes where the cottony bolls of weird blossoms hung like fur muffs on the leafless branches. Surra, her coat hardly to be distinguished from the normal shade of the alien grass, trotted ahead, sending into the air in terrified leaps some of the odd rodent inhabitants of that limited world.

Dort suddenly drew rein, his hand flung up in warning, so that Storm obeyed his lead. Surra was belly flat and hidden in the grass and Baku came earthward, uttering a sharp, imperative call.

"I take it we're sighted?" suggested Storm quietly.

"We are. But we won't see a Norbie unless he wants it that way," Dort returned. "Yaaaah—" he called, dropping his reins on the horse's neck and raising his hands, palm out.

A physical peculiarity of Norbie throat structure prevented any vocal speech that could either be understood or imitated by the off-world settlers. But there was a well-developed form of communication and Dort employed it now. His fingers moved swiftly, though Storm could hardly separate the signs he made. But his message was understood, for a shadow detached itself from the trunk of a tree and stood out, giving Storm his first sight of a native apart from a tri-dee picture.

The Terran had pored over all the films concerning Arzor at the Center. They had been exact and colorful, meant to entice settlers to the frontier world. But there is a vast difference between even a cleverly focused and very lifelike tri-dee and the real thing.

This Norbie was tall by Terran standards, very close to seven feet, looming over Storm himself by close to a full twelve inches. And he was exceedingly lean for his height, with two arms, two legs, regular, even handsome humanoid features, a skin of reddish-yellow not far removed from the shade of Arzoran earth. But there was the one distinctive physical attribute that always centered off-world attention to the forehead at a first meeting between Norbie and alien visitor—the horns! Ivory white, they were about six inches long, curling up and back over the hairless dome of the skull.

Storm tried to keep his eyes from those horns, to concentrate instead on Dort's flying fingers. He must learn finger-talk himself as soon as he could. Then, baffled, he turned his attention to the native's dress and weapons.

A wide band of yoris hide was shaped into a corselet, which

covered the Norbie's trunk from armpit to crotch, split at the sides over the curve of the hip to allow free leg movement. The legs in turn were covered with high-legginged boots not unlike those worn as a protection against the thorn shrubs by the settlers. The corselet was doubled in thickness at the waist by another strip of scaled hide serving as a belt, supporting several pocket pouches decorated with designs made by small red, gold, and blue beads, and the ornamented sheath of a knife close to a sword in length, while in his six-digit hands the hunter carried a weapon Storm already knew. It was longer than any Terran bow he had seen, but it was a bow.

Dress, armor, and ornament were combined in one last article of apparel, a wide collar extending to shoulder point on either side, and almost to the waist in front, fashioned entirely of polished yoris fangs. If those had all been taken by this one Norbie, with only a bow and a knife as weapons, then the hunter would have to be respected in any company of fighting men in the galaxy!

Dort dropped his hands to his saddle horn as the native signed a reply. Then he stiffened as the Norbie set arrow shaft to bowstring with a speed that startled the Terran.

"Look out for your cat!"

Storm hissed Surra's call. She arose out of the masking grass and came to him, the arrow trained upon her unrelentingly. Dort was trying frantic sign-talk. But Storm had his own method of reassurance. Swinging from the saddle pad, the Terran motioned and Surra moved closer, rubbing with feline affection against his legs. Storm went down on one knee and the cat set her forepaws on his shoulders, touching her nose lightly to his cheek.

CHAPTER THREE

torm heard a bird-trill and glanced up to meet the astonished yellow eyes of the Norbie, their vertical pupils expanding visibly. The native spoke again in his thin, sharp twitter, a surprising sound to come from the throat of that large body as his fingers flicked a question at Dort.

"Call in that eagle of yours, too, if you can, Storm. You're makin' a big impression and that can be good for us—"

The Terran scratched Surra under the jaw and behind the ears and then stood up. Spreading his feet a little apart and tensing his shoulder for the shock of Baku's landing weight, he whistled.

Wide wings beat the air as Baku dropped in a series of spectacular turns. But when those powerful talons gripped Storm's shoulder they did not pierce flesh. Under the merciless beams of the Arzor noon sun the blue-black plumage had a metallic sheen, and the patch of bright yellow feathers about the cruel blue-gray curve of the beak stood out as if freshly daubed with paint.

"Saaaa—" The Terran's warning alerted both cat and bird. Feathered head and furred one moved to his signal, and two pairs of predatory, glittering eyes regarded the Norbie with intelligent interest.

"That's done it!" Dort was relieved. "But keep 'em under control when we go into the camp."

Storm nodded, staring at the spot where the native had stood only seconds earlier. The Terran prided himself on his own scoutcraft and ability to become a part of the landscape, but this Norbie was better than the best he had ever seen.

"Camp's down on the river bank." Dort came out of the saddle. "We walk in. Also—" He drew his stun rod from its holster and fired the ready charge into the air. "You don't enter with a loaded rod, it's not considered manners—"

Once more Storm followed the settler's direction. Baku took off into the sky and Surra paced a yard or so before them, the tip of her tail twitching now and then to betray her interest in her surroundings. There was the scent of strange cooking and stranger living smells, as well as small sounds, coming up slope.

A Norbie camp was not pitched on formal lines. Lengths of kalma wood, easily shaped when wet and iron stiff when dried, had been bent by each householder to form the framework for a hemisphere tent. The hides stretched over that frame were piebald mixtures patched together from the fruits of the individual family's hunting. Blues of frawn pelts were joined by clever lacing to the silver-yellow scales of young yoris skins, banded in turn with the red fur of river rodents. The largest tent had a complete border about its base and door flap of jewel-bright bird skins set in a pattern of vivid color.

Storm could see no women as they came down to the cluster of tents. But before each of the dwellings stood Norbie males, young and old, each armed. The scout who had met them on the trail was waiting at the flap of the bird-trimmed lodge.

As if unaware of the silent audience, the off-world men threaded their way to that tent and Dort halted before the chieftain. Storm stood quietly a little behind him, allowing none of his interest in his surroundings to show. Silently he counted some twenty of the rounded tents, and he knew that each housed a full family, which could number up to fifteen or more natives, since a man married into his wife's clan and joined her family as a younger son until the number of his children increased to make him the head of his own family. Judging by Norbie standards this was a town of some size— of the zamle totem—for a stylized representation of that bird of prey was painted on the name shield before the chieftain's lodge.

"Storm"—Dort spoke softly as his hand signed a greeting to the impassive natives—"call in that bird of yours again. These are—"

"Zamle clansmen," the Terran nodded. "So they'll be favorably impressed by *my* bird totem?" Again he whistled to summon Baku, bracing himself for the bird's landing. But this time matters were not to go so smoothly. For, as the eagle came, she screamed a challenge in a way unlike her usual manner. And she did not come to Storm, but threw her body back, presenting her ready talons to the tent as if that hide and fur erection were an enemy.

Storm, startled, hurried forward. Baku had grounded now, walking across the open space before the Norbie chieftain in a crouch, her feathers standing up, wings trailing half open on either side of her black body. She was in a red rage, though the Terran could not see what had aroused her. That is—he did not, until a streak of living green burst from the tent in reply to the eagle's scream of challenge. Luckily Storm got there first, catching Baku by the legs before she could strike at her attacker.

Screeching in a frenzy the eagle beat her wings, tried to turn her talons on her handler, while Storm exerted all his strength of shoulder and arm to keep her fast, striving at the same time to enforce his mental control as well as the grip of his hands. The Norbie chief had caught up his own feathered champion and was engaged in a similar battle until one of his clansmen flung a small net over the angry zamle. When the green bird had been bundled back into the tent and Baku had been calmed, Storm tossed her onto his riding pad, confining her with jesses so she could not leave that perch until he freed her.

Breathing hard he turned to find the Norbie chief beside him, intent on the eagle. The native's fingers flew and Dort translated.

"Krotag wants to know if this bird is your totem."

"It is." Storm nodded, hoping that that gesture meant the same on Arzor as it had on Terra.

"Storm!" Dort's excitement broke through the control he had kept on his voice. "Do you have a wound scar you can show in a hurry? Scars mean something here. That will prove you're a warrior according to their standards—as well as a man with a real fightin' totem. The chief may even accept you as an equal."

If scars would help, the Terran was only too willing to oblige. He jerked at the loosely looped lacing of his shirt, pulling the silky material down to bare his left shoulder and display a ragged white line that marked his meeting with a too alert sentry on a planet whose sun was only a faint star in the Arzor night heavens.

"I am a warrior and my fighting totem has saved my life—" He spoke directly to the Norbie chieftain, as if the other understood and did not need Dort's translation by finger. The other answered in his twittering speech as he moved his hands. Dort grinned.

"You've done it, fella. They'll make drink-talk with us now, seein' as how you're a real warrior."

Krotag's camp supplied them with five experienced tracker-hunters and Larkin was well pleased, though it was plain the natives considered the stampede as an opportunity graciously arranged for their benefit by the Tall-Ones-Who-Drum-Thunder-in-the-Mountains as a means of adding to their clan wealth in horses.

Now as the riders and the Norbies worked in pairs to bring back the widely scattered animals, it became more and more apparent that Storm had been right in his suggestion that the stampede had been planned. Though even the natives found no identifiable traces of the raiders, it was clear that the horses had been separated into small bands and adroitly concealed in canyons and pocket valleys.

The clues to the identity of the stampeder or stampeders were so conspicuously absent that Storm heard some muttering to the effect that Krotag's men, now virtuously engaged in hunting the mounts, might well have hidden them in the first place, so they could claim the stallion and the three or four footsore mares Larkin promised them for their services.

Storm wondered about that a day or so later as red dust churned up by trampling hoofs arose about him until he pulled to one side of the bunch he was helping to head in to the gather point. The Terran adjusted the scarf he had tied over nose and mouth, watching another rider who was a distant dot, yet plain because of his white horse. That was Coll Bister. And by all rights Storm owed Bister some gratitude, for it was he who had found and brought in Rain, the horse the Terran now rode. But the ex-Commando couldn't find any liking for the man. He was one of those most outspoken against the Norbies and in addition he had shown covert hostility toward Storm, for no reason that the Beast Master could understand.

As usual the Terran had kept aloof in the herd camp, using his animals as an excuse for bedding down a little apart from the others. But his skill with horses had won him more ready acceptance than most off-world newcomers could claim. Larkin had turned over to him the breaking of additional mounts to take the place of work horses lost in the stampede, and the men not out on the hunt often gathered to watch him gentle them.

Had he wanted to, Storm might have enjoyed a favorite's position. His particular gifts, his even temper, and his willingness to carry his share of the tedious herd work, were all qualities the riders could readily appreciate. They were willing to accept Storm's reticence, which had hardened at the Center into an encasing shell. To the frontiersmen that ancient planet on which their stock had first been bred was an exotic mystery. It was a great tragedy that Terra was now gone, and naturally a Terran would feel it deeply. The death of his home world tended to lend Storm something close to exiled majesty in Arzoran eyes.

Only with Larkin and Dort Lancin did Storm approach a relationship stronger than just the comradeship of the trail. Dort was teaching him finger-talk and pouring out for his benefit all the Norbie lore he himself had absorbed over the years, displaying toward the Terran the proprietorship of the instructor for an apt pupil. With Larkin the bond was horse, a subject on which both men could talk for hours at the night's campfire.

So he knew Larkin and Dort and liked them in that pallid way that was the closest he was able to come to friendship with one of his own kind nowadays. But Bister was beginning to present a problem, one which he did not want to face. Not that Storm had any fear of physical combat should the other push his dislike that far. Bister bore all the signs of being a top bully, but in a fair fight—in spite of Bister outweighing and overtowering him—Storm was certain of victory.

In a fair fight— Storm's tongue licked dust from his lips behind his scarf. Why had that thought crossed his mind? And why did it bother him just now to see Bister sitting there as if waiting for him to ride up?

Although Storm had never pushed a fight, neither had he ever directly avoided trouble when it was necessary to face it—not before. Why *didn't* he want to come to grips with the problem Bister would present to him sooner or later?

Another rider drew level with Rain and a yellow hand lifted from a braided yoris hide hackamore to sign a greeting. Though the Norbie had followed Storm's example and drawn a scarf over the lower half of his thin face, the Terran recognized Gorgol, youngest of the scouts Larkin had hired.

"Plenty dust—" The native made signs slowly out of courtesy for Storm's beginner's learning. "Ride dry—"

"Clouds—over mountain—does rain come?" Storm signaled back.

The Norbie's head swung so he could look over his lean shoulder at the red rises now to the east.

"Rain comes—then mud—"

Storm knew that Larkin feared mud. Rain in these wastes, the heavy downpours of spring, could make a sticky morass of all level ground, producing dangerous quagmires.

"You bird totem warrior—" That was a statement, not a question. The Norbie youth rode with an easy grace, matching the pace of his smaller black and white mount to Rain's stride until he cantered beside the Terran as if they were practicing such a maneuver for some exhibition.

Storm nodded. Gorgol's left hand went to a cord about his own neck on which hung two curved objects, black and shiny. There was a shy self-consciousness about the native as he dropped his hand again to sign:

"I no warrior yet—hunter only. Have been in high peaks and killed an evil flyer—"

Storm asked the proper question in return. "An evil flyer? I not of this world—I know not evil flyer—"

"Big!" The Norbie's fingers spread to their farthest extent making the sign for great size. "Bird—evil bird. Hunt horse—hunt Norbie—kill!" His forefinger and thumb scissored in the emphatic sign for sudden and violent death, then rose again to tap the trophies swinging against the corselet which covered his breast.

Storm stretched out his hand in polite question and the boy pulled the thong from his neck, passing it to the Terran for examination. The objects strung on it were plainly a bird's claws. And, using the length of Baku's talons in relation to her thirty-four inches as comparison, the creature that had borne them must indeed have been huge, for each claw measured the length of Storm's hand from wrist to the end of the longest finger. He returned the necklet to its proud owner.

"You great hunter," Storm nodded vigorously to underline his finger statement. "Evil flyer must be hard to kill."

Gorgol's face might be half hidden by the scarf mask, but his whole person expressed pleasure as he answered.

"I kill for man deed. Not warrior yet—but hunter, yes."

And well he might boast, Storm thought. If this boy had killed the monster he described while hunting alone—and the Terran had learned enough of Norbie customs from Dort to know that idle boasting was no part of native character—he had every right in the world to claim to be a hunter.

"You be frawn herder?" the Norbie continued.

"No. I have no land—no herd—"

"Be hunter. Kill evil flyer—kill yoris—trade their skins—"

"I stranger," Storm pointed out, making the signs slowly as he launched bravely into expressing more complicated ideas. "Norbies hunt Norbie lands—off-world men do not so hunt—"

The hunting law was one of the few rigidly enforced by the loosely knit government of Arzor, as the Terran had been warned at the Center and again at the space port. Norbie rights were protected. Herd riders could kill yoris or other predatory creatures attacking their stock. But any animal living in the mountains, or in the native-held sections of the plains was taboo as far as the settlers were concerned.

Gorgol objected. "You bird totem warrior—Krotag's people bird totem—you hunt Krotag's land—no one say no—"

Far within Storm a feeling stirred faintly, some emotion, frozen on that day when he had returned from a hazardous three months of duty behind the enemy lines to discover that he was a homeless man. He moved restlessly on the saddle pad and Rain snorted nervously, as if the stallion, too, had felt that painful tug. The Terran's face, beneath his mask, was set in passionless endurance as he fought against that feeble response to Gorgol's impulsive offer.

"You're pullin' it late—" Bister's dust-hoarsened voice rasped not only on Storm's ears but on his awakened nerves. "Sure got you a big bunch this time. The goat here lead you to where he had 'em all salted away nice and neat?"

That new aliveness in Storm rose in answer to the prod of antagonism. He did not like Bister, but he no longer accepted that passively as just another unpleasant fact of his present existence. There might be cause for him to do something positive to counter the other's needling. The Terran did not know that over the edge of the scarf his eyes, usually better controlled, now gave him away. Coll Bister was more alert to small points than he seemed.

The settler pulled his own scarf away from his mouth and spat. "Maybe you don't believe these goats have brains enough to plan it all out—eh?"

Storm was more interested in the idle swing of Bister's right hand. A quirt dragged from the man's thick wrist, a quirt with an extra-long length of a doubled yoris-hide lash.

"We wouldn't have found as many horses as we have if Krotag's men weren't nosing them out for us." Storm's position on the riding pad looked lazy, his hands were well away from the weapons at his belt. But he sensed, with a good moment's grace in which to act, what was coming, as if he had sucked that knowledge out of the air along with the grit and dust.

That dangling right arm rose as the last straggler of the stray bunch trotted by. It could be that Bister was aiming to snap his quirt at the tired yearling. But Storm did not believe that. A sudden pressure of knee sent Rain forward so that the yoris-hide strap did not strike Gorgol's bare thigh, but landed in a stinging slap on Storm's own better protected leg.

Bister had not been prepared for that, nor for what happened next. Storm's well-timed retaliation sent the bigger man to the ground—the arm that had wielded the quirt temporarily numb to the elbow. With an inarticulate roar of rage Bister struggled to his feet only to go down again, sent sprawling by a Commando blow delivered by the edge of Storm's open hand. The Terran had thought out his strategy in advance.

To his surprise Bister did not get up to rush him again. Instead when the big man did rise to his feet he stood still, his chest heaving, his face flushed, but making no move to continue the fight.

"We're not through—" he spat. "I've heard about you, Storm. You Commandos can kill a man with your bare hands. All right. Wait until we get to the Crossin' and let's see you stand up to a stun meetin'! I'm not done with you—nor with those goat pals of yours neither!"

Storm was bewildered enough to be shaken out of some of his self-confident complacency. Bister's restraint now did not fit into the type of character he appeared to be. Neither, Storm was certain, was it a case of the Arzoran rider being just all bluster and no bite. Looking down at that flushed face, into the dark eyes raised to his, Storm wondered if he had completely misread Coll Bister. The man was not in the least afraid, he was confident—and he hated! So why had he refused to continue to fight now? The Terran watched the other swing up into the saddle. He would allow Bister to call the next move in the game—until he learned more about the stakes.

"Remember—" Bister's fingers were busy with his face scarf, ready to jerk the mask up over his square jaw once again—"we aren't through—"

Storm shrugged. Bister doubtless could bear watching, but there was no advantage to be gained from allowing the other to think so.

"Ride your side of the trail," he returned shortly, "and I'll ride mine, Bister. I'm not out to rope trouble."

The other cantered off and Storm turned to find Gorgol watching that retreat. The Norbie drew level with the Terran once more and his eyes held an unmistakable note of inquiry as he signed:

"He challenged but he did not fight—why?"

"Your guess is as good as mine," Storm said and then made more halting finger-talk. "I know not. But he does not like Norbies—" He thought it best to give a warning that might save the boy future trouble with the trail bully.

"So do we know. He thinks we steal horses—hide and then find them for Larkin. Maybe that good trick for Nitra—for wild men of the Peaks. Not for Krotag's men. We make bargain with Larkin—we keep bargain."

"Somebody hid those horses, made yoris come to stampede," Storm observed.

"That true. Maybe outlaws. Many outlaws in mountains. Not Norbies, but raid on Norbie land. Norbie fight—kill!"

Gorgol sent his horse on after the disappearing bunch of strays and Storm followed at a slower pace. The Terran had his own motive for coming to Arzor, for riding into this Basin country. He certainly did not want to become involved in others' quarrels. Larkin's stampede had just happened and Storm could do no less than help the trader out, but he was not going to pursue his trouble with Bister, or get pulled into any fight between the settlers and the Norbies.

The threatened rain broke upon them with a wild drumming of thunder that evening. After its first fury it turned into a steady, drenching downpour. And from then on Larkin's riders had little time to think of anything except the troubles of the trail.

Surra crawled under a tarp on the wagon to join the meerkats, growling her stubborn refusal for any venture into the wet, and even Baku sought shelter. This steady fall of moisture was beyond the team's past experience and they resented it, a state of mind Storm came to share as, ankle deep in mud, he helped to fill the softer spots of the trail with branches and grass, or rode into the swirling waters of a river to rope and guide loose horses along a line of stakes the Norbies had set up to mark a questionable ford.

By the end of the second day of rain the Terran was sure they could not have advanced a mile without the aid of the native scouts. The mud did not seem to tire the Norbies' wiry, range-bred horses, though it constantly entrapped the off-world stock. The natives did not display any weariness either as they dashed about ready with a dragrope or an armload of brush to fill in a bad mudhole.

But on the third day it began to clear, and word was passed that two more days' travel should bring them into the auction town— news they all greeted with relief.

CHAPTER FOUR

The soil had absorbed water like a sponge. Now the heavy heat of the sun drew out in return luxuriant foliage such as Storm would not have guessed this waste could produce. The horses had to be restrained from grazing lest they founder. And the Terran also needed to keep close watch on Ho and Hing who relished digging in the easily excavated earth. It was almost impossible to believe that after six more weeks of such plenty this country would again be close to desert.

"Pretty, eh?" Dort set his mount to climb a small hillock, joining Storm. The yellow-green ground blanket ahead was patterned with drifts of white, golden, and scarlet flowers. "But wait a month or so and"—he snapped his fingers—"all dried and gone. Just sand and rocks, some of the thorn bushes, and the rest a lot of nothing. Fastest changing country you ever saw!"

"Surely the grazing can't disappear that fast in the Basin. Or do you have to move the frawn herds continually?"

"No. Give any of this land water and it'll grow all you need. There's year 'round water in the Basin, and a different kind of grass with long tough roots. You can drive a trail herd through here spring and fall. But you can't hold animals on range in this district. Frawns are big eaters, too—need a wide range. My dad has seventy squares and he runs about two thousand head on 'em 'round the year."

"You were born on Arzor, Dort?" Storm asked his first personal question.

"Sure was! My dad had a little spread down Quipawa way then. He was born here, too. We're First Ship people," he ended with a flash of pride. "Three generations here now and there're five spreads runnin' under our ear notch—my dad's, me an' my brother's, my sister and her man's over in the peninsula country, my Uncle Wagger and his two sons—they have theirs, the Borggy and the Rifts, over on the Cormbal Slopes."

"A good world to come back to—" Storm's gaze swept over the level land eastward to those mountains that had called him since he had first sighted them.

"Yes." Dort glanced at Storm and then quickly away again. "It's good country—wide. A man can ride free here. Me—when I was in the forces and saw Grambage and Wolf Three and some of those other worlds where people live all stuck together—well, it wouldn't suit me." Then, as if his curiosity pushed him past politeness, he said:

"Seems like you knew a country like this once, you act right at home—"

"I did—once. Not the same colors—but desert and mountains, short springs to make a waste bloom—dry, dead summers—hot sun—open range—"

"That burn-off wasn't war—it was plain murder!" Dort's face was flushed, anger against the irredeemable past alight in his eyes.

Storm shrugged. "It is done now." He lifted his reins and the stallion single-footed it down the other side of the hillock.

"Say, kid," Dort caught up with him again, "you've heard about the land grants open for veterans—"

"I was told—ten squares to a qualified settler."

"Twenty to a Terran," the other corrected. "Now me and my brother, we've got us a nice spread on the eastern fork of the Staffa and beyond that the land is clear to the Paszo Peaks. If you aren't going to stay on with Larkin and run herd, you might ride on with me and take a look in that direction. It's good country—dry around the edges maybe—but the Staffa doesn't give out even in high-sun season. You could bite out your twenty squares clear up to the Peaks. Quade has a section there—"

"Brad Quade? I thought his holdings were in the Basin—"

"Oh, that's his big spread. He's First Ship family, too, though he did a hitch in Survey and has gone off-world other times. He's imported horses and tried Terran sheep here. Sheep didn't last, the groble beetles infected them the first year. Anyway, he set up the Peak place for his son—"

"His son?" Storm's dark face remained expressionless, but he was listening very closely now.

"Yes. Logan's just a kid and he and Brad don't rub along together too smooth. The kid doesn't like just herding—goes off with the Norbies a lot and is as good as one of their scouts at tracking. He tried to get in the forces here, raised merry Hades down at the enlistment center when they wouldn't take him because of his age. So Brad gave him this wilder grant down at the Peaks about two years ago and told him to take out his fight on taming that. Haven't heard how he's made out lately." Dort laughed. "Home news took a while catching up with our outfit while we were star shootin'."

"Hey!" Larkin's shout was a summons to them both. "Ride circle, you two, we want them bedded down here—"

Storm rode to the right while Dort took the left. To bed down here meant they would wait to hit the Crossing late tomorrow. Larkin wanted to rest the horses before the auction. As he rode, the Terran was thinking. So Brad Quade had a son, had he, a fact which altered Storm's plans somewhat. He had been willing to confront Quade where and when he found him and have their quarrel out. He still wanted to see Quade, of course he did! Why did the fact that his enemy had a family make any difference? Storm pushed that last puzzle to a dead end without solving it.

He carried through his duties with his usual competence, glad to be busy. The rest of the men were in a festive mood. Even the Norbies twittered among themselves and made no move to leave the camp after they collected their pay. Here the party would split up—the veterans who had joined for the trip at the space port would now ride on to their own spreads or light and tie for the big owners who were coming to buy at the auction, which was also an informal hiring depot. This was one of the two big yearly gatherings that broke the usual solitude of the range seasons, and was a mixture of business, fair, and carnival, attracting the whole countryside.

"Storm." Larkin sat down by the Terran where he was settled cross-legged near the fire, the meerkats wrestling playfully before him, Surra lazily tonguing her paws at his back. "You planning to take up land? Law gives you rights to a nice piece—"

"Not now. Dort was talking about the Staffa River country—running up to the Peaks. I may ride on to see it—" One excuse for remaining foot-loose was as good as another, the Terran thought wearily.

Larkin brightened. "That's good grazin' land—the Peak country. I've been thinkin' some of that lately myself. Me, I've been doin' pretty well at importin' horses. But there aren't goin' to be many more brought in from off-world. Sure, we can buy 'em like these—or other fancy stuff from Argol. But that's a lighter breed, not suited to range work. The old Terran stock is gone. So I've a plan runnin' around in my head. I'd like to round me up some good basic stock—some of these we got right out here in the herd, and some range stuff of at least two generations Arzoran breeding, plus a few mounts out of the Norbie camps. Mix 'em and see what I can do 'bout buildin' up a new strain—a horse that needs less water, can live off scrub-feed ground, and follow a frawn drift without givin' out at the end of one day's trottin'. Now, son, you're a master hand with animals. You ride down there and cast an eye over the Peak country. If you're willin'—look me up here at the fall auction and we'll see about a partnership deal—"

Again that tug deep inside, a blow at the wall he had built around himself. Three times now Storm had been offered a possible future—by Gorgol, by Dort, and now by Larkin. He shifted slightly and used the evasive tactics he had developed as protective armor at the Center.

"Let me see the land first, Larkin. We can talk it over in the fall—"

But long before fall he should meet with Brad Quade—Brad Quade and maybe his son Logan in the bargain.

Partly to get away from his own thoughts, Storm allowed Dort to persuade him to visit the Crossing at night, leaving his team in camp and riding with Lancin and Ransford into a town that made him blink a little, it was so unlike other villages.

Arzoran settlements such as this one were almost a hundred Terran years old now. Yet there was a kind of raw newness about them that Storm had not seen elsewhere. Between the half-yearly explosions of auction week, Irrawady Crossing was close to a ghost town, though it was the only village in several thousand squares of range land. Tonight the town was roaring, wide open. Life here was certainly far removed from the peace Storm had known on Terra, or the regimentation and discipline of the Center.

The four from the trail camp had no more than stabled their horses when they witnessed the end of a personal argument, both men having drawn stun rods with speed enough to drop each other flat and unconscious. And they skirted another crowd moments later, watching another dispute being settled bloodily by fists.

"Boys playful tonight, aren't they?" inquired Dort, grinning.

"Anybody here ever try to activate a stun gun with a blast bolt?" Storm asked. He was astonished at the grim chill of Ransford's reply.

"Sure—that's been done—by outlaws. But any fella who tried to blast wouldn't last long. We don't hold with murder. If the boys want to play rough with a stun—and that sure leaves an almighty headache to follow a guy for hours—or try to change another fella's looks with fists, that's their right. But blastin's out!"

"I saw a couple of riders mix it up with Norbie long-knives once," volunteered Dort. "That was a nasty mess and the winner was sent down to Istabu for psychin'. 'Course Norbies duel it out to the death when they give a 'warrior' challenge. But that's accordin' to their customs and we don't bother 'em about it. Nobody is allowed to interfere with the tribes—"

Ransford nodded. "Tribe wars are somethin' like religion to a Norbie. A boy has to get him a scar in personal combat before he can take a wife or speak up in council. There's a regular system of points for a man to gather 'fore he can be a chief—all pretty complicated. Hey, fella, take it easy!"

A man caromed into Dort, nearly carrying the veteran off his feet. Dort fended him off with a good-natured shove. But the other whirled, moving with better coordination than his weaving progress predicted. Storm went into action as the rod came from the other's holster, not trained at the bewildered Dort, but directly at Storm.

The ex-Commando moved with trained precision. His rising hand struck the man's wrist, sending the stun rod flying before a finger could press the firing button. But the other was not licked. With a tight little strut he bounced forward, to meet a whirlwind attack. The stranger was out on his feet before any of the men passing really understood that a scuffle was in progress.

Storm, breathing a little faster, stood rubbing one hand against the other, looking down at the now unconscious rider. Did local etiquette demand that he now dispose of his late opponent in some manner, he wondered. Or did one just leave a loser where he fell?

He stooped, hooked his hands in the slumberer's armpits, and dragged him with some difficulty—since he was a large man and now a dead weight—to prop him against the side of a neighboring building. As the Terran straightened up he saw a shadowy figure in the dusk turn and walk abruptly away. There was no mistaking Bister's outline as he passed the garish lights of a café. Had this rider been sent against Storm by Bister? And why couldn't, or didn't, Coll Bister fight his own battles?

"By the Great Horns!" Dort bore down on him. "What did you do then? Looked as if you only patted him gentle like, until he went all limp and keeled over like a rayed man! Only you didn't pull your rod at all."

"Short and quick," commented Ransford. "Commando stuff?"

"Yes."

But Ransford showed none of Dort's excitement. "Take it easy, kid," he warned. "Make a parade of bein' a tough man and a lot of these riders may line up to take you on. We don't use blasters maybe, but a man can get a pretty bad poundin' if a whole gang moves in on him—no matter how good he is with his hands—"

"When have you ever seen the kid walkin' stiff-legged for a fight?" Dort protested. "Easiest-goin' fella in camp, an' you know it! Why did you jump that guy anyway, Storm?"

"His eyes," the Terran replied briefly. "He wanted to make it a real fight."

Ransford agreed. "Had his rod out too quick, Dort, and he pulled it for the kid, too. He was pushin'. Only don't push back unless you have to, Storm."

"Aw, leave the kid alone, Ranny. When did he ever make fight-talk on the fingers?"

Ransford chuckled. "It wasn't the fingers he used for his fight-talk—mostly the flat of his hand. I'm just warnin' him. This is a hot town tonight and you're from off-world, Storm. There're a lot of chesty riders who like to pick on newcomers."

Storm smiled. "That I'm used to. But thanks, Ransford, I'll walk softly. I never have fought for the fun of it."

"That's just it, kid, might be better if you did. Leave you alone and you're as nice and peaceful as that big cat of yours. But I don't think she'd take kindly to anyone stampin' on her tail, casual-like. Well, here's the Gatherin'. Do we want to see who's in town tonight?"

Lights, brighter than the illumination of the street, and a great deal of noise issued out of the doorway before them. The structure assembled under one roof, Storm gathered, all the amenities of bar, theater, club, and market exchange, and was the meeting place for the more respectable section of the male population—regular and visiting—of Irrawady Crossing.

The din, the lights, the assorted smells of cooking, drinks, and horse, as well as heated humanity, struck hard as they crossed the threshold. Nothing he saw there attracted Storm and had he been alone he would have returned to the camp. But Dort wormed a path through the crowd, boring toward the long table where a game of Kor-sal-slam was in progress, eager to try his luck at the game of chance that had swept through the Confed worlds with the speed of light during the past two years.

"Ransford! When did you get back?"

Storm saw a hand drop on the veteran's shoulder, half turning him to face the speaker. It was a hand almost as brown as his own. And above it, around that equally brown wrist—! Storm did not betray the shock he felt. There was only one place that particular ornament could come from. For it was the ketoh of the Dineh—the man's bracelet of his own people developed from the old bow-guard of the Navajo warrior! And what was it doing about the wrist of an Arzoran settler?

Without realizing that he was unconsciously preparing for battle, the Terran moved his feet a little apart, bracing and balancing his body for either attack or defense, as his eyes moved along the arm, clothed conventionally in frawn fabric, up to the face of the man who wore the ketoh. The stranger and Ransford had drawn a little apart, and now in his turn Storm shifted back against the wall, wanting to watch them without being himself observed.

The face of the settler was as brown as his hand—a weather-burned brown. But his were not Navajo features—though the hair above them was as black as Storm's own. And it was a strong, attractive face with lines of good humor bracketing the wide mouth, softening the almost too-firm line of the jaw, while the eyes set beneath rather thick brows were a deep blue.

Storm was not too far away to hear Ransford's return cry of "Quade!"

He had caught the hand from his shoulder and was shaking it vigorously. "I just got in, rode herd for Larkin down from the Port. Say, Brad, he's got some good stuff in his new stud string—"

The wide mouth curved into a smile. "Now that's news, Ranny. But we're glad to have *you* back, fella, and in one unbroken piece. Heard a lot of black talk about how bad things were going out there—toward the end—"

"Our Arzor outfit got into it late. Just one big battle and some moppin' up. Say—Brad, I want you to meet—"

But Storm took two swift steps backward, to be hidden by a push of newcomers, and Ransford could not see him. For once it was useful to be smaller than the settler breed.

"Queer—" The veteran's voice carried puzzlement. "He was right here behind me. Off-worlder and a good kid. Rode herd down for Larkin and can he handle horses! Terran—"

"Terran!" repeated Quade, his smile gone. "Those dirty Xiks!" His words became highly flavored and combined some new expressions Storm did not recognize. All worlds, it seemed, developed their own brand of profanity. "I only hope the devils who planned that burn-off were cooked in their turn—to a crisp! Your man deserves every break we can give him. I'll look him up—any good horseman is an asset. I hear you're going out to the Vakind—"

They moved on but Storm remained where he was, surprised and not a little ashamed to find that the hands resting on the belt about his flat middle were trembling a little.

A meeting such as this did not match with the nebulous plans he had made. He wanted no curious audience when he met Quade—and then each of them should have a blaster—or better still—knives! Storm's settlement with his man must not be one of the relatively bloodless encounters of Arzoran custom but something far more decisive and fatal.

The Terran was about to go out when a bull-throated roar rising above the clamor in the room halted him.

"Quade!" The man who voiced that angry bellow made Brad Quade seem almost as slender as a Norbie.

"Yes, Dumaroy?" The warmth that had been in his voice while he spoke with Ransford was gone. Storm had heard such a tone during his service days—that inflection meant trouble. He stayed to watch with a curiosity he could not control.

"Quade—that half-baked kid of yours has been ridin' wild again—stickin' his nose in where it isn't wanted. You pull herd guard on him, or someone's goin' to do it for you!"

"That someone being you, Dumaroy?" The ice thickened into a glacial deposit.

"Maybe. He roughed up one of my boys out on the Peak Range—"

"Dumaroy!" There was the snap of a quirt in that and the whole room was silent, men edging in about the two as if they expected some open fight. "Dumaroy, your rider roughed up a Norbie and he got just what he deserved in return. You know what trouble with the natives can lead to—or do you *want* to have a knife feud sworn on you?"

"Norbies!" Dumaroy did not quite spit, but his disgust was made eloquently plain. "We don't nurse Norbies on *my* spread. And we don't take kindly to half-broke kids settin' up to tell us how to act. Maybe you goat-lovers up here like to play finger-wriggle with the big horns— We don't, and we don't trust 'em either—"

"A knife feud—"

Dumaroy interrupted. "So they swear a knife feud. And how long will that last if my boys clean out their camps and teach 'em a good lesson? Those goats run fast enough when you show your teeth at 'em. They sure have the finger-sign on you up here—"

Quade's hand shot out, buried fingers in the frawn fabric that strained across the other's wide chest.

"Dumaroy—" He still spoke quietly. "Up here we hold to the law. We don't follow Mountain Butcher tricks. If the Peak country needs a little visit from the Peace Officers, be sure it's going to get just that!"

"Better change your rods to blast charges if you ride on another man's range to snoop." Dumaroy twisted out of the other's hold with a roll of his thick shoulders.

"We tend to our own business and we don't take to meddlers from up here. If you don't want to have your pet goats tickled up some, give them the sign to keep away from our ranges. And they'd better not trail any loose stock with 'em either! And, if I were you, Quade, I'd speak loud and clear to that kid of yours. When Norbies get excited, they don't always look too close at a man's face before they plant an arrow in his middle. I'm serving notice here and now"—his glance swept from Quade to the other men about him— "the Peaks aren't goin' to be ruled from the Basin. If you don't like our ways—stay out! You don't know what's goin' on back in the hills. These tame goats who ride herd around here aren't like the high-top clans. And maybe the tame ones will learn a few lessons from the wild ones. Been a lot of herd losses in the last five months—and that Nitra chief, old Muccag, he's been makin' drum-magic in the mountains. I say somethin' bigger than a tribe war is cookin'. And we ain't goin' to have goats camped on our ranges when the arrow is passed! If you've any sense, the rest of you, you'd think that way too."

Storm was puzzled. This had begun as a personal quarrel between Quade and Dumaroy. Now the latter was attempting to turn the encounter into an argument against the natives. It was almost as strange as Bister's early actions. He sensed an undercurrent that spelled danger.

CHAPTER FIVE

The Terran was so intrigued by that problem that he did not see Quade turn until he was aware, suddenly, that the Basin settler was staring at him. Those blue eyes were searching, oddly demanding, and there was a shadow of something that might have been recognition in them. Of course that was impossible. To his knowledge he and Quade had never met. But the Arzoran was coming toward him and Storm stepped back, confident that outside in the half-light of the street the other could not find him unless he willed it.

But Storm did not move so fast that a startled cry of warning did not reach him. Had it not been for that call and perhaps the fact that his attacker was overeager, the Terran might have gone down with a Norbie long-knife driven home between his shoulders, to cough out his life in the dusty roadway. But the ex-Commando had lived long enough under constant danger so that once more his reflexes took over, and he dived to the right, bringing up against the wall of a building, as someone rushed past him. That half-seen figure flashed into the obscuring dark of an alleyway, but the light reflected from a naked blade as he went.

"Did he get you?"

Storm swung around, his hand on his own knife hilt. The light from the Gatherin' showed him Brad Quade standing there.

"Saw that knife swing," Quade elaborated. "Did he mark you?"

Storm stood away from the wall. "Not at all," he answered in the same gentle voice he had used at the Center. "I have to thank you, sir."

"I'm Brad Quade. And you?"

But Storm could not force himself to take the hand the other held out to him. This was all wrong and he could not go ahead with a

scene differing so far from the one he had visualized all these years.
He had been pushed off base and he had to get away fast, no matter
how many would-be assassins lurked in the alley mouths of Irrawady
Crossing. Would his name mean anything to Quade? He doubted it,
but he could not really be sure. Yet he could not give a false one. His
quarrel with this man was not one to be cloaked with tricks and lies.

"I'm Storm," he replied simply, and bowed, hoping that the other
would believe the meeting of hands was not a greeting custom of his
kind, since manners varied widely from planet to planet and his accent ruled him off-world.

"You're Terran!"

Quade was too quick, yet again Storm could not bring himself to
deny anything.

"Yes."

"Quade! Hey, Brad Quade! You're wanted on the com-talk—" a
man hailed from the door of the Gatherin'. As the settler looked
around Storm faded away. He was sure the other would not pursue
him through the town.

Carefully, with attention alerted to any pitfalls or possible ambush
sites ahead, Storm went back to the stable. But he did not breathe
easily until he was mounted on Rain and riding out of the Crossing
with the firm intention of keeping away from that town in the future.

Months before he had worked out an imagined meeting with
Quade to the last tiny detail, a very satisfactory meeting. *He*, Storm,
would select the proper time and place, make his accusation—to a
man who did not fit the pattern of the Brad Quade he had seen tonight. This Quade was not at all the passive villain he had pictured
him to be.

And their business could not be transacted on the crowded street
of a frontier town just after Quade had probably saved his life. He
wanted—he had to have—his own kind of a meeting.

Storm shied from following that line of reasoning. He did not
honestly know why he had run—yes, he *had* run—from Quade tonight. He had come to Arzor only to meet Quade—but which Quade,
the figure he had created to justify his action, or the man he had met?
His actions were becoming as hard to understand as Bister's—

No, Storm's heel touched Rain and the horse obediently broke into a gallop. There was nothing wrong with his motives—Quade deserved what Storm had to bring him. What if the settler's warning *had* saved his life? It wasn't any personal wrong of his own he had come to avenge—he could not cancel Quade's debt to the dead!

But the Terran did not sleep well that night, and he volunteered as a herd-holder as Larkin took the first of the string in to the crossing for showing in the morning. It was midday when the trader returned, well satisfied with the morning's sales. And he brought a stranger with him.

Though Storm did not know the man, the earth-brown uniform he wore was familiar enough, being that of Survey. And he had met other men of that service, had studied under them, in the training camp of the Beast Masters. Nor was he greatly surprised when Larkin beckoned him over.

"Sorenson, archaeologist," the Survey man introduced himself, the crisp galactic speech overlaid with the faint lisp of a Lydian-born.

"Storm, Beast Master, retired—" the Terran replied as formally. "What can I do for you, Specialist Sorenson?"

"According to Larkin you haven't signed up with any outfit yet and you don't plan to apply for a land grant just at present. Are you free for a scout engagement?"

"I'm off-world, new here," Storm pointed out. But he was excited, this was a perfect answer to his immediate problems. "I don't know the country—"

Sorenson shrugged. "I've Norbie guides, a settler pack master. But Larkin tells me you have kept your team intact—I know the work such a team can do and I can use you—"

"I have my team, yes—" Storm nodded toward his bedroll. Surra sprawled there, blinking in the sun, the meerkats chittering beside her, while Baku perched on the rim of the supply cart. "Dune cat, meerkats, African eagle—"

"Good enough." Sorenson only glanced at the animals. "We're heading into desert country. Have you heard of the Sealed Caves? There is a chance they may be located down in the Peak section."

"I've heard, also, that they are a legend."

"We got a little more accurate information recently. That territory's largely unmapped and your services will be useful. We have a government permit for pot-hunting."

"Sounds like a good deal, kid," Larkin spoke up. "You wanted to look over the Peaks. You'll get your pay from me in horses—and you can either sell 'em at auction or you can keep that stallion you've been riding and take the black pack mare for your gear, and let me put up the other two. If you find a likely range down there, stick up your stakes and register it when you come back—"

"Also, you can take your scout pay in a government land voucher," Sorenson added quickly. "Useful if you want to stake out in new country. Or use it for an import permit—"

Storm stirred. He felt pushed, and that aroused opposition. On the other hand, the expedition would take him away from the Crossing and from both the knifer—whoever he might be—and Quade until he could decide about the latter. Also—the Peak country held Logan Quade and he wanted to know more about that young man.

"All right," he agreed, and then instantly wished that he had not, but it was too late.

"Sorry to hurry you, Storm"—Sorenson was all brisk efficiency now—"only we pull out early tomorrow morning. The mountain rains won't last too much longer and we have to count on them for our water supply. That's pretty arid country up there and we'll have to leave it anyway at the beginning of the big dry. Bring your own camp kit—we will furnish the rest of the supplies—"

Over Sorenson's thin shoulder Storm caught sight of a pair of riders rounding the wagon. Ransford—and Brad Quade! At the moment they were looking at the horses, but a slight turn of the head would bring Storm into the settler's line of vision.

"Where do I meet you to move out?" the Terran asked quickly.

"East of town, by the river ford—that grove of yarvins, about five—"

"I'll be there," Storm promised and then spoke to Larkin. "I'll keep Rain and the mare as you suggest. We'll settle for the auction price of the others when I get back."

Larkin was grinning happily as the Survey man left. "Keep your eyes open around the Peaks, son, and stake a good stretch of land.

Give us three-four years and we'll have us some colts that'll beat anything even imported from Terra! That pack mare—she's the best of the lot for a rough trip, steady old girl. Any of your kit you want to store, just leave it in the wagon, I'll see to it—"

Storm was too impatient to wonder at Larkin's helpfulness. He wanted to be out of sight before Quade came away from the improvised corral. But escape was not to be so easily achieved. It was Ransford who hailed him.

"Storm!" That shout was so imperative the Terran dared not ignore it and waited for the other to come up. "Look here, kid, Quade told me about your being jumped by a knife-man in town—what kind of trouble are you in anyway?"

"None—that I know of—"

But the other was frowning. "I tried to find out somethin' about that rider you put to sleep—but nobody knew him. Sure it wasn't him waitin' for you?"

"Might have been—I just sighted a shadow with a knife—never saw his face." Storm longed to get away. Quade was dismounting and he was sure the settler would join them.

"I put Dort to askin' around some," Ransford continued. "He knows men in about nine-tenths of the outfits here for the auction. If anyone is out to get your hide, he'll hear about it—then we can take some action ourselves—"

Why was everyone so interested in his affairs? Storm wanted desperately, at that moment, to snake Rain out of the picket lines, call his team, and ride off alone into the wilderness. He did not want such solicitude, in fact it scraped raw some nerve he had not known he possessed. He asked nothing but to be left alone, to go his own way. Yet here was Larkin—and Ransford—and Dort—and even the Norbie, Gorgol, all with splendid little plans, or concern, or helpful hints for him. Storm could not understand why—any more than he knew why Bister wanted to make trouble for him.

"If anyone is gunning for me," he returned as well as he could without betraying his rising irritation," it won't do him any good after tomorrow morning. I've signed up as scout for a Survey expedition and am leaving town."

Ransford gave a sigh of relief. "That's usin' your head, kid. Maybe this hothead got a skinful of tharman juice last night and when he sobers up he'll have forgotten all about it. Which way you headed?"

"To the Peaks."

"The Peaks—" That echo came from Quade. Then the settler added in a language Storm had never thought to hear another speak again:

"Where do you ride, man of the Dineh?"

"I do not understand you," Storm answered in galactic one-speech. Quade shook his head, his blue eyes measuring Storm astutely.

"You are Terran," he switched to the common tongue of the space-ways, "but also you are Navajo—"

"I am Terran—now a man of no planet," Storm replied shortly. "I do not understand you."

"I think that you do," Quade countered, but there was no abruptness in that, only a kind of regret. "I overheard you saying that you had signed on as a scout with an expedition into the Peak country. That's good land down there—look it over. My son has a holding in that district." His eyes dropped to his hands, twisting his reins. "If you see him—" But Quade did not finish that sentence, ending with another suggestion altogether. "I'd like him to meet you—you are Terran and Navajo. Well, good luck, Storm. If you ever need anything, try my range." His foot was already in the stirrup and he swung into the saddle, moving off before the Terran could answer— if he had wanted to.

"If you do see Logan," Ransford broke the silence, "I hope he's not in trouble up to his chin. That boy's as hard to ride herd on as a pack of yoris! Pity—Quade's the easiest man livin' to rub along with—if you're straight and doin' your job right. But he and his own kid can't be together more'n a week before fire's bustin' out all over the range! Nobody can understand why. Logan Quade's crazy about huntin', and he lives with the Norbies a lot. But the kid never did a crooked thing in his life and he's as decent as his old man. They just can't seem to live together. It's a shame, 'cause Quade is proud of the boy and wants his son for a partner. If you hear anything good about the kid, tell Quade when you come back—it'll mean a lot to him— and he's taken a big likin' to you, too. Well, good luck, kid—sounds as if you've got yourself a good deal. Survey pays well and you can turn their write-off in for an import permit or somethin' like."

Storm was disturbed. He wanted none of the information Ransford had supplied. What did Quade's personal affairs matter to him? In that second brief encounter with his chosen enemy he felt he had lost some advantage he needed badly as a bolster for the future. He had accepted Quade, the enemy, but this other Quade was infringing more and more on his carefully built-up image. He hurried about his preparations for the trip, thankful for the occupation.

Surra sat on his left, the meerkats snuffled, poked, and pried under and around his busy hands as Storm sorted, piled, and made up two packs of his personal belongings. One he must leave with Larkin, the other comprised the kit he would need on the trail. There remained now just one small bundle to explore.

He had left that roll to the last, doubly reluctant to slit the waterproof covering sewed about it on another world, keeping its contents intact for two years. Now Storm sat quietly, his hands resting palm down upon the package, his eyes closed, exploring old roads of memory—roads he had managed to avoid exploring at the Center. As long as he did not cut the waxed cord, as long as he did not actually see what he was sure must be inside—just so long was he in a way free of the last acceptance of defeat—of acknowledging that there was never to be any return.

What did these men of another race here in camp—or those in the town—or those at the Center who had watched him so narrowly for months—that Commander who had so reluctantly stamped his freedom papers—what did any of them know of the voices of the Old Ones and how they could come to a man? How could they understand a man such as his grandfather—a Singer learned in ancient ways, following paths of belief these other races had never walked, who could see things not to be seen, hear things that no others could hear?

Between Storm and the clear beliefs of his grandfather—that grandfather who had surrendered him to schooling as a government ward only under force—there was a curtain of white man's learning. Good and bad, he had had to accept the new in gulps, unable to pick and choose until he was old enough to realize that behind the outer façade of acceptance he could make his own selection. And by that time it was almost too late, he had strayed far from the source of his people's inner strength. Twice after he had been taken away by the authorities, Storm had returned to his people, once as a boy, again as a youth before he left Terra on active service. But then always between him and Na-Ta-Hay's teaching there had been the drift of new ways. Fiercely opposed to those, his grandfather had been almost hostile, grudging, when Storm had tried to recapture a little of the past for himself. Yet some of it had clung, for now there sang through his mind old words, older music, things half-remembered, which stirred him as the wind from the mountains whipped him outwardly, and his lips shaped words not to sound again on the world from which this bundle had been sent.

Slowly, Storm sawed through the tough cord. He must face this now. The outer wrappings peeled off, and Ho and Hing crowded in with their usual curiosity, intrigued by the strange new smells clinging to the contents.

For there were scents imprisoned here—he could not be imagining that. The tightly woven wool of the blanket rasped his fingers, he saw and yet did not want to see the stripes of its pattern, red, white, blue-black, serrated concentric designs interrupting them. And to its tightly creased folds clung the unmistakable aroma of the hogan—sheep smell, desert smell, dust and sand smell. Storm sucked it into his lungs, remembering.

He shook out the blanket, and metal gleamed up at him as he thought it might. Necklace—blue-green of turquoise and dull sheen of silver—ketoh bracelet, concha belt—all masterpieces of the smith's art—the ceremonial jewelry of a Dineh warrior. Old, old pieces he had seen before, made by brown fingers, dust long before he had been born—the designs created by the artists of his race.

Seeing those, Storm knew he had been right in his surmise. Not only had Grandfather somehow known—but he had found it possible to forgive the grandson who had walked the alien way—or else he could not resist this last mute argument to influence that grandson! It might have been his own death that Na-Ta-Hay had foreseen—or perhaps the death of his world. But he had sent this legacy to his daughter's son, striving to keep alive in the last of his own blood a little of the past he had protected so fiercely, fought so hard to hold intact against the push of time and the power of alien energy.

And now out of the night did there come a faint sound of a swinging chant? That song sung for the strengthening of a warrior?

"Step into the track of the Monster Slayer.
Step into the moccasins of him whose lure is the extended bowstring,
Step into the moccasins of him who lures the enemy to death."

Storm did not put the contents of this last packet with the things to be left in Larkin's care. He took up the jewelry, running his fingers across the cool substance of silver, the round boss of turquoise, slipping the necklace over his head where it lay cold against his breast under his shirt. The ketoh clasped his wrist. He rolled the concha belt into a coil to fit into his trail bag.

Then he got to his feet, the blanket folded into a narrow length resting on his shoulder. He had never worn a "chief" blanket in all his life, yet its soft weight now had a warm and familiar feel, bringing with it the closeness of kinship—linking the forgotten hands that had woven it to Hosteen Storm, refugee on another world, lost to his people and his home.

Lost! Dumbly Storm turned to face the east, toward the mountain ranges. He threw his hat down on the blanket roll, baring his head to the tug of the wind from those high hills, and walked forward through the night, doubly lighted by the two small moons, coming out over a little rise that could not even be named "hill." He sat down, cross-legged. There had always been a strong tie between the Dineh and their land. In the past they had chosen to starve in bad times rather than be separated from the mountains, the deserts, the world they knew.

He would not remember! He dared not! Storm's hands balled into fists and he beat them upon his knees, feeling that pain far less than the awaking pain inside him. He was cut off—exiled—And he was also accursed, unless he carried out the purpose that had brought him here. Yet still there was this other hesitation in him. Without realizing it, he reverted to age-old beliefs. He must have broken his warrior's magic. And so he could not meet Quade until he was whole again, once more armed against the enemy—the time was not yet ripe.

How long he sat there he did not know. But now there were streaks of orange-red in the mauve sky. It was not the same promise given by the sun to Terra, but with it came the feeling that his decision had been rightly made.

Storm faced the band of growing color, raising his arms and holding up into that light first his bared knife and then his stun rod—the arms of a warrior—to be blessed by the sun. He pointed them first at the life-giving heat in the sky and then at the earth, the substance from which the Faraway Gods had fashioned the People in the long ago. He had not the right, as had a Singer, to call upon those forces he believed existed, and possibly, this far from the land of the Dineh, the Faraway Gods could not, would not listen. Yet something within Storm held the belief that they could and did.

> "Beauty is around me—
> This one walks in beauty—
> Good is around me—
> This one walks in beauty—"

Perhaps the words he recalled were not the right ones, perhaps he did wrong to pre-empt the powers of a Singer. But he thought that the Old Ones would understand.

CHAPTER SIX

The wind that had drawn Storm to this little height died away. With a soft, coaxing whine Surra pressed against his leg and bumped her head against the hand that had dropped from his knife hilt. He heard the chittering of the meerkats in the grass. Above, a perfectly shaped black silhouette on the dawn sky, Baku mounted to greet the new day in the freedom of the upper air. Storm breathed deeply. His feeling of loss and loneliness dimmed as he returned to the trail camp to make his farewells.

A short appraisal of Sorenson's preparations told the Terran that the Survey man was as competent as Larkin about the details of packing. The party was a small one: Sorenson himself, the settler pack master, Mac Foyle, and three Norbies, among whom Storm was not too surprised to find Gorgol. He raised his hand in greeting to the young native hunter, as he led his pack mare along to be lined with the others.

Foyle eyed this addition to the train with some astonishment, for the meerkats clung to the top of the mare's pack and in addition she bore an improvised perch rigged for Baku. Surra trotted on her own four paws, well able to match the ambling pace of the pack animals.

"Those are a couple of tricky riders you got there," Foyle hailed the Terran. "What are they, young fella? Monkeys? I heard tell of monkeys but I've never seen 'em."

"Meerkats," supplied Storm.

"From Terra, eh?" Foyle tested a lashing, looked over the mare's rig with approval, and then brought up his own riding horse. "Smart lookin' little tykes—what are they good for?"

Storm laughed. "Digging mostly. See their big claws? Those can make the dirt fly when it's necessary. They also bring back what they take a fancy to. You might call them thieves sometimes—" He snapped his fingers at Ho and Hing and they blinked back at him, uncaring.

"Heard about you and your animals back in town. Your name's Storm, isn't it? Heard tell, too, how you knocked out one of Gorlund's riders just pattin' him on the head—or so the boys were sayin'."

Storm smiled. "Commando tricks, Foyle. That rider was loaded and wanted to stretch himself a little, only he did it a bit too wide and in the wrong direction—"

Foyle examined him with a frank stare that climbed from boot soles to the top of his hat. "Bet the boys weren't far wrong either about your bein' thunder and lightnin' all rolled up into one. You aren't so big a fella, but it's the small ones, light on their feet, who can really cause trouble. I'd like to have seen that dust-up, I surely would!" Foyle jerked the lead rope of the first pack horse and that animal obediently fell into line behind.

They went down slope to the river where Surra balked on the bank, spitting her displeasure at the thought of water and wet fur. Storm soothed her and tossed a rope end, to be caught in her teeth after a last cat-curse. Then, with the dune cat swimming along with the horses, they crossed the Irrawady to the field above which the eastern mountains reached into the faint lavender of the sky.

Sorenson not only knew how to organize an expedition, he could also lead it. And Storm soon learned that this was the third and not the first time the Survey Service man had attempted to find the Sealed Caves.

"Water's the problem," he explained. "You can travel this country in the spring, or for about four short weeks in the fall, and live off it. The rest of the time you have to pack water and food for your horses. And that just can't be done, except at ruinous expense, which my department won't authorize on mere rumor alone. We had one successful season before the war, opened a small dig on the Krabyaolo, that's the edge of the Peak country. And a piece of carving was unearthed there that caused an explosion in rarefied circles. So the authorities will grant us a pittance now and then for these short trips. Let me discover something really worthwhile and they might set up a permanent work camp. I've been told that the water supply is better in the direction we're heading this trip—"

"This thing you found—what made it so important?"

"Did you ever see any Lo Sak Ki work?" Sorenson counterquestioned.

"Not that I know of—"

"That's a unique type of carving found in the Lo Sal provinces on Altair Three—very intricate patterning, shows evidence of a long development of civilized art, undoubtedly the result of a lengthy period of experiment and refinement. And it's native to Altair Three. Only this piece we found repeated at least two of Lo Sak Ki basic designs."

"I don't suppose there are too many different designs possible," ventured Storm. "And with about two thousand planets producing art work—twenty-five other nonhuman races of high intelligence into the bargain, as well as all the dead civilizations we have uncovered in space—designs *could* be repeated without being related."

"Logical enough. But see here—" The Survey man used his quirt as a pointer to indicate the ketoh on the Terran's wrist." I take it that is Terran, also that it may represent some lesser known tribal work there, perhaps it has ceremonial significance—"

"It was developed from a bow guard once worn by my people when they were roaming desert raiders—"

"And were those people a dominant nation on your world in the days when separate nations did exist there?"

Storm laughed. "I believe they considered themselves to be so—in error. They did rule a small section of one continent for a few years. But no, they were not a dominant race. In fact their country was overrun by a white-skinned race, representing a mechanized, technical civilization, who considered them barbarians."

"It follows then you would not have found such a bracelet to be an object universally known and worn on Terra?"

"No."

"So what would have been your reaction if say on— Where did you serve during the war, Storm?"

"Lev—Angol—"

"Lev? Good. Suppose while you were on Lev you investigated a mound of rubble and found buried in it the twin to your bracelet—knowing, of course, that no other galactic trooper had been there recently, that no Terran of the present era could have dropped it. What then would have been your conclusions?"

"Well, either a Levite had imported it or there *had* been a Terran there once—"

"Just so. But if all other evidence argued that it had been there since *before* the era of Terran space flight?"

"Either there was earlier Terran space flight than is known to our records, or Terra had off-world visitors herself."

Sorenson nodded vigorously. "You see, you cling instinctively to the idea that your bracelet *must* have come from Terra. Not once have you suggested that an alien developed something of the same design."

Again Storm laughed appreciatively. "You make out a good case, sir. Perhaps it's all a matter of native pride—"

"Or perhaps your instinct is entirely right, and there was space travel at an earlier date. So—here we have a similar problem, a design, well known to a very limited section of Altair Three, is found half the galaxy away in ruins attributed by native legend to a nonnative race. May we not assume that others prospected through the star lanes before Terra colony ships and explorers went out to the same paths? If so, why haven't we met them or their descendants? What ended *their* empire or their confederacy? War? Decadence? Some plague spread from system to system by their ships? Perhaps our answer lies in the Sealed Caves, if we can find them!"

"You are sure you have a good lead this time?"

"Better than just a lead, we have a guide waiting for us in the Valley of Twisted Horns, a man who says he has found at least one cave. Most of the Norbies avoid that section. But their wizards do go in at certain seasons of the year for ceremonial purposes, and war parties can add to their effectiveness by making magic there against their enemies. They believe that a ritual performed near the Caves can render a warrior twice as impervious and the enemy twice as vulnerable, whether that enemy is within striking distance or three days' journey away at the time. Youngsters who want to claim warrior status travel to the Peaks. That young Gorgol joined us for that reason. The place has religious significance. And Bokatan, our guide, is a clan wizard. He's made three such journeys and now he believes that the Sealed Caves people want to issue forth again and that an off-worlder must open the gate for them—hence our expedition has his blessing."

"Has Bokatan power enough to impress other Norbies with that idea?" questioned Storm. "We could run into trouble if he hasn't."

"I believe he has. The alien laws have always frustrated digging here on Arzor. We are not allowed to cultivate the tribes unless they make the first overtures, and we cannot enter their territories unless invited. But this time we're on safe ground. I had to swear to observe a formidable set of conditions before I received my permit and then Bokatan testified for me. A few off-world men have lived as licensed yoris hunters in Norbie territory, and from them, and the settlers for whom the Norbies will work, we have to pick up all we know about their customs. And there are tribes back in the hills who have had no contact with off-worlders or settlers at all, whose whole way of life may differ radically from those we do know something about—"

"You can't live in a Norbie camp without government permission?"

"Oh, I guess it has been done, but the invitation has to come from the Norbie clan involved."

Storm eyed the ranges ahead. He would fulfill his contract with the expedition. But afterwards what was to prevent his cutting loose and striking down south on his own? He had the team and he had learned how to live off the land in far more hostile countries than this one, including some where not only the natives were deadly enemies but also the land itself provided fatal pitfalls for the unwary.

As they traveled, Storm fitted into the wilderness and the duties of a scout as a hand would slip into a well-worn glove. He perfected his finger-talk with Gorgol's eager aid and the assistance of the other Norbies. But repeated failures taught him the truth of what he had heard—that an off-worlder could not hope to learn and use the vocal speech of the natives. His efforts to imitate their twittering actually seemed to hurt their ears.

In spite of their lack of a common oral speech the Norbies adopted him in a way they did not accept Sorenson or Foyle. The Terran tried their bows, displaying his familiarity with that type of weapon, only he discovered that he could not string one made for an adult Norbie. Gorgol's was lighter and when Storm's trial shaft centered in the heart of a deerlike browser, the Norbies ceremoniously presented him with a smaller weapon of his own and a quiver containing five arrows with fire-bright heads, points brilliant enough to have been chipped from gem stone.

"Warrior arrows," Gorgol told him via fingers. "No use second time after they have been dipped in man-blood. You warrior—you can use."

The young native tried to persuade Storm to follow the Norbie custom of tattooing a bright scarlet band about the old scar on his shoulder, urging that any warrior would be proud to display such marks at the evening fire when Norbie men stripped off their corselets, showing for the awe of their untried fellows their marks of valor.

It was usual that Gorgol and Storm were paired as scouts, Baku circling overhead, and Surra ranging in a crisscross pattern to cover both flanks. The meerkats rode in skin bags slung across Rain's back, scrambling out at every halt to go exploring on their own, but returning readily to Storm's call, usually dragging some prize—a succulent root or brightly colored stone—which had taken their fancy, as loot.

This acquisitive habit of theirs was a never-ending source of amusement for the whole party, and there was a demand at each evening's camp for Storm to turn out the bags where the meerkats stored their treasures and reveal what Ho and Hing had thought worth retrieving that day.

Twice they turned up worthwhile items. Once it was an "eye" stone—an odd gem sometimes found in dried river beds. It was shaped like a golden drop, the color of dark honey, with a slitted line of red fire through its middle, not unlike one of Surra's eyes—save for the color. And it changed shades when moved from light to dark—the red slit lightening to yellow, the honey becoming greenish.

But it was the other find, made on the tenth day after they had left Irrawady Crossing, that excited the Norbies. Emptied out of Ho's bag, among other gleanings, was an arrowhead. It was barbed and unlike the others Storm had seen in use by the expedition scouts, for the crystal from which it was fashioned was a milky white. Since the natives would not personally handle any of the meerkats' plunder, the Terran picked it up, balancing it on his hand. Hunting points were always of green-gold stone, war arrows clear crystal with a blue cast—at least those carried by the camp Norbies were. This one's delicate point had been snapped off, but otherwise it was a beautiful piece of fletcher's art.

Dagotag, the leader of the Norbies, examined it carefully as Storm held it out, but he did not offer to touch it. He sucked in his breath loudly, a Norbie preliminary to serious pronouncement, and then made fast finger-talk.

"That be Nitra—over-the-mountains-men. Warrior—this be war arrow. Come to collect honors for Nitra warrior talk—kill strangers—"

"They be enemy you?" Storm signed.

Dagotag nodded. "Enemy us—we Shosonna people. Maybeso enemy you faraway men. Nitra never see faraway men—big trophy bow hand—"

"The Nitra eat THE MEAT?" Sorenson shaped a sign forbidden save in times of stress, and punctuated his question by spitting ritually into the fire three times.

"Not so!" Dagotag's fingers flew. "Take trophy—hang bow hand of enemy in wizard house. But no eat THE MEAT. Only evil men do so. Nitra—good fighters—not evil ones who listen to black spirits in the night!"

"But they might fight us?" Storm persisted.

"Yes—if they track us. But this point—it may be old—of another season. Only we must watch—"

Every Norbie had reached for his skin bedroll and was bringing out his well-protected package of personal war arrows to place the customary five such shafts in their quivers beside the ordinary hunting points.

Storm spoke to Sorenson. "We'll have plenty of warning if they do try to scout us. I have yet to see any living thing creep by Surra undetected." He tossed the enemy arrowhead into the air and caught it. Dragged out of a man's flesh, those cruel, brittle barbs were clearly meant to be left in the wound on the way. It was as wicked a thing as a blaster. Where Ho had found it and how long it had lain there were the important questions. Was it truly the relic of some long-ago raid, or had its owner discarded it that very day because it was broken?

He ordered the dune cat on guard, certain that no scout of the Nitra could win past her. And tomorrow Baku would comb the wastes ahead of them with better eyes than any human or humanoid possessed. The party was reasonably safe from a surprise attack, but there was the matter of an ambush, which could be so easily staged in this country, where the trail threaded through canyons and narrow defiles, along twisted traces where it was sometimes necessary to dismount and lead one's horse. And the farther they bored into the mountains, the worse the going became. He could well understand that only a strong lure could drag anyone into this desolate country.

After Sorenson and Mac turned in, Storm brought out his own bow and arrows. The fire had not yet died down and he held those glittering points in its glow. One by one he touched each to his wrist and pressed, saw the answering drop of blood cloud the crystal tip. Then, when all had been so painted, Storm let the blood fall in a thick dollop to the ground. The age-old offering to secure strong "medicine" for a new war weapon was made. Why did he offer it now—and to what spirit of the Arzoran wilderness?

"Why you do so?" The slender hand in the firelight sketched that inquiry.

He did not know the Norbie word for fortune or luck—but he used the finger vocabulary he did have and tried clumsily to explain:

"Give blood—arrow shoot straight—enemy feel. Blood pay for good arrow—"

"That is true! You faraway man—but you think Norbie. Maybeso Norbie inside man—he fly far—far—be caught faraway—want to get back to his own clan—enter in faraway baby—so come back now. True—true—" The yellow-red fingers tapped lightly on the back of Storm's hand close to that tiny wound. "Here—outside—you be faraway man. Inside, you Norbie come home again!"

"Perhaps—" Storm agreed lest he give offense.

"The sealed ones will know. They came far—far—too. Maybeso they like you—"

Gorgol spoke with the confidence of one who was acquainted with the mysterious, legendary people, and Storm asked another question:

"Gorgol knows the sealed ones?"

His question loosed a flood of story. Gorgol—three seasons back as far as Storm could determine—had left his tribe on his man-trip, to prove himself a lone hunter able to stand with the adult males of Krotag's following. After Norbie custom he had either to engage an enemy tribesman on his own—if he were lucky enough to find a roving warrior of some clan traditionally at war with his people—or kill without aid one of the four dangerous forms of wildlife. Since his "inside man" had suggested such a path in a dream, Gorgol had headed to the eastern mountains, working his way along the same general direction the expedition was now traveling.

There he had come across the spoor of an "evil flyer," the giant bird-thing the Norbies regarded with a wholesome aversion for its unclean habits and respect for its ferocious fighting spirit. Since he could hope for no better kill to establish himself among the men, Gorgol had spent the better part of five days tracking the creature to its nesting ledge high in the mountains. But he had been too eager at his first shot and had wounded it only.

The bird, after the manner of its species, had attacked him, and there had followed a running fight down the side of the nesting peak into a valley where Gorgol had laid an ambush that had successfully finished the flyer. Though he had been injured in the final encounter, he was not too badly wounded. He thrust his leg out into the firelight now, tracing for Storm the blue line of a ragged scar fully ten inches long.

Disabled by his hurt, Gorgol had been forced to stay in the valley of the ambush. Luckily the season was still one of rains and the big dry had not yet begun so there was a trickle of water from the heights. And during his imprisonment in the narrow cut he had discovered a walled-up cave opening, together with other objects made by intelligent beings who were neither Norbie nor settler.

He had left those finds behind him when at last he could hobble, not wishing to vex the sealed ones. But since that day he had remained certain that he had chanced upon one of the doors of the Sealed Caves.

"The sealed ones—they good to men who keep their laws. Put in Gorgol's head how to kill flyer—send water drip to drink while leg bad. Old stories say sealed ones good to Norbies long, long ago. I say this too. Maybeso I die there did not their magic help me! Their magic big—" His hand expanded in the large sign. "They do much—sealed away from sun they sleep—but still they do much!"

"Could you find this valley again?"

"Yes. But not go there unless sealed ones allow. I follow bird. Sealed ones know I come not to disturb them, not to dig them up. They excuse. Go to wake them—maybeso they not like. Must call—then we go."

Storm heard the conviction in that and respected it. Each man had a right to his own beliefs. But this did back up Sorenson's story that the wizard Bokatan had offered to guide them because he believed that the sealed ones themselves were in favor of it. And since the country of Gorgol's hunting adventures was in the same general direction as the territory into which the expedition was heading, perhaps they were going to find the mysterious Sealed Caves after all.

CHAPTER SEVEN

The sun was a warm hand pressing on his bared shoulders as Storm lay on top of an outcrop, his long-vision glasses trained on the pass ahead. He had shed his easily sighted frawn shirt many days ago, having discovered that his own brown skin was hard to distinguish from the rocks.

Now the path of the expedition had narrowed to one choice, a defile leading between climbing walls, a perfect country for ambush. Properly they should travel it by night, except that the footing was none too good and they dared not risk a fall for either man or horse. Already the party followed well-tried Terran precautions for advance into enemy territory, stopping in the early afternoon to graze their horses and feed themselves, and then moving on for an hour after sunset, so that their night camp site was far from the place where they had first—to any spy-scout—bedded down. Whether such elementary tactics would mislead experienced native raiders was another matter.

Storm was certain that they were under observation, though he had no real proof except the alert uneasiness of the team. And he depended upon bird and cat for his first warning against any attack.

Now Baku did come in, voicing a harsh scream, to send winging out of the brush below a whole covey of panic-stricken grass hens. There was someone coming through the defile, a Norbie riding along on a vividly spotted black and white horse. And the white star on its forehead was dabbed with red, a circle centered by a double dot—If this newcomer was not the wizard Bokatan, then he had acquired Bokatan's favorite mount, which had been described to Storm in advance. This would not be too impossible. Storm remained where he was, his bow ready.

"Hoooooooooo!" The call was the twitter of Norbie speech prolonged into a high-pitched hoot. Out of the rock, seemingly, Dagotag arose to meet the wizard. At least the party now had their promised guide.

Before nightfall they had crossed the invisible border of the taboo land, to camp that night on the banks of a swollen stream. The water was red with silt, whirling along uprooted bushes and even small trees. Sorenson surveyed it critically.

"You can have too much of a good thing. We have to depend upon the mountain rains for water. But, on the other hand, flash floods in these narrow gorges can wipe out a party such as ours in a matter of seconds. Tomorrow we'll have to parallel this as long as we can to water the horses. Let us hope the level begins to drop instead of to rise—"

Before noon the next day, not only was the flood dwindling but Bokatan pointed them away from it, using as a guide for their new direction something that excited them all. There was no mistaking the artificial origin of that low black ridge, running at right angles to the northeast.

Strom measured it roughly with his hand, finding it about a foot wide, though raised only a few inches from the ground. It was wedge-shaped with the narrower edge straight up. To the touch it was not stone, nor metal, at least no stone nor metal he had ever seen before. And its purpose remained a mystery. A knife blade made no impression, but under prodding fingers the substance had a faintly greasy feel, though neither dry soil nor leaves clung to its surface. Nor would Surra put paw on it. She sniffed dubiously at the ridge, plainly avoiding contact, sneezing twice and shaking her head in her gesture of distaste.

"Like a rail," Mac commented, and whacked the first pack horse on, though that animal, too, picked a way that did not bring it close to the black ridge.

Sorenson stopped to snap tri-dee prints of the thing though Bokatan urged the party to hurry. "Up!" his fingers counseled. "Up and through the hole in the earth before sun sets—then you may look upon the valley of the sealed ones—"

Already the cliffs rose so high that the light of the sun did not penetrate to the floor of the canyon through which they passed, and gathering shadows thickened almost to dusk as they rode along by the black rail.

Death defiles, that old belief of his people haunted Storm, while his modern training denied it. A man who touched the dead, or their possessions, dwelt under a roof where death had been, was unclean, accursed. This black ridge was like a thread wrought by the dead to draw others into the house of the dead—He blinked, shrugged the blanket about his shoulders, dropping a little behind the rest as he fumbled in his belt pouch for an object he had fashioned during their noon halt.

The Terran did not dismount, but leaned far from his riding pad, holding that small sliver of wood plumed at one end with two of Baku's feathers. It had been shaped with the aid of one of his war arrows after immemorial custom, and now he aimed its point at the alien rail—if rail it was. The prayer stick caught and held in some infinitesimal crack of the substance, standing unwavering, its feathers triumphantly erect.

One magic against another. Storm clicked his tongue to Rain and the horse trotted on to catch up, just as a turn in the canyon brought them to what Bokatan could well term the "hole" in the earth.

If they had not been able to see the brightness of sunlight ahead, Storm would have protested against entering the place. For the tunnel opening was like an open mouth, fanged at the upper arch with regular pointed projections of the same substance as the rail that had led them here. What purpose those projections had originally served, the explorers could not guess. Now they resembled nothing so much as teeth ready to close upon the unwary. And Storm envied Baku who could wing aloft and cross the mountain barrier in the free air.

Though the tunnel was a short one, open at both ends, within it, the air was stale to taste and smell, as if no cleansing wind had ever flown through. Surra took the passage in a rush, the horses pounding after her, until they burst out into the brilliant blaze of the sun again, to find themselves at one end of a much larger valley.

"This is a leg-breaking do, if I ever saw one!" Mac exploded—rightly. For before them was a choked stretch of debris, tumbled blocks of the black material overgrown with generations of vines and brush.

Sorenson dismounted. "Some kind of a building—perhaps a gate-house for defense—" He was reaching for his tri-dee camera when Bokatan pushed to the fore.

"Into the valley now—night come here—bad—"

Reluctantly Sorenson agreed. Storm was already afoot, his horse's reins hooked over his arm, ready to help Mac with the pack train, while the Norbies strung out, scouting the easiest way through the maze before them. Storm, threading a narrow path between banks of the broken black material, decided this was an excellent trap, certainly not any trail to be traveled after dark.

"I'd like to know what happened here." Mac puffed up to join the Terran, towing the gray lead horse of the pack train. "Looks like somebody got real mad and loosed a buster where it would do the most harm—don't it now?"

Storm gazed at the ruins about them for the first time with interest in the debris itself, not just regarding it as an entanglement through which they must worm their way. He still did not care to make too close an inspection, but Mac's suggestion was shrewdly taken. An earthquake might have reduced a stoutly built structure to this, but mere lapse of time—no. And outside of a convulsion of nature there remained only war. Yet nowhere in the tradition of the Norbies was there any reference to war as the reason for the withdrawal of the sealed ones.

"Yes—a buster—" Mac scrambled ahead. "Or maybe a good, big flood."

"Or a series of floods—" That was Sorenson catching up as they paused to rest the horses. "Look there!" Now that he pointed out the high watermarks on the wall of the valley the others could not miss them.

"Do you suppose that tunnel acts as a drain?" hazarded Storm.

"If it wasn't originally intended for that use, it must serve now—and has done so for a good many years. There's a large lake in the valley according to Bokatan—a few flash floods and the overflow must seek an outlet—"

The ruins sprawled for half a mile of hard going. Then they came into the course of a dry river bed fronting a sharp upward slope. The black rail ran straight ahead, to be hidden in the earth of the slope that perhaps had accumulated since the builders of the black wedge had laid it down.

Up the slope they trudged and stood on the verge of a broad dam, which controlled the stagnant-looking, brown water of quite a sizable lake. And beyond the opposite shore of that dank lake was the rest of the valley.

Dotted in the lake itself and along its shores were mounds of weathered and overgrown debris. The remains of a city? Sorenson sighed and pulled off his hat, wiping his arm across his flushed dusty face.

"We may not have found the Caves," he said slowly, "but we have found something. Go ahead and make camp, boys, I want all the shots of this I can get before the light is gone!"

They made camp on an inlet of the lake and Storm took over the job of dampening down the ground with insect repellent. He noticed that the Norbies did not range far away and that the natives piled their hide night shelters well within the circle of the fire glow.

Mac surveyed the wealth of mounds. "If we're going to dig, we have plenty of places to choose from. Only maybe you 'n' me 'n' Sorenson's goin' to have to do most of it. Norbies don't ever take kindly to usin' shovels—"

"About all we can do on this trip is map." Sorenson came down at last to join them. "Maybe open a test trench or two. A couple of small finds to impress the directors would help out a lot. But if this site is as good as it looks, we'd need a more permanent camp and a dozen years to really clean it out. Bokatan"—he appealed to their guide—"this water," he signed, "does it go with the coming of the big dry, or does it stay?"

The Norbie's hands spread in a gesture of bafflement. "Bokatan come only in wet times—no see in dry. But water much—no think go away when big dry comes—"

"I'm inclined to believe that," Sorenson said happily. "That means we *can* think about year around work here."

"If you don't get too much water," Storm returned. "From the evidence of those high watermarks there have been floods clear across this space."

The Survey man refused to be dismayed by that. "If necessary we can pitch camp back against the cliffs to the north. There is an upward slope toward that end of the valley. Surely the whole place is never altogether under water. We've had high rains for the past month and see the size of the lake?"

He was given a chance to test his deductions before dawn the next morning, for the same kind of drenching rain that had bogged the trail herd came to flood the camp. In a hurry, they moved away from the rapidly rising lake. To take refuge on top of one of the mounds of debris was a temptation, but such a move could only prove more dangerous in the end.

While the steady downpour cut the danger of attack from a Nitra war party, the rain bothered the Norbies. Water and war were both gifts of the Thunder Drummers, but this was not good land in which to be caught by water, and, when they witnessed one landslip along the cliff wall, they pressed back to the upper and unknown northern end of the valley.

Three of the Norbies rode in search of higher ground that might lie above the old flood-level marks, and Storm and Mac, working together, pushed the pack horses steadily away from the lake, following the upward slope. Sorenson and Bokatan struck off in the direction of the reputed Caves, for the Survey man was determined to learn all he could if there was danger of their having to pull out entirely.

Usually tractable enough, the pack horses were hard to handle that morning. Storm wished he could have coaxed Surra to serve as an additional drover, but the big cat had disappeared on her own early in the rain and the Terran knew she was going to hole up somewhere out of the wet. Since he had given her no definite orders she would follow her own instincts. He had not sighted Baku since dawn.

Nearly all the horses had scrambled up a steeper rise when the Terran heard Mac shout excitedly. Hoping that the pack master had discovered a good stretch of higher territory, Storm whacked at the last horse in line, his own mare.

Then the world came apart about him. Storm had been under fire on the training range, he had witnessed—from a distance—the obliteration bombing of an enemy stronghold. But this was no man-made fury—it was the raw sword of nature herself striking unleashed.

The rain, now heavier than before, became a smothering blanket under a black sky. He could not even see Rain's ears, head, plastered mane. The gush of water took away his breath, beat about his body.

Lightning—purple fire in jagged spears—thunder claps that left one deafened, battered— Storm's horse reared, fought for freedom, wild with fear. Then the stallion ran through a wall of water and his rider could only cling blindly to his seat, lying along the horse's neck gasping.

They were still in the dark but the rain no longer beat on them, only the fury of its rushing filled the world with sound. Lightning again tore at the sky. And above him, in that flash, Storm saw an overhang of earth break loose and fall. Half dazed, he jumped, stumbled to his knees, and went down, as mud cascaded on him, pressing him flat under its weight until he lost consciousness.

It was dark when the Terran opened his eyes and tried feebly to move—dark with an absence of all light that was as frightening as the silence that now walled him in. But, half-conscious as he was, Storm struggled for freedom. There was a break in the cover over him, and he levered up the forepart of his body.

None of his bones appeared to be broken. He hurt all over, but he *could* move arms and legs, wriggled the rest of him out of the mass of soil that had imprisoned him. Storm tried to remember just what had happened in those last moments before the world caved in.

He called—to be answered by a plaintive whinny, shrill and frightened. Storm called again through the darkness in soft-voiced reassurance, using the speech of the horse tamer, which he had used with Rain since the first moment he had laid hands on the stallion. And, as he spoke, he dug at the earth still encasing his legs, until he could stand up.

The Terran explored about him with outstretched arms—until he remembered the torch at his belt. Snapping its button, Storm aimed the beam straight up. The answering light was faint, oddly paled. He stood by a rock wall—and, as the beam swept down and away from that solid surface, it was swallowed up in a pocket of darkness that might mark the interior of a cave of some expanse. But caught in the torch's beam was Rain, white foam roping his jaws, his eyes rolling wildly.

Storm moved to run his hand along the sweating arch of the horse's neck, conscious now of the smell of this place. Just as they had found it in the entrance tunnel of the valley, so here the air was stale, musty. As he continued to breathe it the Terran felt a growing sickness and an impulse to turn and batter his way out of this cave, or pocket, or whatever it was, that held them. He fought for self-control.

On his right was a second rock wall, and behind him the fall of moist earth in which he had been caught. Then the torch beam glistened at floor level. Runnels of water were sluggishly crawling toward him from under that mass of loose earth, gathering in the slight depressions of the rock floor. As Storm watched there was more movement, a slide of the soil, only this one uncovered a dim spot of light close to the roof—a handsbreadth of metallic gray that might mark the sky.

Storm snapped off the torch, spoke once more to Rain. With great care he climbed, a few inches at a time, to reach that breakthrough, once leaping clear to avoid being carried back by a second slip. But, at last, he got there, thankful to draw in lungfuls of the rain-washed air, clean and sweet without. The soft earth was easy enough to dig and he set about with his hands to enlarge the opening.

He came upon a rock that had to be dislodged with care, and marveled at the chance or good fortune that had saved him and the stallion from such a bombardment, giving them their lives in spite of their imprisonment. Storm's wonder at the narrowness of their escape increased as his nails scraped across an even larger stone, one wedged in the opening as a stopper might be driven into a bottle.

The Terran returned to clawing at the earth heaped about that rock, pushing outward when he could. Now and again he checked the seepage under the wall; the flow was increasing, if slowly. Could a stream, or part of the lake, be lapping outside? He could not remember in which direction Rain had raced in panicked flight—west, north, or east—

A whole block of moist soil tangled with roots gave way before him and rain beat in to soak him in an instant. The moisture felt clean and good against his body, washing the mud and staleness of the place from him.

Worming his way back up, Storm thrust head and shoulders out of the hole. Visibility was limited by the rain, but what he could see made him gasp, for the whole area below bore no resemblance to anything he remembered.

A sheet of water, swirling angrily and pitted by the lash of the rain, lapped at the other side of the barrier on which he half lay. Uprooted trees tossed on that roiled surface and just below him was the body of the black pack mare, anchored to the shore by the weight of a rock that had crushed her head and one foreleg.

On the frail island of her body crouched a small shape with matted fur, clinging despairingly to the bobbing pack. And seeing that refugee, Storm shoveled swiftly at the earth. He ripped off his belt, stripping it quickly of knife sheath and stun rod holster, and on his third toss one end of the belt landed on the pack. The meerkat moved swiftly, climbing that improvised ladder to a point where Storm could scoop the small creature to safety.

It was Hing and she was uninjured as far as his examining hands could determine. What had happened to Ho he did not want to guess, for the bag in which Hing's mate had ridden must now be trapped under the dead mare.

Whimpering, the meerkat clung to Storm, trying in plaintive little cries to tell her misery. He scraped the mud from her fur as best he could, and carried her into the cave to wrap her in the blanket. With her snug he returned to their window on the outside.

It might be dangerous to try to dig out more of the cave-closing slide at present. Such efforts could only let in the lake waters to engulf them. For such work he needed better light and an end to the rain. And both of those might come in the morning. For the present there was nothing to do but wait out the hours. Surely the skies could not go on releasing such a weight of water forever!

The gray of the day became the dark of a starless, moonless night. Storm rested half across the wall, Hing curled against him, watching in vain hopes of seeing some light along the cliff walls that would signal the escape to safety of the others, some indication that he was not the only human survivor of the flood that filled the valley.

Storm must have fallen asleep at last, for when he roused, it was to find weak sunlight on his face. Hing sat by his shoulder making an exacting toilet, chittering with almost human disgust at the unhappy state of her usually well-groomed fur.

The water had fallen away outside, grounding some of the wrack that it had floated. Something as red-brown as the soil, with a wicked mouthful of teeth, was busy at the mare, feasting upon the bounty. Storm shouted and flung a clod of earth at the creature.

As the scavenger flashed to cover the Terran's voice echoed weirdly from the heights. He shouted again, this time with a summoning call. Though he did that again and again, waiting eagerly between each shout until he counted twenty—there came no answer. So he set to work again digging until he was able to get out, skidding down to bring up short against the dead pack horse.

CHAPTER EIGHT

Having salvaged the mare's pack and dumped it in the cave, Storm stationed Hing on guard over what might be the last supplies. The meerkat was not a fighter, but she would keep off the scavengers such as the one he had seen at work earlier that morning. That precaution taken, the Terran splashed out to explore, using a length of driftwood to anchor him on the slippery mud banks. Twice he disturbed scavengers and carrion birds and both times hurried to see what they fed upon.

Once it was the horse Sorenson had ridden, and secondly it was a battered wild thing that must have been swept down the mountain stream. He stopped at intervals to call, to whistle for Baku—but there was never any answer.

As the sun rose higher, its rays sucked up the moisture and Storm was able to flounder about the end of the enlarged lake. The spread of murky water now covered five-sixths of the valley, including the entire lower end through which they had entered. And the Terran found no traces of any survivors, saw no camp smoke, had no answers to his frequent hails.

The mounts of debris were largely covered, only a few projecting above the surface of the flood. On one or two he sighted moving creatures, all small refugees from among the grass dwellers of the valley. He was about to turn back to the cave when he heard the beat of powerful wings and saw a black shape etched against the clear sky—a shape that could only be Baku. Storm whistled and the eagle dropped in her falcon swoop.

She skimmed above his head, thus delivering her usual signal to follow. But the path she pointed lay directly across the lake and Storm distrusted those dark waters full of floating drift and perhaps some unpleasant water-dwelling things he could not sight. He splashed along the verge, sometimes thigh deep, always sounding ahead with his pole. Baku had come to rest on one of the above-surface mounds, one which had been situated far up the dry portion of the valley before the storm. The Terran recognized it as an earlier landmark by a few feet of battered outcrop that still bore some resemblance to a wall. He shouted and Baku screamed in answer but did not rise. His testing pole plunged into a sudden deep and Storm knew he would have to swim to reach that islet. He took to the deeper water gingerly, striking out with care to avoid the flotsam, hating the smell of the mud-thick liquid that slid greasily about his body.

Then he caught at a block, found his feet, and climbed to the top of the island. He had expected to find traces of the flood. But what he faced now was a battlefield! Three dead men lay there, each with a war arrow in him, each lacking a right hand, Sorenson, Bokatan and Dagotag. By the signs, they had died early that morning, perhaps when he was making his struggle to get out of the cave.

His age old racial fear of the dead warred in him with the need to know what had happened and the necessity of providing a last service for these whose lives he had shared during the past strenuous days. Storm walked slowly forward and something else stirred, lifted a tawny head on which the fur was matted with red. The Terran sprinted to the side of the dune cat.

Surra whined. The ragged wound on her head was ugly, but, as Storm discovered thankfully, not dangerous. It looked much worse than it was and the attackers must have believed her dead. Not for the first time the Terran wished that the team had speech in common, as well as their trained rapport. He could only survey the scene and try to deduce what had happened.

It was his guess that Sorenson and the two Norbies had been cut off by the flood and had taken refuge on this hillock that was by far the highest in the vicinity. The attack had come later, after the end of the storm. And the attackers had thoroughly looted the camp, stripped the bodies—all weapons were gone.

Storm brought out his small personal aid kit and went to work on Surra, cleansing her wound. She allowed him to handle her, giving only a little protesting cry now and then. He worked as slowly as he could, trying not to think of that other task ahead of him. But with Surra comfortable he forced himself to it, though he could not repress shudders as he straightened out Sorenson's contorted body and placed the dead Norbies on either side of the Survey man. There was nothing with which to dig graves, but he broke off pieces of the rubble, working with dogged determination, piling the loosened stones and earth over the three, while the sun turned the hillock into a steam bath.

Surra called before he had finished and Storm looked up to see her wavering to her feet. Baku was alive, and Surra, and back in the cave he had Rain and Hing. He knew little of Norbie war customs, but he did not believe that the Nitra—if it had been those wild tribesmen who attacked here—would linger. They might well believe that they had wiped out all members of the exploring party. He must get Surra to the higher land at the north of the valley, which meant using Rain. Storm spoke gently to the cat, planting in his mind the idea that he must go but would return soon which she would sense.

The water had fallen swiftly so that this time he swam only a few feet as he backtracked. He returned to the cave to discover that Hing had been busy on her own, using her particular talent—digging—perhaps in search of edible roots carried down in the earthslide. Because of her activities he was able to clear a path for Rain. There were iron rations among the supplies he had in the pack and purified water in his canteen. Rain trotted down to suck up a drink from the flood and tear avidly at the waterlogged grass.

Towing the stallion loaded with the supply pack, Hing riding on top, and Baku overhead, Storm came back to the vicinity of the hillock. The sullenly retreating waters had now bared a stretch of washed gravel and boulders against the cliff wall about half a mile ahead, and he chose that site for his temporary camp. Leaving the pack with Hing and Baku on guard, he splashed over to the mound.

Rain had accepted Surra from the start as a running companion. The cat on four feet was a familiar part of his everyday world. But whether the stallion would allow her as a rider was another matter. Storm, mounted, maneuvered the horse close to the mound, gentling Rain with hands and voice, and when the mount stood quietly, he called to the dune cat. She staggered to the edge of the drop and sprang, landing in front of the man with a sudden shock of weight.

Somewhat to the Terran's surprise, Rain did not try to rid himself of the double burden. And Storm, with Surra draped awkwardly before him, headed the horse back through the roiled waters to the rapidly enlarging dry stretch beyond.

Once on the gravel bed Storm took stock of his supplies. Before leaving Irrawady Crossing he had pared his personal kit to bare essentials, depending upon Sorenson's preparations for food rations. So what he had rescued from the mare was only a fraction of what they might need before they found a way out of the wasteland and gained some isolated settler's holding or a temporary herd station. There were for weapons his stun rod, the bow the Norbies had given him, his belt knife. And for food, a packet of iron rations he had already drawn upon, a survival of his service days. He had his sleeping roll, the blanket from Terra, the small aid kit he had used for Surra, the torch, a hand heat unit with three charges, and a canteen. But he would have to boil his water from now on; the chemical purifiers had gone with the rest of the party's supplies. However, Storm had done with far less when in the field and the team had learned to hunt game with dispatch and economy.

There was an oversized, rock-dwelling, distant cousin of a rabbit, which they had shot and eaten with good appetite on the trail, a deerlike browser, and the grass hens, which could be easily flushed out, though it took a number of them to satisfy a man. But all Arzoran animals moved with water, and he would have to make the river-fed plains before the big dry closed up the land.

Storm sat cross-legged by the bed of grass he had pulled for Surra's resting. Hing muzzled against him, chittering mournfully to herself. Even the bag in which Ho had ridden was not to be found and she missed her mate. As the Terran stroked her coarse fur comfortingly, he studied the southern end of the valley. Between him and the gateway of the tunnel there was still a vast spread of water. He was walled off from that exit until the flood retreated still farther. Also—Storm pushed Hing down on his knees, reached for the vision lenses lying by him.

He swept that southern range, dissatisfied. There was something wrong there, though he could not decide just what it could be. He had a feeling that there had been a change in what he saw. His gaze traveled along the cliffs. There were places there where an active man could climb, but none where he could take Rain. No, unless there was a gateway in the north, then the tunnel remained their only exit. And to head north was to bore farther into the untracked wilderness.

To be alone was nothing new for Storm. In one way or another he had walked a lonely road for most of his life. And sometimes it was easier to live with his inner loneliness and just the team, than to exist in a human anthill such as the Center. But there was something in this valley that he had never met before, not on any alien, enemy-held planet where he had learned to live in peril, where every move might betray him to an enemy and yet not to quick, clean death. This thing clung to the mounds of rubble—to the walls of rock, and the Terran knew that he had not been greatly surprised to find only the dead waiting on the hillock. This was a place that invited death. It repelled his senses, his body. Had it not been that Surra could not yet travel far, Storm would be seeking a way out right now.

The Terran wanted a fire, not only to dry what was left of his clothing and gear and as a source of physical comfort against the chill of the coming waterlogged night, but because fire itself was his species' first weapon against the unknown—the oldest, and the most heartening. Slowly he began to speak aloud, his voice rolling into the chants, the old, old songs meant to be a defense against that which stalks the night, words that he believed he could not remember, but that now came easily in the ancient and comforting rhythms.

Baku, perched on a stone outcrop yards above Storm's head, stirred. Surra raised her chin from her paws, her fox ears pricked. Storm drew his stun rod. His back was against the cliff wall, he had a shielding boulder on his right—only two sides to cover. With the other hand he worked his knife out of its sheath. Any attack would have to be hand to hand. Had a bowman stalked them the arrow would be already freed from its cord. And his stun ray could take care of a charge—

"Eruoooooo!" That call was low, echoing, and it was one he had often heard and could not repeat.

Storm did not relax vigilance, but neither did he press the control button of the ray, as a figure, which was hardly more than a fitting form against shadows gathering in this part of the valley where the western sun was already cut off by the cliffs, came running toward him. Gorgol, his right arm pressed to his chest, reached the gravel beach and dropped on the edge of Surra's bed. His left hand moved in limited signs which Storm had to watch carefully to translate.

"Enemy—after flood—kill—all dead—"

"It is so," Storm returned. "Let me see to your wound warrior."

The Terran pushed the young native back against the barricade boulder and examined the hurt hurriedly in the fading light. Luckily for the Norbie the arrow had gone cleanly through, and as far as Storm could judge none of the treacherous, glassy barbs had broken off in the flesh. He washed it with the last of the purified water and bound it up. Gorgol sighed and closed his eyes. The Terran brought out a block of concentrated ration, broke off a portion and pushed it into the Norbie's good hand.

When Gorgol opened his eyes again Storm signed the all-important question.

"Nitra gone? Or still here?"

Gorgol shook his head in a determined negative. "No Nitra—" With the ration block clenched between his teeth, he moved his one set of fingers. "Not Nitra kill—not Norbies—"

Storm sat back on his heels, his eyes sweeping out over the mound-studded desolation. For an instant or two his vague fears of this place merged in a flash of imagination—the Sealed Cave people? Or some inimical thing they had left here on guard? Then he smiled wryly. Those men on the mound had been killed by arrows, the wound he had just tended was left by the same weapon. His racial superstitions were at war with all the scientific learning of his lost home-world.

"Not Norbies?"

"No Norbie, no Nitra—" Storm had made no mistake in his first reading of Gorgol's signs. Now the native moved his other arm stiffly, forced his right hand to add to the authority of his left. "Far-away men come—your kind!"

But the arrows? That ritual mutilation of the dead—?

"You see them?"

"I see—I on cliff ledge—water high, high! Men come at end of rain—they wear this"—he tapped the yoris hide corselet protecting his own torso—"like Norbie—carry bows—like Norbie—but not Norbie. Think Mountain Butchers—steal horses—steal frawns—kill—then say Norbie do. Mark dead like Norbie. They shoot—Gorgol fall like dead—only first Gorgol kill one!" His eyes gleamed brightly. "Gorgol warrior now! But too many—" He spread all his fingers to spell the size of the other party. "So when arrow find Gorgol he fall back—be dead—they no climb up to see whether really dead or no—"

"Mountain Butchers!" Storm repeated aloud and Gorgol must have guessed the meaning of the sounds for again he signed an eager assent.

"They are still here?"

"Not so. They go—" Gorgol pointed north. "Think they live there. Not want men to know where they hide—so kill—"

Well, that was one more reason for not heading north when they tried to get out out of here. But Gorgol was still making finger-talk.

"They have rider—he tied—maybe they make kill to feed evil spirits"—he hesitated and then added that horrific sign Storm had first seen Sorenson make— "THE MEAT."

Storm had heard of some Norbie tribes who, for purposes of a dark devil worship—or devil propitiation—ate prisoners they took under certain conditions. To most of the Arzoran tribes this custom was an abomination and there was a fierce and never-ending warfare waged between the ritual cannibals and their enemies. In Norbie minds the quality of evil was so associated with THE MEAT that it was natural for Gorgol to make the assumption he had just offered.

"Not so," the Terran corrected. "Butchers not eat captives. This prisoner—he was from the plains?"

"Rider," Gorgol agreed.

"Any settlers near here? We could find them—tell them about evil men—how they kill—"

Gorgol turned his head slowly so he looked south. "Many suns come up—go down—before reach settlers that way. Maybeso we can go. But not in dark—I not know this country—and Nitra be in hills. Man walk soft, go quick, be very careful—" But he glanced back at the Terran with a kind of level measurement the off-world man did not understand.

"With that I agree," Storm spoke and signed together. The dark was almost on them now. He shared out bedding from his own roll, saw Gorgol was comfortable and then curled up on the grass beside Surra, sleeping as he had so many times before in perfect confidence that the super-acute hearing of the dune cat would warn him of any danger.

It was almost dawn when Storm did wake at her faint signal. He came not only awake but instantly alert, a trick he had learned so far in the past he was no longer conscious of knowing it. Whatever was coming had not aroused Surra's fighting instincts, only her interest. He listened intently, hearing Gorgol's heavy breathing, the rattle of hoof on gravel as Rain stirred. Then that other sound, a pattering noise so faint he could have missed it without Surra's caution.

The light on the gravel bar was gray enough to distinguish objects and he was ready with the stun rod. He aimed at the dusky blot as soon as he was sure it was not a horse. The top-heavy outline against the rocks could be that of only one animal he had seen on Arzor, and they could certainly use the meat such a kill would provide. A minute later he was busy blooding the carcass of a yearling frawn, one which was plump enough to have enjoyed good foraging lately. Though what a frawn was doing alone in this wilderness was a mystery. The animals were plainsbred and ran in herds and they were never, under ordinary circumstances, either found in the mountain or alone.

Gorgol had an explanation when they squatted close to the fire Storm dared to light after he had heaped some rocks together as a screen. Chunks of frawn steak were spitted on sharpened sticks and the Norbie was giving their even browning careful attention.

"Stolen. Evil men put frawns in hiding—perhaps they lose this one when they drive many through—perhaps storm made herd stampede—"

Storm regarded the meat reflectively. There was a side problem to all this stealing of horses and frawns. What in the world—or in Arzor—did the thieves intend to do with their plunder? The market for frawns lay off-world. There was only one space port and all animals loaded there had to be legally accounted for with sales and export papers. Settlers would be the first to detect any newcomer who could not account for his holdings clear back to the moment he set foot on Arzor. What was the profit in stealing meat on the hoof that you had no hope of selling?

"Why they want meat—no sell—" He passed that along to Gorgol, knowing the young native was acute enough to follow his chain of thought.

"Maybeso not sell—big land—" The Norbie waved his left hand wide. "Take frawns far—horses, too. Norbie knows of places where Butchers hide. Norbie take horses from their secret places. Hurol, he of Gorgol's own clan—he take three horses so last dry time. He big hunter—warrior—"

So the Norbies raided the secret caches of the Butchers. Now that scrap of information might lead to something. Suppose the Norbies should be encouraged in that useful occupation, one which appealed so to their own natural tastes? Put a Norbie afoot in the wastes and he could get along. Unhorse an off-worlder without supplies and it was a far different matter. But it all came back to this— how *did* the Butchers intend eventually to profit from their raids?

The situation might almost suggest a hidden space port to handle illicit trade. A hidden space port! Storm stiffened, his eyes very wide and level as he stared unseeingly at the fire. And Surra, catching from him that hidden tension, growled deep in her throat. There *had* been hidden space ports of a sort. He had uncovered one himself and brought in a mop-up squad to deal with it and those who manned it. Such a port established to milk a planet of food supplies—! Eagerly he responded to that familiar spur of the hunt.

Sure—the war was over—officially. He had spent that dreary year at the Center to prove it. But suppose, just suppose that his wild suspicion were right! Then he had another chance—a chance to strike back once more at those who had taken away his world. Storm began to hum under his breath. In that moment his quarrel with Brad Quade was very far away—a thin wisp of a thing out of a half-forgotten story. If he were right—! Oh, Faraway Gods—let him now be right in his preposterous guess!

The Terran turned to Gorgol who had been watching him with close to the same narrow-eyed intensity that Surra's thin pupils mirrored.

"These Butchers—they have horses?"

"It is so," signaled the other.

"Then, as Hurol, let us see whether some of those horses may not carry us!"

Gorgol's thin lips drew back in the half-smile of his people. "That is good hearing. For these have killed our blood, and for that there must be a taking of hands in return—"

In that moment Storm realized how close he had been to making a grave error of judgment, one which might have finished his friendly relations with the native. Had he ridden south as had been his first plan, then he would have outraged custom that demanded a personal vengeance for those killed here. It was a small thing to weigh against the crime he suspected, but it was a good argument to use against that scrap of conscience that recalled the unfinished matter of Quade.

CHAPTER NINE

uch as he wanted to be on the move, Storm desired
Surra to have another day of rest before he put her
to the strain of the trail. And Gorgol's wound also
needed tending. After seeing to his patients, the Terran made his own plans for a scouting trip. First south, because he
wanted to be sure that the Nitra were not between his party and that
retreat route. But before he left, he made other preparations.

Grease from the frawn meat mixed with powdered red dust and a
chalky stuff ground from some small soft pebbles provided him with
a kind of paint and he went to work, streaking face and chest with
splotches and broken lines— War paint or camouflage, it served
equally well on both counts.

Gorgol watched the paint job with keen interest.

"You make warrior magic?"

The Terran glanced down at the stripes on his chest and smiled,
but the movement of lips made no difference in the general ghastly
effect of his new face mask.

"I make warrior magic—my people's magic—"

On impulse he put over his head the circlet of the necklace and
fastened about him, looped over his weapon belt, the concha—the
embellished one of his inheritance. Then he considered weapons.

He could use a bow, having two hands. But Gorgol could not.
And he would not leave the Norbie with no better defense than just
his long-knife. Now he unbuckled the holstered stun rod. Storm
knew that the natives had a deeply rooted prejudice against using another man's weapons—believing that there was a mystical relationship between man and his arms. But there were also occasions of
free gift in which the "magic" of the weapon could be transferred

intact. He did not know the Norbie ceremony, but he could follow his own intuition.

As he had done on the morning he had started on this expedition, Storm held the sheathed weapon to the sky and then to the earth, before he extended it to Gorgol with the sign that signified the weapon was to be a permanent gift.

Gorgol's slit-pupiled eyes widened, but he did not yet touch finger to the rod. Stun ray guns were imported from off-world, they cost what seemed to a native a fabulous amount in trade goods and Norbies seldom bought them, since it was too hard to get fresh clips to recharge them. But the gift of such a weapon was sometimes made by off-worlder to native and that was a very serious and honorable thing.

"Press here—aim so—" Slowly Storm went through the drill, but he knew that Gorgol had worked by the side of settler riders often enough to understand. The Norbie nodded and stood proudly as the Terran rebuckled the holster to the belt of the new owner.

Storm was about to sling his arrow quiver over his shoulder when Gorgol stopped him with an imperative gesture. One-handedly the Norbie transferred half of his hunting points to the Terran's keeping. The war arrows were sacred and could not be given to another lest they fail him in some crucial moment. Now, equipped, painted, a true Navajo again outwardly, Storm saluted with upraised hand and padded away from the camp, Baku taking to the air to accompany him.

An unpleasant smell issued from the water still murky with mud. Where necessary, Storm splashed through shallows. But he worked his way around the drying outer rim of the valley, not attempting to swim the lake. There were dead animals, bloated, floating in the silted liquid. However, he found no trace of the party's horses, of Mac and the third Norbie from the Crossing, or any of the party supplies. Had any of the mounts survived they must have been scooped up by the raiders.

As the Terran approached the southern end of the valley where the tunnel lay, he halted at regular intervals to sweep the ground ahead with his vision lenses. And now he could see that there *was* a change in the outline of the heights there. But it was not until Storm reached the wall of the lake and climbed a slime-encrusted mound of mud-cemented debris that he knew the worst.

The tunnel was gone, obliterated by a slide that would probably yield only to the powerful punch of a boomer, if there were one on Arzor, which he very much doubted. A man probably could climb those heights, fearing all the while to be trapped in another slip of the soft earth, but he could not get Rain through. It was certainly intended by someone or something that there was to be no easy escape southward. Storm felt a queer elation because he had already made his choice before he knew that the door had been slammed shut.

An hour or so later Gorgol accepted the information indifferently. Apparently it was of little matter that Baku was the only one that could now cross into the outer world with any ease. He, himself, was eager to head north. And Storm promised that they would leave Surra and Rain with their supplies in the cliff camp the next morning, he and Gorgol to try to trace the path the wandering frawn had used. For frawns were not climbers and it was certain that any trail the animal had followed into their valley was one a horse could negotiate.

Storm had considered himself, rightly by his standards, to be somewhat of an expert at trailing. But Gorgol was able to pick traces seemingly out of the surface of unmarked rock, guiding them to a thin crevice in the cliff walls where the prints of the frawn's hoofs did show in drying mud. That crevice was narrow to begin with, and it climbed, but not too straightly. Above them Baku quested, sometimes totally lost to sight in the immensity of the sky where she faced no travel obstacles at all.

They came at last to a pocket-sized pass and Gorgol picked from between two rocks there a small hide pouch lined with frawn fabric, smelling of some aromatic herb.

"Faraway men chew—makes powerful dreams—" The Norbie passed the find to the Terran who sniffed inquiringly at the strong odor. It was not unpleasant, but he had never come across it before that he could remember. He was sorry for that ignorance as what he held might be an important clue to the true identity of the outlaws.

"Dream stuff grow on Arzor?" he asked.

"Not so. Wizard use some found in Butcher camp. Made head shake—many dreams—evil. It is a spirit thing—not good."

Storm tucked the find inside his belt. Undoubtedly it was a narcotic of some kind, perhaps with a stronger effect upon the Arzoran natives than upon the original off-world users.

"Through here—with horses—"

A small patch of earth was indented plainly by the prints of horsehoofs, though these were later overlaid with the frawn tracks bound in the other direction. And all the horses had been shod, proving they were not Norbie stock.

On the other side of the pass they found the reason for the wandering of the frawn, a yoris kill, the white bones of a full-grown frawn picked clean. But the killer had not profited greatly, though it had gone to its own death with a full paunch, because the huge lizard lay there too, its sickly yellow corpse thriftily skinned and left as a feast for a pack of small scavengers.

Gorgol slipped from one cover rock to the next, losing little of his agility because of the arm bound across his chest, venturing at length to squat beside that unsavory carcass as the feasters fled. When Storm joined him the Norbie pointed to the reptile's head.

That was a disturbing sight, not because the whole top of the saurian skull was completely missing, but because the Terran knew only one weapon that could cause a death wound such as that. And it was one completely outlawed at the end of the war.

"A slicer!" he breathed. More evidence that his wild guess of yesterday had some base in fact. He glanced at the bow in his own hand and grimaced. A bow against a stun ray was not too impossible odds—but a bow opposed to a slicer was no odds at all—in favor of the man equipped with the slicer!

The Norbie rose to his feet and looked around him. He picked up a stick and thrust it under that wreck of a head, turning up the skull to pry at the lower jaw. Under his probing a sudden stream of greenish liquid fountained high. Gorgol twittered in much the same tone of consternation Hing used upon occasion. Dropping his stick he made finger-talk.

"Yoris' death poison—mating season now."

That meant that the big, ugly reptiles were twice as vicious and far more deadly. During the mating season each of the males would have effective poison fangs to use against rivals, and yoris' venom was often fatal—at least to off-worlders. From now on they must be prepared to kill the lizards on sight without waiting for any attack.

Leaving the carnage on the small plateau, Storm strode to the rim for a survey of what lay below. The land there presented a surprising vista, though perhaps he should have been prepared, having seen the ruins in the lake valley. As far as Storm could see the cliff walls were cut into a series of giant steps—really terraces—most of which were cloaked—or choked—with thick growths of vegetation. Leading from a point to the south, a road had been cut and cleared from level to level—perhaps the trail along which the outlaws drove their stolen animals. For the pass through which he and Gorgol had just come could not have accommodated a herd of any size.

The Terran unslung his lenses to study in detail the floor of this second valley. It was easy to pick out a sizable frawn herd at graze there, the curious loping gait of the animals making them seem almost top-heavy when they moved because of their heavily maned forequarters and high-held horned heads contrasted to the relatively weak nakedness of their sharply sloping hindquarters free of almost all but a tight fuzz of hair.

Frawns—but no horses. And no signs of riders either. The limiting walls of the valley itself perhaps provided an adequate barrier to drifting and canceled the need for any herders—though with the yoris season at its height Storm would have considered guards necessary.

This valley was much wider than the outer one and only the lenses allowed Storm to see that the opposite walls were terraced in the same fashion as those below. The grass was luxuriant and high, and there were no signs of the flood that had devastated the neighboring lowland.

Nor were there any other evidences of what Storm sought. This place might be only a convenient hiding place for stolen herds. If it had not been for the wound on the dead yoris—

Gorgol's hand pressed the Terran's arm. Obedient to that warning, Storm turned his lenses swiftly back to the valley floor. The frawns were no longer grazing. Instead the bulls were tossing their heads, galloping awkwardly to the right, while the cows and young were falling back into a tight knot, heads pointing outward, the typical defense position of their species.

Horsemen! Three of them. And the horses they rode were a dark-skinned stock, a different breed than those of Larkin's string, wiry, smaller animals, such as those Storm had seen in the Norbie camp. However, the men who rode them were not natives. Nor did they wear the almost universal Arzoran settler dress of yoris-hide breeches and frawn-fabric shirts.

Storm went down on one knee, swinging around to follow that group of riders with his powerful glasses. His first sight of those dull black tunics—the black that always looked as if it were coated with gray dust—had confirmed all his suspicions. This was it! Those enemy uniforms, the hidden business in stolen frawns, everything clicked together with a satisfying snap. No wonder they had wiped out the Survey party, striving at the same time to make the deed seem a native massacre! Blame everything on the wild Norbies. A beautiful cover, a situation made to order for the Xiks.

"Saaaa—" Gorgol had learned to imitate the call Storm used for the team, the only sound he had in common with the Terran. The native was energetically stabbing his forefinger into the air northward in a demand for Storm to shift his attention to that point.

The frawns were still bunched, not relaxing their vigilance. However, their very ordinary reaction to the invasion of their feeding grounds was not what interested the native. Some of the force of the storm had stripped a path down the mountain, clearing a haphazard lane of yellow-red earth that ended in a mound on the next to the last terrace. And, hugging that, almost indistinguishable from the ground on which he lay, another was watching the same scene. With the aid of Storm's lenses that spy leaped into full view, and the Terran saw the long, lean body of a Norbie who must be completely concealed from sight as far as anyone on the floor of the valley were concerned. There was something odd about the fellow's head. Those horns, curving back across the hairless pate, they were not ivory white as Gorgol's, as those of all the other Norbies Storm had seen, but dyed a blue-green.

He looked to Gorgol for enlightenment. The young Norbie had flattened himself out on an overhanging rock from which he could get the fullest view of the other native, his chin supported on the injured arm, his features impassive, but his cat-eyes very much alive. Then his lips drew flat against his teeth in the humorless grin that signified anger or battle excitement among his kind, and his other hand, resting on the rock next to the Terran, made the finger-sign for Nitra.

Was that a hidden scout traveling alone? Or did he act as the advance ranger for a war party? Norbie custom allowed for either answer. A youngster out on a personal hunt for a warrior trophy could prospect these ranges on his own. Or a raiding party might have marked down this hidden valley and its secret herds and decided to make the Butchers their prey. From these terraces with their thick cover an ambush attack by expert bowmen could cause a good deal of trouble.

Gorgol's fingers moved again. "One only—"

Though the Terran could not speak Gorgol's language, nor the native do more than imitate the team call, Storm had discovered that he could convey information in a sketchy way, or ask a question with extravagant movements of his lips and be half-understood. He held his lenses still but turned his head to ask:

"War party?"

Gorgol dipped his chin and moved his head from side to side in empathic negation.

"One only."

Storm longed for Surra. He could have set the dune cat to shadow that warrior, make sure in her own way that he was the only one of his kind along the terraces. Now the Terran's own plan for trailing those three riders must be revised. Without Surra to run interference it would be folly to venture down into the lower reaches of the valley and perhaps be cut off from the pass. Yet he wanted to see where those riders were headed.

The Terran worked his way along the small plateau, passing once more the very dead yoris, to reach the northernmost tip. There he dared to get to his feet and lean back against a rust-red finger of rock, sure that he was a part of the stone to anyone who was more than a few rods away.

This valley was surely a wide expanse, roughly in the outline of a bottle, of which the south was the narrowest part. And the outlaws could, and probably had, camouflaged everything at ground level. He could pick out no buildings, no indication that this was anything but virgin wilderness.

Except for that one thing planted there, stiffly upright, sending small sparks of reflected sunlight through a masking of skillfully wrought drapery, a piece of work that made Storm grant those below very full marks.

He judged that sky-pointing length narrowly, knowing that its landing fins must now be sunk well below the surface of the meadowland. That meant that a great amount of labor had been expended—as well as pointing to the fact that the pilot who had ridden down his ship's tail flames into that constricted area had been a very expert one. From the appearance of the drapery it must have been some time since the ship had been landed and apparently built into the general surroundings. If he could see the thing stripped, he might be able to identify the type—though with that slender outline it was no cargo carrier— Storm believed it might be a scout or a very fast courier and supply ship, the kind a man might latch onto during the break-up immediately before surrender for a fast getaway. Whatever its kind, Storm knew that on its scarred side he would find only one symbol. But was he now spying on a secret and well-established colony, set up while the Xiks were still powerful, or just a hideaway for holdouts who had fled the order to lay down their arms?

Gorgol came up beside him. "Nitra go—" He flicked a finger north. "Maybeso hunt for trophies—" His hand remained outspread, his gaze centered on the half-hidden ship. Then his head snapped around and his astonishment was very plain to read.

"What?" he signed.

"Faraway sky thing." Storm used the native term for space ship.

"Why here?" countered Gorgol.

"Butchers—evil men bring—"

Again the thin-lipped fighting grin of Norbie anger stretched Gorgol's mouth.

"Faraway sky thing no come Norbie land." He strained the fingers of his right hand to join the left in making that protest. "Norbie drink blood faraway men—talk straight—swear oaths of warriors. Faraway ship thing only come one place on land—not near mountains where Those-Who-Drum-Thunder be angry! Faraway men not talk straight—here sky thing too!"

Trouble! Storm caught the threat in this. The Norbies allowed the space port to be located well away from the mountains that to them were sacred. And the treaty that had made the settlers' holdings safe to them allowed only that one place of landing and departure for off-world ships. To let the rumor get started that there was a second port right in the heart of their mountains would be enough to break every drink-blood tie on Arzor.

Storm let his lenses swing from their strap, held out his hands to focus Gorgol's attention.

"I warrior—" He underlined that statement by drawing his index finger along the faint scar line on his shoulder. "Gorgol warrior—" With the same finger he touched the other's bandaged forearm gently. "I get warrior scar, not from Nitra, not from other tribe like mine— I get wound fighting evil men—of that tribe!" He made a spear of his finger, stabbing the air toward the grounded space ship. "Gorgol wounded by those evil men—from there!" Again he pointed. "They are of those who eat THE MEAT—" He added the worst symbol the sign language contained.

Gorgol's yellow eyes held the Terran's unblinkingly before he signed:

"Do you swear this by Those-Who-Drum-Thunder?"

Storm drew his knife from his belt, pushed its hilt into the Norbie's hand and then drew it up by the blade until the point pricked the skin encircled in the necklace on his breast.

"Let Gorgol push this home if he does not believe I speak true," he signed slowly with his free hand.

The Norbie drew back the knife, reversed it with a flip of his wrist and proffered the hilt to the Terran. As Storm took the blade from him, he replied, "I believe. But this—bad thing. Faraway man fight evil men his kind—or oath broken."

"It is so. What I can do, I shall. But first we must know more of these men—"

Gorgol looked down into the valley. "Nitra hunts—and the night comes. In the day we can move better—you have not the eyes that see in darkness—"

Storm knew an inward relief. If the Norbie had wanted to keep up with the scout, now it would have been hard not to agree. But this suggestion coming from the native fitted in with the Terran's own wishes.

"Big cat—" Storm suggested, "get well—be able to hunt Nitra while we watch evil men—"

Gorgol agreed to that readily, having seen Surra in action. And with a last detailed examination of the concealed ship, which told him no more than he had learned earlier, Storm started back to the outer valley, to plan an active campaign.

CHAPTER TEN

Although it was close to dark when they returned to the outer valley, Storm set about building a screen of rocks behind which they could shelter a night fire, with Gorgol's one-handed aid. There was, of course, the cave in which he had been imprisoned. But that was the width of the valley away. And, in addition, he shrank from experiencing again its turgid air and the faint exhalation of stale death he recalled only too vividly.

Rain had been turned loose to graze. Should the stallion be sighted from the heights by any lurking Nitra or outlaw sentry he would be thought a stray from the destroyed Survey camp. And with Surra on guard there was no danger of a thief getting close enough to steal the mount. Perhaps he could even be used as bait in some later plan.

Storm suggested as much to Gorgol and the Norbie agreed with enthusiasm. Such a horse as Rain was a treasure—a chief's mount— a trophy to be flaunted in the faces of lesser men.

"There remains the road—" Storm's fingers moved in the fire-light after they had eaten. "The path that we found today is not for herd-driving. We must discover their other road—"

"Such a way does not lie through this valley," Gorgol answered with conviction.

Their explorations before the flash flood seemed to confirm that. The Survey party had discovered no evidence of frawn-grazing around the mounds. Storm drew his knife and with the point began to scratch out a map of the valley as he knew it—in its relation to the outlaws' hold. He explained as he went and the Norbie, used to his own form of war and hunting maps, followed with concentration, correcting, or questioning.

When they had pooled their knowledge of the terrain Storm could see only one explanation for the lack of a connecting link between the valleys—save for the narrow cleft they had explored that day. There must be a way from the southeast or southwest, running between the heights that separated the two cups of lowland.

"In dark—Nitra maybe raid—" Gorgol had been watching their handful of fire thoughtfully. "In dark Norbie see good—night raid big trick on enemy—good against Butchers." He glanced at Storm. "You no see so good in dark—? Maybeso not. But cat—she does!"

The Terran aroused at that half-hint for more immediate action. Norbie scouts would not hang about the outlaw camp too long. The Nitra they had sighted on watch today might well hole up for the first part of the night and then raid the horses of the Xik hideout in the early hours of the morning, a favorite trick of the natives. If a man were on the spot, then he could learn a lot in the ensuing confusion.

However, it was a very thin chance, depending so much on luck and on factors over which Storm had no control. He had taken slim chances before and had been successful. This was like the old days. A well-remembered prickle ran along the Terran's nerves, and he did not know it but the yellow light of the flames gave him something of the look of Surra, Surra when she crouched before taking off in deadly spring.

"You will go." Gorgol signed. "We shall try for the lower way now—wait then for the zamle's hour—"

"You too?"

The Norbie's thin grin was answer enough, but his fingers added:

"Gorgol is now a warrior. This is a good trail with much honor on it. I go—seeing ahead our path—"

They ate of the frawn meat methodically. And to that more tasty food Storm added two of the small concentrate tablets from his service days. If they had to go without food for a full day or more, they would not feel the lack.

He gave Surra her silent orders, noting that the dune cat moved with much of her old strength and litheness, and swung Hing on his shoulder. Night exploits were not for Baku, but the Terran knew that with the coming of light the eagle would be up and questing. Should her aid be required then he could summon her.

They reclimbed the frawn pass and came out once more upon the plateau. Surra charged forward and something half her size scuttled away from the body of the yoris, leaving a musky odor almost as strong as the hunting reptile's stench hanging in the air. The dune cat coughed, spat angrily, plunging on into the growth below as if she must wipe that contagion from her fur.

Storm had to admit to himself within five minutes that, had it not been for Surra and the Norbie's excellent night sight, he would have had to call off his ambitious plan. The thick growth on the ancient terraces cut off the sky, doubled the gloom of the night. He locked hands with Gorgol, his other arm protecting Hing against his body lest she be swept from her hold by low-swinging branches. But somehow, with raw scratches on his face and the welts of lashing boughs crisscrossing his shoulders and ribs, Storm made it to the floor of the valley.

By day he could have used the terraces for cover, and indubitably now both cat and Norbie could have taken that way with ease. But the Terran knew he must keep to the fringe of the open land or give up entirely. Luckily the frawns would bed down for the night well out in the open. Though they would gallop away from a mounted man, to meet them on foot was a different matter, as Dort and Ransford warned him during his early days on Arzor. Frawns were curious and they were hostile, especially in calving season. A man fronted by a suspicious bull and caught afoot was in acute danger.

It was not until they were almost in line with the disguised ship that Storm saw the first light. Perhaps long immunity had made someone careless. But that prick showed clearly from the base of one huge peak whose bulk furnished the major northern wall of the second valley. And there was no mistaking the nature of that blue glare. It was cast by no fire or atom-powered lamp such as the settlers used, but was a type of installation Storm had seen before, half the galaxy away.

Using the grounded ship as a mark point, the Terran fixed the general location of that bright dot. Then he pressed his fingers to Gorgol's wrist, giving the Norbie's arm a slight jerk in one of the simple signals they had agreed to use in the dark. Gorgol's fingers tightened on his twice in assent and Storm dropped his hold, getting down to his knees, with Hing now riding crouched low on his back and Surra to act as his advance guard.

Leaving the Norbie in the screen of bushes, the three worked their way into the open, making for the vicinity of the ship. Luckily the frawns had not grazed this section, and the rank grass grew so high that Storm had to rise from hands and knees at intervals to be sure he was on course. But he came at last to the edge of a pit.

Under his exploring hands the earth was wet, the clay very recently disturbed. He wriggled forward until his head and shoulders projected over the drop, and aimed his torch on its lowest power into the emptiness below. He was right, the digging was recent and it was not yet finished, for only half of the soil had been cleared away from around the fins of the ship. The cruiser had been buried after it had been landed, partly to help conceal it, partly to keep it steady in a proper position for a take-off where there was no cradle to hold it. If a storm here had battered it off fin level, with no port cranes to right it, the ship would be useless scrap until it rusted away.

But this digging now meant that it was about to be recommissioned. Storm wished he knew more about its type. He moved the torch from the nearest half-unearthed fin upward to the body. All ports were sealed. His light went back to the fins again. Had he still been able to order both Ho and Hing, a little judicious excavation under one fin to overbalance the other two, he might have caused trouble enough to spoil Xik plans. But the job below was too big for one meerkat, no matter how willing, in the limited time granted them tonight.

Hing had plans of her own. Scrambling down from Storm's shoulders she patted the soft earth approvingly with her digging paws and half-rolled, half-coasted down into the pit of shadows about the excavation where she went to work vigorously, snorting with disgust when Storm called her back. And she took her own time about obeying, sputtering angrily as she climbed, avoiding the Terran's hand as he would have pulled her to him again.

He tried to restore her good will with an order. She consented grumpily and then chirruped in a happier frame of mind as she scuttled off to the first of the net ties, digging at the stake that held it. There was just a faint chance that the tightly drawn net itself helped to steady the ship in the pit, now that the digging was in progress, and to release the main ropes could rock it off center. Any gamble was worth the effort and this *was* something the meerkat could do.

Storm made his retreat to the terraces backwards, pulling up as best he could the grass he had beaten down. He could not erase all traces of his visit, but what could be done to confuse the trail he did. Surra's paw marks threading back and over his would make a queer pattern for any tracker to unravel, since no native Arzoran creature would leave that signature.

As Storm came back to the bushes Gorgol met him and they locked hands once more, the Norbie giving him a squeeze to indicate he had discovered a hideout. It proved to be a small hollow between two sections of terrace wall that had given way long ago under the impetus of landslips, and they crouched there together with Surra—to be joined sometime later by Hing who nudged at Storm's arm until he accepted some treasure she was carrying in her mouth and cuddled her to him.

They would wait, they had decided, until dawn. If there was no disturbance engineered by the Nitra before that hour, there would be none later. Of course, the scout they had seen that afternoon might have decided that the hideout was too tough a proposition. Storm dozed, as he had learned to sleep between intervals of action, but he was halfway to his feet when a flaming ball arched across the sky—to be followed by another—and then a third.

The first fire arrow struck on fuel and a burst of flame flashed up. Storm heard the high, frightened scream of a horse as the third ball landed. The fire was burning along a line perhaps five feet above the level of the ground—it could be following the top of some wall or corral. Wall or corral—he remembered a precaution Larkin had used on two different nights along the trail when yoris attacks were to be feared—a temporary corral topped with thornbushes to keep the scaled killers at bay. And dried thorn burned very easily.

The shrill whinnies and squeals of the horses were answered by shouts. The distant prick of light they had spotted earlier suddenly grew into a wide slit that must mark an open door.

Gorgol moved, scraping by Storm with a brief tap of a message on the Terran's shoulder. The milling horses had been freed from the burning corral somehow, the thud of hoofs on the ground, as they raced from the fire, carried to the two in hiding. And the Norbie was about to take advantage of the confusion to catch a mount. The native had the stun rod and so was better prepared to defend himself in the darkness where Storm's bow was largely useless.

Now they both heard a high yammering cry that had been torn from no off-world throat—a Nitra in trouble? Yet surely the native would be busy among the horses racing from the blazing corral. The thornbush fire lit up a whole scene as men ran across the area around it, covering the ground in zigzag advance patterns that told Storm all he needed to know about their past activities. Those were troops who had known action, snapping into defense positions with veterans' ease and speed.

Then a light that swallowed up the glow of the fire snapped on—to make a sweeping path reaching almost to the ship. The beam moved, catching and centering on running horses. And did one of those have a figure crouched low on its back? Storm was not sure, but the mount he thought suspicious did dodge out of the line of the light with almost intelligent direction.

Again the light tried to catch the horses, but this time they were not so closely bunched, spreading out—two or three taking the lead by lengths from the others.

There was a crack of sky-splitting thunder and purple fire lashed up from the sod to the far left. Storm's teeth clicked together, he was on his feet, Surra pressed tight against his thigh, snarling in red rage. That was not new either, they had both seen that whip of destruction in action before, lashing out to herd fugitives, only that time the fugitives had not been horses! Gorgol! If he could only call the Norbie back to safety. This was no time to try to catch one of those maddened animals, not with someone using a force beam so expertly. And the native knew nothing of Xik weapons or their great range.

The Terran went down on one knee. He was loath to risk Surra, but he must give Gorgol a chance. With his hands resting lightly on the dune cat's shoulders, his thumbs touching the bases of her large sensitive ears, Storm thought his order. Find the Norbie—bring him back—

Surra growled deep in her throat and the force beam struck

again—this time to the right. Their safety would depend on how far the operator could revolve his beam base, or the full extent of its power. A skillful gunner made force lashing an art and Storm had seen incredible displays on Xik-held worlds.

The cat strained a little against his touch. She had her briefing and was ready to go. Storm lifted his hands and Surra disappeared into the high grass. The air tickled his throat, carrying with it the stench of burning where that man-made lightning had left only scorched earth, black and bare.

Now the first of the horses ran past him—another, a third. He could see them only as moving shadows. Let them pound on at that mad pace into the frawn herd and they would start a real stampede. If only Surra could get Gorgol back—!

Again the power beam slapped the earth, making eyes ache with its burst of force. Horses wheeled, ran back from that horror—but the three leaders had gotten through. And had one of them carried a rider? Gorgol— Where was the Norbie—and Surra? To be caught out there was to be in peril not only from the crack of the lightning flash, but also from the horses now racing in a mad frenzy. There was no possible hope of capturing any one of them.

Storm set himself to watch the play of the beam, trying to judge the farthest extent of its reach. Unless the operator was purposely keeping it keyed to a low frequency, it did not touch near the ship, nor hit the terraced slopes behind the Terran. If the Norbie would only return, they could climb to safety. Storm, as resourceful as he was, had a very healthy respect for the weapons of the enemy.

The slaps of the beam were coming closer together, cutting in a regular fan pattern from their source. It would appear that the operator of the machine was now under orders to work over the whole meadowland between the western wall of the mountain and the ship. The Terran's hands jerked toward his ears as the terrible tortured scream of an animal in dire pain answered one flash. They must be deliberately cutting down the horses! The use of the lash had not been just to stop their getaway!

Were the Xiks sacrificing their own animals to get any Norbies who might be trying to round up the runaways? That form of sadistic revenge went well with the character of the enemy as he knew it.

Storm fought down his wave of rage, made himself stand and watch that slaughter, adding it to the already huge score he had long ago marked up against the breed of alien men out there, if you could even deem them "men."

Horses continued to die and Storm could not control the shudders that answered each agonized cry from the meadow. Surra! Surra and Gorgol. He did not see how they could escape unless they already had won to the terraces.

Hing cried, digging her claws into his skin, her shivering body pressed tight to his chest. Then Storm jumped backward and—in a moment—felt immense relief when soft warm fur pressed against him and Surra's rough tongue rasped his flesh. He fondled her ears in welcome and then caught out in the dark, his fingers scraping across yoris hide—Gorgol's corselet.

The Norbie swung around, only a very dimly seen bulk, bringing his other side against the Terran. He was half-supporting another body, slighter, shorter than his own. Storm's hand was on frawn skin fabric in rags, on flesh, on a belt like his. The rescued one was no tribesman, but someone in settler dress.

Storm located that other's dangling arm and hitched it across his shoulder so that now Gorgol and he shared the weight between them. As they made their way onto the first terrace the limp stranger roused somewhat and tried to walk, though his stumbling progress was more of a hindrance than a help to his supporters.

They struggled up two terraces, pausing for breath at forced intervals. The clamor in the meadow was stilled now, though the force beam still beat methodically back and forth. Nothing lived there—it could not—yet it seemed the Xiks were not yet satisfied.

A third terrace, one more and they would be on a level with the pass. The stranger muttered, and once or twice moaned. Though he did not seem fully conscious and had never replied coherently to Storm's questions, he was more steady on his feet and obeyed their handling docilely.

To climb the terraces and then to force one's way along them was a difficult task. And had not the vegetation proved to be thinner near the upper rim of the valley they might have been held to a dangerously slow pace. The sky was gray when they reached the edge of the plateau where the dead yoris had lain. Surra glided back to give the alert. There was danger standing between them and the pass.

If he could be sure that only a Norbie opposed them, Storm would have given the big cat the order she wanted and let her clear the way. But an Xik outlaw armed with a slicer or some other of their ghastly array of weapons was more than the Terran would let her risk meeting. Storm signed caution to Gorgol to take to cover, working his way on to the pass alone.

Again Surra's acute hearing had saved them. There was a guard stationed there right enough. And he had holed up, well protected in a rock niche, taking a position from which he could sweep the whole approach. There was no advancing until he was somehow picked out of that shell. Storm squatted behind a rock of his own and studied the field. It was plain to him now that the outlaws had been willing to sacrifice their horse herd to insure the death of someone. And a quick process of elimination suggested that that someone was the stranger Gorgol had rescued. He might even be the same man the Norbie had seen earlier in Xik hands, on the day they had accounted for the Survey party.

Doubtless every way out of the valley was now under guard. The next logical move for the enemy would be to start a careful combing of the terraces, driving their prey toward one of the known exits and so straight into the blaster sights of the men stationed there. It was a systematic arrangement that Storm, though it was used against him now, could approve as an example of good planning. But then the Xik forces could never be accused of stupidity.

Who was this stranger—that his recapture was of such great importance? Or was it a case like that of the murder of the Survey people—a killing ordered because no one who knew of this base could be allowed to escape? The why was not important now. What was important was that Storm and those with him win past this check point before that drive started down in the valley or before the one man now ahead could be reinforced.

He had one good trick left. If it worked! Storm's head went down until it rested on his crooked arm. He closed his eyes to the plateau. But he held in his mind the picture of the enemy guard in his rock post—making it as vivid as he could. Clinging to that image, the

Terran drew upon that other sense he had never tried to name, launching a demanding call. Surra he was sure of. Hing could be controlled only by hand and voice, her sly mind touching his on the far edge of the band that united the team. But Baku—now he must reach the eagle. She would be up in the air at dawn, cruising for sight of him. If he could attract her by that unvoiced call—!

That tenuous thing that he could not rightly call power but which tied him to cat, eagle, and meerkats, centered now on that one purpose. For so long they had been united in their life and efforts that surely the bond had been strengthened until he could rely upon it now for the only help that would mean anything to them. Baku—come in, Baku! Storm sent that strong soundless call up into the gray-mauve sky, a sky he did not see except as a place that might hold a wheeling black eagle.

CHAPTER ELEVEN

Baku—Storm's will became a cord—a noose tossed high in the lighting heavens to find and draw down that wide-winged shape. Once before, more than a Terran year earlier, he had summoned the great eagle to a similar task and she had obeyed, with all the power in her fearless body and those raking talons. Now—could he do it again?

Surra crowded against him, he could feel through fur and flesh the tension of the cat's nervous body, as if she had joined her untamed will to his, strengthening his calling. Then the dune cat growled, so almost noiselessly that Storm felt rather than rightly heard that warning.

The Terran raised his head from his arm, opened his eyes to the morning sky. It seemed to him that he had been using his will for hours, but the space of time could not have been more than a few moments. The Xik guard was still there, still half-crouched by one of the rocks he had chosen for his improvised fort, staring downslope, slightly to Storm's left.

"Ahuuuuuuu!" That cry might have been a scream from the furred throat of one of Surra's large kin. Once it had been the war shout of a desert people, now it summoned the team to battle.

The strike of a falcon or eagle is a magnificent piece of precision flying. It is also one of the most deadly attacks in the world. The guard at the pass could have had a second of apprehension, but only a second, before those talons closed in his flesh, the beak tore at his eyes, and the wings beat him close to senselessness.

Storm sped from one side, Surra from the other. The attack was all over in moments. And the Terran stripped from the other's body those weapons that would go a long way to insure the safety of his own party. Then he dragged the body of the guard along to thrust it into a crevice where it would lie hidden unless there were a detailed search. No man would now recognize the badly torn features, but Storm did not need to see that faintly green skin, the welling blood that was a different color from his own, to identify the species of the dead man. The Xiks were humanoid—perhaps more so in appearance than the Norbies, setting aside such small differences as color of skin and texture of hair. But there was a kinship of feeling between the horned and hairless Norbies and the Terran-descended settlers, which could never exist between man and Xik. So far no common meeting ground with the ruthless invaders had been discovered, in spite of patient search. And though they could and did mouth each other's speech understandably, there was no communication between his species and the Xiks that reached below surface exchange of information. Dramatically opposed aims drove the two peoples. Failure upon disastrous failure had followed every contact between them.

The Terran could not control his instinctive aversion as he dragged the body into hiding—and that feeling was far more than his dread of touching the dead—just as he could not and had not tried to smother the rage that ate into him the night before when he had been forced to witness the cold-blooded torture slaying of the horses. There was no understanding the invader mind. One could only guess at the twisted motives that drove them to do the things they did. The destruction of Terra had been one result of their kind of warfare—and perhaps it was just as useless as the continued carnage in the meadow below, for spread throughout the galaxy in numberless colonies the Terran breed had survived the destruction of their first home, while here the prisoner the Xik had thought to catch in the power net was now also on his way to safety.

Gorgol had only been waiting to have their path cleared. Already he was moving at the best pace he could force his charge to maintain across the plateau to the pass itself. The Norbie's greater height was pulled to one side as he supported the wavering stranger. And Storm, having set Surra and Baku to scout duty and having slung the plundered blaster over his shoulder, hurried to lend a hand.

In the increasing daylight it was easy to see that the rescued man had been brutally handled. But not as badly as some captives Storm had helped to release from Xik prison camps. And the very fact that he was able to keep on his feet at all was in his favor. But when Storm came up to steady the shuffling body, Gorgol allowed the full support to shift to the Terran. He had pulled his wounded arm out of its sling, and now he signed swiftly:

"Horses—free—on the side trail. We shall need them—I bring—"

Before Storm could protest he sped away. They could use the mounts right enough. But the sooner they were safe out of this sinister valley, the better. And goodness only knew how far the beaters in that drive for the fugitive had advanced below. The Terran kept on through the pass, staggering a little under the lurching weight of the stranger.

Surra he stationed in the pass. If Gorgol did flush horses up that narrow trail, she would help to herd them in. The big cat was tiring, but she was able to do sentry duty awhile, while Baku would provide them with eyes overhead. Hing scampered along before them, pausing now and then to turn over some flat stone and nose out an interesting find.

A band of aching muscles began to tighten about Storm's legs, his breath came in short, hard gulps that ended in a sharp stitch in his side. Must be out of condition, he thought impatiently—too long at the Center. He tried to plan ahead. Their camp on the gravel bar was too exposed—and they could not push the stranger too far into exhaustion, even if Gorgol did produce horses to ride. That meant they *must* discover a hiding place down in the flooded valley.

Storm knew of only one, much as he disliked it, the cave into which Rain had blundered during the cloudburst. That lay to the east of the pass they now threaded, perhaps a mile from the gravel bed. Surely the water had fallen well below its entrance now. Water— Storm ran a dry tongue over drier lips and turned his thoughts resolutely from the subject of water.

There would be no time to rest in the camp—just gather together their few supplies and mount the stranger on Rain, then get moving at once. And now Gorgol's try for horses no longer seemed so reckless. If successful, it would make very good sense. That is—if the poor brutes hadn't been run until they were almost foundered.

Mounts could mean the difference between disaster and safety for the fugitives.

"You're—not—Norbie—" Though the words came in slow pauses from those cut and battered lips, they startled Storm. He had been unconsciously considering his companion as so much baggage that had to be supported and tended, but that had no individual will. To be addressed intelligently by the stranger surprised him.

The face half-turned to his was a mass of cuts and bruises, so well painted with dried blood that it was hard to guess at the fellow's normal features. Nor did Storm realize that his own attempt at camouflage war paint did almost as well to make him equally a mystery.

"Terran—" He replied with the truth and heard a little gasp from the other, which might have been in answer to that statement or because the stranger stumbled and slapped one dangling hand inadvertently against an outcrop.

"You—know—who—they—are—?"

Storm needed no better identification for that "they." "Xiks!" he returned tersely, using the very unflattering service term for the invaders.

The explosive sound of that word was echoed by the walls of the pass, but above it sounded the pounding of hoofs. Since Surra had given no warning, Gorgol must have been successful. Storm drew the stranger back against the wall and waited.

It would have taken an expert horseman to see any value in the three animals that picked their way down the slope, their heads hanging, the marks of dried foam on them, their eyes glazed. None could be called upon for any great effort now, save that of keeping on its feet and moving. But Gorgol strode after them, the ivory of his horns glowing in the growing light of the morning as he held his head high in this small triumph. He clapped his hands together, the small report loud enough to turn the weary shuffle of his charges into a limited trot. Then leaving them to drift on downslope to the outer valley, he came to help Storm with his charge.

"You have had good hunting!" the Terran congratulated him.

"No time—or hunting—would have been better. The Butchers are foolish—few horses are left to them now—but still they do not try to round them up—" Gorgol replied before he used his hands for the purpose of aiding the injured man.

With the Norbie to take half the burden, the three covered the rest of the distance to the floor of the valley in better time. The horses, too exhausted to graze, stood with drooping heads, while Rain cantered up, full of interest, to inspect the newcomers. Beside the overdriven trio the stallion was a fine sight as he stood, pawing at the sod with one forehoof, the wind pulling at his red mane and forelock.

"That—is—all—horse!" The battered stranger had come to a halt, half-braced against his supporters, but the eyes in his pulped face were all for Rain.

"Think you can stick on him?" questioned Storm. "Sorry, fella, but we'll have to keep moving for a while."

"Can—try—"

Together Norbie and Terran boosted their rescued man up on the nervous stallion. He tried to crook his fingers into the mane for a hold and failed. And Storm, seeing for the first time the condition of those fingers, snapped a few sharp and biting words in the native tongues of at least two worlds.

There was a ghost of an answering laugh from the other. "All that and more," he mouthed. "They play pretty rough, those Xiks of yours, Terran. Once—a long time ago—I thought I was tough—"

He slumped so suddenly that Storm could not have saved him from falling off Rain's back. But the Norbie moved more quickly.

"He is hurt—"

Storm did not need to be told that. "That way—" he pointed. "Beyond the mound where Dagotag and the others lie—a cave in the cliff wall—"

Gorgol nodded, steadying the stranger's now limp body while Storm went ahead, Rain obediently following him.

They located the cave and Storm left the stranger with the Norbie and Hing, then rode back to collect their supplies. On the return trip he was accompanied by Surra and hazed before him the horses from the other valley, knowing that the two mares and the yearling colt would be protected by Rain. And with the stallion alert they would not stray too far from the new camp after they recovered their normal strength.

Gorgol met him at the cave entrance with news he had not expected—which a week earlier would have been exciting.

"This Sealed Cave once." Taking Storm by the arm, the native drew him farther in to point out the unmistakable marks of tools on roof and walls. He waved his hand toward the darkness beyond. "Hidden place—go far in—"

Would the Norbie refuse to stay here now, Storm wondered wearily. The Terran was too exhausted himself to care. Knowing that if he so much as sat down he would not be able to fight off sleep, Storm packed in the supplies and then went to look at the stranger. Stretched out on the floor of the cave, his head pillowed on a blanket roll, the Arzoran seemed to have shrunk in a curious way. His bruised face rested against the blanket, his breath caught a little now and then as if he were a child who had cried himself to sleep.

Storm sent Gorgol for water to be boiled over the fire the native had built, and laid out the supplies from the aid kit. Then delicately, with all the gentleness he could muster, he went to work, first to wash away the blood from those battered features, and then to assess the rest of the stranger's injuries. The other moaned once or twice under the Terran's ministrations, but he did not come to full consciousness.

At the end of a good half-hour's work Storm drew a deep breath of relief. Judging by Xik standards, they had hardly started to use their unpleasant methods of breaking a prisoner. It would be several days before the stranger would have full use of his hands, the lash weals on his back and shoulders would also be tender at least that long, and his face would display a rainbow-colored mask for some time. But there were no bones broken, no disabling wounds.

Leaving his patient as comfortable as possible, Storm went down to the lake, stripped, washed from head to foot, coming back to roll up in a blanket and sleep with the complete surrender of sodden exhaustion.

A tantalizing smell pulled him at last out of the mazes of a dream in which he ran across gradually rising mountains in pursuit of an Xik ship that, oddly enough, fled on human legs and twice turned to look at him with the face of Brad Quade. And he sat up to see Gorgol toasting grass hens on peeled spits over a fire. The process was watched with close attention by a mixed audience of Hing, Surra, and the stranger, now very much aware of his surroundings and sitting up backed by a brace of saddle pad and supply boxes.

Outside it was night, but they saw little of that save a patch of sky framing a single star, for the barrier once left by the landslip had been partly restored to mask their camp from anyone who did not have Baku's powers of elevation. And Baku, as if Storm's thought had once more summoned her, stirred now on a perch on the top of that barrier where she sat staring out on the valley.

But it was the rescued stranger who drew most of Storm's attention. He had been too tired, too absorbed in the task at hand when he had worked over the other, to really look objectively at the man whose wounds he tended. Now, in spite of the bruises, the bandages and the battering, he noted something that brought him upright, betraying surprise as much as Hosteen Storm could ever register it.

Because beneath the bruises, the bandages, the temporary alterations left by Xik treatment, Storm knew those features. He was facing now not just one of his own general human kind, but a man—a very young man—of his own race! Somehow—by some strange juggling of fate—he was confronting across this dusky cave another of the Dineh.

And the other's eyes, the only part of him that was not Dineh—those startling blue eyes—were focused back on the Terran with the same unwavering look of complete amazement. Then the swollen lips moved and that other asked his question first:

"Who, in the name of Seven Ringed Thunders, are you?"

"Hosteen Storm—I am Terran—" He repeated his former self-introduction absently.

The other raised a bandaged hand clumsily to his own jaw and winced as it touched the swelling there.

"You won't believe this, fella," he said apologetically. "But before I took this workin' over, you an' I looked somethin' alike!"

"You are of the Dineh—" Storm slipped into the tongue of his boyhood. "How did you come here?"

The other appeared to be listening intently, but when Storm was finished, he shook his head slowly.

"Sorry—that's not my talk. I still don't see how I got me a part-twin on Terra. Nor how he turned up to help pull me out of that mess back there. Enough to make you think the smoke drinkers know what they're talkin' about when they say dreams are real—"

"You are—?" Storm, a little deflated by the other's refusal to acknowledge a common speech, asked in a sharper tone.

"Sorry—there's no mystery about that. I'm Logan Quade."

Storm got up, the firelight touching to life the necklace on his breast, the ketoh on his wrist as he moved. He did not know, and would not have cared, what an imposing picture he made at that moment. Nor could he guess how the eagerness mirrored in his face a moment earlier had been wiped away, to leave his features set and cold.

"Logan—Quade—" he repeated without accent, evenly. "I have heard of the Quades—"

The other was still meeting his gaze with equal calmness though now he had to look up to do so.

"You and a lot of others—including our friends back yonder. They seemed to like Quades just about as much as you do, Storm. I can understand *their* dislike, but when did a Quade ever give you a shove, Terran?"

He was quick, Storm had to grant him that. Too quick for comfort. The Terran did not like this at all. For a moment he felt as if he had a raging frawn bull by the tail, unable either to subdue the animal or to let it free. And that was an unusual feeling of incompetence that he did not find easy to acknowledge.

"You're on the wrong track, Quade. But how did the Xiks pick you up?" It was a clumsy enough change of subject and Storm was ashamed of his ineptitude. To make matters worse he had a well-founded idea that Quade was amused at his stumbles.

"They gathered me in with the greatest of ease after settin' up some prime bait," Logan answered. "We've a range a little south of the Peaks and our stock has been disappearin' regularly in this direction. Dumaroy and some of the other spread owners around here yammer about Norbies every time they count noses and miss a calf. There've been a lot missin' lately and Dumaroy's talkin' war talk. That sort of thing can blow up into a nasty mess. We've had minor differences with some of the wild tribes right enough, but let Dumaroy and his hotheads go attackin' indiscriminately and we could make this whole planet too hot for anyone who didn't wear horns on his head!

"So—not swallowin' Dumaroy's talk about the terrible, terrible Norbies, I came up to have a look around for myself. I chose the wrong time—or maybe the right, if we consider it from another angle—and found the trail of a big herd bein' driven straight back into the mountains where they had no business to be. And, bein' slightly stupid as my father likes to point out occasionally, I just followed hoofprints along until I was collared. A simple story—with me the simplest item in it.

"Then these gentle Xiks thought maybe I could supply some bits of information that they considered necessary to their future well bein'. Some things I honestly didn't know and, while they were tryin' to encourage my reluctant tongue, somebody pulled a raid on their horse corral and rather disrupted things. I believe that they had considered their situation entirely safe here and that when they were attacked they came unlaced at the seams for a few minutes. I took advantage of a very lucky break and headed for the hills. Then Gorgol here stumbled on me and so—you know the rest."

He waved a bandaged hand and added in a far more serious tone, "What you don't know—and what is goin' to hurry us out of here—is that we're sittin' right on the edge of a neat little war. These Xiks have been deliberately stirrin' up trouble to set the settlers and the Norbies at each others' throats. Whether it's just that they thrive on pure meanness, or whether they have some plans of their own that can only be ripened in a war, is anybody's guess. But they are plannin' a full-sized raid on the range below the Peaks, disguised as Norbies. And in turn a couple of raids on Norbie huntin' camps doublin' as settlers. I don't know whether you know about the Nitra tribe or not. But they're not the type any man with any sense excites. And the Xiks have been twistin' their tails regularly—in a manner of speakin'—pushin' them straight into a stampede that might smash every spread on the Peak Range. Get the Norbies mad enough and they'll unite in a continent-wide drive. Then"—he waved his hand again—"good-by to a pretty decent little world. With all the best intentions in the galaxy the Peace Officers will have to call in the Patrol. There'll either be guerrilla warfare for years, with the Norbies against everythin' from off-world—or else no Norbies. And since I believe that the Norbies are a pretty fine lot, I'm just a little bit prejudiced. So now we're faced with a big job, fella. We have to try and stop the war before the first shot is really fired!"

CHAPTER TWELVE

The pattern fitted, not only with the situation as Storm already knew it, but with tactics the Xiks had used elsewhere in the galaxy. The enemy had apparently learned nothing from their defeat, and were starting their old games over again. Did this handful of holdouts believe Arzor was going to furnish them with a nucleus for a new empire? Yet that vision was no more grandiloquent than the one they had always held and that the Confederacy had had to expend every effort to defeat. Storm sighed. There had been no end after all to the conflict that had wiped Terra from the solar map.

"How many Xiks are there?" He was already occupied with the practical side of the matter.

Logan Quade shrugged, let out a little involuntary yelp of pain, and then added:

"They kept me busy, a little too busy to count noses. Five in the bunch that first downed me. But all of those weren't alien—at least two were outlaws of our own breed. And there was an officer of sorts in command of the questionin'. Him I want to meet again!" The hands in their bandage mittens moved on Logan's knees. "I saw maybe a dozen aliens—about half as many outlaws—they don't mix too well—"

"They wouldn't." The Xiks had had human stooges on other worlds, but it was always an uneasy cooperation and seldom worked. "How many settlers in the Peak country?"

"There're seven ranges staked out. Dumaroy's the largest so far. He has his brother, nephew, and twelve riders. Lancin—Artur—he has a smaller holdin'—though his brother's comin' out to join him as soon as he's mustered out of the Service. They have five Norbies ridin' for them. And our range—six Norbies and two riders m' father sent up from the Basin. Maybe ten-twelve men can be combed out of the small outfits. Not a very big army—at least you'll figure that after being with the Confed forces—"

"I've seen successful move-ins accomplished by even fewer," Storm returned mildly. "But your Peak people must be pretty well scattered—"

"Just let me get to the first of the line cabins and there'll be a talker to call 'em in. We aren't so primitive as you off-worlders seem to think!"

"And that line cabin—how far away?"

"I'd have to take a looksee from some height around here. This is new territory as far as I'm concerned. I'd guess—maybe two day's easy ridin'—fifteen hours if you pushed with a good mount under you."

"Rain's about the only one of those we have. And there'll be a pack of Xiks out to nose our trail." Storm wasn't arguing, he was simply stating the odds as he saw them. "Also, we haven't yet found a way out of this valley that we can take a horse over. The road in was blocked by a landslide."

"I don't care how we do it," Logan fired back. "But I'm tellin' you, Storm, it has to be done! We can't let Dumaroy and the Norbies mix it up just to please those Xiks! I was born on Arzor and I'm not throwin' this world away if it's at all possible to save it!"

"If it's at all possible to save it—" echoed Storm, the old chill of loss eating into him.

"Yes, you, more than all of us, know what those Xiks can do when they play the game according to *their* rules."

Storm turned now to Gorgol and his fingers outlined as much of Logan's story as he could find the proper movements to explain. He ended with the question that meant the most now:

"There is a way out of valley for man—horse?"

"If there is—Gorgol find." The Norbie stripped two of the small birds from his roasting spits, tucked them into a broad leaf and gathered them up. "I go look—" He scrambled over the barrier and was gone.

"You been long on Arzor?" Logan asked as Storm divided up the other birds and brought Quade's portion to him.

"A little over a month—my time—"

"You've settled down quickly," the other commented. "I've seen men born here who can't make finger-talk that fast or accurately—"

"Perhaps it comes easier because my own people once had a sign language to use with strangers. Here—let me manage that."

The bandaged hands were making clumsy work of eating and Storm sat down beside Logan, to feed him bite by bite from the point of his knife. Surra blinked at them in drowsy content and Hing draped herself affectionately over Logan's outstretched legs.

"Where did you get the animals—they're off-world? And that trained bird of yours—what is it?" the younger man asked as Storm paused to dismember another grass hen.

"I'm a Beast Master—and these are my team. Baku, African Black Eagle, Surra, dune cat, Hing, meerkat. They are all natives of Terra, too. We lost Hing's mate in the flood—"

"Beast Master!" There was open admiration in the tone, even if the battered features could not mirror it. "Say—what is this Dineh you spoke of earlier—?"

"I thought you did not understand Navajo!" Storm countered.

Now those blue eyes were very bright. "Navajo," Logan repeated thoughtfully, as if trying to remember where he might have heard the word before. He put up his mittened hand to the ketoh on Storm's wrist, and then lightly touched the necklace that swung free as the other offered him more food. "Those are Navajo, aren't they?"

Storm waited. He had an odd feeling that something important was coming out of this. "Yes."

"My father has a bracelet like this one—"

That was the wrong thing, the words pushed Storm into remembering what he had avoided these past few weeks. Involuntarily he jerked away from Logan's hand, got to his feet.

"Your father"—the Terran spoke gently, quietly, very remotely, though there was danger under the veneer of that tone—"is not Navajo!"

"And you hate him, don't you?" Logan said without accusation.

He might have been commenting upon the darkness of the night without. "Brad Quade has a lot of enemies—but not your sort of man usually. No, he's not Navajo—he was born on Arzor—but of Terran stock—He is part Cheyenne—"

"Cheyenne!" Storm was startled. It was easier to think of Quade, the enemy, as coming from the old, arrogant, all-white stock who had lied, cheated, pushed his people back and back—though not into the nothingness the white man wanted for them. No—never into nothingness!

"Cheyenne—that's Amerindian—" Logan was starting to explain when he was interrupted.

Surra was on her feet, her drowsy content gone as if she had never sprawled half-asleep a moment earlier. And Storm reached swiftly for the blaster he had taken from the pass guard. It was Xik issue but enough like a Confed weapon for him to use. He only wished he had more than one clip for it, but the invaders must be running low on ammunition themselves.

It was Gorgol who squeezed through and the news he brought was not good. Not only had he been unable to prospect for another exit from the valley, but there was a Nitra war party camped in the southern end of the flooded land, and lights showed to the north along the cliffs.

"The horses," Storm decided first, "and water. Get the mounts in here and as much water as we can store. Perhaps we can sit out a search and the Xiks may tangle with those Nitra—"

They worked fast, dousing the fire and widening the opening so that Rain and the three horses from the other valley could be brought into the cave. On their return they found Logan on his feet, using Storm's torch and exploring into the dark tunnel they had all avoided earlier.

"I wonder," he speculated, "whether this hole couldn't run on through the mountain. This might not have been one of the regular Sealed Caves but a passage from one valley to the next. You say you got into this valley through a tunnel—well, couldn't this one be the way out?"

But Storm eyed the dark hole in which the beam of the torch was so quickly lost with no favor at all. The air was dead the farther one moved in from the entrance, and he had a feeling that to go into that unknown region would be merely to walk to one's death. Unless he were driven to it he would have no part of such exploration.

"Queer air—" Logan limped on, one supporting hand against the wall. "Seems to be dead—light plays tricks here too."

And Storm noticed that the horses were huddling together in the middle of the expanse, showing no desire to push into the tunnel—that Surra avoided the dark mouth of the place and Hing, whose curiosity had led her in the past to the most reckless venturing, did not patter along at Logan's heels, but sat on her haunches, rocking from side to side, her pointed nose high, making snuffling noises of suspicion.

With Gorgol, the Terran set about building up the front of the cave, obliterating hoofprints as far back as the edge of the water. Then they loaded to the brim the three canteens and Gorgol's water carrier of lizard skin. From the edge of the still shrinking lake Storm saw those dots of light along the cliffs. If the Xiks had discovered the body of the guard, they might well be more cautious about advancing in the dark.

It was the middle of the night when the fugitives stopped their work of disguising the cave and crawled into hiding. It seemed to Storm, as he settled down to get what sleep he could, that the inert atmosphere of the place was expelling the fresh air that came in through a small opening they had left. And, when he closed his eyes and could no longer sight that scrap of sky, his imagination presented a picture of his being fastened in some box he could not batter open.

"Sealed Caves"—he had always thought that that name had been given because they were actually walled up. But now he could believe that that which sealed them was inherent in the caves themselves. Reason told Storm that they were doing the best thing now, that if they could stay undercover until he and Gorgol, scouting the hills, found a path out, they would have better than a fifty-fifty chance. But his body was tense, every nerve in him resisted holing up here.

Morning came and the three in hiding discovered that the cave had one good property besides offering concealment—it was cool, while the sun in the valley was a bright glare generating dank heat. Logan wriggled up to share Storm's lookout.

"Big dry's comin' early this year," he remarked. "Sometimes works that way when the storms in the mountains are too heavy early in the season. We've more than one reason for gettin' out of here on the gallop."

"The Survey party crossed a river coming in," Storm replied. "High with rainfall, of course, but would it dry up entirely?"

"The Staffa, no. But that runs pretty far south of this region, rises in the East Peak country. I don't know about this other one you mention. To try to make the Staffa and trail it out would just about double your ridin' time and you'd be in the edge of the Nitra raidin' country—"

"Then we had better make our break soon—" Storm stopped almost in mid-word as the fan-shaped piece of valley he could sight from his vantage point was suddenly peopled. Through his lenses those distant figures leaped into clear detail. They were wearing Norbie corselets and boot leggings, but they had not taken the trouble to continue the deception farther than their clothing. That pale greenish skin, the lank, bleached hair hanging in curled rats' tails down to their shoulders in the back, marked two of the riders as Xiks, while their three companions were plainly of the settler race. Two of the latter had bows, but the former were armed with off-world weapons. And one of them bore across his saddle a tube of a dead white color.

Storm had accepted the presence of slicers, the blaster he now half lay upon, the force beam he had seen at its deadly work in the other valley. But still he jibbed at the white tube and what it meant. There were few enough of them, a development produced so close to the end of the war that it had never been in wide use. And certainly the last place the Terran would expect to see it carried casually on horseback was here in the wastes of a frontier planet. Two, captured in outposts so quickly overrun by Confed forces that the defenders had not been able to blow them up and so avoid surrender, had been tested on barren asteroids. And, witnessing the result, the Confed command had ordered that all others found were to be destroyed at once.

The tubes could be used, yes—and the results would be disastrous to the enemy before their sights—only there was in addition an unpredictable backlash of energy, though it might not affect the Xiks as adversely as it did the Confed force that tested the weapons. Built on a principle not unlike that of the disrupters, used to dispose of inanimate material, the tubes were far more powerful than any Confed disrupter of three times their size and range.

"More trouble?" Logan asked.

Storm held out the lenses, steadying them for the other.

"See that tube on the second horse—that's the worst trouble I know." The Terran added what he had heard about that weapon.

"Goin' to make sure of somebody—or somebodies," commented the Arzoran dryly. "I don't particularly care for Nitra warriors. We've had our differences, and until you have a Nitra double-barbed arrow cut out of you, fella, you don't know just how much you can sweat over a little knife work. No—I've never felt kindly toward Nitras. But any disputes we've had have been on a more or less even basis. Usin' that tube against Norbies's more like puttin' up a grass hen against your Surra and tyin' the hen's feet into the bargain."

Storm made signs for Gorgol, repeating as well as he could the information about the Xik weapon. The Norbie nodded that he understood and watched the riders round the lake, to be hidden by a series of mounds linked together by a brush wall.

"Nitra there—last night. Maybeso not so now. Nitra do not wait like bug one sets foot upon! This evil thing—better we take it—"

"Not so," Storm returned regretfully. "Made only to be used by evil men—we touch—we killed!" He used the most emphatic of the death signs.

The rider with the tube appeared on the far side of the end mound. He dismounted, with none of the easy grace of a settler or the litheness of a Norbie, but in a scrambling way that informed Storm that to the alien the animal he had bestridden was merely a means of transportation and no more. Seeing that, the Terran could understand better how the Xiks had been able to cut down the frightened animals in the other valley undisturbed by the brutality of the act.

Having shouldered the tube, the invader climbed to the top of the mound and set about the business of putting together the rubble there to form a base for it. He moved expertly but with no hurry. Yet Storm did not miss that flash through the air, was able to pick out with the aid of the lenses the arrow, head down and still quivering, planted in the soil just a foot short of its target. But that must have been a specially lucky shot as no more arrows hit the mound.

"The Nitra are shooting." Storm passed the lenses again to Logan.

"Poor devils," the other commented, "they must be cornered—they wouldn't take such a chance unless they were."

The other riders burst into sight, with the outlaws well to the fore, urging their mounts in a retreat that held panic as part of its haste.

"Drawing them on—" Storm speculated aloud. "Those idiots are really planning to use that thing!"

He squirmed around on the bank of earth and stone, jabbing a fist at Gorgol's shoulder to urge him down. Another sweep of Storm's arm sent the blaster skidding to the cave floor ahead of him, as he took a grip on Logan's belt and jerked the younger man down with him. Surra? The cat was on the floor—Baku—Baku!

The eagle had gone foraging an hour ago. Storm beamed as best he could a message to keep up—up and safe in the high heavens.

"Get those horses back! All the way back into the tunnel mouth!"

"What's the matter? They set up that thing about a mile from here and facin' the other way—" Logan protested, but he was limping toward Rain, flapping his arms at the mares.

Together they forced the horses back into the mouth of the tunnel. Storm glanced back despairingly at that window on the outer world. But there was no time to close it.

"Get down!" He set the example, throwing himself flat on the floor, and saw Gorgol and Logan obey. "Your eyes! Cover your eyes!" He shouted that to Logan, signed it to the Norbie. Then he lay waiting, his face buried in the crook of his arm.

The heartlessness of the aliens was never more plain than in this move. They would wipe out the pocket of Nitras right enough—but they would also doom most of the living things in this valley into the bargain. The Terran grinned without mirth as he remembered those outlaws riding for their lives. If he knew Xiks they would hardly delay long enough to give their colleagues a good start to safety. The chance for those riders to survive was so slender as to be practically nonexistent.

Surra had flattened herself beside Storm, and Hing was endeavoring to dig her way under him, scraping fruitlessly at the rock floor and whimpering, until he reached out an arm and gathered her in between him and the cat. He heard the horses stamp, but they did not venture out of the tunnel mouth where Logan had driven them. It was as if they were as alert to the warning in Storm's mind as the other animals.

He had nothing to guide him except those army reports. But those, using the terse language of such communications, had been circulated widely among all Commando outfits where the men or beast and man teams engaged in mopping-up activities might chance upon the new and horrific weapon. And service reports were not prone to exaggerate.

Why were the effects of the thing so much worse on non-Xiks? How long now before it would blow? Storm tried counting off seconds in the dark and was not aware he was doing it aloud until he heard a sound that could only be a chuckle coming from Logan's direction.

"I hope you're not makin' us pull this burrow trick for nothin'," the other remarked. "How long before the world comes apart?"

His words might have been a cue. For their world, dark and stuffy as it was, did come apart then. Storm could never later describe what happened to him in that space of time lifted out of the ordinary stream of seconds, minutes, hours. The experience was like being caught up in a giant's hand, rolled into a conveniently sized ball, and tossed up in the air to be caught again. There was no thinking—no feeling—nothing but emptiness, with himself blown through it—on and on—and on—

And it was not wholly physical, that assault upon the stable foundations of his small portion of the planet. One part of Storm clung to the solid cave floor as an anchor for the part that whirled and flew. And inside he was torn because he so clung.

How long did it last? Was he unconscious toward the end of that weird struggle between substance and nonsubstance? Did the rocks about them keep them safe by turning the worst of the unknown radiation? He only knew that they did endure the backlash and lived.

Again he felt the warmth coming from Surra through the icy chill that blanketed the cave. He shrank from the scratching of Hing's claws as she squirmed and kicked.

For a long moment he lay still, as an insect might cower beneath a rock if it could foresee that in a moment that shelter would be lifted and it would be exposed to unforeseeable danger. Then, in the midst of his blinding, unreasoning panic, a spark of resolution sprouted. The Terran lifted his head from his arm and for a terrified minute thought he was blind. For there was no more small slit of sky—nothing but thick darkness—a chill darkness filled with the dead air native to this place.

Storm sat up, feeling Surra rise with him. She growled and spat. And then, out of the dark, Logan spoke with determined lightness:

"I think somebody just slammed the door!"

CHAPTER THIRTEEN

Storm used the torch, aiming it at the mouth of the cave. His mind refused to accept what his eyes reported—there was no longer any opening there. It had been closed once by the landslip—but that had been a different matter, an affair of earth and stone. This was a black oozing over that same earth and stone, a thick stuff in drips and runnels forming a complete curtain across.

"What in the—?"

The Terran heard Logan's amazed demand as he walked closer to that strange wall, focusing the torch on the widest of the black streaks. Storm could recognize the stuff now. It was the substance of that wedge rail the Survey party had trailed into the valley, the stuff that had walled the tunnel of the entrance gorge. Yet now it had been melted as tar might have softened and run from the breath of a blaster. Though he had not noticed it earlier, the building material of the long-ago aliens must have rimmed this cave, to be released by the backlash of the Xik weapon!

Storm handed the torch to Gorgol with a gesture to keep it trained on the widest of the surface streams. He rammed the stock of the blaster against that black runnel with all the strength he could put into a swinging blow. The light alloy of the butt gave off a metallic ring, rebounded with force enough to jar Storm back a step or two, yet the black stream showed no dent or mark.

The Terran reversed the weapon, set its dial to maximum and pressed the trigger. A point of vivid, eye-searing flame bored into the black stain for an instant, until Storm flicked the control. Again there was no impression on the alien coating.

"Nothing happened?" Logan limped around Gorgol to examine the wall for himself. "What is that anyway?"

Storm explained almost absently. He had taken the torch back from Gorgol and was pacing along the front of the cave. Some trick of chance—or could it be that the ancient owners had prepared a booby trap for the unwary?—had cemented the barrier all the way across. Those black streams had run in just the places where they could best weld together rocks and earth. Perhaps Hing might be able to dig her way to freedom, but no effort could clear a large enough space to release the rest of them.

Which left—the tunnel.

Storm traversed the new wall for a second time, hoping against the evidence of his eyes to find some break they could enlarge. He met Logan face to face as he turned back.

"I still don't see what happened—or why!" The Arzoran studied the wall beside him. "If they had turned that little machine of theirs on us, yes. But the tube was facin' the other way—and a mile off at that!"

"The Confed Lab men after the first experiment said the results were a matter of vibration. And this stuff has been molded like plasta-flesh. Must have turned every bit of it in this valley fluid for a time—"

"I hope," Logan stood away from the wall, "that it caught every one of those devils stickin' in it tight! No chance of breakin' through this?"

Storm shook his head. "The blaster was our best hope. And you saw what happened when I tried that."

"All right. Then we'll have to go explorin'. And I would suggest we move now. I don't know whether you've noticed it, but there's been a change in our air."

That quality of staleness that Storm had met on his first imprisonment here was indeed very noticeable. And using the blaster had not helped to clear the atmosphere any. They would have to try the tunnel or face a very unpleasant death where they were.

Packing their supplies on the horses, with Surra padding in the lead beside Storm, they moved reluctantly into the tunnel. The Terran kept his torch on the lowest unit of its force. No use exhausting its charge when he had only one spare cartridge. And by its light they saw that they were out of the natural roughness of the cave into a cutting, which, if it had not been bored by intelligent beings, had been surfaced by them, for the walls changed abruptly from the red stone of the natural rock to the black of the alien material.

"Good thing your vibrations didn't reach this far," Logan commented and then coughed. "If this had been melted we would have been finished."

Just as the period of the Xik attack had been lifted out of normal time for Storm, so did now this journey appear to take on the properties of a march through a nightmare. They must have been progressing at the rate of a normal walking pace, yet to the Terran the sensation of wading through some vast delaying flood persisted. Perhaps it was the inert quality of the air that affected his reactions, slowed his mind. Had it been minutes—or hours—since they had left the cave to enter this long tube where the flat black of walls, floor, roof sucked the air from a man's lungs and the light from the torch?

Then Surra left his side. She was a tawny streak in the torch light, leaping ahead, to be absorbed utterly by the gloom. He called after her and was nearly sent sprawling as Rain nudged against him. The horses were as eager as the cat to hurry ahead.

"Air!"

Storm caught that hint of breeze also. And it was more than just fresh air to battle the deadness of the passage; that puff of wind carried with it its own freshness and scents—strange perhaps, but pleasant. Storm stumbled on at a half-run, hearing the others pounding after him.

There was a turn in the corridor, the first they had found. Then light shone ahead, squares of light. Storm snapped off the torch and headed for that goal. He squeezed past Rain, urged one of the mares aside and nearly stumbled over Surra, who was standing on her hind legs, her paws resting on a crossbar of a grill-like closing, her head blotting out one of its squares.

Storm steadied himself with a grip on the bars, looked ahead.

But not into the open day as he thought he would. Instead he was surveying a section of what might be a garden. Yet there was not one of the plants sprawling there that he could name, not among those in the first bed, at any rate.

In the next—No! Storm's hands twisted tightly on the bar. He had been shaken when he had unrolled the package Na-Ta-Hay had sent him. But not as much as now. That small stretch of good clean *green* grass, the pine a little beyond—not a spizer, nor a candlestick gum, nor a Langful, but a true Terran pine!

"Pine!" He could make a song of that word, a song that would have power enough to pull the Faraway Gods across the void of space. His hands battered at the grill gate and then strove to find the release of its lock—let him through—out to stand beneath that pine!

"Storm—bar—other side—"

Somehow those words penetrated his excitement. There was a bar on the other side of the grid, the mechanism of its lock, as far as he could see through the holes, strange. But there was some way of opening it, there had to be!

The Terran worked his arm through one of the grill openings, pounded with his fist along the bar. His impatience built to a rage with the stubborn thing that kept them prisoners in the tunnel when all that fresh world lay beyond. Then his self-control began to assert itself once more. He withdrew his arm and unsheathed his belt knife.

Half-crouched, Storm flattened his body against the grill once more and picked with the knife point at every possible opening in and around that circle of metal that apparently locked the bar into place. Logan and Gorgol kept back the crowding animals while he worked. The sweat made his hand slippery, until at last he dropped the knife out of reach on the other side of the still-locked barrier. Gorgol's belt knife was too long and Logan's had been taken from him on his capture. There was no use in trying the blaster against the alien material of the portal.

Storm had gone back to the futile pounding when a sudden squeak from ground level—ground level on the opposite side of that obdurate door—startled him into sane thinking again. The squares of the grill might have kept out the rest of them, but Hing had squeezed through and was now watching him with expectancy.

Hing! Storm went down on his knees and schooled patience back into his voice as he chirruped to her. A Beast Master could only control and direct his charges when he was in full control of himself. He had forgotten the first rule of his training and the realization of that frightened him almost as much as the sight of the Xik weapon—more so because this fault lay within him, and it was the first time he had erred since his earliest days in the service.

The Terran forced himself to breathe more slowly and put aside his fear of not being able to master the alien lock. Hing was the important one now—Hing and her curiosity, her claws, the jobs she had been trained to do in the past. Storm blanked his mind, narrowed all his power of projection to one thing—and sent that thought along the path as he had called Baku out of the morning sky to help them clear the pass.

Hing sat up, her long clawed paws dangling in front of her lighter belly fur. Then she dropped to four feet once more, came to the door and climbed it agilely until she was perched on the bar itself, her pointed nose only inches away from Storm's face. Again she waited and chirruped inquiringly.

He could not direct her, send those claws to the right places as he had in the past when she had destroyed buried installations, uncovered and rendered useless delicate machinery. Then the Terran had had models of the necessary kind to practice with, had been able to show Hing and her mate just what they must do. Now he did not even know the type of lock that baffled them. He could only use Hing's own curiosity as a tool, urge the meerkat to solve the mystery. And since she did not have the quick and reaching intelligence of Surra, nor the falcon brain of Baku, implanting the proper impulse was a longer process and a doubtful one.

Storm put all his force into that one beam of will. He did not know that he showed the face of a man strained close to the limit of endurance. And that the two who watched him, without understanding how or why he fought, were held silent by the strain and effort he displayed.

Hing walked a tightrope along the bar. Now she balanced on her hind feet, patting that circle of the lock with her paws. And if Storm did not actually hear the click of her investigating claws on the substance, he sensed them throughout his tense body as he poured out his will.

She raked the disc impatiently and shrilled a protest—perhaps at the stubborn lock, perhaps at his soundless command. But she did not retreat. Bending her head she tried her teeth on the thing, hissed almost as angrily as Surra had done, and went back to picking with her claws. Whether she did puzzle out the pattern, or whether it was only lucky chance, Storm was never to know. But there was a tiny flash of light. Hing squealed and leaped from the bar just as it dropped.

The grill swung open, dragging the Terran with it into the place of growing things. He was too weak from his efforts to get to his feet and was only barely conscious of Gorgol pulling him back out of the path of the horses. Then he was lying on his back, partially supported by the Norbie's arm, gazing up dazedly into a vast space filled with wisps of floating mist.

"What kind of a place—" Logan's voice sounded subdued, with more than a touch of awe.

The air was fresh, not only fresh but filled with scents—spicy, perfumed, provocative odors, as if someone had emptied all the aromatic growing things of a dozen worlds into one limited space and kept them at the peak of production.

And that was just what someone or something had done, as they discovered. Storm, with Gorgol to steady him, got to his feet. He saw Surra squatting on her haunches before a round puffball of a thing studded with cups of purple blooms, her eyes half-closed in ecstasy as she sniffed the delicate but tantalizing fragrance those flowers spread. And the horses had cantered on, stopping to graze on the bank of cool, green grass that had certainly once been rooted on the planet of Storm's birth.

He pulled loose from the Norbie's hold and staggered to the pine, his hands fondling its bark. The scent of the needles, or the resin, was stronger in his nostrils than the more exotic odors about him. It was true this was a pine, standing at the apex of a triangle of mixed Terran vegetation. And with the bole of the tree to steady him, Storm looked ahead, to see the brilliance of roses in full bloom, tassels of lilacs, familiar, unfamiliar, all aflower, all scented, in an unbelievable mixed array.

"What is it?" Logan joined the Terran, his bruised face turned toward the mass of flowers and green as if he too felt some healing quality in it.

"From Earth!" Storm used the old word, sweeping his arms wide. "These are all from *my* world! But how did they come here?"

"And where and what is *here?*" Logan added. "Those surely aren't Terran too—" His hand fell on Storm's arm and he drew the other part way around to face, across a narrow path of the alien black stuff, another mixed garden. And the Arzoran was very right. The oddly shaped—to Terran eyes—bushes with their bluish, twisted leaves, the striped flowers (if those flat plates *were* flowers) were not Terran—not from any world Storm knew.

Gorgol came across the open glade where the horses were. His fingers moved to express his own wonder—

"Many growing things—all different—"

Storm turned again, still putting one hand to the pine as an anchor, not only because of his tired body, but also because the wonder of its being here still made this all part of a strangely satisfying dream.

There were two more gardens or garden plots wedging out from the section directly before the gate grill, and each of them was widely different in the life it supported, save that odd and weird as the growing things appeared, they shared two attributes, none were truly ugly and all were sweet scented.

Logan rubbed his forehead with his bandaged hands and blinked.

"There is something about all this—" He swung about slowly as Storm had done. A flight of brilliant patches that the Terran had thought firmly attached to a bush of ivory white stalks floated free, moved double wings, and skimmed to new perches. Birds? Insects? They could be either.

"They have places on some worlds," Logan pursued his own explanation, "where they keep wild animals—call 'em zoos. It looks to me as if this place were meant to keep specimens of vegetation from a lot of different planets. One, two, three, four," he counted the separate plots about them. "And these are just about as different from each other as you can get."

He was right, Storm could agree to that. Gorgol put out a hand and touched with gentle hesitation one of the ivory stems that had supported the flying flowers. He withdrew his fingers and sniffed at them with some of the same pleasure Surra had shown when she drank in the perfume of the purple cups.

Surra? Storm glanced around, seeking the cat. But she was gone, vanished somewhere into this scented wilderness. He sat down at the foot of the pine, leaning his back against its trunk, his hands flat against the earth that felt like home earth, moist, but firm under his flesh. He could close his eyes now to the riot of those other gardens and their weird beauty, or look up into the tent of green over him and be back again—

Gorgol and Logan drifted away. Storm was glad to be alone. Slowly he slid down the length of the pine bole until he was curled on a mat of needles and he slept, dreamlessly, completely relaxed, though the semblance of day about him never changed to evening.

"—biggest mixture you ever saw." Logan lay on his back, sharing the bed under the pine, while Gorgol dug his fingers back and forth through the same needle padding, shifting the brown harvest of years. It was still day by the light, though they must have been many hours in the cavern.

"I'd say," the Arzoran settler continued, "that a whole mountain was hollowed out to hold this. We counted about sixty different gardens—including two which are mostly water. And then there are the fruit orchards and vines—" He gestured at the remains of their recent meal, a small collection of pits and rinds. "I tell you—this is fabulous!"

"No animal life—?"

"Birds, insects—no animals, except that cat of yours. We caught her rolling in a big patch of gray mossy stuff and acting as if she were wild. Ran away from us as if *we* were Xiks stalkin' her with one of those pop guns of theirs."

"But how could all this keep growing without any attention for years, maybe centuries?" marveled Storm. "You are right, it is, it must have been intended as a botanical garden of specimens gathered from all over the galaxy. This"—he pulled a curl of flame-orange rind between his fingers—"was an Astran 'golden apple.' And the black and white berries were from Sirius Three. But you'd think the place would have grown into a wilderness when it was left. Something continued to control it, kept the growth right, nourished everything properly—"

"Maybe the light is part of it," Logan suggested. "Or the atmosphere. I've noticed one thing." He held out his hand. The bandages were gone and the wounds and burns Storm had tended were not only closed, they were almost healed.

"Show him your arm," Logan signed to Gorgol and the Norbie presented his wounded forearm for inspection. The arrow tear was only a reddish mark, and the native used the limb freely with no sign of discomfort.

"How do *you* feel?" Logan demanded of Storm.

The Terran stretched. He had not really noticed before but, now that Logan had drawn the matter to his attention, he was aware that the weight of exhaustion that had ridden him into this Eden was gone. In fact Storm had not awakened so contented with life for a long time—for years. Like Surra he wanted to roll on the ground and purr his pleasure aloud.

"See?" Logan did not seem to expect an articulate answer. "It's in the air here, all around us. Growth—making us feel alive and vigorous, healed of our hurts, too. Perhaps this place was designed for other uses besides just botanical display."

"Does it also have a door out?"

"We found three doors," Logan returned. "Two are grills, but the third looks the most promisin'."

"Why?"

"Because it has been walled up. The legends of the Sealed Caves suggest it might be an outlet to the outside—"

Storm supposed he should get up and go to inspect that doorway. But for the first time in years a kind of languorous laziness held him in its grip. Just to lie here under the pine, to watch Rain and the other horses at their ease, Logan and Gorgol beside him as relaxed as himself, none of them driven by a need for immediate action—it was wonderful, perfect! He and the others had found a small section of Paradise, why be in a hurry to leave it?

Gorgol sat up, brushed the pine needles from the fringes of his belt. He turned his head, gazing about him with a slow measurement and within Storm a faint, very faint apprehension awoke.

The native's yellow-red fingers moved in short sweeps, with pauses between, as if the importance of what he had to say was making the Norbie doubly careful of his choice of signs.

"This—trap—big trap."

CHAPTER FOURTEEN

rap?" repeated Logan without much interest. But the languor that held Storm was pierced by a fast-growing doubt. Perhaps because he *had* known a variety of traps—and very ingenious ones—in the past, the Terran did not only listen but was receptive to such a warning.

"What manner of trap?" he signed.

"You like here—happy—" Gorgol was plainly groping for signs to convey a complicated idea. "No go—want to stay—"

Storm sat up. "You no want to stay?" he asked.

Gorgol looked about him again. "Good—" He touched the remains of the fruit. "Good!" He drew an exaggeratedly deep breath of the perfume-laden air. "Feel good!" He gave an all embracing twirl of his fingers. "But—not mine—" He ran those fingers through the pine needles. "Not mine—" He flicked the fingers to include the other gardens about them. "No Gorgol place here—not hold Gorgol—" Again he was trying to make limited signs explain more abstract thought. "Your place—hold you—"

The Norbie had something! That alerting signal far inside Storm was clamoring more loudly. What better bait for a trap than a slice of a man's home planet served up just when he believed that world lost forever? Even if a trap were not intended, it was here just the same. He got to his feet, tramped determinedly away from the pine.

"Where's that built-up door of yours?" he demanded harshly over his shoulder, refusing to look back at that wedge of temptation set in familiar green.

"You think Gorgol's right?"

"You don't think about things such as that," Storm answered out of the depths of experience, "you feel! Maybe those who built this place didn't intend it for a trap—" He slapped Rain's flank, making the stallion move from the grass to the roadway that separated the small piece of Terra from its neighbor.

"Surrraaaaa—" Storm shouted that aloud, an imperative summons that he had only had to use once or twice in their close comradeship. And his voice awoke echoes above and around the gardens, while birds flew and flower-colored insects floated, disturbed, to settle again.

Leading Rain by the headstall, the Terran started down the path. The sooner he was away from that bit of his native earth the better. Already a new bitterness was beginning to fester in him and he turned it against the enemy outside. So the Xiks thought they had finished Terra? Perhaps—but they had not finished Terrans!

He hurried, deliberately twisting and turning from path to path, trying to muddle his own trail, so that he could not easily find his way back to that pine-roofed spot. Twice more he called the dune cat. Hing pattered along behind him, stopping now and then to sniff inquisitively or dig, but perfectly willing to move, while the other horses followed Rain. They threaded the narrow roadways between gardens—such gardens. Twice Storm saw foliage he recognized, and both times they were samples from widely separated worlds.

"Left through here"—Logan came up beside him—"around the end of this water place, then behind the one with the scarlet feather trees. I wonder what kind of a world those are from? See—now you're facing it."

Storm followed his directions. The scarlet plumes of the trees arched high against the duller red of the stone wall of the mountain interior. And the black path led directly to an archway that had been carefully bricked up with blocks about a foot square. The Terran could see none of the black sealing material, unless it was used as mortar to set those bricks. Under his hands the wall was immovable, and he examined it carefully, wondering what tool there was among their supplies that could best be used to attack it.

Would the points of their belt knives make any impression on those cracks? He could turn on the blaster, but he was loathe to use up the charge in the most potent weapon they had. Best try knives first.

At the end of a quarter of an hour, his hands slippery with sweat, his control over his temper hard pressed, Storm admitted that knives were not the answer. That left the blaster. It was not a disrupter, of course. But set to highest power it should act upon the blocks, if not upon the stuff that held them together.

Sending the rest of the party back, Storm lay on the path, resting the barrel of the Xik weapon on several stones so that its sights were aligned with a point in the middle of the wall, directly below the highest rise of the arch. He pressed the release button and fought the answering kick of the weapon, holding it steady as Xik-made lightning struck full on the blocks.

For seconds, perhaps a full minute, there was a flareback that beat at Storm with a wave of blast heat. Then a core of yellow showed at the center point of the beam, the yellow spreading outward in a circle. The color deepened. Harsh fumes spreading from that contact point made Storm cough, his eyes stream. But he held the blaster steady for another long moment before he started to depress the barrel slowly, drawing the yellow mark down in a line toward the floor.

As the light began to pulse, he knew that the charge was nearing exhaustion. What if he had guessed wrong and thrown away the blaster without achieving their freedom? Storm held the weapon tensely while those pulsations grew more ragged, until the pressure of his finger on the firing button brought no response.

To his vast disappointment the wall, save for that heat scar, looked as stanch as it had been on his first examination. He could not wait to know the truth. Reversing the blaster so its stock was a club, he ran forward in spite of the lingering heat, to thrust the butt into the scar with all the force of his weight and strength behind it.

There was a shock that made the Terran grunt as the metal stock met the blocks. But it wasn't the blaster that gave. A whole section where the flame had licked moved outward—perhaps not very much. But he *had* felt it give. Heartened he struck again. The section of blocks broke apart, not along the joints where they had been mortared together, but in the middle of the stone squares themselves—proving once again that the building material of the unknown aliens was more enduring than the products of nature.

Before he attacked the second time Storm allowed the wall to cool. The fumes of the ray were gone, almost as if they had been sucked away or absorbed by some quality in the air of the garden cavern. A bush with a lacy covering quivered until its iridescent leaves shook, and Surra, her fur ruffled, her eyes glinting wild and feral, crawled from under it to the roadway and stood panting before Storm.

He rubbed behind her ears, along the line of her pointed fox jaw, talking to her in that crooning speech that soothed her best. She was excited, overstimulated, and he marveled that she had answered his call. One could never be sure with the felines, their independence kept them from being servants—companions, yes, and war comrades, but not servants to man. Each time Surra obeyed some order or summons Storm knew that obedience was by her will and not his. And he could never be sure whether his hold on her would continue. Now, under his gentling, she softened, purred, dabbing at his hands with a claw-sheathed paw. The alien trap had not taken Surra either.

They plundered the fruit gardens for another meal, filled their canteens with purified water from a miniature waterfall in one of the lake lands and waited. Until, at last, with the three of them working, they were able to handle the cooled blocks and break their way through the barrier.

Logan had been right in his surmise. No tunnel reached before them, only the mouth of another cave, and, beyond that, the light of Arzoran day. They led the horses one by one through that break, and Gorgol, who had gone out on a short scout, returned, his hands flashing in an excited message.

"This place I know! Here I slew the evil flyer when I went on my man hunt. There is a trail from this place—"

They came out in a valley so narrow that it was merely a ravine between two towering heights. And the cut was so barren of vegetation that the sun trapped within those walls made a glaring furnace of the depths, so that the contrast between this sere outer world and the delights of the cavern was even more pronounced. On impulse Storm turned back to rebuild the barrier they had broken through, piling the crumbling blocks of stone across the opening. Logan joined in, his healing lips no longer so puffed that they could not shape a smile.

"Let the sealed ones continue to keep their secrets, eh?" He laughed. "This is too good a hiding hole to waste. We may have need of it again."

But how quickly that need was to come they did not dream. Gorgol mounted one of the mares and turned her to the southern end of the valley. Logan swung up bareback on a second horse, they having packed what was left of their supplies on the yearling. Storm was just about to settle himself on Rain's pad saddle when Surra gave her battle cry, bounding ahead of the Norbie's horse, to face the end of the valley, the hair along her backbone roughed, her ears flattened to her skull as she hissed defiance.

Her hiss was answered twofold. Gorgol's stun rod went up as a yellow-gray boulder detached itself from the general mass of rocks before them, produced driving feet, and charged in an insane rage before Storm understood what was happening.

The yoris, meeting the beam of the stun ray head on, gave a choked scream and landed in a skidding heap while Gorgol fought his terrorized horse. The mare Logan was riding panicked, and her rider, still suffering from his beating, with no reins or saddle as an anchor, was thrown, rolling over just as a second yoris came out of a pocket in the cliff and screeched down to join its mate.

Storm's arrow hit a lucky mark, the soft underskin of the lizard's throat, one of the giant reptile's three vulnerable spots. But the thing was not killed outright. Snapping its murderous jaws, it beat against the ground, and Logan threw himself back with a cry, a red stream welling through his boot over the calf. Gorgol beamed the wounded lizard and it went limp. But the Norbie paid no heed to the yoris as he vaulted to Logan's side.

Young Quade had both hands clasped tightly about his leg just above that wound, his face very pale. He glanced up at Storm with an odd emptiness in the brilliant blue of his eyes.

Gorgol drew his knife and cut a length of fringe from his belt. He worked the boot from Logan's leg with a quick jerk that made the other catch his breath. With the cord of fringe he looped a tourniquet above the wound and then passed the ends to Storm to twist tight while he went to the yoris, prying open its mouth to peer within. That examination required only a second. The native stooped to slash at the middle of the lizard, ripping out a great hunk of fatty flesh. He ran back to clap it over the bloody gash on Logan's leg.

"Male"—Logan got the word out between set teeth—"poison—"

Storm was cold inside. There was nothing in his depleted aid kit that could handle this. And he had heard tales of yoris poison, most of them grisly. But Gorgol was signing.

"Draw poison out—" He gestured to the raw gob of lizard fat. "No ride, no walk—be quiet—sick, very sick soon—"

Logan shaped a shadow of a smile. "He's not just fanning his fingers when he says that." His voice sounded oddly thick. "I think I've had it, fella—"

The pallor that crept up under his brown skin was close to gray and his hands and arms jerked in spasmodic quivers that he apparently could not control. A small trickle of blood rilled from the corner of his swollen mouth.

Gorgol went back to the yoris and cut a fresh strip of fat. He motioned to Storm to pull off the first poultice and slapped on the second. With the blood on the discarded lump there was a blue discoloration. The Norbie pointed to it.

"Poison—it comes—"

But could they hope to draw out all the venom that way, wondered Storm. Logan no longer twitched. His head had slumped forward on his chest and he was breathing in quick snorts, his ribs showing under the tight skin as the lungs beneath them labored. His skin was clammy to the touch, with cold perspiration rising in great beads. Storm thought that he was no longer conscious.

Four more times Gorgol changed that poultice of lizard flesh. The last time it came away without a trace of the blue stain. But Logan lay inert, his breathing very quick and shallow.

"No more poison. Now he sleep—" the Norbie explained.

"Will he wake?"

Gorgol studied the unconscious rider. "Maybeso. No thing else to do. No ride, no walk, maybeso this many days—" He held up two fingers.

"Look here," Storm began aloud and then switched to signs. "You tell me how go—I find help—come back—you wait for me in place of growing things—"

The Norbie nodded. "I keep watch—you bring help—tell also about evil ones—"

Together they carried Logan back into the cavern and then Storm proceeded to strip down for a quick journey along the trail Gorgol drew in the dust for him to memorize. He would take Rain but not Surra. Perhaps he would find Baku outside. But he intended to set and keep a pace the cat could not match.

At the last, he took only two of the canteens, a packet of iron rations, and his bow and arrows. Gorgol offered him back the stun rod and he hesitated, refusing it only because he knew the symbolic reliance the Norbie placed upon it. That, and the thought that the Xiks might just invade the valley outside and he had to leave Gorgol the best defense.

Logan was still limp and unresponding when Storm examined him before he left. But the Terran was sure that the other's breathing was better, that his stupor was now close to normal sleep. If he did nothing in the way of exercise to send the remaining poison through his system, he had a good chance for recovery. And all settlers possessed yoris antidote, which Storm could bring back with him.

So, in the hours of the next dawn, the Terran set out, passing the scavenger-stripped bones of the yoris, heading along that trail Gorgol had committed to memory two seasons earlier.

As Storm rode he beamed a silent call for Baku. But, as there came no answering dive from the skies, no rasping scream of greeting, he began to fear that the eagle had not escaped the backlash of the Xik weapon. He missed Surra's scouting, the aid of her keen scent and keener hearing, and he began to realize that he might have come to depend too heavily upon his team.

The path Gorgol had discovered leading out of this slice of valley was a defile that curved around southwest, and should, the Norbie had promised, bring him out of the mountains proper by sundown. Nowhere did Storm find any trace of either Nitra or Xik, though twice he crossed a fairly fresh yoris trail and once marked claw prints in a bank of soft earth that might have been the sign left by the monster of the heights Gorgol called the evil flyer.

He camped that night in a small side gully, a dry camp where he shared with Rain the contents of one of his canteens, and the stallion grazed disdainfully on some bunches of coarse grass already browning to summer death. But the morning came cool and cloudy and Storm pushed the pace, wanting to be out of these gorges if another cloudburst was brewing aloft, his lively imagination painting a vivid picture of what a sudden dash of water down these ways would mean to a trapped horse and its rider.

By midmorning the threatening clouds had not yet released their burden of water, and the Terran was cantering into the fringe of lowland that extended a tongue to the very foot of the Peaks. According to Logan, he should come across the first of the line cabins before nightfall and find within the communicator that would link him to all the range holdings of the district.

But Storm chanced upon the village first. The Staffa had cut a path across this level country and the Terran detoured to follow its west bank, sure that what he sought could not have been located too far from the necessary water. The rounded tent domes of a Norbie camp were a very welcome sight. He reined in, slung his bow so that he could show empty hands for the sentry, and waited. Only no sentry appeared to challenge him, and now, when he let Rain trot closer, Storm could sight no warriors about those tents. The continued eerie silence finally made him halt once more.

Norbie villages were never permanent affairs. You could come across the signs of old camp sites along any river in the right district. But neither was it customary for any clan to ride off and leave their curved roof poles standing, the hide and skin coverings stretched in place. Both possessions counted as part of the families' wealth and were too hard to replace.

By the crimson strings marking the shield pole of the largest tent this was a Shosonna clan, allied to Gorgol's people and friendly to the settlers. Had it suffered a Nitra raid? Storm kept Rain down to a walk and proceeded cautiously toward the tents. More Xik deviltry?

"All right, rider! Stand where you are and keep your hands open!"

That voice came out of the blue—or rather lavender sky—as far as Storm could determine. But the bite in the tone was enough to lead the Terran to obey orders—for that moment anyway. He held up his hands, palm out, searching sky and ground for the invisible challenger.

"We've a far sighter on you, fella—"

So! Storm's pride in his scout's art revived a little. A far sighter could pick up a man a mile or more away. The unknown speaker could have cut him down before he even knew the other was in the country. But who was that unknown? Outlaws talking for the Xiks? Settlers? One guess was as good as another.

Rain snorted, stamped, and half turned his head toward his rider as if to ask what they were waiting for. Storm still watched the lodges before him, the waving grass of the plain, the banks of the stream, searching for some sign of the men he was sure were hidden there. His own impatience approached the boiling point. This was no time to play games of hide-and-seek. The sooner Logan had medical attention the better. And the knowledge of the Xik holdouts must be relayed to the authorities at once.

At last he deliberately dropped his hands. And that might have been an awaited signal, for three men stepped out of the chieftain's tent in the village and began to walk toward him, their stun rods centered steadily on him.

"Dumaroy!" he said under his breath, "and Bister!" That was a combination he did not relish.

Coll Bister had fallen a step or so behind his companions and Storm, giving him his main attention, was sure the other had recognized him. A moment later he had oral proof of that.

"It's that crazy Terran I told you about!" Bister must be purposely raising his voice it carried so well. "Run with the goats all the way down the trail to the Crossin'. Clean off his head, he is. And it looks like he's teamed up with the horned boys for good."

Dumaroy strode ponderously on, an impressive figure physically, and as dangerous in his own way as a frawn bull. Storm knew his type. If the settler had already made up his mind, nothing could change his point of view.

"Why the holdup, Dumaroy?" the Terran asked mildly, in his most gentle voice. "I'm glad to meet you. Back in the Peaks—"

Once before Storm had been a target for a stun rod and had

suffered the consequences. But then he had not taken the beam dead center. This was worse than any blow, almost as bad as the wild tumult he had ridden out in the backlash of the Xik projector. He did not realize that he had fallen from the saddle pad until he was lying dazed on the ground, the sky swirling madly over him and a faint shouting making a clamor in his ears.

He felt hands turn him over roughly, secure his wrists, taking him prisoner as he tumbled into a dark pit of unconsciousness. His last weak thought was that one of the three had shot him without warning. And Bister's broad face was in the picture. Only there was something wrong with that face—something wrong with Bister—and it was important that Storm understand that wrongness, very important to him.

CHAPTER FIFTEEN

The torturing headache that was the result of being stun rayed provided a fierce rhythm over and under Storm's eyes. And his eyes hurt in the bargain when he forced them open. But a feeling of urgency carried over from the past and the Terran fought for control over mind and body. His tentative struggles informed him that he had been staked out on the ground and that every pull he gave to his bonds heightened the pounding in his head.

The time was early evening, Storm judged, as he squinted at the daylight between half-closed lids, and he could hear the coming and going, the inconsequential talk of riders in camp around him. In spite of his sick dizziness the Terran concentrated on picking up what information he could from their conversations.

Piece by piece, half-heard sentences built an ugly picture indeed. Some of what Logan had feared had already come to pass. Dumaroy's main herd had been raided and the trail of the stolen beasts led straight to the Shosonna river bank camp, which the aroused riders had attacked in retaliation. Luckily the Norbies had fled in time and there had been no killing, though when the riders pursued them, two men had been badly wounded by arrows.

Dumaroy was now awaiting reinforcements, determined to track down the Shosonna back in the hills and teach them a drastic lesson. He had sent out a call to rally all able-bodied settlers as there were signs that the retreating Shosonna band had crossed fresh Nitra trails and the original posse feared a uniting of the two native clans against the settlers' expedition.

Let there once be a real battle between Norbie and settler and Xik plans would be well on the way to complete realization. The

holdout outlaws could continue to needle both sides without loss of
either secrecy or any of their own numbers. That is, it might have
worked that way had not Storm reached the settlers. But surely once
he had a chance to tell his story Dumaroy would have to reconsider,
to wait for the Peace Officers. Bister—somehow Coll Bister had an
important part. Storm was as certain, as if he had seen him do it,
that Bister had rayed him before he could give his information.
What sort of a tale had the other concocted while the Terran lay unconscious to explain that raying without warning, to supply a valid
reason for keeping the other prisoner?

That Storm was friendly toward the natives was not strong enough.
Too many of the settlers felt the same way. As a Terran he could be
suspected of mental instability—had Bister played that angle? It was
a hard one to refute. Everyone had heard the rumors out of the Center and Bister had traveled with him from the Port to the Crossing—
Nobody here he could appeal to—

Since the Terran could not raise his head more than an inch or so
his range of vision was necessarily quite limited and those men he
sighted were all strangers. Dort Lancin had a range in the Peak area,
and if the settlers came in at the summons to back Dumaroy, he
should arrive sooner or later. Dort Lancin was a stanch supporter of
the pro-Norbie party and he could speak for Storm. But the Terran
fumed inwardly over the waste of time.

Bister—that was Bister approaching now. On impulse Storm
closed his eyes. A sharp tug on the rope about his ankles sent a
quiver of pure agony through his head and he had difficulty in remaining still. Then followed a similar jerk at the wrists extended
above his head. Scuff of boots on the ground—a grunt. Storm dared
to peek. Bister was standing, his attention distracted by the sound of
galloping horses.

Storm watched the settler as one fighting man measures another—
an enemy—during a momentary truce. The fellow was a puzzle. He
nourished hatred for Storm, had disliked the Terran from the first,
for no reason Storm could fathom. If Bister were true to type, he
would have been only too eager to mix it up physically. Yet Storm
had mastered him without difficulty at their first embroilment
and thereafter Bister had tried to get others to do his fighting for

him—almost as if his impressive body, his cover of trail bully, was only the outer husk of a very different personality.

A suspicion, wild and unfounded, crossed Storm's muzzy mind as he groggily pursued that line of reasoning. Perhaps it was well that the party of horsemen whirled by just then to distract his captor for the Terran gasped. There were those stories Storm had heard in the last weeks of the war when the desperate enemy had emptied out their full bag of tricks and weapons, stories he had heard in greater detail later during the dreary months at the Center when men had sweated out rehabilitation. An aper!

If Bister were one of these fabulous apers—an Xik reconstructed by surgery and every available form of psycho-training to pass as a Confed man—that would explain a lot. He would in fact be the most dangerous "man" Storm had ever faced. For by all accounts an aper gathered under one changed skin as many—or more—varied talents as a Commando Beast Master, and was trained to use every one of his weird gifts.

But those tales had been dismissed as the wildest of barracks rumors. Storm had heard them repeatedly denied, been assured by psycho-medics and intelligence men that such a thing was virtually impossible. Of course, those authorities had hedged with the "virtually."

As if this thought were not startling enough, Storm discovered another frightening thing. Bister had not been just inspecting the captive's bonds a moment ago, he had been loosening them! Bister wanted the Terran free, only Storm was also sure that Bister wanted him dead. The fellow had not dared to betray himself by using any weapon more lethal than a stun rod at their encounter at the Shosonna village. But it would be very easy to knife or otherwise fatally dispose of an escaping prisoner.

So—here was one prisoner who would not escape, even when encouraged. Storm was so lost in that line of reasoning that he was not at first aware of the loud argument not too far away, not until he heard one name mentioned that drove the problem of Bister momentarily to the back of his mind.

"—Brad Quade, and he's breathin' out rocket fumes all the way up river! You'd better take it easy, Dumaroy—he's got a Peace Officer with him and if you go off half set and start a Norbie dust-up you'll have to answer to Galwadi for it! I'm not goin' to head into those hills 'till Quade gets here—"

"You can lick dust off Brad Quade's boots if you want to, Jaffe. No man here's goin' to stop you. Only we aren't goin' to have the Basin tell us here at the Peaks not to protect our own property and go along nursin' these thievin' goats! Every one of you saw that trail. It led right to that village and then off again into the mountains. Me, I've lost my last herd to the goats! And I'll tell that flat to any Peace Officer. As for Brad Quade—if he knows what's good for him, he'll keep his nose out of our affairs. So that kid of his is missin'? Well, I'll lay you five credits right on the line that Logan's been ambushed by goats and his right hand's curin' right now in some Nitra Thunder House! I'm sayin' right now that we're ridin' on come sunup. And anybody here who don't want to do that can clear out now—"

There was a muttering and a few raised voices. Storm, straining to listen, gathered that Dumaroy's private army was not so keen on Norbie chasing as their leader wished.

"All right! All right!" The settler's bull roar deadened the other's clamor once more. "You can just get your horses, all of you, and clear out of here. You, Jaffe, an' Hyke, and Palasco—Only don't you come whinin' to me when you're cleaned out, and there're goat tracks all over your ranges. You just go and talky-talk it out with Brad Quade and let him point his fingers at the goats to give 'em back!"

"And I'm tellin' you back, Dumaroy, that you'll pull the Peaks into a big mess and we'll all be in trouble. You better wait and hear what Quade and the Peace Officer have to say. They'll be here in the mornin'—"

"Get out!" The roar was a red-edged bellow. "Get outta here, you soft riders! I'm not takin' orders from Quade. He may be the big chief back at the Basin, but not here. Clear out—every last one of you!"

Storm was tempted. Should he make a break for it along with the rebel party? He tried to raise his head and was answered by such a thrust of pain as blurred his sight for an instant. There was no hope of his moving quickly enough to elude Bister until more of the ray effects had worn off. But the thought that Quade was moving up river gave him a little hope. No matter what lay between them personally, the Terran had more confidence in the settler than he wanted to admit. And he was sure that Quade, alone of the settlers he had met so far on Arzor, had the force of character and leadership to stand up to the Xik-fostered mess now brewing. Storm must make the escape Bister had set up for him, but make it a successful attempt, one which would carry him and his information into Brad Quade's camp.

Luckily, in the general confusion Dumaroy seemed to have forgotten his prisoner. At least no one came to inspect Storm for signs of life, or prepared to ask questions. That too might have been the result of planning on Bister's part. It was odd, Storm thought, but since that first suspicion of the other's true identity had dawned on him, he had accepted it as a fact. Though he was just as sure if he shouted aloud his belief in this camp he would only prove to the Arzorans that he was indeed one of the crazed Terrans—just another refugee who had finally been pushed over the verge of sanity.

Storm began to fight as well as he could the hang-over of the stun ray, taking care to attract no attention. It was slightly in his favor that he had been staked out on one side of a small hillock that rose between him and the center of the camp. Save for men going to the river for water and a few others spreading out their bedrolls, he was not generally under observation.

At first it was a fight to move his head. He did not dare to draw his hands away from the stakes where they had been pinioned lest somewhere out of his line of sight Bister was waiting for just such a move. But when Storm was able to lift his head without suffering too much pain, he saw that dusk was closing in. Just let night come and he would be willing to risk Bister, though the other had all the advantages on his side.

But before dark Dumaroy at last remembered his prisoner. Storm shut his eyes, counterfeited as best he could the rigid tension of a stun-shocked man.

"He's been under long enough—" Dumaroy was not exactly uneasy but he sounded puzzled. Bister answered and Storm listened for the slightest hint of accent in his voice that might help to unmask the aper.

"He's a Terran. They can't stand up to a ray—don't use 'em much—"

"Maybe. But Starle tells me this fella was a Commando—they're supposed to be a tough crowd. I don't see why you thought you had to ray him out anyway, Coll."

"I came down the trail from the Port with him. He's tricky—and he was half over the edge then—like all Terrans. You've heard the stories about how they blew up after they heard about Terra being given the big burn. This fella got it in his head that everybody was against him—plottin' to get him. Everyone except the goats. He got chummy with them right from the start. When he disappeared so quick from the Crossin', I nosed around a little. He's a Beast Master. You should have seen him gentlin' a string for Put Larkin. Let a fella who can do what he can with animals get in as a Butcher and with the goats lettin' him set up in their territory—and you've got yourself a live yoris by the hind foot! Wouldn't surprise me none to find out he was back of this Shosonna raid. I didn't want him to get away out there before we had a chance to ask some questions. Might be well to put him undercover or you'll have to hand him over to the Peace Officer—"

"He can't ride until he comes to," Dumaroy commented. "Keep an eye on him, Coll, and let me know when he wakes up. Yes, I want to ask him a few questions—"

They moved off while Storm held his body rigid until the ache in his sorely tried muscles came close to matching the ache in his heavy head. So Coll Bister was to keep an eye on him? That would give Bister opportunity to get rid of one Hosteen Storm with as little fuss as possible. If he only had Surra waiting out there in the grass— or Baku—Then Storm took hold of himself firmly, surely he was not so lacking in resources that he had to depend only upon his animals!

The gurgle of the river made a steady sound, backing all the noises of the camp. In this country rivers were necessary. Quade and his party were undoubtedly camped on one bank or the other of this same stream. Storm did not know whether he could muster the strength to sit a horse—even Rain. Could he trust himself to the water instead?

All riders habitually strapped a canteen to their saddles or saddle pads when on the range. But a camp as large as this one, with the men planning to head into the drier mountains, would have in addition other preparations for the transportation of water. And a common one here, Storm knew, was water-toad hide bags that could be slung in pairs across the backs of pack animals.

Such bags were large oval affairs, each made from the entire skin of one of the huge amphibians found in the marshes, tanned and cured for use by the fisher-Norbies of the southern coasts. Almost transparent, the skins inflated like balloons when moistened as they were before being filled. Storm had seen Norbie children make rafts of them at Krotag's camp. With a pair of those to buoy him up, a man's swimming ability would be no great problem; he could float along with the current.

There remained the point of his break out of camp past Bister's sentry-go, and the stealing of one, maybe two water bags. If the posse was going to start out on the Shosonna trail in the early morning, Dumaroy would send one of his riders down to the river to refill those bags. They had to stand through the night hours with the purifying tablets in them or their contents would not be drinkable for half the next day. It was a procedure Storm had followed himself when with the Survey party.

Weakened as he was, Storm believed he could handle one rider, especially if he took the man by surprise. But Bister—Bister remained the big threat. All depended upon chance and his own ability to seize the first possible opening.

He slowly flexed his fingers and wrists, feeling his bonds give. What was left him for a weapon? Only the fact that his enemy—though he might look human, be drilled to think and act human—was not born of the same species. How could Coll Bister, the aper, ever be sure from one moment to the next that he would not make some small slip that would damn him utterly for what he was? Perhaps his hatred for Storm was based on that fear, for Bister could recognize in the Beast Master one who had been selected for that service because of just such off-beat qualities of mind—though probably not the same ones—as those he himself possessed. So Bister might have built up his distrust of the Terran until at present he credited Storm with far higher gifts of perception and extrasensory powers than any living man could hope for. Bister, in his present state of mind, could not be sure *how* Storm would react to anything—even a ray beam. Now the Terran must turn that gnawing uncertainty of his enemy to his own account in the opening move of their private struggle.

Storm waited until he was rewarded by what he had hoped to see, one of Dumaroy's men passing on the way to the river, empty water skins flapping on his shoulders. He allowed him to pass and then staged his act.

With a low moan the Terran twisted, apparently fighting his bonds. The man turned, gaped at him, and came over. Luck was on Storm's side so far; he had not fallen afoul of a quick-witted man. Another moan, low, and as realistic as he could make it—he was a little surprised at his own artistic ability—and the man, dropping his burden, went down on one knee to inspect the captive more closely.

Storm's arm swept up to strike at the side of the other's neck. The blow did not land quite true, he was too weak to deliver it correctly, but it brought the rider off balance and down on top of the Terran. Then the right pressure applied and the fellow, still surprised, went limp. For a long moment of perilous waiting Storm held the flaccid body to him, waiting for the shout, the running feet, and also to gather strength for his next move.

When there was no reaction from the camp, the Terran cautiously rolled out from under the rider and stretched the man in his place. Sweeping up the water skins, he forced himself to walk at an even pace to the river bank. Three—maybe four more yards and he would make it. Then to inflate the water bags—and not to force the air out of them again. He need only secure the mouth of each skin with its dangling cord and he had his improvised raft.

However, the river was a popular place at present. A noisy party was bathing and there were horses being brought down to drink. Storm, the bags crumpled tight in one arm, took to cover, working his way through a reed bank, expecting every moment to have the cry of alarm raised behind him.

What did happen was that he caught sight of Rain among the horses being watered. The stallion was not taking kindly to this shepherding and he was plainly in an ugly mood. A black horse squealed and offered challenge and the red-spotted mount was only too ready to oblige. The rider in charge pushed his own animal forward and used his quirt freely for discipline.

But with Rain that was a very wrong move. The stallion, who had never been touched by a whip since Storm had brought him out of Larkin's corral at the space port, went completely fighting mad. And Rain, though young, was a formidable opponent, as he let loose with both hoofs and teeth.

Storm slipped to the water's edge. The attention of all the men along the stream was on the plunging, screaming horses. He saw Rain dash into mainstream as he himself plunged into the current, the inflated bags ready as a buoy when he needed them. The river, which appeared so lazy from the bank, was provided with a swifter core and Storm struck out into it.

He heard more shouting, saw the red and gray horse break from the water and race, at a speed the Terran was sure few if any of the mounts in the camp could match, through the riders in the general direction of the mountains and freedom. Then the river curved and Storm was carried out of sight.

The excitement of escape gave him the energy to reach the main current, but once in its grip the Terran did little except cling to the puffed skins and hope that Quade's camp was not too far away. Night came and Storm, his head and shoulders supported above the level of the water, shivered under the touch of a mountain-born wind. There was a flick of lightning over those heights, the distant rumble of thunder as a threat. He would have to watch the water about him, be ready to make for the shore before the wash of a flood added to the current.

But it was hard to think clearly and his whole body trailed suddenly behind the bobbing skins. Storm could not judge the passing of time. The thought that he had beat Bister was for the moment a small triumph, quickly dulled.

There were no moons visible in the sky and the stars showed dim and far away between ragged patches of wind-driven clouds. Storm, his cheek pillowed on the clammy skins, was only half aware that he was still waterborne southward. He was nosed by an investigating water rat. But perhaps the scent of his off-world body made the big rodent wary, for the creature only swam beside him for a space.

However, the coming of the rat aroused Storm to make some efforts on his own for the streams of Arzor had larger and more dangerous inhabitants than water rats. And some of them might be less fastidious. He began to kick his legs, attempting not only to quicken his rate of travel, but to steer the odd raft.

Sometime in the dark hours the Terran ran into difficulty. The river made another turn and here drift had built a tongue of tangled flotsam out into the water. Before Storm was conscious of danger a snag pierced one skin and its sudden deflation into tatters plunged him under water, bringing him up with cruel force against the wall of drift.

Somehow he pulled himself up that barrier, fought his way over it at the price of scratches and gouges, until he was able to reach sand and finally meadow turf beyond. He sprawled there face down, too spent to struggle, and went to sleep.

"—bring him around now—"

"It's that Terran, Storm! But what—?"

"Been in the river by the looks of him."

There was light now, the warmth of fire combined with the clearer gleam of a camp atom-lite. There was an arm under his shoulders, holding his head up so that he could swallow from a cup pressed against his lips. There was a strange dreamlike haze over the scene, but one face swam out of that haze, took on reality, perhaps because those features had had a place in so many of his dreams. And this time Storm was able to talk to the man he had come to Arzor to—to kill. Yes, he had come across space to kill Brad Quade! Yet that desire seemed now as remote as a year-old battle in a jungle wilderness, three solar systems away!

"Trouble—" He got that out and the word was such a limited expression of what he must say. "Xik holdouts in the Peaks— Norbies—Dumaroy—Logan—"

He was being shaken, first gently, and then with rougher insistence.

"Where *is* Logan?"

And Storm, caught again in the mazes of his dream, answered with some of his own longing:

"Terra—garden of Terra."

CHAPTER SIXTEEN

When he made better sense later, Storm discovered that the party who had followed Brad Quade into the Peak Ranges did not ride with closed minds. Kelson, of the Planetary Peace Police, a big, slow-speaking man with eyes that Storm decided overlooked nothing, and with a computer bank for a mind, asked a few questions, every one directly to the point.

The Terran had been reluctant to voice his suspicions concerning Bister. Such a story might be accepted by veterans of his own corps who had good reason for knowing that agents could assume a wide variety of cover. But to ask these men who had never come up personally against the Xiks at all to accept the fact that one had been living among them undetected, and without any more proof than Storm was able to offer, was another matter.

To his vast surprise when Kelson drew from him that revelation—with the questions of a well-trained inquisitor as the Terran understood too late—none of his listeners displayed incredulity. Maybe these planet bound settlers were more open to such imaginative flights—as the existence of an aper among them—than were the service officers trained to meet the nonproven with wary disbelief.

"Bister—" Quade repeated thoughtfully. "Coll Bister. Anybody here know him?"

Dort Lancin answered first. "He rode down from the port as trail herder, 'long with me and Storm. Just like the kid here tells it. Seemed just like any other drifter to me. Only I heard about apers when I was with the outfit. Seems like they captured two of them close to the end, wearing Confed uniforms and runnin' a side show to the big muddle. Might have fouled up that whole sector if one of the messes they cooked up hadn't been called to the attention of a section commander in time. After that mix-up a lot of the boys looked close at each other, providin' they weren't born and raised together in the same river valley or such! Bister didn't come in on our ship, and he was a new light and tie with Larkin, never rode for Put before. Don't know where he came from—except Put picked him as a hire rider along with the rest of us."

"Guilt," Kelson observed, "is a queer thing. Bister hated Terrans, and he was probably, as you say, afraid of you, Storm, because you were trained for a duty not unlike his own. If he hadn't been guilty— and afraid—he wouldn't have tipped his hand by his treatment of you. Bister is one man we *are* going to rope *tomorrow*—or rather today—and tight! If Dumaroy's moved out, we'll trail him. But we don't want to tangle with the Xiks. Since they are provided with the type of weapons you report, Storm, we'll need a Patrol ship in here to really mop up. Quade, you'll want to collect your kid anyway—you strike in that direction, angle up with a scout party to the east. I'll ride on with the rest of you and try to head Dumaroy off. I think we can learn a lot more by splitting—"

So they did as Kelson suggested. Quade, with Storm as a guide, and two of the settler's riders, took the side trail after they found Dumaroy's river bank camp deserted and indications that the Peaks settler had proceeded with his plan to trace the Norbies and his missing herd into the mountains.

Storm rode in a dreamy haze. He located his landmarks, made his calculations as to where they must avoid possible ambush. But all of that was handled mechanically by a part of him operating as a robot set to a well-defined task and keeping to the pattern of a work tape. Whether the stun ray had more lasting effects than he had supposed, the Terran could not tell. But nothing about him appeared to have much meaning. He rode beside Quade for a space and answered questions concerning his meeting with Logan, their escape from the Xiks and through the cave of the gardens, and the final disastrous attack of the yoris. Yet to the Terran the conversation was all a part of a dream. Nor was he conscious when Quade began to study him covertly as they bored farther into the wild territory of the foothills.

However much that haziness clouded his mind, it did not prevent an instant reaction to trouble when attack did come. They were in the narrow opening of that gorge leading to the valley of Gorgol's cave entrance, riding single file as the ground demanded. Storm had perhaps five seconds of time to sound the alert. He saw that yellow-red arm move, the blue streaks of painted horns against a domed skull.

"Ahuuuuuu!" The war cry of his people was a warning as bow-strings sang. Then the ground erupted with men about them. A numbing blow just below his shoulder almost sent Storm crashing from his saddle. His left arm hung heavy and limp as a blue-horned Norbie grabbed for his belt.

The Terran struck out with his other hand in a Commando blow but the weight of the falling native dragged him to the ground where they rolled into a pocket between two rocks. For a frenzied space of time Storm fought one-handed to keep a sword-knife from his throat. Only the fact that his first blow had practically disabled the Norbie saved his life. He brought his knee up and toppled the other off balance, rolling over again to send the Nitra senseless, sprawling out into the floor of the valley where the struggle was still in progress.

Storm struggled to his feet, only to collapse again as a stun ray clipped the side of his spinning head. He slid, bonelessly limp, be-hind the rocks and did not feel it when he landed full upon his wounded shoulder driving the cruelly barbed arrowhead deeper into his flesh, snapping off its painted shaft.

Perhaps that second dose of the ray neutralized in a measure the effects of the first, for when Storm opened his eyes, he remembered clearly all that had happened just before his raying.

The bright sunlight had left the gorge and the small passage was chill, chill and very quiet. Shivering, catching his breath at the twinge in his stiff shoulder, Storm somehow dragged himself upright to lean against the small wall of rocks that had protected him. He must have been overlooked, he decided. The Nitra had not mutilated his body after their custom.

There were no bodies in the narrow way, though broken arrows, and churned earth, a splash or two of blood marked the field. Storm staggered into the open and attempted to read the trail. Bootmarks leading away—prisoners forced to walk?

Storm pressed his hand tightly over the ragged hole in his shoulder and squinted down at that mixture of hoof, boot, and Norbie tracks. With one hand out to fend him off from the walls he reeled along, heading for the garden cave.

Just how he reached the mouth of the outer doorway he could not tell. But he *was* there, calling softly for the two he had left behind. There was no reply out of the dark. Storm stumbled on, guided by the light seeping from the garden cavern. The doorway they had half-closed and then reopened was still unblocked. The Terran wavered in and went to his knees on the path between two flanking gardens.

"Logan!" He called weakly. "Gorgol!" He could not get to his feet again. But somewhere there was a pine tree—and green grass—and the fragrance of the hills of home. Storm wanted that as much as he wanted cool water in his throat, an end to the burning pain in his shoulder, cool green grass and the arch of pine boughs over his head.

He was crawling now, and there was an object barring his path, a yellow-red barrier. He touched the softness of flesh, saw Gorgol's face turned up to his, the eyes closed, the mouth a little open. But the native was still alive. Storm could see the beat of a laboring pulse in a vein running beneath one of the ivory white horns. There were no visible wounds; the Norbie might have been peacefully asleep.

"Gorgol!" Storm shook him. Then raised his good hand and slapped the Norbie's face stingingly. Until at last those eyes opened and the native stared bewildered up at him. With one hand Storm asked his question:

"Who?"

Gorgol levered himself up, both hands going to his head. He moaned softly, pressed his fingers hard over his eyes, before he used them to answer.

"I come—go find water—Head hurt—fall—sleep—"

"Rayed!" Storm looked about him. There was no Logan, Surra and Hing were missing, as were the horses.

"Nitra?" He doubted that. Would the Nitra, who could hardly be familiar with a settler's side arm, use the ray on Gorgol?

"Nitra kill with arrows—knife—" Gorgol was signing. Then he caught sight of Storm's wound, that inch or so of arrow shaft showing out of the ragged tear. "Nitra—that! Here?"

"Ambush—down valley—"

"Come!" Gorgol, one hand going again to his head as he arose, stooped to draw Storm up beside him. Supporting the Terran, he led him along through the maze of gardens. Until at last Storm realized that he was indeed lying on a bed of pine needles, looking up once more into the green tent of the Terran tree. Not too far away Gorgol had built a small pile of dry twigs and was now engaged in coaxing a spark from his firestone to ignite it. When a tongue of flame sent fragrant smoke curling up, the native drew his knife and passed its sharp point into the red heart of the fire.

Storm, guessing what was to come, watched those preparations grimly. They were necessary and he knew it. Logan was gone—the animals had vanished—but he must be able to carry on if they were to find either, or trace Quade's scouts. When the Norbie came across to him, the Terran managed a stretch of the lips that curved them briefly into something still far from the smile he intended.

"Arrow stay in—bad!" Gorgol's fingers spelled out the warning Storm did not need. "Must cut out—now."

Storm's good hand, moving restlessly through the carpet of needles on which he lay, closed on a small chunk of dead branch. He clenched his fingers about that in preparation.

"Go ahead!" Though Gorgol could not have understood what were to him meaningless sounds, he read the answer in Storm's eyes. And go ahead he did.

Norbies were deft and the Terran knew that probably this was not the first time Gorgol had operated to cut out an arrowhead from some companion. But to endure the probing, skillful as it was, was hard. And Storm remembered what Logan had said about the Spartan treatment for arrow wounds and what it cost the victim. He was lucky in that three of the barbs on this head remained intact as Gorgol freed the glassy main section, and only one had to be located by deeper knife work.

Breathing hard and with a swimming head, Storm lay quiet at last while Gorgol slapped a mass of pulped wet leaves over the ragged wound and then raised his patient's head to let him sip water in a blessed flood of coolness down his parched throat. As the native settled Storm down again, he held his hands into the line of the Terran's vision and signed:

"Go—look for Logan—see who put Gorgol to sleep—hunt trail of evil ones—"

"Nitra—" Storm was too shaken to raise his hand in the proper movement. But again the Norbie appeared to understand.

"Not Nitra—" He wriggled his own right hand. "Still have bow hand on wrist—Nitra take for Thunder House trophy. Think maybeso Butchers. We see—"

Storm shut his eyes, even on the welcome green of the branch over him. He aroused to a soft, warm weight on his good arm, a snuffling in his ear, and opened his eyes slowly. Over his head was a rustling, and a dark shape moved on a low swinging branch, a sharp beaked head was bent so glittering eyes could regard him.

"Baku!" The eagle mantled in answer to his call, replied with her own harsh cry.

The warm lump on his arm chirruped, and Storm heard Surra's purr rumble louder from beside him. For a moment of lazy content, not yet fully awake, the Terran lay unmoving. Then he tried to lift his left arm to caress Surra and felt the answering twinge in his shoulder, awaking him to full memory. The pain, as he experimented cautiously, was not nearly as bad as he expected. As on his first visit, this slice of a vanished world had worked its magic on him, and he was able to move with a measure of ease. In addition, the leafy plaster the Norbie had applied had dried hard, covering the wound and dulling the pain as if it had narcotic properties.

Gorgol must have returned and left again, for a small heap of objects taken from their supplies was piled not too far away. A battered canteen and one box of rations lay on the woolen blanket that had been his legacy from his grandfather. And beyond was some fruit laid out on a leaf plate.

Storm ate, with the greediness of a thoroughly hungry man. And as the minutes passed he had less and less trouble with his wound.

He was trying to find the full extent of his disability when Gorgol came running lightly down the pathway toward the grassy oasis about the pine tree.

"You have found—what?" Storm demanded eagerly.

"Logan taken by Butchers. Butchers killed by Nitra. Logan—men with you—held by Nitra in other valley. Maybeso kill. Time of big dry comes, Nitra wizard makes magic to Thunder Drummers so rain come again. Kill captives for Thunder Drummers—"

"Nitra think that makes rain again?" Storm tried to put into signs his questions. "Nitra fear rains never come unless kill prisoners?"

The Norbie nodded vigorously. "Thunder Drummers live in high mountains, make rain, make growing things come. But sometimes too much rain—bad. Bad like too much dry. Storms worse in Nitra land than for Shosonna. So Nitra wizards give prisoners to Thunder Drummers—end big dry, not make bad rains if have prisoners to eat."

"How do they give prisoners?"

Gorgol made a wide swinging sweep with one hand, ending in the gesture of one tossing an object out into empty space.

"Throw from high rock—maybeso. Not sure—Shosonna do not spy on Nitra wizards. Many, many Nitra guard around—kill those who watch if not Nitra."

"Where?"

"Nitra camp over ridge. They wait—think they wish to kill Butchers. Also there are Shosonna in hills—maybeso fight with them."

Refugees from the river village Dumaroy had tried to raid? These mountains were getting rather full now, Storm thought with a little smile. For some reason he felt almost absurdly confident. There was Dumaroy's crowd, and the posse now headed by Kelson, unless either or both had run into the Xik holdouts, or Nitras, or been ambushed by the aroused and thoroughly angry Shosonna. But it was the Nitra who interested Storm most at present. Kelson had been warned, and Dumaroy was not too far ahead of the Peace Officer—they would have to take their chances.

But the Nitra were holding Logan, Quade, Lancin and perhaps Quade's two riders. That was Storm's concern. He had one card to play. With the Shosonna or any semicivilized Norbie tribe it might not work. But here he would be dealing with natives who should know very little about off-world men, especially any breed different from the settlers with whom they were only on raiding terms.

He outlined his plan as well as he could for Gorgol's benefit. And, to his pleased surprise, the native did not object, instead he answered readily enough:

"You have wizard power. Larkin say your name mean weapon of Thunder Drummers in his tongue—"

"In my tongue also."

Gorgol nodded. "Also Nitra not see bird totem like this one, nor other animals who follow you. Horses men may ride, zamle they can trap. But a frawn eats not from a man's hand, or rubs head against him for notice. Nitra wizard commands no animals. So you may walk into their camp without meeting arrow. But maybeso you not come out again—that is different—"

"Could Gorgol find Shosonna in the mountains to help?"

"Wide are the mountains. And before sunrise the Nitra wizards make their magic." The Norbie's hands sketched the killing sign. "Better Gorgol use this." From his belt holster he whipped the ray rod. "Use such magic on *them!*"

"You have only one charge left—" Storm pointed out. "When that is used, all you will have is a rod without power—"

"And this!" The Norbie laid his hand on his knife hilt. "But there be much warrior honor in this deed. When the fire of men is lighted, Gorgol can stand forth and tell great deeds before the face of twenty clans, and there shall be none to say it is not so—"

Storm made his preparations carefully. Once more he turned his face into a mask with improvised paint. The folded blanket lay across his shoulder to hide Gorgol's protecting plaster of leaves, its ends thrust through the concha belt. He surveyed himself in a greenish mirror of one of the water garden pools, tearing a rag from a supply bag to hold his untidy hair out of his eyes. And the image the water presented was a barbaric figure, one which certainly should hold attention in the Nitra assembly, even without the addition of the team.

The Terran could not bear Baku's weight on his injured shoulder for the full trip and he had to coax her out of the cavern as he carried

Hing, and Surra walked beside him. Gorgol told him the eagle had
come from the sky the day before, just preceding the attack of the
Butchers, and had vanished into the garden cave where Surra and
Hing had chosen to prowl on their own concerns.

Storm concentrated as he came into the open upon holding the
animals' attention, preparing them to aid him in any necessary attack. Gorgol's night sight aided them again as they climbed a twisting way up to the heights. But tonight there were moons, and when
they won from the maw of the valley, they crossed a brilliantly
lighted slope.

The Terran went slowly, conserving his strength, accepting the
Norbie's assistance over rough places. The wind was changing, bearing with it a low muttering of sound that aped the roll of thunder.
They reached a ledge that Gorgol turned to follow, one hand ready
to lead or support the Terran. And that narrow and perilous path
took them around the spur of an outcrop, through an arch of stone,
onto a wider platform where there was a muddle of dried sticks under an overhang.

Gorgol kicked at some of the rubbish to clear a path and signed:
"Evil flyer."

This must have been the eyrie from which he had pursued the
wounded monster on the day it led him into the valley of the Sealed
Caves. But by all indications the bird had had no mate, nor had its
untidy nesting place been claimed by another.

The nest ledge was above another. With Gorgol's hand on his
belt, Storm swung over by one band and dropped to this, wondering
how often he could equal that feat if called upon to do so tonight.
However, this cutting led on around the side of the cliff and there
was the red of fire beyond, a red that suddenly puffed vivid sparks of
green into the air, along with a suffocating odor.

"Wizards!" Gorgol's fingers wriggled.

As the green sparks cleared, Storm discovered that he was perched
over a table-topped plateau, bare of any vegetation, but mounded
here and there by weather-carved rocks, which assumed odd shapes in
the semidarkness. Lashed to two such pillars were four men—settlers
by their dress—while the space about the fire was crowded by squatting Norbies, intent upon the actions of two of their number who

paced back and forth around the circle of the flames, beating on small tambors they held in their hands, so producing that deep thunder mutter.

Storm studied the scene. Either the Nitra felt secure from attack here or their sentries were very well hidden. He could detect none from his present stand. But there were men squatting beside the pillars to which the prisoners were bound, one each at the very feet of the captives.

"I am going in—" he signaled to Gorgol.

He beamed the silent summons to Baku who must be cruising overhead, felt Surra press reassuringly against him. Then the Terran made a slow descent of the drop immediately below him. As his boots struck the surface of the plateau he shouted aloud the rallying call of the team.

"Saaaaaaaa—"

Out of the black sky Baku dropped, a thing that was a feathered part of the night endowed with separate life. Storm staggered a step or two as she set her claws in the blanket on his shoulder, resting her weight above the green wound. But he recovered swiftly and straightened under that necessary burden.

Then, with Hing wary against his breast, her eyes as bright as his necklace, and Surra, soft-footed beside him, showing her fangs in a snarl that wrinkled her lips, Storm walked confidently into the full light of the fire.

CHAPTER SEVENTEEN

"Comes now the Monster Slayer, wearing this one's
    moccasins,
Wearing the body of the storm born one.
Comes now the Monster Slayer, bowstring extended,
Arrow notched upon it for the flying—
Comes now the Monster Slayer—ready for battle—"

Storm was no Singer, but somehow the words came to his tongue, fitted themselves readily together into patterns of power so that the Terran believed he walked protected by the invisible armor of one who talked with the Faraway Gods, was akin to the Old Ones. He could feel that power rise and possess him. And with such to strengthen him what need had a man for other weapons?

The Terran did not see the Nitra rows split apart to make him a pathway to the edge of the fire. He was not truly aware of anything except the song and the power and the fact that, at this moment, Hosteen Storm was a small but well-fitting part of something much greater than any one man could aspire to be—

He stood still now, bracing himself under the weight of Baku, not noting the pain that weight brought him. Before him was a blue-horned Nitra wizard, his tambor drum raised. But the native was no longer beating it, instead he was staring at this apparition out of the night.

"Ahuuuuuu!" Storm's voice spiraled up in the old war cry of his desert raiding people. "Ahuuuuuu!"

The Nitra wizard thumped his drum, was answered by a roll of muted thunder. However, there was a hesitation in that reply, which

Storm sensed more than saw. The native made talk in his own high-pitched voice. To that the Terran did not reply with finger-talk. This was no time to betray kinship with the settlers and their ways. He turned to face the four prisoners, saw recognition leap to life in Logan's eyes, surprise dawn in Quade's.

"Power is in this one's arm—power is in this one,
The Monster Slayer wears now this one's body—
He walks in this one—"

Surra moved with Storm, matching her soft padding to his deliberate pace. He released Hing from his hold. The meerkat scurried, a gray shadow touched to life by the fire, to the nearest pillar. Rising on her hind legs, she attacked the prisoners' bonds with teeth and claws. Storm gestured and Surra moved as quickly to Logan and his partner at the other post, to chew at the hide thongs about their bodies.

The Nitra priest squalled like an enraged yoris and sprang at Storm shaking his tambor. Baku mantled, her fierce eyes on the native, screaming with rage. She took off into the air and came down to do as she seldom did, attack from ground level, as she had faced the zamle in Krotag's village. And the Nitra gave ground before her bristling fury, so that bird drove man around the fire and there was a shrilling chorus of wonder from the watching warriors.

"Power is now ours!" Storm exulted in a song perhaps only one other within hearing could understand. But if the words were unknown the meaning was clear and as he moved forward again the Nitra cowered away from him.

Quade stepped away from the pillar where he had been bound and Storm saw him shake off cut thongs. Gorgol had played his part back in the shadows. The settler jumped to catch the staggering Logan, but the younger man's hand rested on Surra's head for a moment—an attention the big cat had never before permitted from any save Storm—and he was once more steady on his feet.

"Let us go forth in power—" The Terran's voice arose above the screaming rage of Baku. Surra led the retreat with Quade supporting his son, the riders crowding behind. Hing ran to Storm and climbed his leg, hooking her claws in his breeches.

"Go forth in power—" Storm put full urgency into that order. He moved between the retreating men and the restless Nitra. How long he could hold the natives Storm had no idea, but at this moment he had no doubts that he *could* hold them. Only a very few times in his life had the Terran experienced this inner rightness, this being a part of a bigger pattern that was meant to work smoothly. Once when he first had his orders obeyed as team leader by the animals and Baku—twice during his service days when that team carried through a difficult assignment with perfect precision. But this in its way was again different, for the power flowed through him alone.

"This one walks in power—
This one carries power—
This one works the will of the Old Ones,
The Old Ones who walk in beauty,
This one serves—"

The rescued had gone beyond the rim of the firelight.
"Saaaaaa—"
Baku came to him. The Norbie wizard had a bleeding gash on his forearm and he no longer held the tambor. There was bitter hatred in his eyes and a knife ready in his hand. As Baku settled again on Storm's shoulder the Nitra followed her in the arching spring of an attacking yoris.

He reached Storm only to go down with the stiff jerk of a man who had been rayed. And from the massed warriors there arose a wailing cry. It was then that Storm laughed. This was a night in which nothing could go wrong! Gorgol had used his rod at the right moment as he had earlier used his knife. They were all riding one of the waves of phenomenal luck that sometimes overtakes tides of action and can be used to carry a man on their crest until he is able to achieve the impossible. The Singers were right. At that moment full belief in the unseen powers of his people flooded through Storm, burning away all doubts. He was truly possessed and no Nitra—no—nor Xik—could stand successfully against him!

He withdrew stride by stride backwards to the edge of the light where he must climb to the heights.

"Over here, Storm—" came a low call just before the Nitra pack screeched their fear and anger aloud—though no warrior ventured in pursuit. A hand caught his arm, pulled him up to the cliff wall.

"Where did you come from?" Quade demanded. "We thought you were dead!"

Storm laughed again. The intoxication that filled him still bubbled.

"Far from dead," he said. "But we had better get out of here before they recover nerve enough to come hunting—"

His exultation held as they climbed back to the ledge of the deserted nest, worked their way around to the valley of the Sealed Cave. But at the mouth of that same cave he halted.

"Listen!" His tone was so sharply commanding that the men about him were silent.

And it was not so much a noise that they heard as a vibration, which came to them through the walls of stone, from the earth under their feet.

"The Xik ship!" Storm knew that trembling of old. He had sheltered in hiding to watch the enemy take-off from hidden ports he had been sent to locate and harass. Always there had been that shaking of the earth as the alien ships had warmed to their take-off.

"What—?" Quade demanded.

"The Xik ship—it is getting ready to take off. They may be leaving Arzor!"

Quade, one arm about Logan, put his other hand to the cliff surface.

"What a vibration!"

Too much so. Storm was conscious of that suddenly. The ship he had seen in the hidden valley was no intergalactic transport—it was hardly larger than a converted scout. This tearing was too much! Another Xik craft hidden somewhere near? Only now that throbbing came raggedly—

There was a roar that filled the night, a torch of light that shot miles high from the mountains. Around them the cliffs trembled, miniature landslips started, and they crouched together, men and animals, in a terrified huddle.

"The tubes—they must have blown!" Storm was on his feet again, his hand pressing against his shoulder where the sharp bite of pain gnawed once more. He had been torn out of his self-hypnotism, thrown into the weariness of near exhaustion.

"What tubes?" Logan's question came thinly as if some muffling veil hung between them.

"The Xiks had their ship partly buried for concealment. They were digging her out when you escaped. But if they were pressed for time they might have tried to take her up without being sure of thoroughly clean tubes—or else"—Storm glanced down at the ball of whimpering fur he held, one sorely frightened meerkat—"or else Hing pulled one of her tricks. When they tried to lift the ship, the tubes blasted it wide open!"

"So they blew themselves up!" Brad Quade squared his shoulders. "But there might be something to see to over there, perhaps some of our boys were involved and need help. It might be well to check—"

"One of those other grills in the garden cave—" Logan cut in weakly. "There was a northwestern one pointing in the right direction. If we could find another tunnel from that it would take us straight through—"

Whatever shaking up the mountain had received, the garden cavern remained apparently untouched. Though the newcomers were awed by the bits of strange worlds divided by the black paths, they did not linger. Gorgol sped ahead, the rest trying to match his pace. A quarter of the way around the cavern they came to the grill Logan had found on his first exploration.

They mastered the latch and were fronting another tunnel which, with its curiously dead air and blackness, engulfed them wholly, for this time there was no torch to light the way. Surra pressed on with Gorgol, eyes of cat and native not so baffled by the gloom, the others strung out behind. All were driven by a gnawing desire to be through this passage and out into the normal world of Arzor once again.

It was easy to lose one's sense of direction here in the dark and the tunnel did not run straight. Whether it followed the easy path of some natural fault in the mountain, or whether its long-ago builders had intended the turns to bewilder, Storm could not guess. But after two twists, he was at sea. For all he could determine, they might be heading back into the cavern they had just left. Baku moved restlessly on his shoulder, he lurched to one side, scraping against the unseen wall for support, hearing close by the heavy breathing of one of his companions, and then Logan's assurance, fiercely uttered to his father, that he could keep up in spite of his injured leg.

Another twist, and a spark in the dark ahead, a light that grew to a reflected glow as if some giant fire raged beyond. They hurried on at that promise of escape.

Now the off-worlders caught up with Gorgol and the cat, to look out into a well of fire. Those flames ate along the terraces of the valley of the ship. And the heat from the conflagration beat in at them. Gorgol wriggled through a slit of door and Storm edged after him, giving Baku her flight signal. If there were any way out along the heights, she would find it for them.

Seeing that whirl of flames below, the Terran believed that nothing within that bowl of mountain walls could have survived the blowup of the overdriven ship. Sparks came up in the suck of air as they edged about the small walled space that long ago might have been a sentry point, to put a crag between them and the full force of the heat.

Even here the light approached that of day and they discovered Surra at the head of a flight of stairs. They were hardly more than niches gnawed away by the elements, down which a man could edge only at his peril. But they were a way down with the full bulk of the peak between them and the raging inferno of the blasted valley.

Surra's species were sure-footed. The pumas of the western continent, a breed crossed with her dune cat ancestors in the experimental laboratories, were adept at climbing cliffs and crossing ridges where neither man nor hunting hound dared to follow. However, now she was examining this drop narrowly, advancing one paw as if to test the stability of that first weather-worn step.

Something in its feel must have reassured her, for she flowed down with liquid grace until she came out some hundred feet below in a shadowed space which appeared much larger than the platform on which Storm and Gorgol lingered. Storm hitched over that drop, only he crawled down those niches on his hands and knees. The heat of the opposite valley was cut off, and when he reached the ledge, he saw that from this point a roadway took the down curve, cut into the rock in the obscurity of the dark side of the mountain.

"A road—" Gorgol signed in the moonlight. "Below—a wider one—running so—" He gestured southeast.

Perhaps this was part of that other way into the valley up which the raiders had driven their stolen horses and frawns. If so, its other end should bring them out on the plains.

"Return—" Storm signed. "Bring the others here—"

Gorgol was already climbing, his tall body ascending that ladder easily. Storm went on. Surra quested ahead, scouting in advance. The Terran had a feeling that he must keep moving now—that if he rested, as his body craved, he would not be able to move on again. He started down that narrow pathway hacked in the side of the mountain, overhung in places where the builders had bored a half-tunnel to accommodate the traveler. These peaks might all be honeycombed, he thought, by caverns and tunnels, and other hidden ways of the long-ago invaders. Sorenson had been proved right and Survey must be informed.

Surra came out of the dark and pressed against his legs, making a barrier of her body in a warning of immediate danger. Storm swayed, retrieved his balance, listened. Then he caught the faintest noise—scrape of boot on rock? Metal against stone? Someone was coming up to meet him and that lurker could be anyone from a Nitra scout to an Xik who had escaped from the burning hell of the valley.

There were voices from behind too. The Quades and the riders were coming down under Gorgol's guidance. And the Terran believed that the creeper below must have heard them also. Steadying himself against the rocks, he leaned as close to Surra as he could.

"Find—" That order was a faint whisper, underlined by mental force. She left him noiselessly to go into action—to flush out of hiding any enemy who might set up an ambush on the lower roadway.

At his belt was the only weapon Quade's party had been able to spare him earlier—one of the long bladed hunting knives. Storm drew it, holding the weapon point up as a fencer might hold his épée. So much depended upon the identity of that hidden enemy. Against a Nitra one method of attack, but Xiks did not fight with knives—And what chance had a knife against a blaster or a slicer?

Storm's progress became a stumbling run—with small pauses every five steps or so to listen. Surra had not yet flushed her quarry. A turn in the trail, the way jackknifed back on the level below. The Terran made that turn panting. It never occurred to him to share the struggle ahead with any of the men he had left on the upper trail. Storm was too used to fighting his own battles with only his team to back him. And this tangle with Xik forces had returned him to his service days, so that now, half-dazed with fatigue and the pain of his wound as he was, the enemy ahead was in his mind his own affair.

Another turn and the trail was widening—leveling off. To his left there was a darkened gash leading back into the side of the mountain. And it was here that the sudden beam of light flashed out, caught the last quarter of a yellow-brown tail but did not entrap the rest of Surra.

"Ahuuuuuu!" Storm shouted and cast himself to the left, bringing up with a little gasp of agony against a rock wall. That light flashed again to where he had stood only a second earlier.

His distracting tactics were successful. Surra squalled and attacked in her own way. The flash bobbed crazily and then fell to ground level, making a straight path of light across which Storm must go if he aided the cat.

Then a figure staggered out into the moonlight, with flailing arms. Settler! Or Xik in disguise? Storm moved out toward the torch hoping to turn it on that shape that was trying to ward off Surra. The big cat had not gone in to kill, but to harass, to keep her opponent moving until Storm arrived.

The ex-Commando stooped, picked up the torch awkwardly and then swung well around. There was no mistaking that whirling, dodging figure spotlighted in the beam—Bister!

"Saaaaaa—"

Surra flattened her body to the ledge, her ears back against her skull, her mouth a snarl, her tail lashing as the fur raised in a stiffly pointed ridge along her spine. Though she was between Bister and retreat she did not leap.

Storm saw that the other's hand was going to a weapon at his belt. "Hold it—right there!" he ordered.

The big man, his face patterning his emotions as fiercely as Surra's did hers, leaned a little forward, his hand opening with visible reluctance, rising inch by grudging inch in the beam of light.

"The Terran!" He mouthed the word as if it were obscene, making of it both an oath and a challenge. "Animal—"

"Beast Master!" Storm corrected him in his gentle voice, the one that marked him at his most dangerous.

He thrust his knife into the front of his belt and came on unhurriedly, holding the light on Bister until he was within arm's distance. Then he moved with some of Surra's lightning swiftness, pulling the stun rod from the other's holster, tossing the weapon out and over the edge of the drop.

But Bister was quick, too. His hand streaked for his knife in one last bid for freedom. The fine super-steel of the off-world blade was blue fire in the torchlight as he bent in the crouch of the experienced fighter. And Storm realized that, Xik aper or not, the man facing him could use that weapon.

"Send in your cat, why don't you—animal man!" Bister grinned, his teeth showing in the light almost as sharp and pointed as Surra's. "I'll mark her—just as I'll gut you—Terran!"

Storm backed, raised his hand, and jammed the torch into a small crevice of the rock. He was a fool, he supposed, to fight Bister. But something within him compelled him to front the other—whoever or whatever he might be—with only bare steel between them. It was the old, old war of the barbarian fighting man who was willing to back his cause with the power of his own body.

"Surra—" Storm motioned to the cat. She remained where she was at the top of the down trail, her eyes bright, watching the men facing each other in the path of light. And she would not move unless he so ordered.

Storm's knife was again in his hand. For a moment the weariness of his body was forgotten, his world had narrowed to those two bared blades. He heard and did not mark a cry from uptrail as the men there caught sight of the scene on the ledge.

But if the Terran did not mark that exclamation Bister did. And the big man rushed, wishing to make a beginning and an end all in one attack before the others could move to Storm's assistance.

Storm dodged and knew a small bite of dismay at the slowness of his movement. But, as it had in the Nitra camp, his purpose possessed him, dampening out physical weakness. Only now his body did not obey with the speed and perfection he needed for safety.

Bister was conscious of that, and knew that Storm was not now the same man he had faced between the Port and the Crossing. He struck quickly, with expert precision.

CHAPTER EIGHTEEN

Blade rang on blade as Storm met that attack. But Bister was boring in, confidence behind each move as he forced the Terran to retreat. Storm tried to weave a pattern of small feints and withdrawals that would bring him around so that full glare of the torch beam would strike in the other's face. Bister was well aware of that danger and he did not advance as Storm gave way.

He could end this in a moment, the Terran knew, by one summons to Surra. But he must face Bister out by himself—standing on his own two feet, steel against steel—or else he could never command the team again.

Time had no meaning as their boots shuffled warily on the rock ledge. After his first leap of attack was countered, Bister, too, became careful, willing to wear down the slighter Terran. Storm felt a small wet trickle under the blanket on his shoulder and knew that his wound must have reopened under that protecting plaster of leaves. That trickle would drain his strength even more, put weights on his feet, just when he needed all the agility he could command.

It was he who was being forced into the path of the light, and once Bister had him blinded in the full glare of that beam he would be pinned helplessly. His thoughts raced, assembling all he knew of the apers. They had been given bodies to resemble his own, training that would make them react as closely as possible to the human. Yet still inside they must remain truly Xik, no matter how conditioned their cover or they would be of no use to their superiors. And the Xik—what set of circumstances would throw an Xik fighter off guard, rattle him badly? What would be his worst fears, his ultimate terror? Why had there always been war to the end between them and the human species?

Storm shuffled, danced, evaded by a finger's small breadth a wily rush that would have pushed him into the danger zone. Why *did* the Xik fear and hate the Terrans? What was the deep-set base of that fear and could he play upon it now?

His thoughts were cut by the clash of steel meeting steel as the hilt of his own weapon was driven back almost to his breast and the jar of that blow numbed his arm for an instant. All the sixth sense that Storm drew upon when he worked with the team was alert behind the defenses of his well-trained body.

Then—as if that flash of knowledge came from some source outside his own mind—Storm knew, knew the weakness of the Xik, because in a manner it was his own weakness by racial inheritance, a weakness peculiar in turn to the Dineh also, a weakness that could also be a kind of strength, so that men clung to it for the security they desired.

"You stand alone—" He spoke those words in Galactic, his tone level. "Your kind have blown themselves up back there, Bister. There is no ship waiting to take you from Arzor. Alone—alone—one among the many who hate you. Never shall you see your home world again! It is lost among the nameless stars."

He knew in that same burst of understanding why the Xik had destroyed Terra—they had hoped to kill the heart of the Confederacy with that one bold stroke. But because the races bred on Terra differed, because her colonies were already mutating from their original breed, that scheme had failed.

"Alone!" He flung that single word with an upthrust of his Singer voice, trying to put into it the power he had felt when facing the Nitra wizard. Bister was alone, and so was Storm. But in this moment the agony of the old loss was dulled for the Terran. He could use that taunt as a weapon, and it carried no backlash to tear him in return.

"Alone!" He could see Bister's eyes, dark, wide, and he saw, too, that small flame of desperation deep in them. Beneath his aper disguise the Xik was stirring. Storm must bring that alien up to the surface, set the buried self to struggling against the disciplined outer shell.

"No one to back you here, Bister. No cell brothers, no battle mates. One Xik left alone on Arzor to be hunted down—"

All the scraps of briefing the Terran had heard concerning the invaders and their customs came flaming into his mind, clear, distinct, lying ready to his use, as his feet circled in the motions of the duel.

"Who will cover your back, Bister? Who will raise the name shout for you? None of your brothers shall know where you died or mark your circle on the Hundred Tablets in the Inner Tower of your clan city. Bister shall die and it shall be as if he never lived. Nor will he have a name son to take up his Four Rights after him—"

Coll Bister's mouth hung open a little and there was the glisten of moisture on his forehead, shiny on his cheeks and jaw. That alien spark in his eyes grew stronger.

"Bister shall die and that is all. No awakening for him by the Naming of Names—"

"Yaaaaah!"

The aper charged. But Storm had been warned by a momentary tenseness in his enemy's body. He swerved with much of his old spontaneous grace. The other's blade caught in the silver necklace on the Terran's breast, scored stingingly across his chest. And the force of Bister's body striking his drove Storm back to the very edge of the ledge.

For fear of being forced over the drop Storm grappled, knowing his danger. The aper was unwounded, strong enough to crush the Terran's resistance. Storm could only use all the tricks of Commando fighting that he knew. One of them brought him out of that grip and reeling back to safety under the undercut.

Bister gave a shrill whine. His eyes were nonhuman now, filled only with the fear and loss Storm had hammered into his alien brain. Every belief that had bolstered his kind when they went into battle had been ripped to tatters by an enemy he hated above all others. He lived only for one thing now—to kill—not caring if his own death was the price he must pay for success.

And because he had slipped over the edge of sanity he was more dangerous and yet easier to handle. Storm backed and Bister followed, his crooked fingers grasping at the air before him.

Storm raised his own hand, flat, ready. Then he pivoted and what he had worked for happened. Bister blundered into the direct beam of the torch. For a moment his crazed eyes were blinded and Storm's blow landed, clean and unhurried, as he might have delivered it on the drill field.

The aper gave a light cough that was half grunt and collapsed slowly forward, going to his knees, and then on to his face, to lie unmoving. Storm reeled back until his good shoulder met rock and he was supported by it. He watched Surra creep, her belly fur brushing the ledge, to sniff at Bister. She snarled and would have raised a paw with claws ready to rake, but the Terran hissed an order at her.

Brad Quade crossed the path of the light, knelt beside the aper. He turned the man over, felt for a heartbeat beneath the torn shirt.

"He is not dead." Storm's voice was thin and faraway even in his own ears. "And he is truly Xik—"

He saw Quade rise quickly, come toward him. Tired as he was, the Terran could not bear to have the other touch him. He drew away from the wall, to avoid Quade's outstretched hand. But this time his will did not command his body and he crumpled, one hand falling across Bister's inert body as he went down.

The picture had been part of Storm's dreams. Yet now that he opened his eyes and lay without strength to move on the narrow bed, it was still there, covering one wall with a bold sweep of colors he knew and loved. There were the squared mesa of the southwestern desert on his own world, above that the symmetrical rounded cloud domes first developed by Dineh painters when they worked with sand as their only material. And there was a wind blowing about that mesa. The Terran could almost feel it as he saw the hair of the painted riders whipped about their faces, the manes of their spotted ponies pulled across their eyes. The mural covered the wall beside his bed and Storm slept with his head turned toward it so that those riders in the wind were the first thing he saw when he had strength enough to raise his heavy eyelids. The artist who had created that scene had ridden in the desert winds of home, been torn by their force, had known well the scent of wool

and sage, of twisted pine, and the dull, sun-heated sand. To watch that
painting was like waking under the pine tree in the cavern of the gardens, and yet this was more closely Storm's than the tree, the grass,
the flowering things of his lost earth. Because this was a thing of
beauty brought to life by one of his own blood. Only an artist of the
Dineh could have pictured this—

The painted wall was far more real to him just then than those
who came to tend his body. For Storm, the medic from the port and
the silent, dark-faced woman who came and went were both shadows without substance. Nor was he able to emerge from his picture-
world to answer Kelson's questions when the Peace Officer had
appeared beside his bed—the Arzoran was far less distinct to Storm
than the nearest spotted pony. He did not know where he was, nor
did he care. He was content to share his waking hours and his longer
periods of dreaming with the riders on the wall.

But at last those periods of wakefulness grew longer. The dark
woman insisted upon piling pillows to bolster his shoulders, lifting
him so that he could not watch the wall in comfort. And he realized
that she spoke to him shortly, even sharply, in the Dineh tongue, as
one might who was impatient with a child proving stubborn. Storm
tried to cling to his languid dreams—only to have them torn from
him abruptly when Logan limped in. The mask of bruises had faded
from the other's face, so that Storm traced there something more
than just the signature of Dineh blood, a teasing resemblance to a
memory he could not quite recall.

"You like it?" The younger Quade looked beyond Storm to the
mural, that section of Terran desert, untamed, but captured for all
time on an Arzoran wall.

"It is home—" Storm answered truthfully and knew how revealing both words and tone were.

"That is what my father thinks—"

Brad Quade! Storm's right hand moved across the blanket that
covered him, its thin brownness crossing one familiar stripe to the
next. His covering was Na-Ta-Hay's legacy, or if not, one enough
like it to be its twin. Na-Ta-Hay and the oath he had demanded of
Storm—and Brad Quade's death lay at the core of that oath.

The Terran lay hoping for the familiar spur of anger to toughen his resolution. But it did not come. It was as if he could feel only one thing now—longing for that pictured land. Yet even if there was no anger to back it, the oath still rested on him and he must do what he had come to Arzor—

Storm had half-forgotten Logan, but now the younger man rose from the chair he had chosen and moved forward to the mural, his eyes on those wind-battered riders. There was a shade of wistfulness in his face, and none could ever doubt his kinship with the men pictured there.

"What was it like?" he asked abruptly. "How did it make a man feel to ride so across that country?" Then he was conscious of the hurt that memory might deal, and a darker flood crept up his clean jawline. He turned his head to the bed, his eyes troubled.

"I left that life," Storm picked his words with care, "when I was a child. Twice I returned—it was never the same. But it stays, deep in one's mind it continues to live. The one who painted that—for him it lived. Even here, far across the star lanes, it lived!"

"For her—" Logan corrected softly.

Storm sat up, away from his bolstering pillows. He could not know how stone-hard his face had become. He did not have a chance to voice his question.

Another stood in the doorway, the big man with the compelling blue eyes, the man Storm had come to find and yet did not want to meet. Brad Quade walked to the foot of the bed and looked down at the Terran measuringly. And Storm knew that this was to be the last meeting of all, that in spite of his queer inner reluctance, he must force the issue and be ready to face the consequences.

With some of his old speed of action the Terran's hand went out, caught at the knife in Logan's belt, and jerked it free, resting the blade across his knee, its point significantly toward Brad Quade.

Those blue eyes did not change. The settler might have been expecting that very move. Or else he did not understand what it implied. But that Storm did not believe.

He was right! Quade knew—accepted the challenge—or at least recognized the reason for it, for the other was speaking:

"If there is steel between us, boy, why did you bring me out of the Nitra camp?"

"A life for a life until our last accounting. You kept the blade out of my back at the Crossing. A warrior of the Dineh pays his debts. I come from Na-Ta-Hay. Upon Na-Ta-Hay and upon his family you have set the dishonor of blood spilled—and other shame—"

Brad Quade did not move, except to step closer to the foot of the bed. When Logan stirred, he signaled with his hand in an imperative order that kept his son where he was.

"There is and was no blood spilled between the family of Na-Ta-Hay and me," he replied deliberately. "And certainly no shame!"

Storm was chilled. He had never believed that Quade would deny his guilt when they at last faced each other. From his first sight of the settler he had granted him the virtue of honesty.

"What of Nahani?" he asked coldly.

"Nahani!" Quade was startled. He leaned forward, his big brown hands grasping the footrail of the bed, breathing a little faster as if he had come running to this meeting. And Storm could not mistake the genuine surprise in his tone.

"Nahani," repeated the Terran deliberately. Then struck by a possible explanation for the other's bewilderment, he added:

"Or did you never know the name of the man you killed at Los Gatos—?"

"Los Gatos?" Brad Quade stooped, as if striving to bring his blue eyes on a level with the dark ones Storm raised to meet them. "Who—are—you?" He spaced those words with little breaths between, as if each were forced from him by that sharp point still in Storm's hold.

"I am Hosteen Storm—Nahani's son—Na-Ta-Hay's grandson—"

Brad Quade's lips moved as if he were trying to shape words, and finally they came:

"But he told us—told Raquel—that you were dead—of fever! She—she had to remember that all the rest of her life! She went back to the mesa for you and Na-Ta-Hay showed her a walled-up cave—said you were buried in it—That nearly killed her, too!" Brad Quade whirled, his broad shoulders undefended to Storm's attack. He balled his hands into fists, brought them down against the wall as if he were battering something else, a shadow not concrete enough to take the punishment he craved to deal out.

"Blast him! He tortured her on purpose! How could he do that to his own daughter?"

Storm watched that sudden rage die as Quade's control snapped into place. The fist became a hand again, reached out to touch with delicate tenderness, the edge of the mural.

"How could he do it? Even if he were such a fanatic—" Quade asked again, wonderingly. "Nahani wasn't killed—at least by me. He died of snake bite. I don't know what you've been told—a twisted story apparently—" He spoke quietly and Storm slumped back against his pillows, his world unsteady. He could not fan dead anger to life. Quade's sober voice carried too much conviction.

"Nahani was attached to the Survey Service," Quade said tiredly. He pulled a chair to him, dropped into it, still eyeing Storm with a kind of hungry demand for belief. "I was, too, then. We worked together on several assignments—and our Amerindian background led us to close friendship. There was trouble with the Xik on some of the outer planets and Nahani was captured in one of their sneak raids. He escaped and I went to see him at the base hospital. But they had tried to 'condition' him—"

Storm tensed and shivered. Quade, seeing his reaction, nodded.

"Yes, you can understand what that meant. It was bad—he was—changed. The medic thought perhaps something could be done for him on Terra. He was sent home for rehabilitation. But during the first month, he got away from the hospital—disappeared. We learned later that he made his way back to his own home. His wife and son were there, a two-year-old child.

"Outwardly he appeared normal. His wife's father—Na-Ta-Hay—was one of the irreconcilables who refused to acknowledge any change or need for change in the native way of life. He was fanatic almost past the point of strict sanity. And he welcomed Nahani back as one rescued from the disaster of becoming Terran in place of Dineh. But Raquel, Nahani's wife, knew that he must have expert help. She got word of his whereabouts to the authorities without her father's knowledge. I was asked to go with the medic to pick him up because I was on leave and I was his friend—they hoped I could persuade him to come in peaceably for treatment.

"When he discovered we were coming, he went on the run again.

Raquel and I followed him into the desert. When we found his hidden camp, he was already dead—of snake bite. And when Raquel returned to her father's place for her baby, he was like a wild man—he accused her of betraying her husband, of turning traitor to her people, and drove her off with a gun.

"She came to me for help, and with guards we went to get her child—only to be shown a grave, the walled-up cave. Raquel collapsed and was ill for months. Afterwards we were married, I resigned from the service and brought her to my home here, hoping in new surroundings she could forget. I think she was happy—especially after Logan was born. But she only lived four years—And that is the true story!"

The knife lay by itself on the blanket. Storm's hands were over his eyes, shutting out the room, allowing him to see into a place that was dark and alive with an odd danger he must face by himself, as he faced Bister back at the Peaks.

A blurred column of years stretched out behind him—separating him from that long-ago day when Na-Ta-Hay had impressed his bitter will upon a small awed boy to whom his grandfather was as tall and powerful as one of the fabled Old Ones—between now and the day just after he had landed at the Center when Na-Ta-Hay's spirit seemed to spread like a shadow across all his memories and dreams of Terra, his now destroyed homeland. He had clung to that shadow of a man, and to the oath he had given, making them anchors in a reeling world. Storm had fostered a hatred of Quade because he had to have some purpose in life, though even then something deep within him had tried to repudiate it. He saw it all now—so clearly.

That was why he had shrunk from pressing the dispute at his first meeting with the settler. As long as he could postpone this settlement, so could he continue to live. After it, his life would no longer have any purpose.

Na-Ta-Hay had stood in his memory as a symbol for all that was lost. To cling to the task the other had set him had, in a strange way, kept Terra alive. They had been right at the Center in their distrust of him, he had *not* escaped the madness of the worldless men, only his had taken another and stranger turn.

Now he was empty, empty and waiting for the fear that lurked just beyond the broken barrier to crawl in and possess him utterly. Na-Ta-Hay had left him no anchor, only delusion. Now he stood on the same narrow edge of sanity where Bister had walked. For his kind, like Bister, *had* to have roots. Roots of a land—of kin—

Storm did not know he was shivering, huddling down into his pillows, seeking oblivion, which would not come. His hands dropped from his face to lie limp on the lightning patterned slashes of the blanket, but he did not open his eyes. For he felt he dared not see that mural now, nor look at the man who had told the truth and made him face his own complete loss.

Warmth ringed his wrists, fingers tightened there as if to drag him out of the encroaching darkness.

"Here, too, is the family—"

At first the words were only sounds—then the meaning came, the words repeated themselves in his empty mind. Storm opened his eyes.

"How did you know?" He begged assurance that true understanding of what he needed had prompted the choice of just those words, not chance.

"How did *I* know?" Brad Quade was smiling. "Are the Dineh the only wise ones, son? Is there only one tribe who seek roots in their own earth? This was your home—always waiting. Your mother helped to make it. You have merely been a little late in arriving—about—let me see now—some eighteen Terran years!"

Storm did not try to answer that. His eyes went once more to the mural. But now it was only a painted wall, nostalgic, beautiful, not meant to hold a man in spell. He heard a quiet laugh from the doorway and glanced up. Logan must have gone—now he was back. He stood there with Baku riding his shoulder as she had so often ridden Storm's, with Surra flowing about his legs. The big cat came and put her forepaws on the bed and surveyed Storm round-eyed, while Hing chittered from the crook of Logan's arm.

"Rain is in the corral. He'll have to wait a few more days for your reunion—" Brad did not yet loose his hold on Storm's wrists. "Here is your family—this is also the truth!"

Storm drew a single, long, shaky breath that was very close to something else. His hands lay quiet, drawing strength from that warm clasp.

"Yat-ta-hay," he said. He was tired, so very tired, but the emptiness was filled with a vast and abiding content he was sure would never ebb again. "Very, very good!"

LORD OF THUNDER

CHAPTER ONE

Red ridges of mountains, rusted even more by the first sere breath of the Big Dry, cut across the lavender sky of Arzor north and east. At an hour past dawn, dehydrating puffs of breeze warned of the new day's scorching heat. There would be two hours—maybe three, yet—during which a man could ride, though in growing discomfort. Then he must lie up through the blistering fire of midday.

The line camp was not too far ahead. Hosteen Storm's silent communication with the powerful young stallion under him sent the horse trotting at a steady pace, striking out over a strip of range where yellow grass waved high enough to brush a rider's leg. Here and there Storm spied a moving blot of blue, the outer fringe of the grazing frawn herd. His sense of direction had not failed him when he took this short cut; they were nearing the river. In the Big Dry no animal strayed more than half a day's distance from a sure supply of water.

But he had come close to the edge of prudence in staying so long in the hills this time. One of the two canteens linked to his light saddle pad was as dry as the sun-baked rocks at his back, had been so since midmorning of the day before, and the other held no more than a good cup and a half of water. The Norbies, those wide-ranging hunters native to this frontier world, had their springs back in the mountain canyons, but their locations were clan secrets.

Perhaps here and there an off-world settler would be accepted by a clan to the point of sharing water knowledge. Logan might—Hosteen's well-marked black brows pulled in a fleeting frown as he thought of his Arzoran-born half-brother.

When Hosteen had landed on Arzor a half planet-year earlier, a veteran of the Confederacy forces after the Xik war, it was as a homeless exile. The last battle of that galaxy-wide holocaust had been a punitive raid to turn Terra into a blue, radioactive cinder. He had had no idea then that Logan Quade existed or that Brad Quade—Logan's father—could be any more to him than a man he had once sworn to kill.

In the end, the hate-twisted oath demanded of him by his grandfather on Terra had not made Storm a murderer after all. It had been broken just in time and had led him to what he needed most—new roots, a home, kin.

Only happy endings did not always remain so, Hosteen knew now. His emotion was more one of exasperation than disappointment. Though he had appeared to drop into a place already prepared to contain him as easily as his vanished Navajo kinsmen used to fit a polished turquoise into a silver setting, yet another stone in that same setting had come loose during the past few months.

To most riders, the daily round of duties on a frontier holding were arduous enough. There were the dangerous reptilian yoris to hunt down, raiders from the wild Nitra tribe of the Peaks to keep off, a hundred and one other tangles with disaster or even sudden death to be faced. But none of that satisfied Logan. He was driven by a consuming restlessness, which pulled him away from a half-done task to seek out a Norbie camp, to join one of their wide ranging hunts, or just to wander back into the hills.

There was a flicker of black just within eye range in the sky. Hosteen's lips pursed as if for a whistle, though no sound issued from between their sun-cracked, blood-threaded surfaces. The black dot spiraled down.

The stallion halted without any outward command from his rider. With the peerless swoop of her kind, Baku, the great African Eagle, came in to settle on the pronged rest that formed the horn of Hosteen's specially designed trail saddle. The bird was panting, her head turned a little to one side as one bright and keen-sighted eye regarded Hosteen steadily.

For a long moment they sat so in perfect rapport. Science had fostered that link between man and bird, had tested and trained man, bred, tested, and trained bird, to form not just a team of two very different life forms but—when the need arose—part of a smoothly working weapon. The enemy was gone; there was no longer any need for such a weapon. And the scientists who had fashioned it had vanished into ash. But the alliance remained as steadfast here on Arzor as it had ever been on those other worlds where a sabotage and combat team of man, bird, and animals had operated with accurate efficiency.

"Nihich'i hooldoh, t'assh 'annii ya?" Hosteen asked softly, savoring the speech that perhaps he alone now along the stellar lanes would ever speak with fluency. "We're making pretty good time, aren't we?"

Baku answered with a low, throaty sound, a click of her hunter's beak in agreement. Though she relished the freedom of the sky, she wanted no more of its furnace heat in the coming day than he did. When they made the line camp, she would willingly enter its heat-dispelling cavern.

Rain, the stallion, trotted on. He was accustomed now to transporting Baku, having fitted into the animal pattern from off-world with his own contribution, speed and stamina in travel. Now he neighed shrilly. But Hosteen had already caught sight of familiar landmarks. Top that small rise, pass through a copse of muff bushes, and they were at the camp where Logan should be on duty for this ten-day period. But somehow Hosteen was already doubting he would find him there.

The camp was not a building but a cave of sorts in the side of a hillock. Following the example of native inhabitants, the settlers who ran frawns or horses in the plains set their hot weather stations deep in the cool earth. The conditioners, which controlled atmosphere for the buildings in the two small cities, the structures in the small, widely separated towns of the range country, and main houses of the holdings, were too complicated and expensive to be used in line camps.

"Halloooo." Hosteen raised his voice in the ringing hail of a camp visitor. The recessed earth-encircled doorway of the living quarters was dark. From this distance he could not tell whether it was open or closed. And the wider opening to the stable, which would give the imported horses a measure of protection, was also a blank.

But a minute later a red-yellow figure moved against the red-yellow earth at the side of the mound, and sun glinted brightly on two curves of ivory-white, breaking the natural camouflage of the waiting Norbie by revealing the six-inch horns, as normal to his domed skull as thick black hair was to Hosteen's. A long arm flashed up, and the rider recognized Gorgol, once hunter of the Shosonna tribe and now in charge of the small horse herd that was Hosteen's own personal investment in the future.

The Norbie came out of the shade of the hillock to reach for Rain's hackamore as Hosteen swung stiffly down. Brown Terran fingers flashed in fluid sign talk:

"You are here—there is trouble? Logan—?"

Gorgol was young, hardly out of boyhood, but he had already reached his full growth of limb. His six-foot, ten-inch body, all lean, taut muscle over hard, compact bone, towered over Hosteen. His yellow eyes, the vertical pupils mere threads of black against the sun's intrusive glare, did not quite meet those of the Terran, but his right hand sketched a sign for the necessity of talk.

Norbie and human vocal cords were so dissimilar as to render oral speech between off-worlder and native impossible. But the finger talk worked well between the races. An expert, as most of the range riders had to be, could express complex ideas in small, sometimes nearly invisible movements of thumb and fingers.

Hosteen went into the cave camp, Baku riding his shoulder. And while the coolness of the earth wall could only be a few degrees less than the temperature of the outside, that difference was enough to bring a sigh of content from the sweating man, a cluck of appreciation from the eagle.

The Terran halted inside to allow his eyes to adjust to the welcome dusk. And a single glance about told him he had guessed right. If Logan had been here, he was now gone, and not just for the early-morning duty inspection of the frawn herd. All four wall bunks were bare of sleeping rolls, there was no sign the cook unit had been used that day, and the general litter of a rider, his saddle, tote bag, and canteen, were absent.

But there was something else, a yoris hide bag, its glittering scaled exterior adorned by a feather embroidery pattern that repeated over

and over the conventionalized figure of a Zamle, the flying totem of
Gorgol's clan. That was the Norbie's traveling equipment—which by
every right should have been stowed in a bunk locker at the Center
House fifty miles downriver.

Hosteen stretched out his arm to afford Baku a bridge to the
perch hammered in the wall. Then he went to the heating unit, measured out a portion of powdered "swankee," the coffee of the Arzor
ranges, and dialed the pot to three-minute service. He heard the
faintest whisper behind and knew that Gorgol had deliberately trod-
den so as to attract his attention. But he was determined to make the
other give an explanation without asking any questions himself, and
he knew that it was unwise to push.

While the heating unit was at work, Hosteen sailed his hat to the
nearest bunk, loosened the throat lacings of his undyed frawn fabric
shirt, and pulled it off before he sought the fresher and allowed water vapor to curl pleasantly and coolly about his bare chest and
shoulders.

As the Terran came out of the alcove, Gorgol snapped the first
swankee container out of the unit, hesitated, and drew a second,
which he turned around and around in his hands, staring blank-eyed
down at the liquid as if he had never seen its like before.

Hosteen seated himself on the edge of a bunk, cradled the swankee cup in his hand, and waited another long moment. Then Gorgol
smacked his container down on the table top with a violence close to
anger, and his fingers flew, but not with such speed that Hosteen was
unable to read the signs.

"I go—there is a call for all Shosonna—Krotag summons—"

Hosteen sipped the slightly bitter but refreshing brew, his mind
working faster than his deliberate movements might indicate. Why
would the chief of Gorgol's clan be summoning those engaged in
profitable riders' jobs? The Big Dry was neither the season for
hunting nor for war—both of which pursuits, dear to the tradition
and customs of the Norbies, were conducted only in the fringe
months of the Wet Time. In the Big Dry, it was rigid custom for the
tribes and clans to split into much smaller family groups, each to re-
sort to one of the jealously guarded water holes to wait out the heat
as best they could.

All tribes with any settler contacts strove to hire out as many of their men as riders as they could, thus removing hungry and thirsty mouths from clan supply points. To summon *in* men in the Big Dry was a policy so threatened with disaster as to appear insane. It meant trouble somewhere—bad trouble—and something that had developed in the week of Storm's own absence.

Hosteen had ridden out of the Quade Peak Holding eight days ago—to set up his square stakes and make his claim map before recording it at Galwadi. As a veteran of the forces and a Terran, he was able to file on twenty squares, and he had set out his stakes around a good piece of territory to the northeast, having river frontage and extending into the mountain foothills. There had been no whisper of trouble then, nor had he seen any signs of movement of tribes in the outback. Though, come to think of it, he had not crossed a Norbie trail or met any hunters either. That he had laid to the Big Dry. Now he wondered if more than the rigors of Arzoran seasons had wrung the natives out of the country.

"Krotag summons—in the Big Dry!" Even in finger movements one could insert a measure of incredulity.

Gorgol shifted from one yoris-hide booted foot to the other. His discomfort was plain to one who had ridden with him for months. "There is medicine talk—" His fingers shaped that and then were stiffly straight.

Hosteen sipped, his mind working fast and hard, fitting one small hint to another. "Medicine talk"—was that answer to shut off more questions or could it be the truth? In any event, it stopped him now. You did not—ever—inquire into "medicine," and his own Amerindian background made him accept that prohibition as a thing necessary and right.

"How long?"

But Gorgol's straight fingers did not immediately reply. "Not to know—" came reluctantly at last.

Hosteen was still searching for a question that was proper and yet would give him a small scrap of information when there was a clear note from the other end of the cave room, the alerting call of the com, which tied each line camp to the headquarters of the holding. The Terran went to the board, thumbing down the receive button.

What came was no new message but a recall broadcast to be repeated mechanically at intervals, set to bring in all riders. There *was*
something going on!

"You ride then for the hills?" he signed to Gorgol.

The Norbie was at the doorway, shouldering his travel bag. Now
he paused, and not only the change of his expression showed his
troubled mind. It was evident in every movement of his body. Hosteen believed the native was obeying an imperative order, greatly
against his own will.

"I ride. All Norbies ride now."

All Norbies, not just Gorgol. Hosteen digested that and, in spite
of himself, vented his surprise in a startled hiss. Quade depended
heavily on native riders, not only here at the Peak Holding, but also
down at his wider spread in the Basin. And Quade was not the only
range man who had a predominance of Norbie employees. If they
all took to the hills—! Yes, such an exodus could cripple some of the
holdings.

"All Norbies—this, too, is medicine?"

But why? Medicine was clan business as far as Hosteen had been
able to learn. He had never heard of a whole tribe or nation com-
bining their medicine meetings and ceremonies—certainly not in
the season of the Big Dry. Why, the river lands could not support
such a gathering at this time of the year—let alone the arid mountain country.

But Gorgol was answering. "Yes—all Norbies." quivers—that was
unheard of!

"Also the wild ones?"

"The wild ones—yes."

Impossible! There were tribal feuds nursed for the honor of
fighting men. To send in the peace pole for a clan, or perhaps—
stretching it far—several clans at a time, was one thing. But for the
Shosonna and the Nitra to sit under such a pole with their war arrows still in the the quivers—that was unheard of!

"I go—" Gorgol slapped his travel bag. "The horses, they are in
the big corral—you will find them safe."

"You go—but you will return to ride again?" Hosteen was bothered by the suggestion of finality in the other's signs.

"That lies with the lightning—"

The Norbie was gone. Hosteen walked back across the room to lie down on a bunk. So Gorgol was not even sure he would be back. What did he mean about that lying with the lightning? The Norbies recognized divine power in shadow beings who drummed thunder and used the lightning to slay. The reputed home of these God Ones was the high mountains of the northeast. And those same mountains also hid the caverns and passages of that mysterious unknown race who had either explored or settled here on Arzor centuries before the Terran exploration ships had reached this part of the galaxy.

Hosteen, Logan, and Gorgol, together with Surra, the dune cat, and Hing, the meercat of the Beast Team, had discovered the Cavern of the Hundred Gardens, a fabulous botanical preserve of the Sealed Caves. That, and the ruined city or fortification in the valley beyond, was still under scientific study. It was easy to believe that there were other Sealed Caves in the hills—and also easy to understand that the Norbies had made gods of the long-vanished and still-unknown space travelers who had hollowed out the Peaks to hold their mysteries.

Hosteen could spend hours speculating about that and not turn up one real fact. Now it was better to sleep through the day heat and ride out at night to answer the return order from the holding. For all Hosteen knew, that summons might have been sounding for days, which could account for Logan's absence. He turned on his side and willed himself to sleep.

That mental alarm clock that had been conditioned into him during his service days brought him awake hours later. To come out of the cave into the dusk of evening was walking into a wall of heavy heat, but it was not as bad as sunlight. He allowed Rain to splash in the shallows of the river before he swung up to the riding pad. Baku's world was not that of the night, but she accepted it at his urging, climbing into the star-encrusted sky.

The Center House was three nights' ride from the line camp. And two of the days in between Hosteen had to spend in improvished shelters, lying flat on the earth to get what coolness the parched soil might provide. Shortly before midnight on the third night, he rode up to the blazing light of his goal. The unusual glare of atom lamps was another warning of emergency.

"Who's there?" The suspicion-sharp hail out of the gate shadows made the Terran draw rein. Then from his right a furry body materialized beside the snorting stallion, reared on its haunches, and drew a paw with sheathed claws along Hosteen's boot.

"Storm," he answered the challenger and dismounted to caress Surra. The rasp of the dune cat's tongue on his hand was an unusually fervid greeting, which awoke answering warmth within him.

"I'll take your horse." The man who came from the gate carried an unholstered stunner. "Quade's been waitin', hopin' you'd make it soon—"

Hosteen muttered a brief thanks, more interested in the fact that there were other men in the courtyard. But there were no Norbies, not a single one of the native riders he was used to seeing there. Gorgol had been right; the Norbies had all pulled out.

With Surra rubbing against his thigh, now and then butting him playfully with her head, he went to the door of the big house. Tension was alive in the cat, too. She had sometimes been like this on the eve of one of their wartime forays. Trouble excited but did not worry Surra.

"—continent-wide as far as reports have come in—"

Maybe Surra was exhilarated by the present happenings, but the tone of that voice told Hosteen that Brad Quade was frankly worried.

CHAPTER TWO

Within the house, Hosteen found himself fronting a distinguished gathering that included most of the settlers in the Peak country—even Rig Dumaroy, whose usual association with Brad Quade was one of uneasy neutrality. But, of course, in any Norbie trouble Dumaroy would be present. He was the one large holder in the frontier country who was prejudiced against the Arzoran natives and refused to hire any of them.

"It's Storm—" Dort Lancin, who had ridden in with the Terran on the military transport almost a year ago, waved two fingers in greeting, a sign that was also a hunter signal for watchfulness.

The tall man standing by the com board glanced over his shoulder, and Hosteen read a shadow of relief on his stepfather's face.

Dort Lancin, his older and more taciturn brother Artur, Dumaroy, Jotter Hyke, Val Palasco, Connar Jaffe, Sim Starle—but no Logan Quade. Hosteen stood inside the doorway, his hand resting on Surra's head as the big cat nuzzled against his legs.

"What's going on?" he asked.

Dumaroy, a wide and rather vindictive grin on his face, answered first.

"All your pet goats have lit out for the hills. Always said they'd cross you up, always said it—now you see. And I say"—his grin faded, and he brought his big hand down on his knee in a resounding slap—"there's trouble brewing up there. The sooner we fort up and send for the Patrol to come in and settle this once and for all—"

Artur Lancin's level voice, threaded with weariness, cut across the other's bellow with the neatness of a belt knife slicing through frawn fat. "Yes, you've been broadcastin' on that beam all night, Dumaroy. We received you loud and clear the first time. Storm," he addressed the younger man, "you see anything different out in the hills?"

Storm flipped his hat up on the daryork horn rack and unfastened the belt that supported his stunner and bush knife as he replied.

"I think now what I did *not* see is important."

"That being?" Brad Quade was pulling a fresh swankee container from the unit. He brought it over and then, with a fingertip touch on Hosteen's shoulder, guided him to a foam chair.

"No hunters—no trails—nothing." Hosteen sipped the restoring liquid between words. He had not realized how bone-aching tired he was until he sat down. "I might have been riding in an empty world—"

The two Lancins watched him narrowly, and Dort nodded. He had hunted with the Norbies, was welcome in their villages, and well understood the strangeness of an empty country.

"How far did you go?" Quade asked.

"I made the rounds to set up markers." Hosteen brought his claim map from the inner pocket of his shirt. Quade took the sheet from him and compared its lines with the country survey chart that was a mural for one wall of the room.

"Clean up to the gorge, eh?" Jaffe commented. "And no hunter sign?"

"No. I thought it was because of the Big Dry retreat—"

"That wouldn't come quite this early," Quade replied. "Gorgol brought in your cavvy of mounts four days ago, took his bag, and rode off."

"I met him at the line camp."

"What did he tell you?"

"That there was a clan summons out—some sort of intertribal gathering—"

"Durin' the Big Dry?" demanded Hyke incredulously.

"I told you!" Dumaroy pounded with his fist this time, and Hosteen heard a snarling rumble from Surra. He sent a mental command to silence the cat. "I told you! We're sittin' right here on the only free runnin' water that keeps on runnin' through the worst of the Dry. And those goats are gonna come down and try to butt us out of it! If we've the sense of water rats, we'll go up and clean 'em out before they can get organized—"

"Once before you moved up to clean out Norbies," Quade said coldly. "And what did we find out—that the Norbies weren't responsible for anything that had happened—that there was an Xik holdout group behind all our stock losses!"

"Yeah—and is this another Xik trick? Callin' in all the tribes now?" Dumaroy's hostility was like a fog spreading from him toward the other man.

"Maybe not Xik this time," Quade conceded. "But I refuse to make any move until I know more about the situation. All we are sure of at present is that our Norbie riders have quit and are heading for the mountains at a time when they are usually eager to work, and that this has not happened before."

Artur Lancin stood up. "That's sense, Dumaroy. We aren't goin' to stick our heads into some yoris' mouth just on your say-so. I say we do a little scoutin'. Meanwhile, we rustle up riders from the Basin or even pick up some drifters from the Port to tide us over. With the Dry on, the herds aren't goin' to move too far from the river, and we'll need only a yoris patrol and some count work. My granddad got through, ridin' on his own, with just his two boys to back him in the First Ship days. None of you here look too soft for the saddle now."

"That's right," Sim Starle agreed. "We'll keep our coms on a circle hookup and with the alert on. Anybody learns anything, he sends the word out on the beam. I'm for sittin' quiet until we're sure about what's happenin' and why. Maybe these Norbies are havin' them a medicine powwow—and that's none of our danged business!"

Hosteen, sinking deeper into his fog of weariness, watched the settlers leave for their 'copters, to fly back to the scattered holdings of the Peak country. He was still too torpid to move when Brad Quade re-entered, having seen off the company. But he roused himself to ask the one question bothering him most.

"Where's Logan?"

"Gone—"

The tone of the other's voice pulled Hosteen out of his lethargy of fatigue. "Gone! Where?"

"To Krotag's camp—at least that's what I think—"

Hosteen was on his feet now. "The young fool! This is medicine business, Gorgol said so—"

Brad Quade turned. His face might seem impassive to an outsider, but it did not hide his feelings from Hosteen. "I know. But he has drunk blood with Kavok, Krotag's first son. That makes him a clansman—"

Hosteen bit back his protest. "Medicine" was tricky. A man could be an adopted clansman, living in blood brotherhood with a Norbie, but that might not cover prying into the inner beliefs of the natives. There was no use putting his thoughts and fears into words. Brad Quade knew all that and more.

"I can make it back up to the washes. How much of a start has he?"

"No. This was his choice; he took it with his eyes open. You won't ride after him. Tomorrow, if you will, I want you on the way to Galwadi in the 'copter."

"Galwadi!"

Brad Quade picked up the claim map. "You have this to record, remember? Then—have a talk with Kelson. He knows Logan." Quade ran one hand through his thick black cap of wiry hair. "I wish Kelson had got that bill through the Council—Logan was so keen on that Ranger business they talked about. If that had gone through, maybe he'd have had a job he'd really settle down to. But you can't make the Council hump just the way you want them to—even when you prod. Anyway—you see Kelson and try to get a line on what's happening. There may have been an official clamp on Norbie news—I suspect that. And I'd better stay here for now. Dumaroy's just hotheaded enough to try one of those dangerous schemes of his if there's no one to talk him down—and just one incident might set off big trouble."

"What do *you* think is happening?"

Brad Quade hooked his thumbs in his wide rider's belt and stared at the floor as if he had never seen such a pattern of river stones before. "I have no idea. This is 'medicine' right enough—but it's unique at this time of the year. The Quades were First Ship people. I've found nothing in our family records like this—"

"Gorgol told me the peace poles were up for the wild tribes."

His stepfather nodded. "I know; he told me, too. But just to sit and wait—"

Hosteen made one of his rare gestures of feeling toward this man he had once sworn to kill, resting a brown hand on the other's wide shoulder.

"To wait is always the hardest. Tomorrow night I will go to Galwadi. Logan—he is Norbie under the skin, and he has drunk blood with the Zamle Shosonna. That is a sacred thing—big medicine—"

Brad Quade's hand came up to cover Hosteen's for a moment of shared warmth. "Big enough—we can hope that. Now, you look like a two-day marcher in the flats. Get to bed and rest!"

To wait—Hosteen felt the first pinch of his own private kind of waiting as he sat in the 'copter boring through the night sky on the way to Galwadi. Behind him he left everything that counted on Arzor—a soft-furred, keen-eyed cat with a coat of yellow and a brain that perhaps matched his own in intelligence, though that intelligence might be of a different order, a horse he had trained, Hing, the meercat, a small, tumbling, clownish animal that had waddled four half-grown kits out for his inspection earlier that very evening, Baku, perched on the top corral bar, bidding him farewell with a falcon scream. And a man, a man whom he had once respected even while he hated him and whom he would now follow anywhere, anytime, and for any purpose. He left all those in what might be the heart of enemy territory if their forebodings crystallized into the worst of futures.

To all outward seeming, there was no tension in Galwadi. Hosteen, coming from the land registration office, eyed the traffic on the street speculatively. The hour was far into dusk, and the small city, which had been dead in the day's heat, was alive now, the streets and shops busy. But whether he could hire any riders here was another question. To get new light-and-tie men at this season was a problem. There were several gather-ins in the lower town, and those would be a starting place for his quest. But first—dinner.

He chose a small, quiet eating place and was surprised at the wide array of dish dials he was offered. Food on the holdings was usually plentiful but plain, with little variety. The few off-world luxury items were carefully saved for holidays. But here he was fronted with a choice such as was more usual in a Port city catering to off-world visitors. Then he noted a Zacathan in the next booth and realized that a restaurant in the capital needs must satisfy the alien government representatives as well as the settlers.

Deciding to plunge, Hosteen dialed three dishes he had not tasted since his last service leave. He was sipping at a tube planted in a dalee bulb when someone paused by his table, and he glanced up to see Kelson, the Peace Officer of the Peak section.

"Heard you were looking for me, Storm."

"Tried your office com," Hosteen assented. He was a little at a loss as to how to word his question. Should he just bluntly ask what was up—if there was any news being withheld from the holdings? But Kelson continued.

"Coincidence. I was trying to reach you. Called the Peaks—Quade said you were here registering your squares. You've decided to settle in the Peak country then?"

"Yes—horse breeding with Put Larkin. He's off-world now. Heard of a new crossbreed on Astra—Terran blood interbred with the local species of duicorn. Can stand up to desert heat there—or so the breeder claims."

"So they might do for the Big Dry here, eh? It's a thought. But your range isn't open yet—"

What did that matter, Hosteen wondered. No one would start on holding work until the rains came. But Kelson was beckoning to someone across the room.

"There's a problem—maybe you can help us," the Peace Officer continued. "Mind if we join you? Time's essential in this one—"

The man who came up was an off-worlder of a type usually not seen on a frontier world. His sleek form-fitting tunic, picked out with a silver-thread pattern, and the long hose-breeches of flat black were those of a business executive on one of the densely populated merchant worlds, and fashionable though they might have been on his home planet, they were as incongruous here as they were ill-becoming to his pudgy figure. Ridiculous as he might look in this Ar-zoran restaurant, one did not think him a figure of fun when one observed his craggy face, saw the square set of a determined and forceful chin and the bleak eyes that were those of a man used to giving orders. Hosteen recognized the breed and stiffened—it was one with which he had little sympathy.

"Gentle Homo Lass Widders, Beast Master Storm." Kelson made the introductions, using the title of respect from the inner planets for the stranger, who seated himself without invitation across the table from Hosteen and proceeded to survey the Terran with an appraisal the other found insolent.

"I am not of the forces now." Hosteen corrected Kelson perversely. "So it is not Beast Master—today I light and tie for Quade."

"You're a holding head rather since an hour ago, aren't you? You've located your stakes. Have you set up a brand?" Kelson asked.

"Arrowhead S," Storm replied absently. "And what do you wish of a mustered-out Beast Master, Gentle Homo?"

"About a month, maybe more, of your time and services," Widders rapped out in the clicking Galactic basic of the business worlds. "I want to have you—and your team—guide me into the Blue section—"

Hosteen blinked and looked to Kelson for confirmation that he had really heard that idiotic statement. To his surprise, the expression on the Peace Officer's face read that this stranger from one of the hothouse worlds meant exactly what he said.

"It is a matter of time, Beast Master. I understand we must get into that country within the next two weeks if we go at all before next season."

Hosteen did not blink this time. He merely replied with the truth. "Impossible."

"Nothing," returned Widders with his irritating confidence, "is impossible, given the right man and credits enough. Kelson believes you are the man, and I can provide the credits."

There was no use giving this madman a blanket denial; he would not accept that. Listen to his story, get the reason behind this insane plan, then prove to him its utter folly—that was the only way to proceed.

"Why the Blue?" Hosteen asked as he spooned up some lorg sauce and spread it neatly over a horva fritter.

"Because my son's there—"

Again Hosteen glanced at Kelson. The Blue was unknown. Those mountains, which were its western ramparts, were known, and appeared on the maps of the Peak country. But what lay behind that barrier existed only as a series of hazy aerial photos. The treacherous air currents of those heights had kept out 'copter surveys, and the territory was the hunting ground of the feared wild Norbie cannibals, hated, shunned, and fought by their own kind of generations. No one—government man, settler, yoris hunter—had ever gone into the Blue and returned. It was posted off limits by government order. Yet here was Kelson listening to a proposal to invade the forbidden section as if Widders was doing no more than suggesting a stroll down a Galwadi street. Again Hosteen waited for enlightenment.

"You're a veteran of Confed forces, Storm. Well, my son is, too. He served with a Breakaway Task Force—"

Hosteen was a little jarred. To find an inner planet man among the Breakaways—those tough, very tough, first-in-fighters—was unusual.

"He was wounded, badly, just before the Xik collapse. Since then he has been on Allpeace—"

Allpeace, one of the rehabilitation worlds where men were rebuilt from human wreckage to live passably normal lives again. But if young Widders had been on Allpeace, how had he gotten into the Blue on Arzor?

"Eight months ago a transport left Allpeace with a hundred discharged veterans on board, Iton among them. On the fringe of this system, that ship hit a derelict hyper bomb." Widders might have been discussing the weather if you did not watch his eyes and note that small twitch of lip he could not control.

"Just a month ago a lifeboat from that ship was discovered on Mayho, this planet's sister world. There were two survivors. They reported that at least one more LB left the transport, and they cruised with her into this system. Their boat was damaged, and they had to set down on Mayho. Their companion headed on here to Arzor, promising to send back help—"

"And didn't arrive," Hosteen stated instead of questioned.

But Kelson was shaking his head. "No—there is a chance she did arrive, that she crashed in the Blue. Weak signals of some sort were recorded on robot coms in two different line camps out in the Peaks. A cross check gives us a Blue landing point."

"And your local climate would mean death to any survivors out there without adequate supplies or transportation at this season," Widders continued. "I want you to guide me in—to get my son out—"

If he *was* on that LB and is still alive, Hosteen added silently. But he made his oral reply as plain as he could.

"You are asking the impossible, Gentle Homo. To go into the Blue at this time is simply suicide, and there is no possible way of getting behind the Peaks during the Big Dry."

"Natives live there all year around, don't they?" Widders' voice scaled up a note or two.

"Yes, the Norbies live there. But their knowledge of the country is not shared with us."

"You can hire native guides, anything you need. There is no limit on funds—"

"Credits can't buy water knowledge from a Norbie. And there is also this—right now the tribes are making medicine in the Peak country. We would not be able to ride in under those conditions even in the Wet Time when all the odds are in our favor."

"I've heard about that," Kelson said. "It has to be looked into—"

"Not by me!" Hosteen shook his head. "There's trouble shaping up back there. I'm down here partly to report it and to try and hire riders to replace our Norbies. Every native has pulled out of the Peak country during the past week—every one—"

Kelson did not appear surprised. "So we heard. And they are moving northeast."

"Into the Blue." Hosteen digested that.

"Just so. You were a short way into that country when you discovered that Xik nest. And Logan—he's hunted along there. You're the only two settlers who have any ground-level information we can use," Kelson added.

"No." Hosteen tried to make that negative sound final. "I'm not completely crazy. Sorry, Gentle Homo, the Blue is closed country—in more ways than one."

Widders' eyes were no longer bleak. There was a spark of anger in their gray depths. "If I refuse to accept that?"

Hosteen slipped a credit disk into the table slot. "That is your privilege, Gentle Homo, and none of my business. See you later, Kelson." He rose and walked away from Widders and his problems. He had his own to deal with now.

CHAPTER THREE

That's it—" For some reason Storm could not sit still but strode up and down the length of the big main room of the holding while he gave the results of his mission to Galwadi. "I hired just one rider, and I had to bail him out of Confinement—"

"What had he done?" Brad Quade asked.

"Tried to wipe off the pavement of a street, using the aeropilot of the Valodian minister for a mop. The minister was rather upset about it—his protests got Havers twenty days or forty credits. He'd lost his last credit at Star and Comet, so he was sweating out the twenty days. Had served three of them when I paid his fine. He seems to know his business, though."

"And you saw Kelson?"

"Kelson saw me. He's blown all his rockets and is spinning in for a big smash if you ask me." Unconsciously Storm dropped into the old service slang.

There was a soft growl from the shadows, where Surra picked up his mood of irritation and faint apprehension, translating it into her own form of protest.

"What did he say?"

"He had an inner-planet civ in tow. They wanted a guide into the Blue—right now!"

"What?" Quade's incredulity was as great as Hosteen's own had been back in Galwadi.

Swiftly he outlined Widders' story.

"That could all be true, though why he's so sure his son was on board that LB—wish-thinking, I suppose." Quade shook his head. "A Norbie might just make it. Only you're not going to find a Norbie who will try, now now. On the other hand—" Quade's voice trailed off. He was sitting quietly at his file desk, two of Hing's kits curled up in his lap, a third cuddled down on his shoulder. Now he looked to the map on the wall. "On the other hand, that might be just the direction in which we should do some prospecting."

"Why?"

"Dort Lancin made a swing up the valley in his 'copter. He spotted two clans on the march, and they weren't just shifting camp. They were moving with a purpose—so fast they had left a stray mare—"

Storm stopped pacing, eying his stepfather with startled interest. For a Norbie to abandon a horse under any circumstances, except to save life, was so unheard of as to join in magnitude Widders' desire to enter the Blue.

"Heading northeast?" He was not the least surprised to be answered by a nod.

"I can't understand it. That's worse than Nitra country—that's where they eat THE MEAT." He made the Arzoran sign for the cannibal tribes. "No Shosonna or Warpt or Fanga would head in that direction. He'd be ritually unclean for years—"

"Just so. But that's where they're going—not raiding parties but the clans, with their women and children. So I agree this much with Kelson—we ought to know what is going on back there. But how any of us could get in—that is a different matter."

Storm went to the map. "'Copter would crack up if those wind currents are all they're reported to be."

"They are, all right," Quade returned with grim emphasis. "You might—with a crack pilot—do some exploring along the fringe under the right conditions and weather. But you couldn't make any long survey flight into that region. Any exploring party would have to go on horses or afoot."

"The Norbies do have wells—"

"Which are clan secrets and not shared with us."

Storm was still tracing the lines of the mountains on the mural map. "Did Logan ever learn any well calls?"

Though the human voice box could not duplicate Norbie speech, nor a Norbie produce anything like a Galactic basic word, there was a rarer form of communication that some of the Arzor-born settlers—those initiated deeply enough into native ways—could understand, even if they could not imitate it themselves. Long, lilting calls, which were almost like songs, were a known code. These were used by native scouts as warnings or reports, and it was common knowledge among the riders that some were used only to signal the appearance or disappearance of water.

"He might have."

"You're sure he is riding with Krotag?"

"He wouldn't be allowed to join any other clan."

The meercats awoke, squeaked. Again Surra growled, alert to the tension behind that quiet answer. Then the big cat padded soft-footed to the door.

"Someone's coming—" Storm stated the obvious. Surra was familiar with every living thing at the holding, human, animal, Norbie. She was waiting now for a stranger.

The dune cat's phenomenal hearing and her better than human nose had heralded the newcomers long before they reached the door, where Quade now stood in the cool gloom of very early morning to welcome them. A path of light from the window picked out the green tunic of a Peace Officer, and a moment later the visitor's hail came in Kelson's voice.

"Hallo—the holding!"

"The fire is waiting!" Brad Quade called back the customary answer.

Storm was not in the least surprised to see that Kelson's companion was Widders, who, in his finicky civ dress, looked even more out of place in the comfortable but rather rough-hewn main chamber. Its chief decorations were trophies of Norbie weapons on the walls, its heavy furnishings were made out of native wood by settler hands, and a few off-world mementos of Brad Quade's roving past as an officer of Survey were scattered around.

Widders crossed the threshold with an authoritative stride and then halted quickly as he fronted Surra. The big cat regarded him with a long, wide-eyed stare. Storm knew that she had not only imprinted the civ's appearance on her memory for all time but had also made up her mind concerning him, and that her opinion was not in any way flattering to the off-world Gentle Homo. Majestically, she moved to the far side of the room and leaped to the low couch, which was her own particular seat. But she did not curl up at ease; instead she sat upright, the nervous tip of her fluffy fox tail just brushing her foretoes, her vulpine ears at attention.

Storm busied himself at the heating unit to produce the inevitable cups of swankee. His early tension was increased now. Kelson had brought Widders here. That meant that neither the off-worlder nor the officer had given up the wild scheme about the Blue, but Quade's word would carry weight. Hosteen did not believe that the others were going to be satisfied with the outcome of the interview.

"Glad you came," Quade said to Kelson. "We've a problem here—"

"I have a problem, Gentle Homo," Widders cut in. "I understand you have a son who knows the outback regions very well, has hunted over them. I'd like to see him—as soon as possible—"

Quade's face showed no signs of a frown, but just as Hosteen knew Surra's emotions, he was aware of the flick of temper that brash beginning aroused in Brad Quade.

"I have two sons," the settler replied deliberately, "both of whom can claim a rather extensive knowledge of the Peaks. Hosteen has already told me of your wish to enter the Blue."

"And he has refused to try it." Widders was smoldering under his shell. He was not a man used to, or able to accept, opposition.

"If he had agreed, he would need remedial attention from a conditioner," Quade returned dryly. "Kelson, you know the utter folly of such a plan."

The Peace Officer was staring into the container of swankee he held. "Yes, I know all the risks, Brad. But we have to get in there—it's imperative! And chiefs such as Krotag will accept a mission like this as an excuse—they can understand a father in search of his son."

So that was it—a big piece of puzzle slipped neatly into place. Hosteen began to realize that Kelson was making sense after all. There was a reason for exploring the Blue, an imperative reason. And Widders' quest would be understandable to the Norbies, among whom family and clan ties were close. A father in search of his missing son—yes, that could be a talking point, which normally would gain Widders native guides, mounts, maybe even the use of some of the hidden water sources. But the important word in that was "normally." This was not a normal Big Dry, and the clans were acting very abnormally.

"Logan has blood drink-brothers or a brother with Krotag's clan, hasn't he?" Kelson pushed on. "And you"—he looked to Hosteen—"are a hunt and war companion of Gorgol."

"Gorgol's gone."

"And so has Logan," Quade added. "He rode off five days ago to join Krotag's drift—"

"Into the Blue!" Kelson exclaimed.

"I don't know."

"The Zamle clan were in the First Finger." Kelson put down his drink and went to the wall map. "They were in camp here last time I checked." He stabbed a forefinger on one of the long, narrow canyons striking up into the Peaks, almost a roadway into the Blue.

Storm moved uneasily, picked up a wandering meercat kit, and held it cupped against his chest, where it patted him with small forepaws and chittered drowsily. Logan had gone with the clan. The reasons for doing it might matter, but the fact that he had gone mattered more. The boy might be condemned by his own recklessness, facing more than just the perils of the Big Dry.

Continuing to stare at the map without really seeing its configurations, Hosteen began to plan. Rain—no, he could not ride Rain. The stallion was an off-world import without even one year's seasoning here. He'd need native-bred mounts—two at least, though four would be better. A man had to keep changing horses in the Big Dry. He'd need two pack animals per man for water transport. Other supplies would necessarily be concentrates that did not satisfy a body used to normal food but which provided the necessary energy to keep men going for days.

Surra? Hosteen's head turned ever so slightly; he linked to the cat in mental contact. Yes—Surra. There was an answering thrust of eagerness that met his wordless question. Surra—Baku—Hing had her maternal duties here, and there would be no need for her particular talents as a saboteur. With Baku and Surra, maybe no chance became a small chance. Their senses, so much keener than any human's or Norbie's, might locate those needful wells in the outback.

Now Quade broke the short silence with a question, deferring to his stepson with the respect for the other's training and ability he had always shown. "A chance?"

"I don't know—" Storm refused to be hurried. "Seasoned mounts, concentrates, water transport—"

"Supplies can be flown in by 'copter!" Widders pounced at the hint of possible victory.

"You'll have to have an experienced pilot, a fine machine, and even then you dare not go too far into those heights," Quade declared. "The air currents are crazy back there—"

"Dumps stationed along the line of march." Kelson's voice held a note almost as eager as Widders'. "We could plant those by 'copter—water, supplies—all the way through the foothills."

The idea became less impossible as each man visualized the possibilities of using off-world transportation in part. Yes, supply dumps could nurse an expedition along to the last barrier walling off the Blue, providing there was no hostile reaction from the Norbies. But beyond that barrier, much would depend upon the nature of the territory the heights guarded.

"How soon can you start?" Widders demanded. "I can have supplies, an expert pilot, a 'copter ready to go in a day."

Again the antagonism Hosteen had felt at their first meeting awoke in the younger man.

"I have not yet decided whether I shall go," he replied coldly. " 'Asizi," he said, giving Quade the title of Navajo chieftainship and slipping into the common tongue of the Amerindian Tribal Council, "do you think this thing can be done?"

"With the favor of the Above Ones and the fortune of good medicine, there is a chance of success for a warrior. That is my true word—over the pipe," Quade answered in the same language.

"There is this." In basic, Storm again addressed both Widders and Kelson. "Let it be understood that I am undertaking this expecting trouble. On the trail, the decision is mine when there comes a time to say go forward or retreat."

Widders frowned and plucked at a pouted lower lip with thumb and forefinger. "You mean, you are to be in absolute command—to have all the right of judgment?"

"That is correct. It is my life I risk, and those of my team. Long ago I learned the folly of charging against too high odds. The decisions must be mine."

A hot glance from those coals that lay banked behind Widders' eyes told him of the civ's resentment.

"How many men do you want?" Kelson asked. "I can spare you two, maybe three from the Corps."

Storm shook his head. "Me alone, with Surra and Baku. I shall strike up the First Finger and try to locate Krotag's clan. With Logan—and Gorgol, if I am able to persuade him to join us—there will be enough. A small party, traveling light, that is the only way."

"But I am going!" Widders flared.

Hosteen answered that crisply. "You are off-world, not only off-world but not even trail-trained. I go *my* way or not at all!"

For a second or so it seemed that Widders would hold stubbornly to his determination to make one of the party. Then he shrugged when glances at Kelson and Quade told him they believed Hosteen was right.

"Well—how soon?"

"I must select range stock, make other preparations—two days—"

"Two days!" Widders snorted. "Very well. I am forced to accept your decision."

But Storm was no longer aware of him. Surra had flowed past the men to the door, and the urgency she broadcast brought the Beast Master after her. Dawn was just firing the sky but had not lit the mountains to a point where man and cat could not see that burst. Very far away, just on the rim of the world, a jaffered sword thrust up into the heavens. Lightning—but it was out of season for lightning, and those flashes descended and did not pierce skyward as these had done. They were gone before Storm could be certain he had seen anything of consequence.

Surra snarled, spat. Then Hosteen caught it, too, not truly sound but a vibration in the air, so distant and faint as to puzzle a man as to its actual existence. Back in the Peaks something had happened.

The scream of an aroused and belligerent eagle deadened the small sounds of early morning. From her perch by the corral, Baku gave forth another war cry that was answered by the trumpeting of Rain, the squeals of other herd stallions, the neighing of mares. Whatever the vibration had been, it had reached the animals, aroused in them quick and violent reaction.

"What is it?" Quade came out behind Storm, followed by Kelson, less speedily by Widders.

"I think 'anna 'Hwii'iidzii," Storm found himself saying in Navajo without really knowing why, "a declaration of war, 'Asizi."

"And Logan's back there!" Quade stared at the Peaks. "That settles it—I ride with you."

"Not so, 'Asizi. It is as you have said before. This country is ripe for trouble. You alone perhaps can hold the peace. I take with me Baku. If there is a need, she can come back for you and others. Logan, more than any of us, is friend to the clans. And the blood-drink bond is binding past even a green-arrow feud."

He watched Quade anxiously. It was not in him to boast of his own qualifications, but he knew that his training and the control of the team gave him an advantage no other man now in the river valley had. Quade knew Arzor, he had hunted in the Peaks, but Quade and Quade alone could keep the settlers in line. To be caught between whatever danger lay in the Blue and a punitive posse headed by Dumaroy was an additional peril Storm had no mind to face. He had had a taste of Dumaroy's hotheaded bungling of a similar situation months earlier when the Xik holdout post had been the object of the settlers' attack.

Somehow Brad Quade summoned a ghost of a smile. "There is that in you which I trust, at least in this matter. Also—perhaps Logan will listen to hanaai, the elder brother, where he closes his ears to hataa, his father. Why this should be—" He was talking to himself now.

The horses were quieting, and the men went back to the house, where they consulted maps, located dump sites. At last Kelson and Widders bedded down for the day heat before flying back to Galwadi to set up the supply lift. Hosteen lay down wearily on his own bed only to discover that he could not sleep, tired as he was.

That flash in the Peaks, the ghost of sound or air disturbance that had followed it—he could not believe they were signs of some phenomenal weather disturbance. Yet what else could they be?

" 'Anaasazi"—the ancient enemy ones," he whispered.

Half a year ago, he, Gorgol, and Logan had found the Cavern of the Hundred Gardens, where the botanical treasures of as many different worlds grew luxuriantly and unwithered, untouched by time, just as the unknown aliens had left them in the hollow shell of a mountain ages earlier. There had been nothing horrible or repelling about those remains of the unknown civilization of space rovers. In fact, the gardens had been welcoming, enchanting, giving men healing and peace. And because of the gardens, the aliens had since been considered benevolent, though no further such finds had been made.

Archaelogists and Survey men had picked into the roundabout mountains, tried to learn something more from the valley of ruins beside the garden mountain—to no avail so far. However, one mountain had hidden beauty and delight, so more mountains might contain their own secrets. And the mountains of the Blue were the essence of the unknown. That strange premonition of danger that had awakened in Storm at the sight and sound of the early morning could not be eased. He was somehow very certain his goal was not a fanciful garden this time.

CHAPTER FOUR

esterday Hosteen had reached the first of the dumps, strategically located where a crevice gave him and his animals cover during the day. But he was not making the time he had hoped. In this broken country, even with Surra's keen eyesight and the horses' instinct to rely upon, he dared not travel too fast at night, and the early morning hours, those of the short dusk, were too few.

But so far, he had had tracks to follow. Trails left by the Norbies crossed and recrossed, made by more than one clan, until in some places he discovered a regular roadway. And he found indications that backed Dort Lancin's initial report—the natives were pushing onward at a pace that was perilous in this season. One could almost believe they ware being herded on into the hills by some relentless pursuer or pursuers.

There had been no recurrence of the phenomenon in the Peaks, and neither Surra nor Baku had given Storm any more than routine warnings. Yet the vague uneasiness was with Hosteen still as he picked his way along the dried stream bed that bottomed this gorge, his horses strung out with drooping heads.

An alert came from Surra. With a jerk of the lead rein, Hosteen brought the horses against the cliff wall and waited for another message from his furred scout before taking cover himself. Then he heard a trill, rising and falling like the breathy winds of the Wet Time. It was a Norbie signal—and, the Terran hoped. Shosonna. But his stunner was now in his hand to serve if he were wrong.

There—Surra had relaxed. The sentry or scout ahead was not a stranger to her. Hosteen believed that the native had not sighted the dune cat. Her fur was so close in color to the ground that she could be invisible if she wished it so.

Hosteen plodded forward once more, leading his horses, not wanting to ride in the thick heat until he had to. One more hour, maybe less, and he must hole up for the day. But, at a second alert from his feline scout, he swung up on the saddle pad. There was a dignity to be maintained between Norbie and outlander, and mounted man faced mounted native in equality, especially when there might be a point of bargaining ahead.

The Terran called. His voice echoed hollowly back from canyon walls, magnified and distorted until it could have been the united shout of a whole party. One of the wiry black-and-white-coated range horses from a Norbie cavvy came into view, and on it sat Gorgol. The Norbie rider did not advance. His face was expressionless. They might have been strangers meeting trailwise for the first time. Nor did the native's hands loose the reins preparatory to making finger talk. It was Hosteen who gave the first hand gesture.

"I seek Logan—this is a matter not to be denied."

Gorgol's vertical slits of pupils were on him, but he did not acknowledge Hosteen's message. When his rein hand moved, it was in a swift finger wriggle of rejection and denial.

"Logan is with the clan." Hosteen stated that as a fact.

"Logan is of the clan," Gorgol corrected, and so eased Hosteen's worries by a fraction. If the boy was "of the clan," his formal adoption was in force and he was not a prisoner.

"Logan is of the clan," Hosteen agreed. "But he is of the clan of Quade, also. And there is a clan matter he must be concerned with— a task to be done—"

"This is not the season for the herding of frawns or the gathering of horses," Gorgol countered. "The clan goes to the heights on a matter of medicine—"

"We also have our medicine, and no man denies his clan call. I must have speech with Logan on this matter. Would I have ridden into these hills in the Big Dry, I who cannot whistle up the water, were it not a matter of medicine?"

Gorgol was plainly impressed by the sense of that, but when

Hosteen would have ridden on, he urged his own mount crosswise to bar the path.

"This is clan talk. Krotag will decide. Until then—you wait."

There was no use in pushing further. Hosteen looked about him. The wait might last an hour—or a day. If he had to stay, he needed protection for the time when the sun would pour down, turning earth and rock into a baking oven. And Gorgol must have read his need, for now the Norbie pulled his mount around.

"Come," he signed. "There is a wait place ahead. But there you must stay."

"There I will stay," Hosteen agreed.

Gorgol's wait place surprised Hosteen. It was a camp site improved by the Norbies, a semipermanent structure of sorts compared to their usual skin-tent villages. Rocks and storm drift, carried along the canyon floor in the Wet Time floods, had been cobbled into an erection large enough to shelter most of a clan, the walls rising above the pit, which gave the coolness of the inner earth to those sweating out the furnace hot hours of the day. Hosteen found more than enough room for his horses, and soon Surra slipped in and Baku swooped down to pick a temporary perch. Hosteen shared out the water and provisions he had renewed at the dump. If he held to the trail marked for him, he would be able to stock up again in two days. But dealing with the clans might throw off his schedule.

He lay on his back on the cool earth and went over their nebulous plans for the hundredth time. Not only would the 'copter lay down dumps ahead, but it should be waiting at their last rendezvous this side of the Peaks to be used in primary exploration for a way through the mountain barrier—providing the Norbies could not or would not guide an off-world party into the Blue.

After a while he must have slept, for he aroused with a start. Surra was pawing at his arm, giving the old signal from their days in the field. She was alerting, not warning, and he expected Gorgol. But the Norbie who dropped down into the shelter was a youngster not yet wearing a hunter's trophy.

"Yuntzil!" Hosteen turned up both thumbs in the warrior's

greeting. Gorgol's younger brother was manifestly pleased by this gesture from one wearing warrior's scars, even though of an alien race.

"I see you, one with honorable scars," the boy's slim fingers flashed in the last light of dusk. "I come bearing the signs of Krotag. The Feathered One says: 'There is a time of medicine in the hills, and the fires of friendship burn low. If the brother of our brother rides here, he does so knowing that medicine is a chancy thing and may rend the unbeliever, even as it holds the bow of defense before the believer—'"

A warning, but not an outright refusal to allow him to proceed. Hosteen had that much. He stretched his hands into the funnel of light from the doorway so that Yuntzil would have no difficulty in reading the signs he made slowly and with care.

"This one is no unbeliever. To each man his own medicine and the wisdom not to belittle the belief of another. I do not ride under Krotag's medicine, but I have my own." He had taken the precaution that morning before his meeting with Gorgol to put on the heavy turquoise and silver necklace that was part of his inheritance from the past. On their first quest together, when they had faced the Xiks, he had worn that as well as the ketoh bracelet, and he knew that the Norbies now considered both ancient ornaments as talismans of power.

"If the brother of our brother believes, then let him come. He may speak with Krotag."

So they rode through the dusk. But Yuntzil did not keep to the main canyon Hosteen had chosen as the straightest route through the foothills. Perhaps a mile beyond the shelter, he turned abruptly to the left, passed behind an outcrop chimney, and brought the Terran into a narrower way. Surra stayed with Hosteen since the Norbie's mount showed fear of the cat. But Baku was aloft again, and from the eagle Hosteen gained the information that an encampment was not too far ahead.

Silently he thought out his message. To keep the eagle out of sight of any prowling scout, as a set of eyes in reserve, was only a sensible precaution. And he also knew that if and when he gave the order, Surra would melt into the shadows behind them, to be an unseen prowler he would defy any native to locate. She had proved many times in the past that her mutant feline senses were superior to those of any creature, man or animal, that Arzor possessed.

"Now!" As unspoken as his order to Baku, the Terran instructed the dune cat.

The dusk was thick, bringing its coolness after the enervating fire of the day. But ahead was a splotch of light—the camp. Hosteen followed Yuntzil, riding easily. All the horses had been watered before they left the clan shelter, but they quickened their pace, suggesting the necessary liquid was waiting ahead—one of the famous hidden springs, perhaps.

The tall, lean silhouettes of Norbie bodies moved between Hosteen and the fire. He could sight no tent shelters. This might be a scout camp or a hunters' rendezvous, save that Yuntzil had given his invitation in the name of the chief. The young Norbie dismounted, and now he waited, his hand outstretched for Hosteen's reins. If he had noted Surra's disappearance, he did not remark upon it.

Leaving his horses behind him, the Terran walked confidently into the full light of the fire, his sensitive nostrils twitching at the strong, almost unpleasant scent of the burning of bone-dry branches that had been packed from some distance to feed those flames. Falwood, sacred to medicine talks, did not grow in the mountains.

"Hosteen!" A smaller figure separated itself from the tall natives. Like them, he wore the high boots of yoris hide, still attached scales glittering in the greenish light. A wide band of the same hide, this time descaled and softened, made a corselet, covering his body from arm pit to crotch, and over that was the second belt of a warrior from which was suspended the twenty-inch knife of an accepted clansman. Logan had finished off his native dress with the customary yoris-fang collar, which extended from shoulder point to shoulder point and dipped down to belt length across his chest. Above it, his red-brown skin, many shades darker than that of the Norbies, glistened with a sweaty sheen. His head was uncovered, the hair held back from his face by a scarlet band. He was a barbaric figure, somehow more so than the natives about him.

Sighting him free and at ease in the Norbies' camp. Hosteen felt his anxiety and tension crystallize into irritation. He noted the shade of defiance on his half-brother's face, guessed that Logan thought the Terran had come to take him home.

Making no answer to Logan, looking beyond him to the waiting warriors, Hosteen held his hands well into the light of the fire and talked with the deliberate, fully rounded gestures of an envoy.

"There is one who is as the Zamle, whose arrows have drunk blood and their points then been powdered into nothingness many times over, who has hunted the yoris in its den and the evil flyer of the heights, alone, with only the strength of his hands and his medicine. I would speak with that one who stands among you wearing in this life the name of Krotag, leader of warriors, guardian of hunters."

A Norbie moved. The rich beading of his belt glittered more brightly than his scaled leg coverings. His horns, not the ivory-white of the others, were ringed with red.

"There is one named Krotag in this life," his hands acknowledged. "Here he stands. What is wanted of him?"

"Aid." Hosteen's one word answer was, he hoped, enough to intrigue the Norbie's curiosity.

"What manner of aid, man from the river country? You have entered these hills not at our bidding but of your own will. This is a time when those of our blood are to be busied with hidden things. You were warned that this was so—yet still you have come. And now you ask aid. Again I say, what manner of aid?"

"The manner of aid that those of the clans will understand, for this also is a kind they have rendered many times in the past among themselves and to others. Lost in these hills of yours is a stranger—"

Hosteen saw Logan start, but he paid no attention to that reaction.

"Here stand only those of the Zamle feather—and you. We have heard of no stranger lost. In the Big Dry who goes into the heart of the fire?"

"Well asked." Hosteen caught that up. "Who goes into the heart of the fire? Many ask that now—naming clans and tribes!"

Krotag's hands were still. None of the warriors behind him moved. Hosteen wondered if that frankness had been a mistake. But he knew that his motives would be judged by the openness of his speech at this meeting, and totally to ignore the unnatural exodus into the mountains on the part of the clans would be a faulty beginning.

"There are secret things belonging to our people, just as there are secret things that are yours," Krotag signed.

"That is the truth. A man's medicine is his own concern. But it is not of medicine I have come here to speak. It is of an off-world stranger who is lost—"

"Again we say—no such stranger has been spoken of." Krotag's finger exercises were emphatic.

"Not here, not even in the Peaks—"

"Yet you head into this country. Why, since you say that the man you seek is not here?"

"The Peaks are thus." Hosteen made a cup of his left hand; the forefinger of his right ran about the outer ridge of that cup in one swift sweep. "Beyond there is other country—"

It was as if he had brought out of hiding some potent "medicine" of his own, medicine embodied with the power of turning Norbies into pillars of stone as rigid as the canyon walls about them.

"This is the story." The Terran broke into the heart of Widders' tale, refusing to be daunted by the rigid and now unfriendly regard of the natives. With an economy of gesture he told of the reputed landing of the LB, the possible survival of some of those on board. And as he moved his fingers in the complex patterns demanded by that exposition, Hosteen was aware of a change in his audience, a relaxation of tension. They were absorbed in what he had to say, and they believed him. But whether they were willing to give him passage into the Blue on the strength of this was another matter and one, he thought, that would not be settled speedily. He was right about that, for when he had done, Krotag replied.

"This is something to be thought on, brother of our brother. The fire is yours." He stepped aside, his men following his example, leaving a clear passage to the strong-smelling smoke and flames.

Hosteen completed the hospitality ritual, walking on, as he held his breath against gusts of nose-tickling smoke, to take his stand within the circle of heat that was pleasant as a symbol but uncomfortable in fact. When he glanced around, the natives had vanished.

Only Logan stood there, watching him levelly with suspicion of hostility.

"You're sharp on the count-off with all this," he commented.

"If you mean this is a piece of fiction designed to get you back, you're off orbit course," Hosteen replied tersely. "It's all true. Widders' men are ~~not~~ *out* now planting supply dumps through the Peaks. He's oath-sure his son is back in the Blue—"

"You aren't goin' to be allowed in there, you know."

Hosteen shook his head. "I don't know, nor do you. They were going to take you with them, weren't they?"

Rather to his surprise Logan shook his head. "I don't know. I only hoped."

"What's going on? Have you any idea?"

"Something that has never happened before and that breaks straight through tribal custom. Hosteen, when you went in with the archaeologist to explore those valley ruins, didn't he have a medicine man for a guide, a Norbie who said that the Old Ones wanted their secrets to be revealed now?"

"Yes. Nothing came of it, though. Those Xik holdouts got the medicine man the same time they wiped out our camp after the big flood."

"But a secret was revealed—we found the Cavern of the Hundred Gardens. Well, the word's out now that the Old Ones are callin' in the clans, plannin' something big. The Norbies have sent out peace poles; every feud has been buried. And the cause is somewhere back in the Blue. But the whole thing is 'medicine.' Let our authorities in, and they will blow it and the tribes wide open. A wrong move now could set every Norbie against us. We'll have to walk small and quiet until we are sure of what we're facin'. I thought Krotag might take me in so I could learn somethin'. I know what those Norbie haters such as Dumaroy could do with a chance to botch up a 'medicine' talk—"

"Which is exactly why 'Asizi is sitting on the blast pin down in the valley now. Didn't think of talking this over with him before you blew, did you?"

Logan flushed. "I know—I know—You think I should have done that. But it doesn't work out—we'd have talked and then maybe argued. We don't think in the same paths. Brad Quade—he's a big man—the kind of man the valley people need. Me—I'm a wild one—I can't want just the holding and building up the herd and being my father's son! Maybe it was the same with Father when he was young. He signed up with Survey, didn't he, and went all over the star lanes? Well, when I was old enough to try somethin' like that, there was the war on—no Survey, and they said I was too young for the Service. So I took to goin' with the Norbies. Sometimes it seems as if they're more my kind than people like Jaffe or Starle.

"Then—well, I guess. I counted too big on that plan of Kelson's for a Ranger force. He promised me the first enlistment in that. It fell through—just like we thought it might. So, maybe I was sore about that. Anyway, I went back to huntin' with the clans—that's how I heard about this.

"And it blew up so suddenly that I knew I didn't dare wait and get in a chew-over about it. I had to ride with the clan then or not at all. The river valley—there's too much talkin' there and not enough doin'! This time I know I was in the right!"

Hosteen shrugged. Argument now was wasted time, and he could understand Logan's frustration. As the younger boy had the wit to see, the inherited strain that had taken Brad Quade into space in his own youth was now working in his son. "I will agree that you did as you thought best. I'm here not about that but for Widders—"

"And to do some nose-pokin' for Kelson—"

"If I make a report to Kelson, that is no more than you were going to do. Think straight, ach'ooni." Deliberately he used the word for brother-friend. "We both know that this situation may hold the seeds of trouble, not only for the settlers but also for the clans. Before, we faced the Xik, and this may be something of the same again. To search for a missing man in the hills is an excuse that the Norbies may accept."

"All right. I'll back you."

"And join me?"

For a moment Logan hesitated. "If they do not turn you back here and now—"

They sat down away from the fire and somewhat ceremoniously shared a drink from Hosteen's canteen, action that would express their present accord to any watching clansmen. As Hosteen rescrewed the cap, Krotag stalked toward them.

"We have thought on this matter of your search." His fingers worked in sharp jerks. "For the time, you ride with us—until we may consult with 'medicine.'"

"As Krotag wishes." Hosteen bowed his head formally and then eyed the chief with a straightness that demanded equality. "As I accede, do you also when the times comes—"

Krotag did not reply. Two youths were throwing sand on the flames. The rest of the men were bringing up their mounts, preparing to ride out.

CHAPTER FIVE

Hosteen smeared the back of his hand across his chin and winced as the cracked and tender skin of his lips reacted to that half-unconscious action. He had given the major portion of his water to the animals, and he had not asked the natives for any of their dwindling supply. Unless within the hour he could strike across the country to the waiting dump, he would be in real trouble. Whether this was a carefully planned move of discouragement on Krotag's part, he did not know, but his suspicions of that were growing. He had no doubts of reaching the cache—Baku's aerial survey would guide him—but soon his mounts would be past rough travel. And trail-tough though he was, Hosteen doubted if a man on foot could make that journey.

Well, there was no use delaying the test any longer. He sent his range horse up along the line of march, past Norbie warriors to Krotag. In the fore he matched pace with the native chief.

"There comes a time for the parting of trails." Hosteen addressed Krotag with outer assurance. "He who does not whistle water must seek it elsewhere."

"You do not ask it of those who know?"

"In the Big Dry who asks water of friends? It is then more precious than blood. He who sent me to find his son has also sent water—lifting it ahead through the air."

Would Hosteen's policy of the complete truth defeat him now? The air travel of the settlers was unquestioned in the lowlands, tolerated in certain higher districts. But from the first, only one space port had been conceded by the Norbie, who argued that Those-Who-Drum-Thunder in the mountains must not be looked down on from the air. And perhaps a 'copter in these hills would be resented, especially now.

The Terran could read no emotion on the Norbie chieftain's face, though those eyes continued to study him for a long moment. Then fingers moved.

"Where lies this water brought through the sky?"

Following native custom, Hosteen pointed with his chin to a line lying southeast of their present track. Krotag spoke over his shoulder, the shrill twittering bringing out of line and cantering ahead two warriors, followed by Logan.

"No one may deny water when it can be found." Krotag repeated the first law of his people. "But this is country in which the wild ones roam, and you have many horses. So it is wise that you do not ride alone. These shall be added bows." With a thumb jerk he indicated the measure of security in Krotag's choice. Both were familiar natives.

Gorgol and his own son Kavok—Hosteen felt a small measure of security in Krotag's choice. Both were familiar with settler ways, had ridden for Quade. Once he had thought that he was on a basis of friendship with Gorgol, though the happenings of the past days had made the Terran more wary of claiming any sure standing with the young warrior.

Logan crowded his mount forward. "I would ride, too."

Again Krotag appeared to consider the point before he gave assent. Then the native line plodded on in the evening dusk just as they had ridden through the two nights since Hosteen had joined them, while he drew aside his horses, the extra mounts and the pack mares. Surra, responding to his suggestion, was already ranging along the side gully they must use to cut back to the wider canyon up which Quade and he had planned his entrance into the Blue.

The overland trail was rough, and at night they had to take it slowly. Logan rode beside Hosteen.

"How far are we from this dump?"

"I don't know—maybe a day. Depends upon the angle of the split when I joined the clansmen."

"We'll have to hole up in the day—"

That was what had been plaguing Hosteen as the hours crawled by. He searched all the latter part of the night for some feature of the countryside that could be adapted for a sun shelter, and he was not alone in that search, for Gorgol and Kavok rode with the width of the gorge between them, as if looking for some landmark.

There was a twittering call from Kavok, which, though they could not understand its import, brought the settlers to him. The young Norbie had dismounted and was down on one knee, running his hand along what looked to Hosteen to be undisturbed surface soil. Then he walked ahead, leading his horse, as if he followed some very faint trail.

They came away from the main cut they had taken into a side ravine, which slanted sharply upward. Kavok went down on his knees once more and dug into the side of the ravine with his long hunting knife, an occupation in which Gorgol speedily joined him, leaving Hosteen and Logan completely mystified.

Surra flowed down the side of the cut. She stopped short a yard or so away from the hole the two Norbies had already excavated, and nose wrinkled, she growled deep in her throat. Gorgol glanced over his shoulder, sighted the cat, and touched Kavok, nodding from Surra to the excavation. Hosteen caught the sudden surge of hunting interest from the feline mind. Beyond the flying knives, the busy hands of the natives, there was something alive, and that quarry was attracting all Surra's feral love of the chase and the kill.

The earth under the scraping hands of the Norbies suddenly caved in, and both of them jerked back as a hole appeared, growing wider as if they had laid bare an underground chasm. Their knives were still at ready, but not to dig, rather to defend themselves against attack. Hosteen, warned by their attitude, drew his stunner. Gorgol flung out a hand in a gesture of waiting.

Surra, her belly fur brushing loose earth, the tip of her tail twitching with anticipation, crept forward with feline caution, her broad paws placed and then lifted in succession with the precision of the stalking huntress.

The Norbies gave her room, and Hosteen lost mind touch. Now the big cat was all hunting machine, not to be turned from the chase. She would answer to no order or suggestion while in this state. Her furred head, fox-sharp ears pricked, hung out over the opening.

Then, as if she were melting into the loose sand and earth, she was gone, down into the unseen pit the Norbies had opened.

Gorgol squatted back on his haunches, and Hosteen caught at his shoulder in a tight and demanding grip.

"What lies below?" the Terran demanded.

"Djimbut pit!" Logan replied before Gorgol could raise a hand to answer.

"Djimbut?" Hosteen repeated, unable to connect the word with anything he knew. Then he remembered a pelt of close-curled black fur, as beautiful in its way as the frawn hides, which served as a wall hanging back in Quade's Basin holding. But that had been the skin of a big beast—one close to Surra in size. Was the Terran cat about to attack such an animal in its own den?

He elbowed Gorgol aside and recklessly launched himself feet first into the hole, one hand holding the stunner close to his chest, the other fumbling for his atom torch as he slid into darkness.

Hosteen landed with a jar on a heap of sand and earth. He crouched there, listening for any sound, becoming more and more conscious of the coolness of this place. He even shivered slightly as he pushed the button of the torch and discovered that he was in the center of a hollowed area of some size.

As the Terran slued about on the sand pile, the narrow beam of the torch swept across a tunnel mouth large enough to give Surra passage or to accommodate a man on his hands and knees. Hosteen scrambled for that, again to crouch in its entrance listening.

Sounds came clearly enough—growl, rounding out into a spitting, yowling challenge that was the dune cat's. Then, in answer, a queer kind of hum ending in a series of coughing grunts, broken by what could only be sounds of battle, enjoined and fiercely fought. Somewhere beyond, that tunnel must widen into a passage or chamber big enough to provide a field for a desperate struggle. Hosteen was head and shoulders into the passage when the coughing grunts deepened into a weird moaning, which was clipped off short. And into his mind came the vivid impression of Surra's triumph, just as his ears caught a singsong rise and fall, which she uttered to proclaim her victory aloud.

Three yards, a little more, and he was in another chamber. Here the smell of blood combined with a thick, musky scent. His light beam caught Surra kneading with her forepaws a rent and blood-sticky heap of fur, her eyes yellow balls of nonhuman joy when the light caught them. She sat upright as Hosteen knelt beside her, tonguing herself where a long red scratch ran across her shoulder. But her battle hurts were few and ones she herself would tend.

The Terran flashed his light about to discover a series of openings in the walls, and his nostrils took in not only the hot blood scent and the odor of the dead animal but also other smells issuing from some of those holes. The place was large—whether the result of the djimbut's burrowing or because the animal had located and used some natural fault in the earth, he was not sure. But he was able to get to his feet and stand with the roof of the chamber still well above his head. And the space, apart from the other openings, was at least ten by twenty feet, he estimated.

Surra gave a last lick to her wound scratch and then hunkered down to sniff along the battered body on the floor, growling and favoring the corpse with a last vindictive slap of forepaw. Hosteen centered the torch on the black bundle. The dead creature was as large as Surra, perhaps a fraction bigger, the chunky body equipped with four legs, which were short and clawed, the talons on the forelimbs being great sickle-shaped armaments he would not have wanted to face. But the head was the alien feature as far as the Terran was concerned. The skull was rounded without visible ears. In fact, as he leaned forward to inspect it more closely, Hosteen had difficulty in identifying eyes—until he glimpsed a round white bulb half concealed by thick curls of fur. The lower part of that head—the mouth and jaws—was broad and flat, tapering into a thin wedge at the outmost point, as if the creature had been fitted by nature with a tooth-rimmed chisel for a mouth.

"Djimbut all right." Logan made a hands and knees progress into the big chamber. "Surra did for him—good girl."

Those yellow eyes half closed as the dune cat looked at Logan. Then a rumble of a purr answered his frank praise.

"We're in luck," Logan continued. "Got us about the best waitout anyone could find in these hills—"

And that had been the reason for the action Hosteen discovered.

The lair of the djimbut was not just the tunnel and its two connected chambers. It was also a series of storerooms opening off the big room, an underground dwelling so constructed as to be heatproof even when they had to wreck most of the protected opening to get the horses under cover.

The damp chill faded, but the men and the Norbies quartered in the storerooms and the horses in the main chamber had a hideout from the sun that was the best protection Hosteen had found since he left the outer valley. And the seeds and roots stored up were sorted over by the natives, a selection given to and relished by their mounts and the rest taken over by their riders.

Hosteen chewed at a yellow-green pod. The flint surface splintered, giving him a mouthful of pulp, which had refreshing moisture. Gleams of sun reached them through the broken walls, but they were well out of its full heat, and they dozed off for the day.

The Terran did not know just what brought him awake with the old, instant awareness of his Service days. His head, resting on earth, might have picked up the vibration of a distant tread. He levered himself up in the cubby he shared with Logan, hearing the restless movements of the horses. A mind cast for Surra told him that the cat was either not in range or deliberately refusing to answer. But the patches of sky he could see were those of early evening. And somewhere beyond, there were riders approaching.

Hosteen's hand went out to cover Logan's mouth as the younger settler slept on his back, bringing him to silent wakefulness. In answer to the question in the other's eyes, the Terran motioned to the outer chamber.

Together they crawled out among the horses to discover Gorgol before them, his hand gripping the nose of his own mount to discourage any welcoming nicker. That told Hosteen what he wanted to know. With his free hand he signed, "Enemy?" and was answered by a vigorous assent from the Shosonna.

They were certainly not in any good position to meet an attack. To get the horses up out of the burrow again was a difficult task at best, and to be jumped while so employed—Hosteen made a mind cast for Surra. He was sure the cat had already left the djimbut burrow. Baku must have flown on to the cache and be waiting there for them. She had not returned the evening before, and her wings made her free from the toilsome march the rest must take. But with Surra one part of the team was still in reach.

"Who—?" He turned to Gorgol for enlightenment.

"Wild ones."

"The peace poles are up," Logan's hands protested.

Gorgol tossed his head in the equivalent of a human shrug.

"These may be far-back ones—they want horses."

The Shosonna and other lowland tribes had their own methods of recruiting their studs. Their young men hiring out as herd riders, their yoris hunters, could trade for the horses they wanted to build up clan herds. For the wild Norbies of the high country, envious of their fellows but fearful of venturing down to contact the settlers, there was another way of acquiring the wonder animals to which the Arzoran native-born had taken with the same ease and fierce joy that Hosteen's own Amerindian ancestors had welcomed the species when the Europeans introduced them to the western continental plains. The wild ones were horse thieves of constantly increasing skill.

And to such thieves, the trail of this party must have been a heady inducement. Any experienced tracker crossing their traces would know that four riders had a total of nine horses with them, counting the pack horses and extra mounts—a windfall not even the raising of a peace pole could save. And here the enemy could simply wait them out with lack of water as the lever to pry them from their refuge.

Which left only Surra. Hosteen said as much, and Gorgol twittered to Kavok before he signed:

"The furred one is not here. Kavok saw her go when the sun was still a sky bead. Perhaps she is beyond your call—"

Hosteen leaned against the now crumbling wall of the burrow, closed his eyes, and threw all his strength and energy into one long call, noiseless, quick, and, he hoped, far reaching enough to touch minds with the cat.

With the snap of one pressing an activating button on a com and receiving an answer, he made the break-through. There were the few moments of seeming to see the world slightly askew and weirdly different—which told him that they had made contact. Then he gave his instructions and had agreement from Surra. Distance meant little to her, and her form of reckoning was not that of a man. He could not tell how far she now was from the wrecked burrow nor how long it would take her to track down the enemy, waiting out there, and deliver the counterstroke that could mean the difference between life and death for those underground. But before she went into action, she would report.

"Surra is movin' in?" Logan asked in a half whisper.

Hosteen nodded. The strain of making that contact was still on him. Gorgol's head was up, his finely cut nostrils expanded.

"They are all about us," he reported.

"How many?" Hosteen demanded.

The smooth head, its ivory horns seeming to gleam in the gathering twilight, swung in a slow side-to-side motion before the Norbie answered:

"Four—five—" He flicked one finger after another as he located the raiders with his own kind of built-in radar. "Six—"

That finger count reached ten before it stopped. Cramped as they were in this earth bottle, those odds seemed impossible. Kavok had no arm room to use his bow. And while Logan and Hosteen had stunners and Gorgol another that had been Hosteen's gift on their first war path months earlier, the weapon of the settlers was a defensive device for which one had to see a good target.

Surra was ready!

Hosteen signed a warning. Kavok had dropped his useless bow, drawn his knife. Leaving the horses, they pushed to the foot of the improvised ramp down which they had brought those animals in the early morning.

"Now!" Hosteen's lips writhed in an exaggerated movement that he knew Gorgol would recognize at the time his order flashed to the waiting cat.

Surra's shrill, ear-splitting scream tore the air. In answer came the terrified neighing of horses, not only from behind but also from the opening ahead. They heard the drum of racing hoofs and the high twittering of Norbie cries.

Hosteen broke for the ramp. Outside, he rolled behind a rock, then pulled himself up to survey the ravine. Surra yowled again, and he saw a figure with blue-dyed horns stand recklessly out in the open fitting arrow to bow cord. The Terran thumbed his stunner button and beamed the narrow ray for the skull wearing those blue horns. The Norbie wilted to the ground in a lank fold-up of long, thin arms and legs.

Another broke from cover, thrusting into the open, his head turned on his shoulders, his whole body expressing his terror as Surra's head and forequarters rose into view. The cat ducked back into cover as Hosteen fired again. Surra was doing her part—driving the wild tribesmen into the waiting fire like the expert she was in this form of warfare.

CHAPTER SIX

orgol stooped above one of the still Norbies and lifted the head from the gravel by a painted horn.

"Nitra," he identified.

Kavok thrust a booted toe under another of the attackers and rolled him over.

"They still live—" he commented, fingering his knife as he surveyed the limp body, his thoughts as plain as if he had shouted them aloud in Galactic basic.

Warrior trophies were warrior trophies. On the other hand, these unconscious enemies, now flat on sand and gravel or looped over the rocks where they had been stun-rayed as they tried to evade Surra, were by custom the property of those who had brought them down. Hosteen, Logan, and Gorgol had the sole right to collect horn tips to display at a Shosonna triumph drumming.

"Let them remain so," Hosteen signed to both Norbies. "The peace poles are up. If the Nitra break the laws of Those-Who-Drum-Thunder, do the Shosonna also work evil?"

Kavok thrust his knife back into its sheath. "What then do we? Leave these to recover from your medicine fire so that they may trail us to try again?"

"The cool of night will be gone and the sun rising before they wake from their sleep," the Terran answered. "And we take their horses. They must make day refuge in the burrow or die. I do not think they will try to follow us."

"That is true," Gorgol agreed. "And also it is right that we do not break the peace. Let us be on our way that we may find your water place before *we* greet the sun."

The mounts of the Nitra had been prevented from bolting by

Surra's presence down canyon. Now, sweating and rolling their eyes fearfully, they were caught and fastened to the horses of Hosteen's pack train. And the party was well on its way across country, leaving its late opponents slumbering by the ruins of the djimbut burrow, before the night had completely closed in.

In the false dawn they came upon Widders' dump, where a section of the far tip of Finger Canyon widened out. The Norbies whistled in surprise, for they fronted a bubble tent of plastaglau, its blue-gray surface opaque and heat-resistant. From a rock beyond, Baku took off to fly to Hosteen. There was no other sign of life there.

Logan glowered at the off-world mushroom squatting arrogantly on Arzoran earth.

"So—what does this civ think we are? Pampered pets from the inner worlds?"

The Terran shrugged. "What he thinks does not matter—it may be that he considers this to be necessary shelter. What he brings is more important—we need those supplies."

But he, too, was startled by that tent, unwanted and unreal in its present setting. It gave the appearance of more than just a dump, though their plans had not called for any base here.

"You say we ride for water—this is an off-world live place!" Kavok's protest came on snapping fingers. Hosteen disliked the hostility in that outburst. Widders had made just the stupid mistake that settlers on Arzor tried to avoid. Some off-world equipment and weapons the Norbies accepted as a matter of course. But a strange dwelling set down in the heart of their own territory without any agreement beforehand—that was an aggravation that, in the present precariously balanced state of affairs, might well send them all packing out of the Peaks—at the very best. Why Kelson had allowed Widders to commit this might-be-fatal mistake Hosteen could not understand.

He came up to the plasta-glau hemisphere and smacked his hand with more than necessary force against the close lock, taking out some of his irritation in that blow. There was a shimmer of fading forcefield, and he could see the small cubby of the heat lock open before him.

This thing imported from off-world must have cost a small fortune. To set up camp here did not make sense, and things that did not make sense were suspicious. Hosteen's foot pressure on the balfloor of the lock activated the forcefield, sealing him in before a second barrier went down, making him free of the interior.

Perhaps this was only a utility bubble, intended for what an inner-planet man would consider the most rustic living, Hosteen thought, for there was only one big room. The supplies he sought were piled in boxes and containers in its center. But around the slope-walled perimeter he saw fold beds—four of them!—a cook unit, a drink unit, and even a portable refresher! No, this could not have been intended as a one-day camp!

He persuaded the Norbies to enter, brought in the horses, and set up a line of supply boxes to mark off a temporary stable, since that was one need the designer of the bubble had apparently not foreseen. The quarters for settlers and natives were correspondingly cramped, but Hosteen knew they could weather the day now with more comfort than they had known even in the depths of the burrow.

Gorgol and Kavok examined their new housing with suspicion, gradually overcome by interest. They were already familiar with the conveniences of cook and drink units, and having seen Hosteen and Logan make use of the refresher, they tried it in turn.

"This is a fine thing," Kavok signed. "Why not for Norbie, too?" He looked inquiringly at the settlers, and Hosteen guessed the young native was trying to reckon in his mind the amount of trade goods it might take to purchase such a wonder for the clan.

"This be a fine thing—but see—" Hosteen opened the control box of the cook unit, displaying an intricate pattern of wiring. "Do this break, one man maybe in Galwadi, he could fix—maybe he could not. Some pieces might have to come from beyond the stars. Then what good is this?"

Kavok digested that and agreed. "No good. Many yoris skins, many frawn skins to be paid for this?"

"That is so. Quade, our blood-father" he made the sign for clan chief—"he is a man of many horses, many fine things from beyond the stars. That is so?"

"That is so," the Shosonna agreed.

"Yet, Quade, our blood-father, he could drive all his horses and half his frawn herd in the Peaks to the Port, and there he would have to give them all up for a place such as this, a place that, when it broke, no man could have mended without giving many more horses, many frawn hides—"

"Then this is not a good thing!" Kavok's reaction was quick and emphatic. "Why is this here now?"

"The off-world one who seeks his son, he is not used to the Big Dry, and he thinks that one cannot live—as perhaps he could not—without such a thing."

"He is truly an off-world child of little knowledge," was Kavok's comment.

Baku sidled along the edge of a box she had selected for a perch. Now she mantled, her wings a quarter spread, and gave a throaty call. Surra was already at the door.

"Company." Hosteen drew his stunner. But somehow he did not believe they were about to face another native raiding party. Baku's warning was of an air approach, and he expected a 'copter.

What he did not foresee as he strode out to the patch of ground already bearing the marks of several landings and take-offs, was the size of the flyer making an elevator descent there. The 'copters, used sparingly by the settlers because of the prohibitive cost of replacement parts and repairs, were able, at best, to hold three or four men crowded together, with a limited space for emergency supplies or very valuable cargo. The machine now agleam in the early-morning light was a sleek, expensive type such as Hosteen had never seen on any frontier world. And his estimation of Widders' wealth and influence went up again. To transport such a craft to Arzor must have cost a small fortune. No wonder that with such a carrier the civ had been able to send in a bubble tent and all the other trappings of a real safari.

Nor was the Terran too amazed to see Widders himself descend the folding ladder from the flyer's cockpit. He had at least changed his off-world clothing for more durable coveralls such as a pilot wore. And he had belted about his slight paunch an armory of gadgets such as Hosteen had not seen since he mustered out of the Service.

"So you finally got here!" Widders greeted him sourly. Glancing around, he added in a petulant spurt of words, "Where're all those horses you were sure we needed so badly?"

"In there." Hosteen nodded toward the tent and was amazed at the answering flood of dusky color on the other's craggy face.

"You—put—animals—in—my—tent!"

"I don't lose horses, not when our lives depend on them," the Terran retorted. "Nor would I sentence any living thing to a day in the sun during the Big Dry! Your pilot had better taxi over under that overhang if he wants to save this 'copter. At this hour you can not hope to get back to the nearest plains shelter—"

"I have no intention of returning to the plains region," Widders replied, and he meant that. Short of picking him up bodily, Hosteen realized, and putting him forcibly into the 'copter, there was no way of shipping him out—for now.

However, one day in the crowded and now rather stale-smelling interior of the tent might well induce the civ to reconsider his decision. There was no use wasting energy fighting a wordy battle now when time and nature might convince him. Hosteen relayed his warning to the pilot and left the civ to enter the tent by himself.

When he came in with the pilot, an ex-Survey man who held tightly to a position of neutrality, Hosteen walked into tension, though there were as yet no outwardly hostile gestures or words. Widders swung around to face the Terran, the dusky hue of his face changed to a livid fury.

"What is the meaning of this—this madhouse?"

"This is the Big Dry, and during the day you get under cover or you cook. I mean that literally." Hosteen did not raise his voice, but his words were delivered with force. "You can really bake to death out among those rocks. You wanted native guides—this is Kavok, son to Krotag, chief of the Zamle clan of the Shosonna, and Gorgol, a warrior of the same clan, also my brother, Logan Quade. I don't know any better help we can get for Peak exploration."

He watched the struggle mirrored on Widders' face. The man's natural arrogance had been affronted, but his necessary dependence on Hosteen prevailed. He loathed the situation, but for the moment there was nothing he could do to remedy it. His acceptance came, however, with poor grace.

The Norbies and the settlers luxuriated in the conditioned temperature of the bubble, but Hosteen wondered privately just how much overloading the conditioner could take. Widders probably had the best. But no one from off-world could possibly realize the demands of the Big Dry unless they experienced them firsthand.

"Storm!" He roused at that peremptory hail from the bunk Widders had chosen some hours earlier.

Stretching, Hosteen sat up and reached for his boots. He, Logan, and the pilot had taken the other bunks. The Norbies had chosen to use their rolled sleep mats on the floor.

"What is it?" he asked now, without too much interest in what he expected would be Widders' complaints, his mind more occupied with what Krotag might feel if he came upon this camp without explanation. They were only here on sufferance, and the Shosonna could well force them back into the lowlands.

"I want to know what plans you have made for getting us back into the Blue."

Hosteen stood up. Both Gorgol and Kavok were awake, their attention switching from Widders to the Terran and back again. Though the Norbies could not understand the words of the off-world men, they could, as Hosteen had learned in the past, often make surprisingly accurate guesses as to the subject of conversation.

"Plans? Gentle Homo, on an expedition such as this, you cannot make definite plans ahead. A situation may change quickly. So far, we are here—but even to remain here is in question." He went on to outline what they might fear from Krotag, making plain that the camp itself could arouse the ire of the natives. "So—it must be as we originally decided, Gentle Homo—you will return to the lowlands."

"No." Flat, nonequivocal. And again Hosteen understood that he might, with some expenditure of force, remove the civ from this camp, but he could not give the order to raise the 'copter and fly Widders back to the river lands. The pilot would not obey him. On the other hand, the Terran's best answer, to wash his hands of the matter completely and go back himself, was impossible, too. He could not leave Widders on his own here to cross the natives and perhaps provide the very reason for the trouble Quade and Kelson were laboring to avoid, that Logan had risked his life to stop. Widders sensed Hosteen's position, for he rapped out:

"Now—where do we go from this point, Storm?"

He unhooked a small box, one of the many items looped to that fantastic belt of his, and held it before him, thumbing a lever on its side.

On the wall of the bubble tent appeared a map of this region of the Peaks, containing all the settlers knew of the country. Hosteen caught a twittering exclamation from Kavok, saw Gorgol eye the lines. The latter had some map lore gathered as a rider.

Time—Hosteen decided—was the factor now. Even if Krotag ordered them out, the chief had yet to reach them to do so. The Terran addressed the pilot.

"How well is the 'copter shielded? Can you take it up before sundown?"

"Why?" demanded Widders. "We have a direct find on board."

A direct find! Now how had Widders managed to have such an installation released to him? So far as Hosteen knew, those were service issue only. But that machine, which would center on any object within a certain radius, did cut down the element of time loss in search to a high degree.

"Can you take off before sundown?" Hosteen persisted. It was not the possible loss of time in sweeping an unfamiliar territory in search of the LB wreck that worried him now—but how long they might have before Krotag or other Norbies sighted this camp.

"We're shielded to the twelfth degree." That admission came with visible reluctance from the pilot. Hosteen did not blame him. Flying in a twelve-degree shield was close to the edge of acute discomfort. But that was his problem, and he could refuse if he wanted to—let Widders and his hired fly-boy fight it out between them.

"What's all this about shielding?" Widders broke in.

Hosteen explained. If the 'copter was shielded so that the pilot dared to take off before dusk, then they could make one flight over the edge of the Blue at once, before the coming of any Norbies. Widders grabbed at the chance.

"We *can* lift now?" He rounded on Forgee, the pilot.

"*We?*" repeated Hosteen. "Do you propose to go also, Gentle Homo?"

"I do." Again that adamant refusal to consider anything else expressed in every line of his face and body. Widders set the map broadcaster down on a supply box and advanced, to thrust a forefinger violently into the picture so that the shadow of his hand blotted out a fourth of the territory. "Right here—your officials have pinpointed the LB broadcast as best they could."

Gorgol scrambled to his feet, his twittering squeaked high. Momentarily, the Norbie had foresaken finger speech to register angry protest in his native tongue. Then, as if he recollected the limitations of the off-worlders, he flexed his fingers before him and began a series of gestures so swift and intricate that Hosteen had difficulty in reading them.

"This off-world man wishes to go *there*? But that is not for strangers—it is medicine—the medicine of those who eat THE MEAT—This cannot be done!"

"What does he say?" Widders demanded.

"That that is cannibal territory and dangerous—" But Hosteen was certain Gorgol feared more than cannibals.

"We knew all that before we came." Widders was contemptuous. "Does he think his cannibals can bring a 'copter down by bows and arrows?"

Forgee stirred. "Look here, Gentle Homo, this Blue is tricky. Air currents in there have never been charted. And what we do know about them is enough to make a man think twice about trying to get very far in."

"We have every safety device built into that flyer that human ingenuity can or has devised," Widders flared, "including quite a few that never reached this back-water world before. Come—let's take off and see for ourselves what this Blue is like."

Kavok half crouched by the doorway. His knife was out and ready in his hand, his enmity so openly displayed that Hosteen was startled.

"What—?" The Terran's hand sign was addressed to Gorgol, and the Norbie replied, less swiftly, with the attitude of one pushed into a corner.

"Medicine—big medicine. The off-worlder cannot go there. If he tries, he will die."

"That answers it." For the first time Logan entered the conversation. "Gorgol says that is medicine country—you can't fly over it now."

Widders' contempt was plain as he raked Logan from head to foot in one long stare of measurement and dismissal, assessing the other's Norbie dress and rating him low because of wearing it. Under that stare Logan flushed angrily, but when he moved, it was to stand beside Kavok by the door, his hand hovering over the butt of his stunner.

"That is true." Hosteen spoke carefully, his position now, he thought, that of a very thin and breakable wall between two male yoris at mating season. "There is no arguing with 'medicine.' If the Norbies have declared that country out of bounds for such a reason, we *are* stopped."

He had never underrated Widders' determination and self-confidence, he had only underrated the man's recourse to action. Widders did not go for his stunner, a move that would have alerted them. Instead he snapped a small pellet to the floor of the tent at a point midway between Hosteen and Gorgol and the two now guarding the door. A flash of light answered—then nothing, nothing at all.

CHAPTER SEVEN

"Calling District Station Peaks—come in—D.S. Peaks—come in!"

There was a frantic note in that repetition that reached Hosteen through the fog in his head. He was also aware of moisture on his cheek and the rasp of a rough tongue. He opened his eyes to discover Surra crouched over him, striving to bring him back to consciousness by her own method.

Gorgol and Kavok sat on the floor, their elbows propped on their bent knees, each with his head between his hands. Beyond them, Logan was up on a swing seat pulled out from the table, one hand to his head, the other holding the call mike of a com to his lips as he got out, between gasping breaths not far removed from moans, his air appeal—

"D.S. Peaks—come in! Come in!"

As Hosteen squirmed up to a sitting position, a red-hot lance of pain cut through his head just behind his eyeballs. And every movement, no matter how cautious, brought on another throb of that agony. He had been stun-rayed once, but this was worse than the after effects of a blasting from that most common of stellar weapons. To get to his feet was an action beyond his powers of endurance, but he managed to slide across to the table edge, to look up at Logan.

"What—are—you—doing?" The shaping of words brought on further pain, and he wondered at Logan's persistence in trying to use the com.

His half-brother glanced down, eyes wide and painfilled in a face that was a mirror for the punishment he was taking.

"Widders took off—in 'copter—trouble—" Logan's hand dropped from his head and gripped the edge of the table until his knuckles stood out as pale knobs.

Hosteen remembered and began to think again with some measure of clarity. Widders had knocked them all out with an off-world gadget, then had taken off in the 'copter, flying straight for the forbidden territory. The Norbies could and probably would be affronted enough by the invasion of their medicine country to retaliate. And settlers such as Dumaroy would return any attack from the natives without trying to negotiate. A fire might have been kindled here and now that would sear this whole world as fatally as Terra had been scorched by the Xik blast.

The Terran hitched away from the table, biting his lip against the torture inside his skull, managing to reach Gorgol. The Norbie's eyelids were tightly closed; there was a thin beading of moisture along the hairless arch of his forehead. It was plain he was feeling all that Hosteen did, if not more, since one could not assess the reaction of alien physiology to an off-world weapon.

But there was no time to waste in useless sympathy. Hosteen touched the native's forearm with all the gentleness he could muster. There was a whistle of sound from Gorgol. His eyes came open and moved in their sockets to focus on the Terran as if he dared not try to turn his head.

Somehow Hosteen balanced himself in that hunched position so that he could free his hands for talking.

"The off-worlder has gone. We must—"

He was not allowed to finish. Gorgol's head thumped back against the wall of the tent. He gave a small, stifled trill, and then his fingers moved in answer:

"He has done evil—much evil—and we have allowed it. There will be a judging—"

"I have done evil." Hosteen signed. "For it is I who listened to his story and brought him here—though I did not know he would come. You carry no blame in this matter—none of us knew that he would attack us to get his desire—"

"He flies the sky thing into the medicine country. Those-Who-Drum-Thunder, loose the lightning arrows, will be swelling in their wrath. This is not good—evil! Evil!" To finger signs Gorgol added a thin wailing of his own untranslatable vocal sounds.

Kavok's eyes opened. He spat with much the same hissing hate as

Surra mustered upon proper occasion. But before Gorgol could continue, they were interrupted by words—spoken in good Galactic basic—issuing from the mike Logan still held.

"TRI calling base camp—" There was a smug note in that voice that aroused Hosteen's temper to the point of seething. "TRI calling base camp—"

He lurched across the space between wall and table, fighting off the sickness the pain of that effort cost him. Then he wrenched the mike away from Logan and leaned weakly against the table edge as he called:

"Widders!"

"So—you've come around!" The voice out of the air held a trace of amusement that did nothing to dampen the Terran's temper.

Hosteen fought for control, achieved enough to demand:

"Are you already into the Blue, Widders?"

"On our way right up to that check point. How's your headache, Storm? Told you I was doing this myself—I know *my* business—"

"Widders—listen, man—turn back—turn back right now!" The Terran knew even as he made that plea he was urging uselessly. But in that 'copter was the pilot, and surely Forgee had been long enough on Arzor, had been well enough trained by Survey, to realize the danger of what they were doing. "Forgee—don't be a fool! Get back in a hurry. You're breaking 'medicine'—not just of one clan, but of all the tribes! Turn back before they spot you. You can be planet-banned for a stunt like this—"

"My, Storm, that headache must be a bad one," Widders began lightly. Then the steel ripped out of the sheath as he added: "These natives won't even see us—I have a shield force up—and we are going in to the check point. Nobody—nobody, Storm—is telling me what I may or may not do when my son's life may be at stake. We'll keep you informed. TRI signing off—"

There was the click of a broken connection. Hosteen put down the mike. He looked at Logan, and the younger man's face was drawn, sickly pallid under its weathering.

"He's going right ahead—"

Gorgol was on his feet, standing unsteadily with one hand braced against the wall of the tent. With the other he signed:

"Krotag—we ride for Krotag—"

"No!" Hosteen answered and saw the stiffness in Gorgol's expression. The Terran indicated the mike. "We call the Peace Officer. He will bring in the law—"

"Off-world law!" Gorgol's whole body expressed his contempt.

Logan pushed away from the table and stood, weaving, yet free of support, using both hands. His Norbie dress did not look strange as he gestured, and the smooth flow of his signs was akin to the ceremonial speech of a chief meeting.

"Last wet season there was Hadzap, who came down into the herds of Quade, not asking for hunter's rights—which those of Quade's clan would have freely granted as is the custom. But he came in secret, without speech, and slew, taking only hides. And these he carried to the Port and would have sold to off-world men, asking for those things that he believed would make him greater in the clan. Was this not a shame upon all those of the Zamle totem? Yet did Quade's clansmen come to take Hadzap for judging under off-world laws? No—not so. Quade sent me to Krotag to ask for speech between one clan chief and another as is rightful custom. And Krotag replied—let it be so—you, Kavok, riding with me to report to Quade as was right and proper, for we are both sons to chiefs.

"Then Quade came and Krotag, and they sat down together. Quade telling of what had been done. But when he had finished, he rode out to your camp leaving Hadzap to the justice of Krotag, nor did he afterwards inquire what punishment had been set—for this is as it should be when chief deals with chief. Is this not so?"

"That is so," assented both Norbies.

"You may say now that this evil committed by an off-worlder is greater than the evil wrought by Hadzap. In that you are right. But do not think that we do not also consider it an evil. Did not this person of no totem strike us down also, for he knew that we would have prevented him by force from what he would do. And the Peace Officer will deal with him after our laws, even as Hadzap was dealt with by yours, for this is a grievous act and one that will harm both settlers and Norbies."

"This is truth," Gorgol agreed. "Yet Krotag must be told—for he gave you the right to ride here, and he, also, will be answerable to others for this evil act."

"That is so," Hosteen agreed. "Let one of you ride for Krotag, and we shall remain here, trying to call our Peace Officer through the air talker—"

"And you swear it on the blood that you will wait here?" Gorgol looked from Hosteen to Logan. "Yes, it is so, for you are not of those who give their word and then make nothing of it for reasons of their own. I ride—let Kavok stay—since other than Zamle men may come and he can talk under the truce pole should that be needful."

They took alternate shifts at the com after Gorgol departed, trying to reach the Peaks office with their calls—but silence was their only answer. Nor did Hosteen's periodic demands upon the 'copter bring any reply from Widders or Forgee. The Terran tried to deduce how far into the Blue the flyer could go before the two would have to return to escape the day heat—without much success.

"They could even set down somewhere in there and take cover," Logan pointed out.

"Once a fool, always a fool—that's what you think of the civ? That's cannibal territory—he's been warned—"

"Widders is the type who wouldn't expect any danger from natives," Logan retorted. "And he's armed with about every possible defensive gadget he could find. I wouldn't put it past him to have smuggled a blaster in on that 'copter! He'd believe he could stand off any Norbie attack."

And Logan was entirely right. Widders would think himself invulnerable as a modern, civilized man coping with natives armed only with primitive weapons. But, as all civs from off-world, he would thereby seriously underestimate the Norbies if he relied on mechanics to defeat those who had mastered nature in the Arzoran outback.

"Sleeee—" The hissing whistle cut through the open door of the bubble tent and startled both men.

Hosteen went out. There had been no alert from Baku or Surra, which meant the newcomers must be known to both members of the team. But he was angry at himself for not having briefed both cat and bird to give warning of any arrival.

It was not until the riders filed out of shadows into the open floor of the canyon that Hosteen recognized Krotag heading a party of warriors. The Terran waited in the path of light from the doorway, not advancing to meet the chief when he dismounted. He must take his cue from Krotag. This was no time for excuses or explanations. The native leader must have had the story from Gorgol—and he must already have been on his way here or he would not have arrived so soon after the messenger left. What action he would take was his decision, and according to custom Hosteen must wait for the Norbie's verdict.

The Terran stepped back as Krotag came up, allowing the chief to enter the tent, and then he gave way for a second tall figure.

Unlike the warriors, this native wore no arms belt or protective shield collar of yoris fangs. Instead, his bony frame was covered with a striking tunic fashioned of black-and-white feathers woven skillfully into a net foundation of frawn yarn. His horns were stained dead black, and each of his deep-set eyes were encircled by an inch-wide ring of black paint, which gave his face a skull-like aspect, daunting to the beholder. In addition to his feather tunic, he wore a short knee-length cloak, also a feathered net, but this of a brilliant yellow-green. And around his neck, on white cords, was slung a small black drum.

"I see you who wears the name of Krotag." Hosteen signed formal salutation.

"I see you—stranger—"

Not a good beginning, but one he had to accept. Hosteen looked at the Drummer.

"I see also the one who can summon the bright sky arrows," he continued. "And this one also wears a name?"

Silence, so complete that they could hear from outside the stir of a horse. Then the Drummer's hands came out before him, palms up, while those black-ringed eyes caught and held Hosteen's in a compelling stare.

Hardly aware of his action, the Terran raised his own hands, moved them out until palm met palm, and so they stood linked by the touch of flesh against flesh, Hosteen and the Norbie medicine man. Once before in his life the Amerindian had felt a power, not human and far beyond the control of any man, fill and move him.

Then he had been swept up and used by that power to bring prisoners out of a Nitra camp. But at that time he had deliberately evoked the "medicine" of his own people. And now—

Words came out of him, words the Drummer could not understand—or could he?

"I have a song—and an offering—
In the midst of Blue Thunder am I walking—
Now to the straight lightning would I go.
Along the trail that the Rainbow covers—
For to the Big Snake, and to the Blue Thunder
Have I made offering—
Around me falls the white rain,
And pleasant again will all become!"

Bits, fragments, dragged from the depths of memory by some power—perhaps borrowed from this Drummer. No true Song, just as Hosteen was no true Singer, yet those words stirred the power where it lay coiled deep in his body—or his mind.

Hosteen blinked. The maze of colors that had rippled before his eyes was gone. He fronted an alien face with round skull-set eyes. Only for a moment was there a flicker in those eyes, a belief or an emotion or a thought that matched what Hosteen felt. Then it was gone, and Hosteen was only a Terran settler fitting his hands to those of a Norbie medicine man. The hands drew away from his.

"This one wears the name of Ukurti. You are one who can also summon clouds—younger brother."

"Not so." Hosteen disclaimed any wizard powers. "But on my world, and long ago, my grandfather was such a one. Perhaps he laid upon me something of his own at his passing—"

Ukurti nodded. "That is as it should be, for it is a burden laid upon us who have the strength to pass it to those who can bear it well in their own time. Now there are other matters—this one who has taken the airways into the medicine country rashly and against the laws of your people and mine. This, too, is a part of your burden, younger brother."

Hosteen bowed his head. "This burden do I accept, for it is partly by my doing that he came into this country, and his rashness and evil are as mine."

"That one has gone in—he will not return." Krotag's gestures were emphatic, but he eyed Hosteen with a mixtures of wonder and exasperation.

"That is not for our deciding," corrected Ukurti. "If he is found, you, my younger brother, must deal with him—that we lay upon you."

"That do I accept—"

There was a crackle of sound, not from without but from the mike before Logan. He jerked it up to mouth level.

"Come in—come in!"

"TRI calling base camp—"

Hosteen leaped across the tent and tore the mike from Logan's grasp.

"Storm here—come in TRI—"

"—sighted the LB. Going down for look—on side of mountain—" The din of static half drowned out the words.

Hosteen made an urgent hand signal to Logan and watched his brother snap on the locater. If Widders kept talking, that ought to give them a fix on the present position of the 'copter.

"LB all right—going down!"

"Widders—Widders, wait!" But Hosteen knew that his protest would never be heeded by the men out there. Logan's fingers relayed the information to the Norbies.

"So he has found what he has sought," the Drummer replied. "It may be that his quest wins the favor of the High Dwellers after all. We shall wait and see—"

Hosteen clung to the mike, calling at intervals, but without raising a reply—until, at last, it came with forceful clarity.

"We are going to look for evidence of any survivors. Forgee—Forgee!" The voice grew as shrill as a Norbie pipe, carrying a note of surprise that deepened to alarm. "No! Fire—fire down the mountain. Forgee—they're coming—Storm! Storm!"

"Here!" Hosteen tried to imagine what was happening out there.

"Fire at 'em, Forgee. Got that one!"

"Widders! Are you under attack?"

"Storm—we can't hold 'em off—the fire's spreading too close. We're going to make a run for it—can hold out in the cave—"

"Hold out against what?" There was no answer from the mike.

"Those-Who-Drum-Thunder have answered," Krotag signed. "This is the end of the evil doer."

"Not so. They may still be alive," Hosteen protested. "We can't leave them there—like that—"

"It has been decided." Krotag's reply was final.

"You," Hosteen appealed to Ukurti, "have said this man is my burden. I cannot leave him there—without knowing the truth of what has happened to him—"

Again it was as if the two of them stood apart from space and time in some emptiness that held only Norbie medicine man and human—that they were in contact in a way Hosteen could never explain.

"The truth was spoken—the burden is yours, and you are not yet loosened from it. These off-worlders have no part of what lies in the Blue, and they have been punished. But I do not think that the pattern is yet finished. The road lies before you; take it without hindrance—"

"If my brother walks this road, then do I also," Logan's, hands flashed.

Ukurti turned on the younger man the measuring regard of his paint-ringed eyes. "It is said rightly that brother should shoulder brother when the arrows of war are on the bow string. If this is your choice, let this road be yours also and no one—save the High Dwellers—shall deny it to you."

"This is spoken on the drum?" Using finger speech, Krotag asked Ukurti.

"It is spoken on and by the drum. Let them journey forth and do what is set upon them. No one can read the path of his beyond-travel. This is a thing to be done." His fingers tapped a small patter of notes on the drum head, a rhythm that sent a crawling chill up Hosteen's back.

From the dark beyond the doorway came Surra, slinking belly to earth, her eyes slitted, her ears tight to her skull. And behind her, Baku, her beak snapping with rage—or some other strong emotion.

Last of all Gorgol, stalking like a sleep walker, his eyes staring wide before him. The Drummer gave a last tap and broke the spell.

"Go—you all have been chosen and summoned. Upon you the burden."

"Upon us the burden," Hosteen agreed for all that strangely assorted group of rescuers.

CHAPTER EIGHT

irage?" Logan asked dazedly, perhaps not of his gaunt, hard-driven companions but of the very world about them.

Having won through the cauldron of rocky defiles on foot, for the way they had come was not for horses, it was indeed hard to believe in this valley—the land sloping gently before them, widening out in the distance until they could no longer see the wall heights that guarded it to the west because here the yellow and yellow-green vegetation of the river lowlands was lush. There was no sign of the searing Big Dry cutting down grass and bush. And in the distance there was the shimmer of water—either a curve of river or a lake of some size.

Gorgol braced himself on his folded arms and surveyed the countryside with an expression of awe, while Hosteen sat up, his back against a rock wall still warm enough to feel through his shirt, though this was twilight. Three, four, five days they had spent in hiding, the nights in winning through to this point, where the Blue was at last open before them.

And on the last night only Gorgol's knowledge of the outback had saved them. All water gone, the Norbie had searched the ground on hands and knees, literally smelling out a clue, until he scooped the soil from a small depression. He buried there a hollowed reed with a twist of dried grass about its tip, sucking at the other end with an effort that left him gasping, until after a half hour of such labor he brought liquid up from the source he alone suspected.

Surra whined, nudged against Hosteen, her nostrils expanding as she took in the scents arising from this oasis of the wild. At least to the cat, this was no hallucination, and Hosteen was willing to rely upon her senses sooner than upon his own. Gorgol opened a small pouch on his warrior belt and brought out a pencil-shaped object. He pressed it against one finger tip to leave a small dot of glowing green. Then he drew marks crisscross on his hollow cheeks, in no pattern Hosteen could see, that glowed, making of half his face a weird mask. He held the crayon out to the Terran.

"We go in peace, so this we must do—"

"For the wild men?"

"Not so. For them we must continue to watch. But for Those-Who-Drum, now we bear the marks of peace in their sight."

Hosteen took the soft stick, applied to his own skin a netting of lines, and passed it along to Logan. To every race their customs, and he was willing to follow Gorgol's lead here. The paste on his face stung a little and left the skin feeling drawn and tight.

Although they were now painted for peace, they entered the valley with the caution of raiders. Hosteen guessed that in spite of peace poles passed between age-old enemies, Gorgol's distrust of the wild and rumored cannibal tribes, whose hunting territory this was, still guided his actions.

Baku had flown ahead to the water. Surra padded down the slope before them, blending, in the twilight, with the vegetation, until Hosteen could only follow her movements when she chose to establish mind contact with him. The cat was alert and wary, though she had found nothing suspicious. Now the men followed her, keeping to cover as much as possible.

If there was native life in this valley, it would locate not too far from the water. Yet, water they themselves must have and soon. The heat clung on the upper slope, harsh on their parched bodies. Then Hosteen noted that Gorgol was catching at the headed stems of tall grass, crushing them in his hands and holding the resultant mass to his lips, chewing, spitting. The Terran followed the Norbie's example. He discovered the moisture so gained was a bitter juice, but it eased the dryness of his mouth.

As they went, he looked about them, trying to guess which of the mountains within sight could be that on which Widders had located the LB. The fix from the camp com had guided them here—but now they would have to find the actual wreckage—

Hosteen tensed. His hand went up in a gesture to freeze both of his companions. Surra had given warning. Between them and the water were strange natives. The three flattened against the ground, and now the Terran regretted the luminous paint on their faces, which might be a source of betrayal.

So far, the others did not suspect their presence. Surra stalked them as they moved steadily along to the south. Hosteen made contact with Baku and knew that the eagle, in turn, would pick up the enemy party.

There were small night sounds. The creatures of the tall grass had not yet gone into Dry Time burrows. Their squeakings and chirpings were loud in Hosteen's ears when he lay on the ground, acutely aware of every small noise, every movement of bush or grass clump. But this was the old, old game the Terran had played so many times during the war years when eyes, noses, keener natural senses than his own, had formed the scouting team, he being the director of activities.

Now, the party of natives had been trailed out of range. The three again had an open path to the water. Hosteen's signal sent them skulking from one piece of cover to the next, working their way through the steadily increasing gloom to the lake—for lake was what Baku reported that body of water to be.

They arrived at the edge of growth of reeds and endured silent torment when insects closed in in a stinging, biting fog. But it was worth that painful, slow progress through mud and slime-coated growing things to plunge their hands into water, scoop up the warm, odorous, and oddly tasting liquid, not only to drink but also to freshen their dehydrated and peeling skins.

Revived, they shared the sustenance tablets brought for emergency rations.

"That mountain—" Logan said. "We'll have to find the right one."

"It is there." To their surprise Gorgol finished his signs with an assured point to the north. "Medicine—and the fire—" But he did not explain that.

Hosteen remembered the night when he had stood in the yard of the Peak holding and watched that flash of light to the north, the flash that had been accompanied by the vibration in the air. That seemed like a long time ago now, and he was visited by an odd reluctance to set out for the mountain Gorgol had set as their goal.

Filling their canteens, they left the lapping waters of the lake, continuing around its perimeter, with Baku aloft in the bowl of the night sky and Surra ranging in a wide pattern back and forth across the line of their advance.

Twice more they took cover to escape Norbie parties. And it was in the last quarter of the night that they began to climb. Bulking big before them so that it cut away the stars was a mountain.

Sound came, first as a faint thumping, then in an ever increasing roll. Drums! Drums with the same compelling power as the small one Ukurti had carried but with far greater range. Logan came up level with Hosteen.

"Village—" He raised his voice to be heard over that roll.

Eastward, Hosteen believed. And he trusted that the drums meant some ceremony was in progress, a ceremony that would keep the villagers safely occupied at home for the few precious hours remaining of the sheltering night.

Surra located the 'copter, her report bringing them to the flattened area of burned-over ground in which lay the twisted, fire-warped framework of the off-world flyer. And not too far away was the half-charred body of the pilot, a burned stump of arrow still protruding from between his shoulders.

"We haven't much time until daybreak. Widders spoke of a cave. We'll separate and look for that," Hosteen said.

Together with Surra, they fanned out from the burned ground upslope. Long line of vegetation ash ridged that rise, puzzling Hosteen by the uniformity of their width and the straight thrust of their lengths. It was almost as if an off-world flamer had been used here—

The Xik? Another holdout group hidden in this remote and forbidden land, just as that other had been when he and Logan had stumbled into their secret base? Those Xiks had used a flamer in their all-out attempt to get Logan when he escaped, destroying their stolen horse herd recklessly in the hope of finishing off one man who could blow wide open their concealed operations on this frontier world. Yes, it was conceivable that another Xik Commando force could be holed up here.

The flamed furrow came to an end abruptly. Here was blackened earth, vegetation charred into powder, and there normal grass, a bush standing high, swaying a little in the predawn wind. Had the flames been aimed up from below, then? But Hosteen had passed nothing in a direct line with the destroyed 'copter and these fire scores that could have produced them. If it wasn't a flamer—then what? Hosteen skirted a bush and began again his hunt for any cave opening, though half mechanically, his mind still partly occupied with the riddle of the fire.

An eye-searing flash lashed the ground only yards ahead, and he stumbled back as flames crackled and bushes flared into torches in the night. Another breakout of the same fire to his left sent Hosteen south and east, running with the fire licking at his heels. He had never seen anything like this before, but the certainty grew, as he fled before the reach of the long red tongues, that the blazes were being used with a purpose, and that purpose— In spite of the heat waves at his back, a chill held the Terran. He was being herded! Someone or something was using a whip of fire to drive him, just as a plains rider used a stock whip to control a stray from the frawn herd.

He stumbled on, striving to pick a way over the now well-lighted ground to avoid any misstep that would leave him the helpless prey of the rage behind him. A small gorge opened ahead, and the Terran made a running leap to cross it, coming down in a panting heap on the far side. When he would have struggled to his feet once more, an arrow quivered deep in the earth by his right hand in blunt warning.

Hosteen hunched together, drawing his feet under him, preparing to spring for freedom if he saw a chance. A ring had closed about him, not of fire but of natives. Unlike the Norbies of the lowlands, these warriors were shorter, closer to Terran build. Their horns were charcoal-black arcs over their skulls, and the same black had been used to draw designs on their faces, not with the aimless crisscross lines that Gorgol had used for peace paint but in intricate and careful patterns.

If he had had a chance in those first few seconds for an attempt at defense or escape, he had lost it now. Whirling out of the flickering half light came one of the native hunters' most effective weapons— a cord net made of the tough, under-the-surface roots of the yassa

plant, soaked in water until the mesh was greasy slick. Once en-
meshed in that, even a fighting yoris was helpless, as helpless as Hosteen Storm at this moment.

Ignominiously packaged, he was transported downslope to a village, a village that was no collection of skin-covered tents, like those
of the nomad Norbies he had known, but of permanent erections
with heavy logs rolled shoulder high to form walls, above them a
woven wattle of dried vine and reed, with high-peaked thatched
roofs.

Out of nowhere had come a Drummer, a medicine man wearing a
feather tunic and cloak but in a vivid metallic green, the tunic crossed
on the breast with a zigzag, sharp-angled strip of red. And the drum
he thumped, as he led the procession carrying the prisoner through
the village, was also red. Torches were set up along the way, their
flames burning a strange, pale blue. Then Hosteen was out of the
open, staring up into the shadows of one of the peaked roofs, as he
was dumped roughly on a beaten earth floor.

House—or was it more temple? He tried to assess the meaning of
what he saw. There were no sleep rolls in evidence, but in the center
of the one huge room was a pit in which burned a fire of the same
blue as the torches. And there were cords passing from one to another of the heavy support timber columns the length of the building, lines on which hung bark and shriveled things, together with
round objects—

A Thunder House! And those were raid trophies—the heads and
hands of dead enemies! Hosteen had heard of that practice as being
usual among the Nitra clans. But this building was larger, older, far
more permanent than any Nitra wizard tent. The Terran tried to remember every scrap of information he had been able to garner
about the Nitra and to apply it to what he could see about him now.

Those warriors who had brought him in were settling down
about the fire pit, passing from one to the other a bowl that probably held the mildly intoxicating clava juice, and they showed signs of
staying for some hours to come.

The clan Drummer had taken his place on the stool to the north,
keeping up a little deep, grumbling sound on his knee drum. That,
too, followed the custom of the outer-world tribes—the northern

stool for him who drums for the Thunder Ones; the southern stool, still vacant here, for the head Chief of the village or clan.

Hosteen closed his eyes, fixed mind and will on contact with the team, but to no avail. There was nothing—no trace of Surra or Baku—along the mental lanes. He had never quite been able to gauge the range to which his silent command call could reach in relation to either eagle or cat. But this present silence was more than worrying. It carried with it an element of real fear. A man who depended heavily upon the support of a cane could fall helplessly when that cane was snatched from his hand.

The Terran swallowed, as if he could swallow down his rising uneasiness. Had he, through the years, become so wholly identified with the team, so dependent upon them, that he would be a cripple when they did not answer his call? That thought bit deep, so deep he was hardly aware of the Thunder House and those in it until a commotion by the door made him open his eyes and turn his head as well as he could in the confines of the net.

Another party of natives brought a second prisoner, and the Drummer now beat out a heavy tattoo that needed no translation, so filled with triumph was its sound. A minute later the tangled and still struggling captive was dumped beside Hosteen, the lines of his net made fast to the same pillars that held the Terran.

"Hosteen!"

He could barely make out Logan's features, marked still with smears of the luminous paint.

"Here. Gorgol with you?"

"No, haven't seen him since we split up. There was a fire all around, and I blasted out ahead of that. Ran right into this net—they had it strung up waiting between two trees."

Organization, Hosteen granted them that, very efficient organization. Did they have Widders stowed away somewhere here, too? And what was the purpose of their mountain firetrap? Just to capture anyone trying to get up in the heights?

"One thing." Logan broke through the other's mental speculation. "Just before that brush fire walled me off, I saw it."

"It?"

"The LB—it must have been the LB. And from the look I had, it didn't crash when it landed—at least it wasn't smashed up any to show."

"You didn't get a chance to examine it closely though?"

"No," Logan admitted. "Something else queer—"

"That being?"

"There was stuff piled all around it—spears, bowls, hides. And somebody had killed a horse, left it lying with its throat cut and its skull bashed in, right up against the boat— Not too long ago, either."

"Sacrifices."

"Could be. Because the LB came out of the sky, d'you suppose? They can't have seen space ships back here."

"Maybe—but then why attack the 'copter when it came in for a landing," countered the Terran. "If they had no experience with sky craft, one kind could be classed with the other. Unless—"

Unless, his mind raced, they did know the difference between an object from space and one merely traversing Arzoran skies.

"They could have contact with the plains, know the difference between flyers and space ships." Logan was thinking in the same direction.

Or, Hosteen's suspicions suggested, they could have contact with spacers. The fire weapon still posed a puzzle past his present ability to solve.

"This is a Thunder House." Logan had been surveying his surroundings.

"I noticed some similarities with Nitra customs," Hosteen returned. "See anything you know?"

Logan was the expert on native Arzor. Perhaps he could pick up some clue to their future or their captors' intentions. Norbie clans were fond of ritual and tied by custom. There could be a pattern here that would fit with what Logan knew.

"They keep some Nitra ways," his half-brother agreed. "The two stools, north and south, the east and west doors. And—watch that hunter coming in. See how he walks in and out among the pillars and not in a straight line? To do that would mean he was boasting before the powers. Their Drummer, he's going into action now—watch!"

In the eerie light of the blue fire, the Drummer was still pounding his knee drum with two fingers, keeping up a barely audible tap of sound. With the other hand, he had tossed into the air above the fire pit two small white things that floated and soared upward on a puff of the warmer air until they were lost in the gloom of the roof.

"Prayer feathers—or rather fluff," Logan explained. "Those warrior trophies are the same as Nitra, too." He regarded with wry distaste the display of dried hands and skulls. "That's the same way the blue horns hang them—"

"But does the Nitra Drummer do that?" demanded Hosteen sharply.

The medicine man had risen from his stool and put down his drum. Now he stood by the fire, the gaze of all the seated natives centered upon him. From the neck folds of his tunic he pulled a cord from which hung a tube some twelve inches long. It glistened not only with the reflection of the fire but also seemingly with a radiance of its own.

With ceremony the Drummer pointed this to the four points of the compass beginning at the north. And then he aimed one end directly at the air over the fire pit.

A fine spray spread from the end of the tube, carrying glittering, jeweled motes into the air. The motes gathered and formed an outline composed of tiny, spinning gems.

"A five point-star!" Logan cried out.

But already the design was changing, the motes spinning, reforming, this time into a triangle, and then a circle, and finally a shaft that plunged straight down into the fire pit and was gone.

"No Nitra does that!" Logan breathed.

"Nor a Norbie either," Hosteen replied grimly. "That's an offworld thing, of a kind I have never seen before. But I'll take blood oath it isn't native to Arzor!"

"Xik?" Logan demanded.

"I don't know. But I have a suspicion it won't be long before we find out."

CHAPTER NINE

Hosteen tried to flex cramped muscles within the cocoon of net that held him. The night was gone, and none of their captors had so much as come into the quarter of the Thunder House where he and Logan were tethered. Yes—the night was gone.

Daylight struck in places through the thatch and walls of the upper part of the medicine house, but the heat was no greater than it would have been in grazing season on the plains. Within the valley, the Big Dry did not exist at all!

"Sun—but no heat—" he heard Logan mumble. "That lake—"

"Couldn't control the weather," Hosteen countered. They had rivers on the plains, sources of water that did not fail, yet there living things still must take cover during the day.

"Something does," Logan returned obstinately.

Something did. What could control weather? There was one place on—or rather in—Arzor where there was controlled weather and controlled vegetation—the garden mountain into which Logan and Hosteen had blundered on their flight from the Xik—where the Sealed Cave people had set out growing things from a hundred different planets and left them to flourish for centuries. Controlled weather—that was not Xik, that was Sealed Cave knowledge!

"The Sealed Caves—" Hosteen repeated aloud.

"But this is in the open, not in a cave!" Logan's thoughts matched with his. "How could they control the open?"

"How did they fashion that cavern?" Hosteen asked. "But if there are more remains of that civilization here, it could explain a lot."

"The 'medicine,' you mean?"

"Yes, and maybe those tricky air currents that have defeated Survey exploration in here."

"But the Norbies have always avoided the Sealed Caves."

"In the outer Peaks they have, but here we can't be sure the same taboo holds. We can't even be sure that somewhere on Arzor, it might be right here, the Old Ones themselves don't exist still. Don't the legends say that they retired to some of the caves and sealed the openings behind them—eventually to issue forth again in the future?"

Hosteen did not quite believe that, though. That some wild Norbies were exploiting Sealed Cave knowledge—that was possible. That the mysterious and long-gone forerace among the stars could linger on here directing the activities of a primitive tribe or tribes—no, somehow that did not fit. The men, or creatures, who had designed and created the Cavern of the Hundred Gardens could have nothing in common with warriors who kept skulls and right hands of their defeated enemies to adorn their temples. There was a contradiction in mental processes there.

Again Logan's thoughts followed the same path. "I'd rather believe the Norbies were heirs," he said slowly.

"Unworthy ones, I think. Maybe the answer lies on that mountain."

"We'll probably never get a chance to learn it," Logan's reply was bleak. "I think we were cut out of the herd to supply some spectacular touches to a big Drum Feast."

Hosteen had long ago reached the same conclusion. And his struggles against his bonds had proved to him the folly of trying to beat the Norbie system of confining prisoners. One could only fall back on the rather grim thought that as long as one was still alive, there was a small measure of hope.

"Listen!" Logan's head bobbed up as he tried vainly to raise himself a few inches from the floor.

Drums were sounding, more than one now, with a pause between each roll. Hosteen, listening intently, thought he could distinguish a slightly different note in each one of those short bursts.

Norbies had been in and out of the Thunder House all morning, but now a large party entered from the south. Then came a thin,

wiry native, his black horns tipped with red, a shoulder plate necklace, not of yoris teeth but of small and well polished bones, covering most of his chest. He took the Chief's stool.

Hosteen's view of the scene was from floor level, but he sighted
the second party entering from the west, a peace pole held up osten-
tatiously. Drummer and Chief walked behind that. When a second
and then a third such delegation arrived through the western door,
Hosteen realized this was not a gathering of a clan but a meeting of
tribal representatives, and from tribes once enemies.

Five, six such delegations now, a handful of warriors ranked
behind each chief and medicine man. The seventh—Hosteen
started—Krotag and Ukurti led that.

The Drummer of the village was at the north stool. Now he beat
a thunderous roll on his knee drum, and two youths broke from the
villagers' group, brought out between them a block of wood, square,
polished with the sheen of years', perhaps of centuries, handling.
Planting this before the fire pit to the north, they laid upon it a leafy
branch of the sacred fal tree, then scuttled back to the anonymity of
the shadows behind their Drummer.

"Speeches now," Logan half whispered in a lull of drumming.

Speeches there were, and Hosteen longed for the power to translate that whistling-twittering. In turn, the village Drummer and the
Chief arose, walked to the block, struck it across the top with the fal
branch, and launched into a burst of oratory, from time to time striking the block again with the fal wand to emphasize some point. Then
each of the visiting chiefs and drummers followed their example.

Hosteen's head ached, his mouth was parched and dry, and he lay
gasping, hardly conscious of the continuing drone at the center of
the Thunder House. He wanted water and food—but more than
anything, water. Twice he tried to reach Baku, Surra—to no avail.
The cat and the eagle might have escaped out of the valley, and he
began to hope that they had.

Any chance he and Logan might have had now diminished to the
vanishing point. He had thought of Krotag and the Shosonna as possible allies. But Krotag had been the second one to make a speech.
Whatever tied the Norbies together in this peace pact was strong

enough to withstand any leanings toward friendship with settlers that the plains natives might have once had.

How long that conference lasted neither Hosteen nor Logan could have told. The former was afterwards sure he had lapsed into semiconsciousness from fatigue, lack of water, and the smoky fumes of the fal twigs the Norbies kept feeding into the fire. When a sharp prod in the ribs roused him into full wakefulness, all traces of sunlight were gone and the gloom of night was cut again by blue torches.

One of the same youths who had dragged out the speech block leaned over him and thrust a tube through the mesh of the net and between the Terran's lips. He sucked avidly, and liquid filled his mouth. If it was water, some other substance had been added, for it tasted sweet and yet sharp, like an off-world relish, and Hosteen sucked and swallowed greedily, his thirst vanishing, his mental torpor fading as he did so. Then the tube was jerked roughly from his lips, and he licked them for the last lingering drop, feeling energy creep back into his body. Logan was similarly fed and watered. Beyond the captives stood both the village Chief and the Drummer, watching the process with an air of impatience, as if eager to push on to some more important task.

A ripple of fingers on drum head brought in a guard of warriors, tough, seasoned fighting men, Hosteen judged from their attitude and the bone necklets they wore. Once more the ropes holding the nets were loosed, and the prisoners, still helpless in their lashings, were rolled like bales into the full torchlight.

Another warrior came out of the shadows, bearing across his shoulder the loops of their arms belts, their canteens. It would seem that where they were going their equipment was to accompany them. And for the first time, Hosteen remembered Logan's grisly description of what he had seen about the grounded LB—sacrifices. Were they about to join the horse, to do honor to whatever power these Norbies imagined the star ship escape craft represented or held?

They had been carried into the village, but they were to walk out. Nets were whirled off their stiff bodies, a loop rope dragged tight about their chests and upper arms. Hosteen stumbled along for a step or two, trying to make his cramped limbs obey. Then two of his captors caught him by the shoulder on either side as supports and herders.

For the first time he saw the females of the village well behind the lines of warriors. Yes, some ceremony was in prospect, one intended for all the tribesmen and their visitors—for under each peace pole, which they had seen in the Thunder House earlier and which now were planted here in the open, was a grouping of strangers.

The two men were half led, half dragged along a well-worn trail leading from the village toward the dark bulk of the mountainside down which the fire had hunted them into their captors' nets. Behind, as Hosteen saw when he glanced back once, trying to pick out Krotag's group, the villagers and their guests fell in to form a straggling procession, carrying torches.

As they advanced, the smell of burned vegetation battled with that of fal wood. And they crossed those curiously straight furrows where the flails of flame must have beaten, either during their own chase or earlier.

Now the drums were beating. Not only that of the village medicine man but also those of all the visiting Drummers—with a heavy rhythm into which their marching steps fitted. And the beat of the drums became one with Hosteen's pumping blood, a heaviness in his head—

Hypnotic! Hosteen recognized the danger. His own people could produce—or had produced ages ago—spells as a part of their war chants and dances, spells to send men out to kill with a firm belief in the invincibility of their "medicine." This was not a pattern unique to Arzor.

He tried a misstep to break the pattern of the march. And perhaps because he had been indoctrinated during his Service training against just such traps, the Terran succeeded in part—or was succeeding—until the mountain came alive in answer to those with whom he marched.

That was what appeared to happen. Was it sound—vibration pitched too high or too low for human ears to register except on the very border of the senses? Or was it mental rather than physical? But it was as if all the bulk of earth and rock exhaled, breathed, stirred into watchful wakefulness. And Hosteen knew that this was something totally beyond his experience, perhaps beyond the experience of any off-worlder—unless Widders had met this before him.

Beat, beat—in spite of his efforts of mind, will, and squirming body held tight in the vice grip of the warriors who marched with him—Hosteen could only resist that enchantment feebly. That he was able to recognize and fight it at all was, he thought, a slender defense. Beat, beat—feet, drums— And again the mountain sighed—sighed or drew in a breath of anticipation—which? This was no earth and rock but a beast crouched there waiting, such a beast as no human could imagine.

The stench of the burned stuff was stronger. Then there was a last crescendo from the united drums—a roll of artificial thunder echoing and reechoing from the heights. They stopped and stood where they were, facing upslope toward the unseen top of the mountain. Then, as the drums had acted as one, so did the torch bearers move, stamping their lights into the earth, leaving them all in the dark, with only the far stars pricking the cloudless sky.

There was not a sound as the last echoes of the drumbeats died. Would the beast who was the mountain make answer? Hosteen's imagination presented him with a picture of that creature—sky-high—waiting—Waiting as Surra could wait, as Baku could wait, with the great patience that man has lost or never had, the patience of the hunter.

The waiting Norbies—the waiting mountain—and waiting prisoners—

Again that breath, that sound that could not be heard, only felt with each atom of his tense body.

Then—

Lightning—great, jagged, broken blades of lightning stabbing up into the sky, lighting the slope. It played about the round knob that Hosteen saw for the first time clearly as the crest of the mountain—knob, one part of mind remaining undazzled told him, that was too round to be natural. A crown of lightning about the rock head of a crouching beast. Then—the whips of blazing light cracked down, cut and fired, and the smoke of those fires carried to the waiting throng. Crack, lash—but behind that was no natural force but intelligent purpose. Hosteen was sure of that as he stood blinded by the flashes.

Xik—this could not be Xik. The installations that must govern this display were no Xik flamers, nor anything he had seen or heard of on other worlds. Yet Hosteen's mind balked at associating this weapon for horrible destruction with the same civilization that had produced the beauty of the Cavern of the Hundred Gardens.

As swiftly as it had begun, it was over. Brush was in flames at widely separated places on the upper slopes, but the fires did not spread far. And now the drums began once again their marching tap. Hosteen's guards pushed him ahead. However, this time the bulk of the villagers remained where they were, only the local Chief, his guards, the Drummer, and their captives climbed anew.

Once more they passed the burned frame of the 'copter. The recent fiery lashes must have struck it again, for the tail assemblage was now a molten mass, glowing as the metal slowly cooled. Past the 'copter—on and up—

Gorgol, Surra, Baku—had they somehow escaped both the nets of the natives and the lightning? Hosteen tried to call again, only to meet that curious deadness in response, as if there had never been any way he could communicate with those intelligent brains so different from his own.

"LB just ahead," Logan called out.

Hosteen sniffed the sickly sweet smell of decay—decay of vegetable and animal matter—the sacrifices, if sacrifices they were meant to be. And were he and Logan now being taken to join those? The Terran knew a trick or two he could use at the last, even with his arms bound—

The slaughtered horse was visible in the flicker of a dying brush fire, behind it the shape of the LB. And as Logan had reported, there were no signs of a fatal crash landing. The escape boat might have been set down as easily as if it landed on the mountainside by directing radar. Survivors? Or had the survivors already gone the path he and Logan were traveling?

Hosteen so expected a battle at the site of the LB that he was startled when they did not pause there. The Drummer tapped, blew a puff of the prayer fluff in the direction of the craft, but they did not approach it.

No—the mountain was still waiting. And again in Hosteen's imagination it took on the semblance of a slightly somnolent yet watchful animal—yet an animal with a form of intelligence.

Up again—and now the slope was steeper, rougher, so that Hosteen and Logan were hauled and dragged by their guards' ropes, struggling to keep their feet at times. Once Hosteen went to his knees and refused to respond to the tugging, striving to combine his need for a breathing spell with the chance for a look about.

Since they had left the LB, they had crossed several of the burned furrows, but these were of an earlier date, since they did not smoke. And now more and more rocky outcrops broke through the vegetation carpeting the slopes. The brush was left behind, and they were surrounded by rock. There was a narrow cleft where they felt their way up a niche stair, the prisoners scraped along painfully by their guards.

The cleft brought them to a ledge almost wide enough to be termed a small plateau. In the rock of the cliff that backed it was a dark opening. But this was not their goal, for the party struck eastward to the right, following the width of ledge around a gentle curve Hosteen judged to be the base of the mountain's dome crest, though that must still climb some hundreds of feet above.

Daylight was coming, and he hoped the strange immunity that protected the village and the valley held here, too—that they need not fear the rising of the sun. Or was that to furnish the manner of their ending, death by exposure to the fury of its rays on a sacred mountain?

Already they were out of sight of the cave opening, and here the ledge extended from curving cliff wall to an edge that overhung a frightening drop to unguessed depths. The smooth path under his boots reminded Hosteen of another mountain road that had appeared to run from nowhere in the heights at the mountain of the Garden. That had been a relic of the Sealed Cave civilization, and on it Hosteen had nearly met death in the person of the Xik aper, the last of his breed on Arzor.

The ledge road ended as if sheared off by giant knife stroke. To their left was the circle of another doorway into the cliff wall—but this was sealed by what appeared a smooth slate of rock. The Drummer sounded his ritual signal—perhaps in salute to whatever power he deemed lurked behind that barrier.

And when the echo of that died away, the Chief of the village took the captives' arms belts from the guard. With deliberation he broke the blades of their long hunting knives and showed his familiarity with the use of stunners by crushing their barrels with a rock ax the Drummer produced. Having destroyed the outlanders' weapons, he whistled, and two of the guards went into action.

Planting palms flat against the surface of the closed door, they exerted full strength, straining muscles on arms and shoulders.

The barrier gave, split vertically apart. Into that opening the Chief tossed the ruined weapons, the belts of the prisoners. And then the two captives were thrust forward with such force that they hurtled helplessly into a thick dark against which the light of day at their backs made little impression.

CHAPTER TEN

Hosteen brought up against an unseen wall with force enough to bruise flesh, to drive breath out of his body in a gasping grunt. He was on his knees, trying to regain both breath and balance when Logan crashed into him, and they both went to the rock surface under them. There was absolute darkness now. The Norbies must have resealed the cave.

The Terran knew of old that particular type of airlessness, that dead feeling—it was found in the passages of the Sealed Caves, long closed to man, perhaps always intended to be closed to his species. This was certainly a relic of the Sealed Cave civilization.

Breathing shallowly, he lay still and tried to think.

"One of the old caves," Logan broke silence first. "It smells like one anyway—"

"Yes."

"Any chance of getting loose?"

Hosteen, moving his arms, was rewarded by a slight give of his bonds.

"Might be." He continued his efforts.

"Ha!" That was an exclamation of triumph from Logan. "That does it! Here—where are you?"

A hand, moving through the thick blanket of no light, clutched at Hosteen's shoulder and moved swiftly down to the coils of rope about him.

"They weren't very clever with their knots." Logan's fingers were now busy behind Hosteen's back.

"I don't think"—the Terran sat up, massaged his right wrist with the fingers of his left hand—"we were meant to stay tied or they would have left the nets on us. Now—let's just see—"

He had no idea how big the cave was or how far they were from the outer door. Nor was he too sure in which direction that door lay. The odd quality of this dark and the lifeless feel of the air did weird things to alter a man's sense of direction—even, Hosteen suspected, influenced his clarity of thought. He stood for a long second or two, trying to orientate himself before he moved in a shuffle, half crouched, to sweep the floor with one hand, while the other was out before him as insurance against coming up short against another wall.

"Stay right where you are," he ordered Logan.

"What's the game?"

"They threw our belts in after us, broke our weapons, but I've an atom torch on that belt. And they didn't damage that, at least not while I was watching—"

Sweep—sweep—finger tips scraping on stone, nails gritting—then the smoothness of hide worked into leather! The Terran squatted, drew his find to him, knew by touch it was Logan's, and looped the belt around his shoulder for safe keeping.

"Got yours," he reported. "Mine can't be too far away."

Once more sweep—sweep. His fingers were growing tender. Then they rapped against an object, and there was a metallic sound. He was holding a ruined stunner. Only a few inches beyond that—his belt!

Hosteen slipped it hurriedly through his hands, locating radar compass, a pouch of sustenance tablets, the small emergency medical kit, to find in the last loop next to the empty knife sheath the pencil-slim eight-inch tube he was looking for. He pushed its wide fan button and blinked at a blinding answer of light.

"Whew!" Logan's exclamation was tinged with awe.

They were in a cave right enough, and the interior walls and roof had been coated with that same dull black substance they had seen in the passages to the caverns of the gardens, the building material of the unknown star travelers.

In a tangle by the door, now closed so that even the seam of its opening was invisible, were objects that certainly did not date back to the period of the Sealed Caves. Hosteen went to examine the exhibits. Their own broken bladed hunting knives and Logan's smashed stunner lay there, but there were other things—another stunner, another belt, this one heavily weighted with a third again as much equipment as the one he had worn into the Peaks.

Hosteen picked that out of the dust.

"Widders!" He got to his feet and held up the torch so its glow covered as much of the cave as possible. But there was no sign of the civ—if he had preceded them into captivity here.

"Maybe there's another passage here—" Logan drew his half-brother's attention to a jutting of wall at the left where a shadow might mask an opening. And it did—there was a dark hole there.

Logan gathered up the rope of their bonds and coiled it belt-wise about his waist. They had no weapons—or did they? Hosteen hefted the belt that had belonged to Widders. Knife and stunner were gone from their sheaths, but he remembered the off-world weapon that had subdued them when the civ had started on his mad quest into the Blue. And there was a chance some similar surprise might be part of this equipment.

"Do we go?" Logan stood at the mouth of the tunnel.

Hosteen had located a pouch envelope on Widders' belt. He shook from it into his hand a ball an inch and a half in diameter, with a small knob projecting from its smooth surface. It had the appearance of a small antiperso grenade. He looked from it to the sealed door in speculation. A full-sized antiperso grenade was a key to unlock a piece of field armor, planted in the right way at the right time, and Hosteen had planted them so. What effect would a grenade one third the regular size have on the cave door?

"Find somethin' interestin'?" Logan asked.

"Might just be." Hosteen outlined in a terse sentence or two what he thought he held and its uses.

"Get the door down with that?"

Hosteen shrugged. "I don't know—might be chancy. We don't know the properties of this alien cave-sealing material. Remember what happened that other time?"

Months before, the back lash of an Xik weapon used miles away had reacted violently on the alien coating of just such a cave, locking them into what, except for chance, might have been a living tomb. They had escaped then, but one could not depend on personal "medicine" too long or too hard.

"I say, try the back door first." Logan indicated the passage.

And that made good sense. Widders was not in the cave, and if he had been a prisoner here, he might have taken that way before them. There had been many indications that the Unknowns had been fond of under-mountain ways and were adept at boring them.

They sorted over the equipment, dividing up the grenades, ration tablets, supplies. Water—they had no water save that in the canteens, but at least they were not exposed to the baking sun.

No passage ran beyond that wall. They found instead a steeply sloping, downward ramp where there was no dust to cushion the black flooring. They advanced slowly. Hosteen ahead, the torch in one hand, a sweat-sticky grenade in the other.

The Terran heard Logan sniff as one might scent-danger.

"Water—somewhere ahead."

For a moment Hosteen's imagination painted for him the picture of another pocket paradise like the Cavern of the Hundred Gardens. But where there had been the aromatic odors of clean and spicy things to tantalize them then, here was a dank breath not only of dampness but also of other and even less pleasant smells.

Along the walls the torch picked up beads of moisture, which gave black prismatic flickers of color. Logan ran his finger along to wipe out a cluster, then rubbed it vigorously on the edge of his yoris-hide-corselet with an exclamation of disgust.

"Slime!" He held the finger to his nose. "Stinks, too. I'd say we might be on our way straight down into a drain—"

The drops on the wall coalesced into oily runlets, and the nephritic odor grew stronger. Yet the air was not still. There was a draft rising, bringing with it a fog of corruption.

All the way down they had seen no indication that anyone had come before them. But now they reached a point where there was a huge blotch across the slope of the wall, where the runlets had been smeared together, through which new trickles were now cutting paths. The damp had prevented the drying of the splotch.

"That wasn't done too long ago," Logan observed. He put out his own hand, though he did not touch finger to the wall, to show that the top of the smear was at shoulder height. "Someone or something could have fallen and slipped down there—"

Hosteen swung the torch closer to floor level. Logan's deduction was borne out by still undried marks.

"And that"—Logan pounced upon one of the damp spots—"was the toe of a boot!"

Again his tracker's eye was right. Only the toe of an off-world boot could have left that well-defined curve. Widders? Or some survivor from the LB holding up in this mountain maze against the danger of the natives waiting outside?

"He went down—he did not come back—whoever he was," Logan observed.

"Meaning that he might not have been able to retreat? Well, we either go on or try to break that door down with a grenade. Have any second thoughts on the matter?"

"Go on." Logan's answer was prompted. "We have stingers in these." He tossed a grenade into the air and caught it deftly.

They went on, watching floor and wall for any further traces of the one or ones who had taken that passage before them, but sighted none. Only the damp increased until the air was half-foggy moisture. And where, in the upper regions, that moisture had been chill, here it was increasingly warm, warm and odorous. There was a musky taint, which set Hosteen to sniffing, hinting of life ahead.

The passage was no longer a steep descent; it was beginning to level off. And now the dripping walls supplied a thin stream of water carried in a depression down the center of the floor, flowing ahead. The torch caught the edge of an archway that led out—out where—into what?

As they went through it, Hosteen switched the beam of the torch from a diffused glow into a single spear point of concentrated light. He thought he could see a shadowy point somewhere far to the right, which could be shoreline or wall. But below was a spread of oily water on which patches of floating stuff turned rainbow-hued when the light caught them, fading into dullness as they moved out of its beam once more.

The passage, which had brought them here, ran on out into the water, as a wharf or pier of rock, obviously artificially fashioned. And along its surface at intervals were rings of the same rock standing on end as if waiting for mooring ropes. Mooring ropes—for

what manner of craft? Who had sailed this lake or river and for what
purpose?

Together they walked slowly along that wharf—the bare rings,
the greasy, ill-smelling flood that washed sluggishly along its side—
The Cavern of the Hundred Gardens had been alien—alien but not
inimical. Here there was a difference. Again Hosteen could not rec-
oncile the minds that had created the gardens and those that had engineered these borings in the mountain of the Blue.

"What kind of ships?" Logan asked suddenly. "Who were they
and why did they want ships here? The Gardens—and this place—
don't match."

"They are not the same," Hosteen agreed. "Kwii halchinigii
'ant'iihnii—"

"What?"

"I said—this place smells of witchcraft."

"That is the truth!" Logan commented with feeling. "Where do
we go now? Somehow I don't fancy swimmin'."

They had reached the end of the wharf and were gazing out over
the sluggishly flowing water, trying to catch some landmark in the
beam of the torch. But save for those vague shadows far to the right,
there was nothing to suggest this place had any boundaries beyond.

It was when Hosteen swung the torch left to pick out a continu-
ation of the wall through which they had come that they sighted
a possible exit. A beach of sorts extended along this side of the
cavern—several yards of coarse sand and gravel between the foot
of the wall and the lapping of the dark water. And along the wall itself were dark shadows, which might or might not contain the
openings to further caves or passages. It was more inviting to in-
vestigate than the water, for Hosteen agreed with Logan's comment moments earlier—this was not a place to tempt a swimmer.
The very look of that opaque flood suggested unpleasant things
lurking below its encrusted surface.

They retreated along the wharf, leaped from it to the fringe of
beach. Here and there stones of some size were embedded in the
gravel—or were they stones? Hosteen stopped and toed one of
them over with his boot. The black eye holes of a skull stared back at

him. Curving horns rooted in the bone told him that a Norbie had died here. Some time ago he judged by the condition of the bone.

"In the Name of the Seven Thunders, what's that?" Logan caught at Hosteen's arm, dragged the torch forward. And again its gleam picked out details of bleached bone.

But such bone! Hosteen found it hard to picture that great head ever enclosed in flesh. Half buried in the gravel as the skull now was, the angle of that fanged jaw as long as his arm, the huge pits of eye sockets, were like nothing he had ever seen on Arzor or on fifty other planets either.

"Three eyes!" Logan's voice sounded weirdly over the lisping lap of the water. "It had three eyes!"

He was right. Two eye sockets abnormally far to each side were centered by a third midpoint above the jagged toothed jaw. Three eyes!

On Terra there had been monsters in the far past whose bones had endured out of their own era into the time of humankind, so that man had dug them free of earth and rock and set them up in museums to marvel at. Perhaps this was one of the ancient things that had once dominated Arzor, its kind long since vanished from the planet. Yet Hosteen did not think so. Those three eye sockets were a distortion, alien.

"It must have been a monster!" Logan was down on his knees scraping at the gravel gingerly, as if he did not want to touch the bone with his bare hands. And now Hosteen surveyed the exposed skull narrowly. He went back, picked up the Norbie one by a horn, and brought it to rest beside that three-eyed thing, comparing one to the other.

"What's the matter?" Logan wanted to know.

"Shil hazheen—"

Logan looked at him in some exasperation. "Talk so a fella can understand, won't you?"

"I am confused," Hosteen obligingly translated. "This is impossible."

"What is?"

"This skull"—Hosteen pointed to the Norbie—"is crumbling

away from age, perhaps from damp. Yet it is of a native, a type of Arzoran life that exists today. Compare it with this other one. The three-eye is no different; they could be of the same age—"

"What are you tryin' to say?"

Hosteen spoke of the early giant reptiles on Terra, of the chance that this might have been a relic of pre-intelligent life on Arzor.

"Only it doesn't look old enough—that's what you mean? Well, couldn't the Norbie have been old, too?"

"That might be so—to each planet its own history. Only on Terra such monsters had vanished long before the first primitive man had evolved. And surely Norbie legends would mention these if they had shared the same world at the same time."

"The plains people have always been afraid of the Blue."

"But not for any reason such as monsters, for they do talk of those giant killer birds and every other known natural menace."

"Which means—?"

"That if these things were alive only a short time ago, historically speaking, say a century or so in the past, they might have been confined to underground places such as this, known only to victims trapped here."

"And that some three-eye could be waitin' right around the next bend now?" Logan got to his feet and brushed sand from his hands. "That isn't the most cheerful news in the world?"

"I could be wrong." But Hosteen was not going to relax any vigilance on that count. And how much advantage would an antiperso grenade give him over sudden death watching through three eyes?

They went on down the beach at a slower pace, using the torch on every dark spot before them, alert to any sound. Yet the lap of the water, the crunch of their boots on the coarse gravel was all they heard.

So far none of those shadows had concealed any further openings. But they were well away from the wharf when Logan again caught at Hosteen's touch hand, directing the beam higher on the wall.

"Somethin' moved—up there!"

Out into the path of the light flew a winged creature uttering a small, mewling cry. The light brought into vivid life yellow wings banded with white.

"Feefraw!" Logan named one of the common berry-feeding birds to be found along any mountainside. "But what is it doing in here?"

"It could be showing us a way out." Hosteen aimed his light straight for the spot from which the bird had come. There was an opening deeper than any of the shallow crevices they had discovered so far. The feefraw must have gotten into the mountain somewhere, perhaps down this very passage.

The bird circled around in the path of the beam, and now, as if guided by the light, went back to the hole above, where it settled down on the edge, still mewling mournfully.

"Back door?" Logan suggested.

"No harm in trying it."

An advantage of that hole was that it certainly did not look large enough to accommodate the bulk of any creature with a skull as big as the one they had found. One could travel that road without fearing a monster lurking behind every rock ahead. Hosteen tucked the torch into the front of his shirt and began to climb toward that promising niche.

CHAPTER ELEVEN

T hey stood together in the opening of another cave. Could they hope by the evidence of the bird that it was the mouth of a passage, a passage giving upon light, air, and the clean outer world?

If this was a passage, it was not a smoothed, coated one, made ready for use by the Unknowns. Here there was no black coating on the walls, only the rough purple-red of the native stone. But there was a way before them, and as they started, the feefraw cried and fluttered along behind as if drawn by the torch light.

Unhappily the way did not slope upward but ran straight, in some places so narrow that they had to turn sidewise and scrape through between jutting points of rock. But the air was a moving current, and it lacked the strange quality of that in the alien ways.

Logan sniffed again. "Not too good."

It was back, the musky taint that had been strong before they came out into the cavern of the river. Musky taint, and damp—yet Hosteen was sure they had not circled back. They could not have returned to the beach beyond the wharf.

The feefraw had continued to flutter behind. Now its mewling became a mournful wail, and it flew with blind recklessness between the two men and vanished ahead down the passage. Hosteen pushed the pace as they came out into a gray twilight. He snapped off the torch, advanced warily, and looked down onto a scene so weird that for a moment he could almost believe he was caught in a dream nightmare.

They were perched in a rounded pocket in the wall of another cavern—but a cavern with such dimensions that perhaps only an aerial survey could chart it. Here, too, was water—streams, ponds, even a small lake. But the water was housed between walls. The floor of the cavern as far as he could see in the grayish light, was a giant game board. Walled squares enclosed a pond and a small scrap of surrounding land, or land through which a stream wandered. For what purpose? There were no signs of cultivated vegetation such as a farm field might show.

"Pens." Logan's inspiration clicked from possibility to probability.

Those geometrically correct enclosures could be pens—like the home corrals of a holding in the plains. But pens to confine what—and why?

They squatted together trying to note any sign of movement in the nearest enclosures. The vegetation there was coarse, reedy stuff, as pallidly gray as the light, or low-growing plants with thick, unwholesome-looking fleshy leaves. The whole scene was repellent, not enticing as the Cavern of the Hundred Gardens had been.

"This has been here a long time," Logan observed. "Look at that wall there—"

Hosteen sighted on the section Logan indicated. The walls had collapsed, giving access to two other enclosures. Yes, and beyond was another tumbled wall. The pens, if pens they had been, were no longer separated. He stood up and unhooked the distance lenses from his belt. The light was poor, but perhaps he could see what lay beyond their immediate vicinity.

He swept the glasses slowly across the territory from right to left. Pens, water, growing stuff, the same as those that lay below them. There was a difference in the type of vegetation in several places, he thought. And one or two of the enclosures were bare and desertlike, either by design or the failure of the odd "crop" once grown there.

The walls were not the only evidence of once purposeful control, Hosteen discovered, as his distance lenses caught a shadowy pile at the far left. It was a building of some sort, he believed, and said as much to Logan. The other, taking the lenses in turn, confirmed his guess.

"Head for that?" he wanted to know.

It was a logical goal. At the same time, surveying those "pens," Hosteen was aware of a strange reluctance to venture down into the walled squares and oblongs, to force a way through the sickly and

sinister-looking growth they held. And Logan put the same squea-
mishness into words.

"Don't like to trail through that somehow—"

Hosteen took back the glasses and studied the distant building.
The murky dusk of the cavern's atmosphere made it somehow un-
substantial when one attempted to pin down a definite line of wall
or a roof or even the approximate size of the structure. This was like
trying to see clearly an object that lay beyond a misty, water-
splashed window. And perhaps that was part of the trouble—the
dank air here was not far removed from fog.

There was certainly no sign of any movement about the place,
just as there was none in the pens, save the ripple of some wandering
stream. Hosteen did not believe that intelligence lingered here,
though perhaps other life might. And the building might not only
explain the purpose of the cavern but also show them some form of
escape. Those who had built this place had surely had another mode
of entrance than the narrow, ragged rock fault that had led the settlers in.

"We'll try to reach that." When he voiced those words, Hosteen
was surprised at his own dubious tone.

Logan laughed. "Devil-devil country," he commented. "I'd like it
better takin' this one with some of our boys backin' our play. Let's
hope our long-toothed, three-eyed whatsit isn't sittin' down there
easy-like just waitin' for supper to walk within grabbin' range, and
me without even a knife to do any protestin' about bein' the main
course. Waitin' never made a thing easier though. Shall we blast off
for orbit?"

He swung over the lip of the drop with Hosteen following. Their
boots thudded into the loose soil as they fell free for the last foot or
so and found themselves in one of the walled patches where the bar-
riers were at least ten feet tall. Had it not been for broken areas, they
might not have been able to make their way from one pocket to the
next, for what remained of the walls was slick-smooth.

Twice they had to form human ladders to win out of pens where
the boundaries were still intact. And in one of those they discovered
another bony remnant from the past—a skull topping a lace of ver-
tebra and ribs, the whole forming skeletal remains of a creature

Hosteen could not identify. There was a long, narrow head with a minute brain pan, the jaws tapering to a point, in the upper portion of which was still socketed a horn, curving up.

Logan caught at that and gave it a twist. It broke loose in his hand, and he held aloft a wicked weapon some ten inches long, sharp as any yoris fang and probably, in its day, even more dangerous.

"Another whatsit."

"Someone was collecting," Hosteen guessed, walking around that rack of bones. He thought that was the reason for the pens—the water. Just as the Cavern of the Hundred Gardens had represented a botanical collection culled from at least a hundred different worlds for their beauty and fragrance, here another collection had been kept—reptiles, animals—who knew? This could have existed as some sort of zoo or perhaps stockyard. Yet where the gardens had flourished over the centuries or eons after the disappearance of the gardeners, this had not.

"We ought to be glad of that," was Logan's quick reply to the Terran's comment. "I don't fancy bein' hunted when I can't do any markin' up in return. This would make a good huntin' trophy." He balanced the horn in his hand, then thrust its point deep into the empty sheath where his knife had once ridden. "Bet Krotag's never seen anythin' like it."

"Those broken walls—" Hosteen sat side by side with his half-brother on the unbreached one of the skeleton enclosure. "Suppose whoever was in charge here left suddenly—"

"And the stock got hungry and decided to do somethin' about it?" Logan asked. "Could be. But just think of things that could smash through somethin' as tough as this!" He slapped his hand on the surface under him. "That would be like seein' a crusher alive, wild, and rarin' to blast! Glad we came late—this would be no place to 'first ship' when that breakout was goin' on."

They kept on their uneven course over walls and through pens. The tablets of emergency rations they had chewed from time to time gave them energy and put off the need for sleep. But Hosteen knew that there was a point past which it was dangerous to depend upon that artificial strength, and they were fast approaching the limit. If they could find refuge in the building ahead, then they could hole up for a space, long enough to get normal rest. Otherwise, the bolstering drug could fail at some crucial moment and send them into helpless collapse.

On top of the last wall they paused again, while Hosteen turned the beam of the torch on the waiting building. Between their present perch and that there was a line of slim, smooth posts set in the earth. But if they had been put there to support a fence, the rest of that barrier had long since disappeared. And as far as the two explorers could see, the way to the wedge-shaped door in the massive two-story structure was open.

Slipping from the wall, they were well out toward those posts when Hosteen halted and flung out an arm quickly to catch at Logan. Memories of safeguards on remote worlds stirred. Because one could not see a barrier was no reason to believe there was none there. If the creatures confined back in the pens had burst through the walls, the keepers of this place must have possessed some form of defense and protection to handle accidents. A force-field now, generated between those poles, he warned. Logan nodded.

"Could be." He caught up a stone and hurled it through the space directly before them. It struck with a sullen clunk on the wall beside the door of the building, passing the pole area without hindrance.

"If it ever was there—it must be gone now."

The evidence was clear, yet a part of Hosteen walked in dread as they advanced. Instinct, rained and tested many times in the past, instinct that was a part of that mysterious inborn gift making him one with the team, argued now against this place. He fought that unease as he stepped between the poles.

His hands went to his ears. He cowered, threw himself forward, and rolled across the hard ground in an agony that filled his head with pain, that was vibration, noise, something alien enough so that he could not put name to it! The world was filled with a piercing screaming, which tore at his body, cell by living cell. Hosteen had known physical pain and mental torment in the past, but nothing had ever reached this point—not in a sane world.

When he was again conscious, he lay in the dark, huddled up, hardly daring to breathe lest that punishment return. Then, at last, he moved stiffly, levered himself up, conscious of light at his back.

He looked over his shoulder at a wedge-shaped section of gray. Wedge-shaped! The door in the building! He had reached the building then. But what had happened? He forced himself to remember, though the process hurt.

The pole barrier—a sonic, a sonic of some sort! Logan—Logan had been with him! Where was he now?

Hosteen could not make it to his feet; the first attempt made his head whirl. He crawled on his hands and knees back into the open and found Logan on the ramp that led to the doorway, moaning dully, his eyes closed, his hands to his head.

"What was it?" They lay side by side now within the first room of the building. Logan got out the question in a hoarse croak.

"A sonic, I think."

"That makes sense." Sonics were known to frawn herders, but the devices were not in general good favor. Such broadcasters had to be used by a master and were not easily controlled. The right degree of sound waves could keep a herd in docile submission, a fraction off and you had a frenzied stampede or a panic that could send half your animals to their deaths, completely insane.

"Still working—but it didn't kill us," Logan commented.

"Tuned in for a different life form," Hosteen pointed out. "Might not kill them either—just stun. But I don't want another dose of that."

Their experience of crossing the barrier had wrung the last of their drug-supported strength from them. They slept, roused to swallow tablets and drink from the canteens they had filled at one of the pen springs, and drifted off to sleep again. How long had lethargy lasted they could not afterwards decide. But they awoke at last, clear-headed and with a measure of their normal energy.

Logan studied two sustenance tablets lying on his palm. "I'd like me some real chewin' meat again," he announced. "These things don't help a man forget he's empty—"

"They'll keep us going—"

"Goin' where?"

"There must be some way out of here. We'll just have to find it."

They had explored the building. If the keepers of the pens had left in such a hurry that they had not had time to care for the future of their captive specimens, still they had taken the contents of the rooms with them. No clues remained among those bare walls as to the men or creatures who had once lived here. That the building had been a habitation was proved by a washing place they found in one room and something built into another that Hosteen was sure was a cook unit. But all else was gone, though holes and scars suggested installations ripped free in a hurry.

When they reached the top floor of the building, they found a way out onto the flat roof, and from that vantage point they studied what they could see of the surrounding cavern.

At the back of the structure there were no pens. A smooth stretch of ground led directly to a passage-opening in the cave wall—a very large one.

"That's the front door," Logan observed. "Straight ahead—"

"Straight ahead—but with something in between." Hosteen pivoted, surveying the surrounding terrain. He was right; the posts marking the sonic barrier made a tight, complete circle about the building. To reach the tempting "front door" meant recrossing that unseen barrier. And to do that—

Also, why did he keep thinking that there was a menace lurking out there? The only living thing they had seen in any of these burrows was the feefraw that had somehow found its way into this deserted world. The bones of the creature that had once been penned here were old enough to crumble. Yet whenever he faced those walled squares, his flesh crawled, his instincts warned. There was some danger here, something they had not yet sighted.

"Look!" Logan's hand on his shoulder pulled him around. He was now facing the entrance to the big passage. "There," his half-brother directed, "by that side pillar."

The sides of the passage opening had been squared into pillars, joined to the parent rock. And Logan was right; here was a dark bundle on the ground at the foot of one. Hosteen focused the distance lenses. The half light was deceiving but not enough to conceal the nature of what lay there—that could only be a man.

"Widders?" Logan asked.

"Might be." Had that crumpled figure stirred, tried to raise a hand? If that were Widders and he had crossed the sonic barrier, he could have been knocked out only temporarily.

"Come on," Hosteen called, already on his way from the roof.

"Make it quick," Logan answered.

That could be their best defense—a running leap with impetus enough to tear a man through the beam. Hosteen knew of no other way to cross without the shields they did not possess. Having tested the straps of their equipment, they toed the mark just beside the outer wall, then sprinted for the pole line.

Hosteen launched himself, felt the tearing of the sonic waves as he shot through them, landed beyond, to roll helplessly, battling unconsciousness. Logan spiraled over him with flailing arms and legs and lay now beyond.

Somehow the Terran fought to his knees. It seemed to him the shock this time was less. He crawled to Logan, who was now striving to sit up, his mouth drawn crooked in his effort to control his whisper.

"We made it—"

They crouched together, shoulder touching shoulder, until their heads cleared and they were able to stand. Then they headed for the man by the pillar.

Hosteen recognized the torn coverall. "Widders! Widders!" He wavered forward, to go down again beside the quiet form. Then his eyes fastened on one outflung hand unbelievingly.

Skin over bone, with the bone itself breaking through the tight pull of the skin on the knuckles! Fighting his fear of the dead, the inborn sense of defilement, he took the body by one shoulder, rolled it over on its back—

"No—no!" Logan's cry was one of raw horror.

This thing had been Widders, Hosteen was sure of that. What it was now, what anyone could swear to, was that it might once have been human. The Terran thrust his hands deep into the harshness of the sand, scrubbed them back and forth, wondering if he would ever be able to forget that he had touched this—this—

"What did—that?" Logan's demand was a whisper.

"I don't know." Hosteen stood up, one hand pressed to his heaving middle. His instinct had been right. Somewhere here lurked a hunter—a hunter whose method of feeding was far removed from the sanity of human life. They must get away—out of here—now!

He grabbed for Logan, shoved him toward the passage Widders must have been trying to reach when he had been pulled down. There was a horror loose in this place that had not died long ago in those pens—if it had ever been confined there.

They ran for the open passage and sped into the dark mouth of the tunnel. And they fled on blindly into that thick dark until there was a band of tight, hard pain about their lower ribs and the panic that had spurred them could no longer push their tired bodies into fresh effort. Then, clinging together, as if the touch of flesh against flesh was a defense against the insanity behind, they sat on the floor, dragging in the dead air in ragged, painful gasps.

CHAPTER TWELVE

T his—is—an—open—passage." Logan's warning came in separated words.

He was right. There was nothing to prevent that which had hunted Widders from prowling into this dark tunnel. Perhaps even now it lurked in the dim reaches ahead.

The arm Hosteen had flung about Logan's heaving shoulders tightened spasmodically. He must not let panic crowd out reason— that would deliver them both over to death. They had to keep thinking clearly.

"We have the grenades and the torch," he reassured himself as well as his companion. "Widders did not have his equipment—no light or weapon. It was a miracle he got even this far."

The shudders that had been shaking Logan were not so continuous.

"Scared as a paca rat caught in a grain bin!" The answer came with a ghost of the old wry humor Logan had always summoned to front disaster. "Never broke and ran like that before, though."

"That was enough to make both of us bolt," Hosteen replied. "You didn't see me holding back any, did you? But now I think we are past the trapped paca rat stage."

Logan's hand tightened on Hosteen's forearm in a grip of rough affection and then fell away. "You're right, brother. We've moved up a few steps in the panic scale—maybe now we're on the level of a frawn bull. But I want to be a tough yoris before we face somethin' alive and kickin'."

"Two yoris it is," Hosteen agreed. "I'd say keep straight ahead, but at less of a scamper."

He fingered the atom torch indecisively. If he switched that on, would the beam signal a lurker? But the advantage of light over dark won. With the enemy revealed in the light, they would have a chance to use their grenades.

As the passage continued to bore ahead through the stuff of the mountain, Hosteen marveled at the extent of the under-the-surface work. More than just the first mountain must be occupied by this labyrinth. He was sure they were well beyond the height up which the Norbies had originally driven their captives.

There were no signs that anything had come this way before them, and the first stark shock of Widders' end lost some of its impact on their minds. Hosteen sighted a gray glimmer ahead and switched off the torch so that they could approach another tunnel mouth warily.

Here projections hung down from overhead and stood up out of the floor of the passage, so they passed between two rows of pointed objects as thick as a man's leg. And set in a curved space well above their heads were three ovals of a blood-red, transparent substance through which light streamed in gory beams.

What lay beyond the opening was sun heat—the sun heat of the parched outer world, where the Big Dry reigned uncontrolled.

They hunched down between those pointed pillars, shielded their eyes against the punishing glare, and tried to pick out some route across that seared landscape.

In the shimmer of the heat waves there was a thin line of poles running—with a gap here and there—into the distance, just as the poles had marked the sonic barrier before the pens.

Hosteen used the lenses to trace that line, but the glare of that open oven was as deceptive as the foggy murk of the interior cavern.

"We'll have to lay up and wait for dark." Logan drew his knees up to his chest and folded his arms about them. "Nothin' could last for a half hour out there now."

How far did that guiding line of poles stretch? Could one find shelter at the end of that path before the coming of another day? And was this indeed open country?

"Open country?" Hosteen repeated questioningly.

"You think this might be another controlled cavern, to hold things enjoyin' bein' baked?"

"There are those poles—they must have run a sonic through here once." Hosteen pointed out the obvious.

"And there are a lot of gaps in that now, too." Logan squinted to study the way ahead. "Do we go back—or do we try it?"

"I'd say try it—at least part way. If night does come here, we can try and turn back if we can't see an end within safe travel distance."

"That makes sense," Logan conceded. "We wait."

Hope was thin. Much depended now on whether this was another cavern under weather control—the wrong kind of control for them—or the open. For human eyes, there was no looking up into the inferno that marked the possible sky. Hosteen had thought that the heat and glare when they first reached the end of the passage had been that of early afternoon. So they would wait for a night that might never fall or start the long trail back to that distant cave into which the Norbies had sealed them.

Uneasily they slept in turn, keeping watch as the time crept lead-enly by. Suddenly, Hosteen was aroused from a doze by Logan's shaking.

"Look!"

Where the light had been—a yellow-white their eyes could meet only with actual pain—there was now a reddish glow. The Terran had seen its like too many times to be mistaken. Yes, there was a night out there, and it was now on its way. They need only wait for true dusk and then follow the road marked by the pole line.

They ate, drank sparingly of their water, and waited impatiently for the red to deepen to purple, the purple that meant freedom. But as they waited, Hosteen walked forward between the projections, his senses alert—to what? There was no sound out of the desert ahead, nothing moving there.

With the lenses he could follow the pole line well ahead—bare rock, the poles, with gaps in their marching line. No vegetation, no place for any living thing he had seen yet on Arzor. Yet, inside him, there was a growing fear of that sere landscape, a tension far higher in pitch than any he had known before in any of the tunnels and caverns they had traversed.

"What is it?"

Startled, Hosteen looked back over his shoulder. Logan had been testing the fastening of the canteens. But now he, too, was staring with narrowed eyes into the open.

"I don't know," the other answered slowly. "This—is—strange—"

They had run in open horror and fear from the place where Widders lay. Now, as the Terran weighed one emotion against the other, he was sure that the sensation he was experiencing was not the same as they had known earlier. Where that, in part, had been physical fear, this was a more subtle thing, twitching at mind and not at body.

"We'll go—" Logan did not make a question of that, rather a promise that was half challenge to what lay ahead. His jaw was set, and the stubbornness that had made him go his own way so often in the past was in the ascendant now, setting him to face what he shrank from.

"We'll go," Hosteen assented. Every fiber of his body fought against his will in this. What had begun as an uneasiness was now a shivering, quivering revolt of one deeply rooted part of him against the iron form of his determination. Yet, he knew that he could not refuse to go out there and face whatever waited, for if he did, he would be broken in some strange, inexplicable way that would leave him as crippled as if he had been shorn of a leg or an arm.

Dusk—they moved forward, shoulder to shoulder, coming out of the tunnel mouth. Logan caught at Hosteen and dragged him half around.

For a wild second or two the Terran thought he was facing the source of his subtle fears. Then he guessed the truth. The tunnel mouth had been carved into a weird and horrible image. They had emerged from a fanged mouth, the open gullet of a three-eyed monster fashioned after the skull they had discovered on the shore of the underground lake. The eyes glinted—those were the oval red patches they had sighted from within. The wrinkled snout—Hosteen did not doubt for a moment that the artist who had designed that portal knew well a living model.

"Could that be the full size of three eyes?" Logan found his voice and attempted some of his old lightness of tone.

"Who knows—at least we came out instead of going in."

"And we may regret that yet!"

They trotted on, away from the mask doorway. Underfoot, the space bordered by the pole line was smooth, though Hosteen's torch did not show any trace of paving. Anyway, it provided good footing for the pace they must set, until midnight told them whether they could advance or must retreat into three eyes' waiting jaws.

Not a sound, not a stir of breeze. But—Hosteen stopped and swung the pencil beam of the torch off the path before him to a pool of shadow under a pinnacle of rock to the left. Light on rocks—just that, bare rocks. Yet, the moment before the ray had touched that surface, he had been certain something lurked there, slinking around that pile, sniffing its way toward the pole path. He could have sworn he heard the pattern of its gusty breathing, the faint scrape of talon on rock, the sound of a stone disturbed!

"Nothin' there!"

Logan, also? Had he heard, sensed, believed something had been out there?

"To the left!" Logan's hand was on his wrist now, bringing the torch beam about, to shine it directly into a crevice in the ground. Of course! The thing must be crouching there, just waiting for them to draw opposite and then—!

Bare rock—empty crevice, nothing!

"There—there has to be somethin'." Logan's words were marked with the determination to hold his emotions in check. "They had a sonic barrier for protection, didn't they?"

"Once they had it," replied Hosteen.

Ghosts—spirits? The ghosts of the builders of this road, the artist who had carved that dragon mask—or of the weird life that had lived on this sun-rusted plain from which the builders protected themselves in their journeyings?

He started on, Logan matching him step by step. They started slowly and then their speed built, as the need to get past all those rock outcrops, all those sinister crevices and dips, ate at their self-control.

Croaking—or was it husky breathing? There—! Hosteen was sure this time he had spotted the danger point, not too far ahead in a shadow pool by a hillock. He gripped a grenade in one hand, ready, brought the torch up with the quick flick of a stunner draw, aiming the light as he might the stupefying ray.

Rock—only rock.

"Steady!" Hosteen was not even aware he had given himself that command aloud.

If his imagination was at work, perhaps he could bend it to his own purposes. Suppose there was some living thing out there playing games, able to project an impression of its presence where it was not in order to confuse enemies? Hosteen's training of the team had made him open-minded in matters dealing with mental relationships between men and animals—and, who knows, perhaps some of the same techniques could work between man and alien?

That faculty, which had tied him to Surra, Hing, and Baku, in part to the stallion Rain and other non-mutant-bred living creatures, could he use it to detect what was behind this nerve-breaking attack? Something assured him that this was an attack, far more subtle and devastating than any physical thrust out of the night.

Just as a blindfolded man might feel his way cautiously through unknown territory, so did Hosteen reach out to try to contact what lay waiting out there. Intelligence—was he dealing with intelligence, alien but still to be reckoned so by human standards? Or did he front some protective device set up to warn off intruders, just as the sonic barrier had been erected to protect the rulers of the pen cavern?

A touch of what—awareness? The Terran was sure he had met that, so sure that he paused and slowly pivoted toward the dark space from which that twinge of contact had seemed to come. Was it his imagination that supplied the rest? He could never have offered any proof, but from that instant Hosteen believed that he had had a momentary mental meeting with someone or something that had once lived in communication with the builders of this mountain maze, as he lived in concert with the team.

And he believed it so firmly that he strove to hold to that thread, to impress upon that unknown creature his desire for a meeting, as he could in part impose his will on the team. Only, the frail and fleeting contact was snapped almost as quickly as it was made.

What flooded in to follow was the anger of an aroused guardian or an embattled survivor—an attack through mental and emotional gates so intense that, had it persisted, perhaps both men would have broken under it.

Shadows boiled, twisted, crawled, slunk in upon them. The light beam stabbed each menace into nothingness, only to have another take its place. Logan called out hoarsely, snatched up stones clawed loose handfuls of soil to hurl them at that invisible menace now ringing them in. And it built up and up!

There was rage in this—as if behind some unclimbable barrier the three-eyed monster of the caverns raced back and forth, eager to get at them. And it was when that impression grew on Hosteen that he gasped out an order:

"Stand still!"

Logan froze, his arm half up to throw a rock.

"We go on—"

Hosteen obeyed his own order, his legs moving stiffly, his active mind arguing against such folly. There—there *was* something crawling across the path just ahead—waiting—ready— To the left— two—converging on the strip through which the men must pass within moments. They were surrounded.

Logan shuffled along. Sweep, sweep—the torch opened the secrets of shadows. But the pressure against the intruders was reaching the point past which Hosteen was afraid he could not hold.

With a snarl Logan faced left, his hand went to his belt, and he lobbed one of the grenades into the dark. The resulting burst of light left them blinded for a second or two.

Then—nothing! As there had been the explosion, so now there was an answering burst of energy in their minds. Then, only empty land under the night sky—a landscape now without any life in it.

Shaken, they stood breathing hard with rib-stretching gasps and then began to run. Again their road approached the foot of a mountain, and they could reach that before the sun rose.

Underfoot, the trail was rising slowly but steadily above the surface of the ground. When Hosteen turned the light on that road, they saw that now it was fashioned of the black substance used elsewhere to coat tunnel walls.

They were well above the general level of the valley when the road ended in a wide wedge of black, the narrow end of which touched against a solid cliff wall in which there was no discernible break. To all their inspection with hand and torch, there was no door there, no way ahead. This was the end of the trail they had been following for so long.

"A landin' mat for 'copters, d' you suppose?" Logan asked after they had made a second circling exploration of the wedge. He was sitting cross-legged on the smooth black surface, his hands resting on his knees. "What now—do we start back?"

Privately the Terran doubted if they could now make that return trip before the day broke. Though they had not come so far in actual distance, their struggle with the shadows had been exhausting. He knew that fatigue of both mind and body rode him, made him flinch at the thought of back-tracking. Yet if they wanted to live, they must do that before sunrise.

He had hunkered down on the pavement and was flashing his torch back forth across its surface for no conscious reason. Then his eyes sighted the pattern there, and his dull mind became alert. There was a circular strip of glassy, glossy black, which began at the point where the road met the wedge and then spiraled around and around until it ended in a circle just large enough for a man to stand upon.

Why he went into action then he could never afterwards explain. It was all a part of the weird influence of this place. He only knew that this he must do at once.

Crossing to the beginning of that spiral, he began to walk along the route it marked, around and around, approaching the center point and concentrating upon keeping his boots firmly planted on the slick surface, in no way touching the duller borders.

Dimly he was aware of Logan asking questions, demanding answers. But that sound, the words, meant nothing now. The most important thing in the world was to walk that path without deviation or error. The circle in the center could not be rightly entered in any other way, and it was a door.

Door? demanded another part of his brain. How? Why?

Hosteen fought down all questions. To walk the spiral slowly, cautiously, with all his powers of concentration, with no careless boot-toe touch beyond its border, he had to fit one foot almost directly before the other, balance like a man walking the narrowest of mountain ledges. This way only was it safe. Safe? He dismissed that query also.

Hosteen was in the circle now, turning to face the way they had come, toward those other dark mountains under which must lie the cavern of the pens, all the rest of the holdings of the forgotten alien invaders. Then he stood waiting. For what? clamored common sense.

Dark—and the sensation of being totally free from the boundaries set by time and space and everything mankind used to measure distance in two dimensions.

Then light and another path to be walked, another spiral, this glowing—not to be taken by one booted foot set carefully ahead of the other but mentally. And with the same concentration he had given to his action on the wedge, so did he now do this. He was at its center, with another kind of light rising in a haze all about him.

CHAPTER THIRTEEN

The process was like waking from a deep sleep. Hosteen fought a groggy disorientation, became aware of where he was and that he no longer stood in the open on a wedge under a starred sky. Instead, his boots were planted on a block of glassy material, and around him was another kind of light, a rusty glow that had no visible source unless it was born out of the air.

"Logan!" He demanded an answer, yet knew that none would come. In this place he was alone, alone with the knowledge that his species was not of this place—or time—that he was in strange exile.

The training the Terran had had acted against panic. He had followed an alien road but one that had had purpose—and it had brought him here. Now he must discover where "here" was.

Leaping from the block, Hosteen looked about. He was in a very small room—a room of three walls meeting in sharply angled corners. And those walls were unbroken by any openings of windows or doors. Again panic threatened as he faced the possibility of being imprisoned in this box. There was no spiral path to lead him out, only the block, the three walls, the ceiling over his head, the floor under him. And to his sight, walls, floor and ceiling were solid.

But eyes were not the only sense organs he possessed. Hosteen approached the nearest wall and ran his finger tips along its stick surface. It was glassy smooth to the touch and a little warm—where he had expected the chill of stone.

He walked the full length of that wall until his fingers pointed into the sharp angle of the corner. Then Hosteen turned along the second. He had reached the mid-point of that when there was a change in the surface not perceptible to the eye. Three depressions appeared, not quite the size or shape of his fingers, since he pushed in with room to spare. But he was reminded of the finger locks used on inner-system planets, locks that would open only to print patterns of their owners' flesh ridges. If this was such a lock, he had no hope, for the fingers—or appendages—which had set it had long since vanished from Arzor. But the Terran pressed his fingers into those hollow desperately, hoping for but not really expecting action.

A tingling in each of those three fingers, spreading up across the back of his hand, reaching his wrist, now into his forearm. A tingling—or was it a sucking—a pull of strength out of his tendons and muscles to be absorbed into those glassy pits of the wall? Hosteen supported his wrist now with his other hand because, when he tried to withdraw his fingers, he found them gripped in a suction beyond his power to break.

He leaned against the wall, twisting his right wrist with the aid of his other hand, striving to break that contact, feeling strength seep out of him as clearly as if he could watch the draining process in action along every vein, through every finger-tip pore.

Then the wall shivered, shimmered, to break from ceiling to floor. A strip of surface three feet wide where his hand had touched vanished, and he fell through, then crawled out of the triangular box to lie on the floor of another, much larger space. At least he was out of the cage!

Logan! Logan left back there on the plain to await the sun—and the burning death of the Big Dry. Logan! Would he—*could* he—take the same escape road Hosteen had found?

The Terran wavered to his feet, nursing his right hand and arm against his chest. The skin was pallid, the hand itself numb, and his utmost efforts to move the fingers resulted only in a slight twitching. Heavy and cold, he thrust it inside his shirt against his bare chest. But for a moment he forgot that as he looked around him.

The dusky, reddish light of the box was lightened here into the golden radiance he had remembered from the Cavern of the Hundred Gardens. With the hope of another such find, Hosteen stumbled forward to a waist-high barrier just a few feet ahead. Then he was looking down from a galley into, not the gardens of his hopes, but into a vast assembly of machines and installations. And from it rose a subdued hum, a vibration of air. These installations were not only in working order, they were working!

Yet, nowhere down those rows could he see any tenders, no human or robot inspectors as one might find in off-world machine plants.

"Started—then left to run—forever?" he whispered.

For what purpose?

He started along the gallery, hunting a way down to that center hall. The room was a vast oval, and his entrance had been at one end. Now as he skirted that waist-high barrier, watching the space below, Hosteen continued to marvel at the size and complexity of the installations.

The Terran's own training had been in psycho-biology. An Amerindian had an ancient tie with nature and the forces of nature, which was his strength, just as other races had come to rely more and more on machines. It was upon such framework that his whole education had been based, his sympathies centered. So, both inborn and special conditioning had made of him a man aloof from, and suspicious of, machines. One had to be anti-tech to be a Beast Master.

Now his disinterest in machines was growing to a repulsion as he looked down into the well of the vast chamber. The minds that had conceived and produced the Gardens he could understand. He might, though he did not find any kinship with them, grasp the motives of the pen keepers—they had dealt with living things. But these installations put a wall between him and those who had once been active here.

His growing dislike was not blunting his powers of observation. Hosteen believed that only a small number of the machines below were in use. He passed by whole sections where there were none of those subtle waves of power rising or falling. Then he saw the platform.

He was raised not more than a Terran foot or so above the floor of the main hall, and it was backed by a tall boarding, reaching almost to the balcony on which he stood. There were lines in relief on that boarding, running in intricate tangles. One made an irregular circle, and it glowed—glowed with a pulsating light of the same mauve that made fair Arzor sky different from Terra's lost blue.

Two other lines also showed color. One, a golden yellow, began in a straight column near the foot of the board and ran up to a mid-point, where, though there was a many-branched channel of the same tubing above, it stopped. And this pulsated with a faster beat. The third—Hosteen caught sight of the third, his attention riveted on it, startled.

That was a spiral leading to a dot. And as he watched, the light grew brighter, until its brilliance was more than his eyes could bear. The light traveled along that spiral, approached the dot, flashed there for an eye-searing second or two.

Then, the whole pattern of spiral and dot was lifeless, dead as the hundred other designs of tubing on that board. But he had not been mistaken. The light had been there—had been so bright he could not watch it, any more than a man could watch the sun of the Big Dry.

Hosteen turned and began to run back toward the triangular box from which he had emerged.

Logan—that shining swirl on the board could mean that Logan had taken the spiral and circle path out of the valley! He could be coming here!

The Terran's wild pace was such that he brought up against the now solid wall of the cubby almost as he had crashed against the inner wall of the cave where the Norbies had sealed them in to begin this adventure.

"Logan!" he shouted and heard the sound deadened, swallowed up in the reaches of the hall. Hosteen pounded on the wall with his good hand, drew the still numb right fist out of his shirt and tried to feel for any hollows on this side of the wall.

Pits for fingers. He had found them—this time with the digits of his left hand. He hesitated to deaden that too, as the right now was—to render himself helpless. But to get Logan out—free from the desert trap. Hosteen pushed his left hand against the smooth surface, fitted three finger tips into the waiting depressions, and waited, not without an inward shrinking, for the tingling—the sucking.

This time the response came more quickly, as might a lock long unused respond more rapidly to the second turning of a key. The panel faded, was gone— He looked into the cubby to see bare walls, empty space—nothing else.

Hosteen had been so sure he would again face Logan that for a moment he could not accept that emptiness.

"Logan!" Again the cry, which had come with the full force of his lung power, was muted, flattened into an echoing murmur of sound.

Already the gap in the wall was forming into its old solidity. He had been so sure. Hosteen lifted his numbed right hand uncertainly to his head. His distrust of the machines, of the power he did not understand, was a hot fire in him, a heat that reached into his cold, blanched fingers. He crooked them with a supreme effort, felt nails scrape the skin of his forehead.

The spiral on the board—it *had* been a miniature of the design in the valley, the pathway that had deposited him in this place. And he was certain that when the tube had glowed, it had signaled the use of that path, or another like it. So—perhaps that board held the secret!

Hosteen lurched away from the now solid wall and started along the other arm of the balcony, searching for a way down to the platform. In the end, he found the exit, an unobtrusive opening back against the hall wall, giving on a series of notched steps. He held the guard rail of that steep stair, noting with a fierce joy that the lack of feeling in his hand was ebbing—though to raise it was still like trying to raise a leaden weight attached to his wrist.

Now he was on ground level, picking a way among the machines to the platform. The majority of the installations were encased in block coverings, and these towered well above Hosteen's head as he hurried down the aisle.

There was no dust here as there had been in some of the tunnels, no sign that this chamber had been in existence for eons, perhaps abandoned for centuries. Yet, he was sure all of this was a part of the vanished Sealed Cave civilization.

Hosteen had almost reached the platform when he paused, took cover. A hum came from ahead, rising from a low note, hardly to be distinguished from the general voice of the machines, to a sound more impressive than his own shouts on the balcony—as if this sound was normal here, the voice of man not.

On the tube encrusted board another design had glowed into life. First blue—then white, bright enough to make him cover his eyes.

When he looked again, there was a man on the platform, facing the board!

"Logan!" His lips shaped the name, but luckily he did not call aloud, for that was not Logan.

The stranger was taller than Hosteen's half-brother, and he was not wearing Norbie dress. In fact, those green coveralls were familiar. That was the Service Center uniform Hosteen himself had worn for over a year at the Rehab station, where the homeless forces of Terrans had been held until they could either be assigned to new worlds or put through pyscho-conditioning.

Slowly the Terran edged around the boxed installation. The LB had been transporting Rehab men when it had crashed out on the mountain. Could this be a survivor, driven into the maze as Logan and he had been? Yet, the actions of the man on the platform were not those of a lost and bewildered castaway; they were the assured motions of a tech on duty.

His head turned from side to side as if he studied the twists and turns of that web of tubing. Then he moved half face to Hosteen.

Unmistakable human features, but painted over with the patterns of a Norbie Drummer—red circles about the eyes, a complicated series of lines on each cheek—just as Hosteen had seen on the faces of the warriors of the Blue. And slung about the other's neck was a small "medicine" tambour. An off-worlder who united in his person the make-up of a primitive medicine man and the actions of one understanding and tending the complex controls of a vanished civilization!

The stranger stretched out both hands and moved them across a line of small bulbs in a carefully governed sweep. To Hosteen's watching, he did not actually touch any, merely passed the flat of a palm over them.

And the board answered. That line of yellow light bubbling in the vertical shaft broke through whatever barrier had controlled it and threaded up and out through a dozen, two dozen filaments, each branching and rebranching until the lighted whole was the skeleton of a leafless tree. The soaring light reached the very top of the board. And around him Hosteen was conscious of an ingathering of energy, a poising of power to be launched.

Far away, but still awesomely loud, there was a clap of thunder, pounding on in a series of receding rolls. Hosteen cowered against the machine.

He closed his eyes for a second and felt as if he stood in the center of a storm's full fury. He could sense, if he could not see, the savage lash of lightning across a night-black sky under clouds as heavy as the rocks over which they clustered. And, small, weak man-thing that he was, he was, he could only seek shelter from elements to which man was nothing.

Yet, when he opened his eyes again, there was only a man in a faded coverall watching a light pulse through a transparent tube. The stranger's hand swept again over the bulbs. And the tree began to die, the yellow shrinking, retreating along the filaments, leaving the tubes empty. Once more it was only in the trunk from which the branches arose.

The storm ended. But the stranger was still intent upon the board. He paced along it, sometimes pausing for long moments, inspecting this and that pattern of webbing. Once or twice he put out a finger to trace some loop of tube. And Hosteen thought that perhaps he was unfamiliar with the function of that particular hookup.

At last he came to the end of the platform nearest the Terran and stepped up upon a small dais. To his right now was another line of bulbs. Holding his hands a foot apart before those, the man brought palm against palm in sharp clap, as if applauding some triumph. Then—

Hosteen stepped away from the shadow of the machine that had sheltered him. The dais was empty, just as empty as if the man was as immaterial as that which had hunted them in the dry valley.

The Terran could accept his journey via the spiral path. But this was something else, more akin to the old magic that his grandfather had talked of before Terra became a roasted cinder.

He made himself mount the platform, go to the dais. There was no break in the flooring, no possible exit for a solid human body. Just as he had recoiled in spirit from the machines in the hall, so was he now repulsed by this device. Yet, as he had been impelled to follow the spiral path in the valley, so now his hands moved against his will. He copied the gesture the stranger had used, palm met palm in a half-hearted clap.

Again the terrible giddiness of being nowhere on earth, or in any dimension known to his species, held him. But a spark of triumph battled fear—again he had used one of the tricks of this place boldly.

Hosteen opened his eyes. Ahead was daylight—not the artificial light of a cavern but true and honest sunlight. He was in a mountain tunnel heading to the outer world.

A murmur of sound ahead, and Hosteen dropped to his hands and knees, making the rest of that journey with all the caution of his Commando training. Daylight—the hour was well into morning he believed. Yet, there was no glare as there had been in the valley of the wedge or that was common in the country outside the wall of the Blue.

Had the devices of the Sealed Cave people put some film of protection between this taboo world and the blistering Dry sun? Had the same knowledge that had bored the tunnels and the caverns also brought weather control to the open? But this was no time for speculations.

Hosteen lay belly-flat at the tunnel mouth, then chose a crab-like crawl to take him out into the open and behind one of the abutments guarding the doorway.

Norbies were drawn up downslope, not in serried rows but in small groupings, each fronted by a flagged truce pole, headed by a Chief and a Drummer. Such a meeting of clans and tribes would amaze any settler. There were Norbies standing clan next to clan down there between whom there had been ceremonial blood feuds from long before the first Survey scout ship had discovered Arzor for Confederation star maps. Only a very big medicine could bring about such a truce against all ancient custom.

Shosonna, Nitra, Warpt, Ranag from the south—even Gousakla, and they were a coastal people who must have crossed a thousand miles at the worst season of the year to appear here. There were other totems of both clan and tribe Hosteen had never seen or heard described.

Counting, Hosteen made that tally of different poles more than a hundred, and he knew he could not see them all without emerging from his hiding place. By rude reckoning, every tribe on this continent must be represented!

The Drummers were busy, the beat of their individual tambours blending into a rhythm that stirred the blood. Lean yellow bodies swayed back and forth, answering that call, though not a booted foot stirred. Hosteen could smell the fug of burned vegetation, could sight trails of smoke. Only recently the whips of lightning had again been laid about the shoulders of the mountain.

Thud—thud—a crescendo of sound. Then, after a final crash, silence. Into that silence fell a delicate counter-tapping—as rain might come in a more gentle fashion after the growl of thunder.

Into the open some distance below came the man from the hall of machines. His fingers played on the taut head of his own drum, making that thin trickle of sound. And his tapping was picked up by first one and then another of the medicine men in that company.

CHAPTER FOURTEEN

The off-worlder threw both hands high above his head, a head that under the sun shown as brightly red-gold as the fires of the lightning.

He began to speak, and he did not use the hand signs of the settlers. The twittering bird notes—which authorities had sworn could not be shaped by human vocal cords or lips—poured from him. He was talking to the Norbies in their own tongue!

Shrill cries broke his first pause. Truce poles were tossed in the air until the fluttering of their totem streamers whirled in a crazy dance of ribbon strips.

Hosteen's mouth straightened into a hard line; his face was graven, without expresison, save that his eyes were watchful, as watchful as those of a man facing a death peril.

The signs were the same from world to world, race to race, species to species. This orator had the Norbies in the grip of a spell woven by his words. And he was inciting them to action! Their "big medicine" was working—alive! The trouble Quade and Kelson had smelled in the plains now walked openly in the Blue. Walked? No rather spoke with drum and voice—to urge what?

Hosteen's own inability to understand more than the emotions being aroused was a torment. But his doubts were resolved. Magic, if you wanted to call it that—but something his own inheritance recognized—was drugging their minds to provide a free path for unreasoning action, which could be used by that man in the off-world uniform with a Norbie painted face.

"Ani'iihii—" Hosteen spat.

Sorcerer was the right name for this witch man shaping disaster and death out of the words, as the witches of Terra long ago had shaped a man's death from a lock of his hair ceremoniously buried in a grave.

The drums replied with a beat that awoke a response in Hosteen's own hurrying blood. Just so, generations ago, halfway across the galaxy, had men of his own race drummed and danced before raiding. This was preparation for war.

And with such a collection of tribes, there could be only one answer to the identity of the intended enemy—the scattered holdings of the plains settlers, strung out thinly with leagues of open range land between each Center House, ripe for plucking by strike-and-run fighters. Norbies were warriors by tradition and training. It would take very little to turn them into an efficient guerrilla force that could wipe off-worlders from Arzor before they were aware of their danger.

The very nature of the country would fight for the natives at this season. Their carefully kept water secrets would make them far more mobile than any Patrol expeditionary force the settlers could call in.

Hosteen rubbed his forearm across his face. Nightmares out of the past provided spectres to follow a man for years. He had served on the fringe of a war that had involved not only worlds but solar systems, had seen the blotting out of nations and planets. Yes, the Patrol could be called in to end such a hit-and-run war—but afterwards, Arzor, as they knew it now, would cease to exist.

There was a final boom of drum—the orator was returning to the ledge of the tunnel, the Norbies ebbing back into the valley. Back to their village—to arm, to plan? Why? Hosteen could not pick the answer to that out of their twittering.

He worked a grenade out of his belt pouch. The stranger was on the ledge. Hosteen waited for a challenge, for some attack. But the other was staring straight before him, his eyes wide. He walked with a stiff, rocking pace. If he had locked the Norbies in some spell of eloquence, he was as tightly enchanted himself. Glancing neither to right nor left, he entered the passage.

This was the mountain on which the LB had landed. Hosteen watched the Norbies withdraw, tried to think. The LB—and Widders' story of those weak signals picked up by line camp coms. Just suppose the craft's com could still broadcast! A message might be sent to alert the plains!

The stranger could be hunted later—but to get to the LB now was worth the risk.

Surra—Baku—Gorgol. None of them had been brought to the village while Logan and he had been there. Were the three still at large?

Hosteen sent out once more that unvoiced, unheard rallying call of the team—tried to locate some mental radiation from bird or cat to reinstate once again their tight compact, so that man, cat, and eagle would not be three alone and adrift but a weapon, a defense such as Arzor, with all its hidden secrets, did not know.

"Baku!" He sent thought spinning like a lasso into the sky, striving to reach the mind behind those falcon-sharp eyes. But there was no answer.

"Surra!" Now he deserted the upper spaces and withdrew to the ground in search of one walking velvet-footed. "Surra!"

The answer he had ceased to hope for came like a stab of fire.

"Where?" His lips shaped the word as the query flew back along that tenuous thread of thought connection.

Impression of dark—of rock-walled passages. The cat must be somewhere within the mountain. Yes, Surra was there. And she lay in wait for some living thing now moving toward her. The orator?

The frustration that had rasped Hosteen moments earlier vanished. He worked the numbed line of mental contact just as he had the fingers of his numbed hand. Surra was an important part of him; without her, the composite entity that was the team was crippled, helpless as a man shorn of some important sense organ.

And he knew from the quality of her response, fierce, demanding, that that that lack had been hers also.

"The one coming"—he sent his message—"trail but do not take. Keep in touch with me."

Surra would take the stranger under surveillance. Hosteen was free to reach the LB. He swung down from the ledge and worked his way along the slope, using every bit of cover and scoutcraft he knew.

Drums again, faint—they must be in the village. He used a springy bush to lower himself into the clearing, where the sweet-sick scent of decay hung heavy. The offerings were still heaped about the rounded sides of the craft; the escape port on the top was closed.

Had it ever been opened or was the LB still sealed with a passenger list of dead men? The presence of the stranger argued that at least one of the castaways had escaped.

Hosteen climbed a sapling, which bent under his weight, allowing him to land near the tail. Slamming his hand down on the pressure lock of the hatch, he waited tensely.

With a squeak of protest, the port began to lift slowly. Hosteen's one fear vanished as he seized the edge of the door and forced it straight up. The LB had opened after its landing on Arzor; he was not about to enter a tomb.

The interior space of such a craft was limited, and from abandon-ship drill in the Service he knew its layout. Pushing between two rows of acceleration bunks set against each wall, he reached the nose, where the auto and hand pilots and the com set were to be found.

Side lights had gone on when he opened the hatch, showing him the wiring was still in order. Hosteen hunched into the small space before the com. He flicked the switch to open and was rewarded with a promising click-click of an expanding broadcast aerial, the purr of a working com. With finger on button, he tapped out the message he had composed on the way downhill.

The landing signals of this ship had registered months ago on the pickups of two line camps. Only because those camps were rarely visited had the signals gone undetected so long. He tapped out his warning twice by hand, setting it so on a repeat wire. Now that would go on broadcasting at ten revolutions an hour until it was turned off, and he intended to see that was impossible unless the com or the ship was destroyed.

Hosteen made adjustments, resealed the shield panel, and then went to explore the rest of the craft in the faint hope of discovering a weapon. But the stores' compartment was open and empty. Save for the plasta foam pads on the bunks, there was nothing left.

He was standing directly under the escape hatch, preparing to leave, when a roll of thunder startled him. Only reflex action saved his life as he slammed his hand on the seal button of the port.

Thunder again, but now muted into a distant mutter by the protection of the hull. The LB trembled under-a blow. Hosteen scrambled for the pilot's seat, thumbed on the visa-screen—to view a roaring holocaust. If the fire that had lashed the mountan before had spared the LB, it did so no longer. The craft shook and reeled under streams of flame.

Would the insulation intended for the protection of space flight hold against this fierce concentration of energy? The force of that attack was twisting the ship around, might push it on down the slope.

Had the broadcast from the com alerted the stranger in the mountain, the message been picked up by some device of that other civilization? Hosteen was sure that this attack came from the Sealed Cave armory.

Surra! Hosteen braced himself in the shuddering cabin as he strove to reach the cat. But once more he met only the solid barrier he had found that night when he had been prisoner in the Norbie village. Perhaps the fire cut off contact. A reasonable explanation if not a comforting one.

The LB was no longer on an even keel. Hosteen caught one of the stanchions supporting the nearest bunk. The visa-screen told him the whole craft was encased in wildly ranging flame. He was trapped with no defense but the walls of the ship.

He stretched out on a bunk and snapped the acceleration webbing to hold his body in place. If that bath of energy did roll the LB over a cliff, he could have that small protection.

The nose of the craft tilted down and the whole hull quivered as the dive picked up speed. Then there was a bone-wrenching crash as the ship met some obstruction head on. The visa-screen went blank. And the com—he thought that the com had not survived either. How many broadcasts had it made before the end? Enough for one full message to reach beyond the Peaks?

Hosteen lay sweating on the bunk, the LB now more vertical than horizontal. The cabin lights flickered, dimmed, then brightened again in a crazy dance of light and dark. Though the LB no longer moved, would a shifting of his own weight send it into another slide?

Freeing himself from the webbing, the Terran gingerly swung his feet to the floor, keeping a grip on the stanchion. The steeply sloping deck did not move as he clawed his way to the pilot compartment to discover chaos behind a buckled wall. The com was dead. Well, if this attack had been to silence the warning, the enemy had won the first skirmish. That didn't mean he would also win the war.

Without the visa-screen. Hosteen was blind. Did the fire still bathe the ship? He wedged into one of the tilted bunks again, rested his forehead on his crooked arm, and bent all the energy left in his mind and body into a concentration aimed at Surra.

"Here—" The word she could not form aloud was a whisper in his brain.

"The man?"

"Here—" A repetition of her first answer or an assurance that she still had her quarry under observation?

"In the mountain?"

"So—"

"Then stay—follow—" he ordered.

Maybe his ability to reach the dune cat meant that the fire no longer ringed the LB. But to get to the hatch now required some acrobatic maneuvering. And when his first attempt to open the port did not succeed, Hosteen knew the starkness of dread. Had the flames sealed his escape hole?

Then, though with protest, the hatch moved as he beat on it with one frantic fist, holding to his support with the other. Smoke swirled in a choking blue fog, burning his eyes, strangling him with coughing until the air filter of the cabin thinned it.

Smoke, heat, but no sign of active flames. Hosteen retreated to rip and pry at the plasta foam covering of the bunks, removing the stuff in tattered strips. Half of these he draped over the rim of the hatch opening, pushing the material through to lie across the heated shell of the LB. The rest he took with him as he climbed out on the temporarily protected area.

The side of the LB bore the lick marks of fire, and around it the ground was charred black. Upslope, small blazes still crackled in bushes.

Hosteen worked fast, tying lengths of the plasta foam about his feet and legs above knee level. The tough synthetic fabric would be a shield against the heat. With more scraps mittening his hands and covering his arms, he crawled up the tail of the LB, leaped for the top of a fire-blackened rock, and started the climb back to the tunnel ledge.

Back in the mountain Surra would be his eyes, a part of himself projected. He could track the stranger, perhaps find Logan. Logan!

All he could do to warn the plains had been done. The holdings would have to take their chances while he faced the heart of the trouble here and now.

Tap—tap—tap—

The Terran was an animal, startled, snarling in defiance, his teeth showing white between tightened lips as Surra's could upon occasion. He stood still, watching that figure come out of a copse that had escaped the lick of the fire.

A cloak spread like huge wings of a mantling bird—a Drummer! And there was no knife in Hosteen's belt, no stunner. He had only his two hands—

However, the other had no more. By tradition, the Norbie would be unarmed—depending upon his power for his protection. And no native would raise hand against a Drummer, even one of an enemy tribe. The vengeance taken by "medicine" was swift, sure, and frightful.

But if this one depended upon that custom now, he would have a rude, perhaps fatal awakening. Hosteen had to get his hands on the tambour the native carried, silence it before the Drummer could use it to arouse the warriors.

The Terran tensed for another leap. His body arched up; his bandaged hands caught up burned and fire-scorched wood. He moved with the sure speed of a trained fighting man.

Tap—tap—

There had been no acceleration in that soft patter, no deepening of the beat. No settler understood drum talk, but Hosteen wondered. He had expected an outburst of alarm when he was sighted. What he heard as he charged was a calm sequence of small sounds—like a friendly greeting. Instead of throwing his body forward in a tackle, he halted to face the enemy squarely.

"Ukurti!"

Fingers lifted from the tight drumhead—moved in talk.

"Where do you go?"

Sharp, to the point. Hosteen tugged at the wrappings on his hands, freed his fingers to reply:

"To the mountain."

He dared not risk evasion, not with this Drummer whom he knew to be not the witch doctor of scoffing off-worlders but a real power.

"You have been to the mountain once."

"I have been once," Hosteen assented. "I go again—for in this mountain walks evil."

"That is so." The quick agreement surprised Hosteen.

"He who drums for the Zamle totem says that?"

"One who drums, drums true, or else the power departs from him. In the mountain is one who says that thunder answers his drum, that he brings lightning to his service."

"It has been heard, so has it been seen." Again Hosteen kept to the strict truth.

"Fire has answered; that is truth. And because of this warriors bind arrowheads to war shaft, chant songs of trophies to be smoked in the Thunder Houses."

"Yet this is not good."

"It is not good!" Ukurti's head pushed forward; his paint-ringed eyes on either side of his boldly arched nose were those of Baku sighting prey before she was quite poised for the killing swoop. "This one who wears the name of Ukurti has been to the place of sky ships' landing and has seen the powers of those who ride from star to star. They, too, drum thunder and raise lightning of a kind—but it is not born of the true power of Arzor." His booted foot stamped the black ground, and a tiny puff of ash arose.

"Before them, others walked the same trails—even here on Arzor.

To the strangers their power, to us ours. This is an old trail, newly opened once again. And in it lie many traps for the heedless and those who want to believe because it serves their false dreams. I who bear the name of Ukurti in this life and who have the right to speak of this power and that"—again he stroked the drumhead gently, bringing a muted purr of sound from its surface—"say that no good comes of a trail that leads to blood running free on the ground, the blood of those who have shared water, hunted, eaten meat with us, and welcomed in their tents my people."

"And he-who-drums-thunder here says that this shedding of blood is right—that the war arrow is to be put to the string against my people?"

"That is so."

"For what purpose does he demand a shedding of blood?"

"That his power may eat and grow strong, giving many gifts to those who serve it."

"But his power is not the power you follow."

"That is so. And this is an evil thing. Now I say to you, who also have a power that is from beyond the stars and lies within you, go up to this man who is of your own kind and set your power against him."

"And you will not drum up those to hunt me?"

"Not so. Between us is a peace pole. It has been set upon me to—in a small way—smooth your trail."

"You knew I was here—you were waiting for me?"

"I knew. But no man explains the working of his own medicine. This is a thing of my power."

"Pardon, Drummer. I do not ask the forbidden." Hosteen's fingers made swift and contrite apology.

"But from here you walk alone," Ukurti continued.

"Do all the clans walk the trail leading to the running of blood?" Hosteen ventured.

"Not all—yet," but the Drummer did not enlarge upon that.

"And this I must do alone?"

"Alone."

"Then, Drummer, give me of your luck wish before I depart."

Hosteen signed the formal request made by all Norbie warriors leaving a clan camp. He waited. Did the other's favor reach to actually invoking his power for an off-world alien or did his aid only consist of standing aside to let Hosteen fight his own battle? The difference could mean a great deal to the waiting Terran.

CHAPTER FIFTEEN

A breeze swirled ash, cooled earth, drove away the smoke and stench of fire, and pulled at the edge of the Drummer's feather cloak. Ukurti stared down at the tambour, which he held in both hands, as if he were reading on the tightly stretched skin of its head some message. His fingers tapped out a small burst of sharp notes while he spoke. Though that twittering was unintelligible to Hosteen, he thought he detected in it a rhythm that could be either a blessing or a curse. Then Ukurti's hands left the drum and made signs the Terran could understand.

"Go in power, one who knows the song of the wind, the whisper of growing things, the minds of beasts and birds. Go in power; do what must be done. In this moment the war arrow is balanced upon a finger. So light a thing as this wind may wreck a world."

It was more than Hosteen had dared hope the Drummer would ever grant him—not the blessing and good will for a warrior departing into danger but the outright promise of one wizard to another who also dealt in things unseen, a promise of power to be added to power.

In return, he accorded Ukurti the salute of upraised palms, which was the greeting of equal to equal, before he turned and started for the waiting tunnel mouth.

But in his hurry the Terran was also cautious. Ukurti had said nothing of any other natives being on the mountain, but that was no reason to disregard the possibility of more Drummers or warriors being drawn to the fire about the LB.

Hosteen reached the ledge of the tunnel without being sighted or trailed. And there he met Surra's warning. The stranger was returning in haste to the outer world. Coming to see the result of the fire attack?

The Terran had the grenades. But a dead enemy could not talk and might well provide a martyr whose influence after death could unleash destruction across the plains. A prisoner, not a dead man, was what Hosteen desired. With Surra's aid he could have that future captive already boxed. Only—

This was like running against an invisible wall. There was no pain such as the sonic barrier had spun around those who strove to pass it. No pain—only immobility, a freezing of every muscle against which Hosteen fought vainly. As helpless as he had been in the net of the Norbies, so was he again, held so for the coming of the enemy.

Helpless as to body, yes, but not in mind. Hosteen gave Surra an order. How far away was that chase—the man running to inspect his catch, the cat, unseen, unsensed by her quarry, padding at an ever quickening trot behind?

Just as Hosteen could plan, he could also hear. Ukurti had not been alone on the mountain. The whistle of more than one Norbie reached him, unmuffled by the morning wind. He did not credit the Shosonna medicine man with any treachery—such a promise as the other had given him when they parted would damn the Drummer who made it in false faith. No, his being held for the kill was not Ukurti's doing.

Surra—and Baku. He must try again to reach the eagle. Cat and bird might be his only defensive weapons.

The cat he made contact with—the bird, no answer. And now the stranger broke from the tunnel mouth.

Taller than the Terran, his skin whitely fair under the paint of the natives, his hair ruddy bright, he stood there breathing hard. With both hands, he held at breast level a sphere that Hosteen eyed apprehensively. It was too like the antiperso grenades.

Then it was the other's eyes, rather than his hands and their burden, that drew the Beast Master's attention. Back at the Rehab Separation Center more than a year ago, he had seen that look in many eyes, too many eyes. Terran units brought in from active Service at the close of the war to discover their world gone—families, homes, everything lost—had had men in their ranks with such eyes. Men had gone mad and turned their weapons on base personnel, on each other, on themselves. And taking a cue from that past, Hosteen schooled his voice to the bark of an official demand.

"Name, rank, serial number, planet!"

There was a stir far down in the set glare of those eyes. The other's lips moved soundlessly, and then he spoke aloud.

"Farver Dean, Tech third rank, Eu 790, Cosmos" he replied in Galactic basic.

A tech of the third rank, 700 in his Service—not only a trained scientist but one of genius level! No wonder this man had been able to understand and use some of the secrets of the Cavern people.

Dean advanced another step or two, studying Hosteen. The face paint disguised much of his expression, but his attitude was one of puzzlement.

"Who are you?" he asked in return.

"Hosteen Storm, Beast Master, AM 25, Terra." Hosteen used the same old formula for reply.

"Beast Master," the other repeated. "Oh, of the Psych-Anth boys?"

"Yes."

"Nothing here for you, you know." Dean shook his head slowly from side to side. "This is a tech matter, not one for the nature boys."

Nature boys—the old scoffing term that underlined the split between the two branches of special Service. If Dean already had such hostility to build upon and was mentally unbalanced— Hosteen put away that small fear. At least the tech was talking, and that slowed any drastic action.

"We had no orders about you either," he stated. If Dean thought this was a service affair, so much the better. And how did the tech hold him prisoner? Was the device controlling the stass field in that sphere the other nursed so close to his chest? If that were so, Hosteen had a better chance than if his invisible bonds were manipulated by some machine back in the mountain.

Dean shrugged. "Doesn't concern me. You'll have to blast off— this is a tech affair."

His attitude was casual, far too casual. Hosteen smelled and tasted danger as he had a few times before in his life:

"Can't very well blast off while you have me in stass, can I?"

The other smiled, the stretch of facial muscles pulling the pattern lines on his cheeks into grotesque squares and angles.

"Stass—the nature boys can't fight stass!" His laugh was almost a giggle. Then he was entirely sober. "You thought you could trick me," he said dispassionately. "I know the war's over; I know you aren't here under orders. No—you're trying to orbit in on my landing pattern! I've life—life itself—right here." He loosed his hold on the orb with one hand and flung palm out in a florid gesture. "Everything a tech could want! And it's mine—to have forever." He giggled again, and that sound following the coolness of his words was an erratic break to frighten a man who had witnessed many crack-ups at Rehab.

"Forever!" Dean repeated. "That's it—why, you're trying to planet in! You want it, too! Live forever with every power in your hand when you reach for it." The fingers of his outheld hand curled up to form a cup. "Only a tech got here first, and the tech knows what to do and how to do it. You're not the first to try to take over—but you're easy. I know just how to deal with your kind." He fingered the sphere, and Hosteen choked as the stass field squeezed in upon his throat.

"I could crush you flat, nature boy, just as flat as an insect under a boot sole. Only—that would be a stupid waste. My friends below—they like amusement. They'll have you to play with."

The stranger touched a circlet fitting in a tight band, about his throat. Then he called aloud, and his shout was the twittering whistle of a Norbie.

Hosteen watched the tunnel entrance behind Dean. "Now!" He thought that order.

A flash of yellow out of the dark and the full force of Surra's weight struck true on Dean's shoulders. His whistle ended in a shriek as he fell. The stass sphere rolled out of his hand, but before the now free Hosteen could seize it, it hit against a rock and bowled over the rim of the ledge to vanish below.

"Do not kill!" Hosteen gave his command as man and cat rolled back and forth across the stone. He moved in on the melee, his limbs stiff, numb, almost as numb as his hand had been after his experience with the alien door lock.

Surra spat, squalled, broke her hold, pawing at her eyes. Dean, yammering still in the Norbie voice, made another throwing motion, and the cat retreated. He looked up at Hosteen, and his face was a devil's mask of open, insane rage. With a last cry he headed for the tunnel as Hosteen tackled him. The Amerindian's cramped limbs brought him down too short; his fingers closed about a leg, but with a vicious kick Dean freed himself and vanished into the passage, the pound of his boots sounding back as he ran.

Surra was still pawing at her eyes. Hosteen grasped a handful of loose hair and skin on her shoulders and pulled her to him. The Norbies Dean had summoned could not be far away. There was only one retreat from this ledge—back into the mountain after Dean. He hoped that some taboo would keep the natives from nosing after.

A head crowned with black horns rose into sight. The Norbie attacked in a scuttling rush, knife in hand. Then Hosteen was fighting for his life just within the passage entrance. He forced heavy feet and hands into the tricks of unarmed combat that had been a part of his Commando training, rolling farther into the dark, his opponent following.

Pain scored a hot slash along Hosteen's side as the heart thrust the other had aimed missed. He pulled loose and brought down his hand on the native's neck just above the collar bone. As the Norbie fell back with a choking gasp, Hosteen pried the knift hilt out of his hand.

There was a whir in the air, and an arrow cut the frawn fabric of the torn shirt at the Terran's shoulder. On his hands and knees, Hosteen scrambled back, hearing Surra's whining complaint as she went ahead. There was more than one archer taking aim now into the tunnel. He could see the arcs of their bows against the daylight. But the odd dark that blanketed the Sealed Cave workings was his protection. Keeping low, he escaped the arrows flying overhead, and none of the natives ventured in—he had been right about the taboo.

When he judged that a turn in the passage cloaked him from feathered death, Hosteen paused, snapped on his torch, and called

Surra to him. What Dean had done to the cat Hosteen did not know. Her eyes were watering and she was in distress, but Hosteen's simple tests confirmed the fact that her sight was not affected and that she was already beginning to recover.

But Surra's ire was fully aroused, and she was determined to trail Dean—which agreed with Hosteen's desire. He wanted to catch up with the renegade tech. And with a knife now in his belt sheath and a better understanding of the man he hunted, the odds were no longer all in the other's favor, though reason told the Terran that a length of metal, well wrought and deadly as it was, was no defense against the bag of tricks the tech might have ready.

The dune cat padded on with confidence. She knew where she was going. Only that did not last. In a stretch of tunnel where there was no break in the wall, Surra stopped short, then circled slowly about, sniffing at the flooring, before, completely baffled, she vented her disappointment in a squall such as she would give upon missing an easy kill.

Hosteen beamed the torch at the floor, more than half expecting to see one of the spiral and dot inlays there. But there was no such path here, no band of bulbs on the wall to open one of those weird other-dimension doors. This was simply another secret of the passages that Dean knew—to the bafflement of his enemies.

Could the tech come and go from any part of the caverns at his will? Or were there "stations" from which one could make such journeys? Hosteen wished now that he had investigated more closely the place into which he had dropped when he had used Dean's door on the platform.

There was nothing to do now but wander through the passages in hope of finding such a door or return to the surface, where he did not doubt he would find the Norbies waiting. How had Surra come into the mountain—by another tunnel?

The Terran squatted down and called the cat to him. With his hand on her head, he strove to have her recall her entrance into the passages.

Those very attributes that made her so effectively a part of the team worked against him now. Surra had been thoroughly aroused by Dean's counter to her attack. She had put out of mind everything but her desire to run him down. And now she was interested only in that and not in what seemed to her to be meaningless inquiries about the passages. The patience Hosteen had always used in dealing with the team held, in spite of his wish for action.

Dean—free in these burrows to use the knowledge of the installations. And Logan—When Hosteen thought of Logan, it was like the burn of a blaster ray across his flesh. The one small hope the Terran clung to was the tube on the board that had lighted. Even if Logan had not arrived in the big hall, he might have escaped the death of the Dry day and be wandering elsewhere in this maze.

"Baku—Gorgol." Since Surra would not respond to Hosteen's first questions, he tried a more oblique approach. And now her concentration on Dean was shaken.

"High—up." As always the answers were not clear. Human mind groped to find a better touch with feline.

"Up—where?" the Beast Master urged.

There was a moment of withdrawal. Was Surra refusing, as she could do upon occasion? Then the cat's head moved under Hosteen's hand, and her muzzle raised as if drawing from the air some message he could not hope to read.

"That one is gone for now—but we shall hunt him," Hosteen promised. "But to so hunt, the team is needed. Where is Baku?"

That had made the right impression. Too long they had been tied together; they both needed the security of that relationship.

Surra made no answer but pulled out of his touch and started down the passage with some of the same determination she had displayed in the trailing of Dean.

No man could ever have traced his way through the labyrinth where Surra now played guide. They went from passage to passage, bypassed caves and chambers where evidence of the aliens was present in installations, fittings, and objects whose purpose Hosteen could not grasp in a glance or two and which interested Surra not at all. However, the cat appeared to know just where she was going and why.

Their way had led down and up again so many times that Hosteen was bewildered, though he came to believe that they were no longer under the same mountain. Finally, Surra cut out on one of the worked tunnels where the walls were black coated and came into a cleft of bare, untooled rock. Here man had to take cat's path on his hands and knees.

There was a last narrow crevice through which Hosteen crawled to light, air, and the fresh scent of growing things—a small valley into which the Big Dry had not ventured any more than it did into that of the native village. Hosteen sat down wearily to look about.

Now that he had a chance to study the vegetation, he saw a difference. This was a green-green world—not yellow-green, nor red-green, nor brown-green—as the vegetation of Arzor was elsewhere. And where had he ever seen foliage such as that of a small bush a hand's distance away?

A thunderbolt swooped down on black wings from the sky! Baku settled on the ground and came toward the Beast Master, her wings half spread, uttering a series of piercing cries. And the warmth of her greeting was part of their belonging.

But when her clamor was echoed by a sharp whistle from the bushes, Hosteen tensed, his hand going to his knife. That Norbie signal had come to mean danger.

Surra stretched out in a patch of open sunlight, blinking her eyes, giving no alarm. As Hosteen got to his feet, Gorgol came into the open. The young Norbie showed some damage. A poultice of crushed leaves was tied in a netting of grass stems about his left forearm, and there was a purple bruise mottling that side of his face, swelling the flesh until he could see only through a slit of eye. The threads knotting his yoris-tooth breastplate together had broken, and a section was missing.

"Storm!" he signed, and then put out his hand, drawing finger tips lightly down the Terran's arm as if he needed the assurance of touch to accept the other's appearance.

Baku had taken to the air, then settled down again on Hosteen's shoulder. And he braced himself under her weight as she dipped her head to put that beak, which could be such a lethal weapon, against his cheek in quick caress.

"Where are we?" Hosteen glanced at the mountain crests reared to the sky about the pocket of earth that held them. He did not recognize any of them, could not have told in which direction their tunnel wandering had brought them.

"In the mountains," Gorgol signed, an explanation that did not explain at all. "We ran far before the fires."

"We?"

Gorgol turned his head and pursed his lips for another whistle. For a moment Hosteen hoped Logan had found his way here too. But the man coming out of a screen of lacy fronds was a stranger.

Rags of green uniform still slung to a lath-thin body, a body displaying dark bruises such as Gorgol bore. Only it was a human body, and there were no horns, only a mop of brown hair on the head.

"So—Zolti was right," the stranger said in a voice that shook a little. "There was help here all along—we could have made it out—home."

Then he was on the ground as if his long legs had folded bonelessly under him, his face buried in his scratched and earth-streaked hands, his sharp shoulder blades shaking with harsh, tearing sobs he could not control.

CHAPTER SIXTEEN

Who is this one?" Hosteen asked Gorgol.

"I do not know, for he has not the finger talk," the native signed in return. "We came together on the mountain, and he led me on a path through the flames. I think that he is one who has run in fear for long and long, and yet still will fight—truly a warrior."

Hosteen signaled with a twitch of shoulder, and Baku took off for a perch on a nearby rock. The Terran sat down beside the stranger and laid his hand gently on the bowed back.

"Who are you, friend?" He used the Galactic basic of the Service, but he was not greatly surprised when broken words came in Terran.

"Najar, Mikki Najar, Reconnaissance scout—500th Landing force."

His voice had steadied. Now he dropped his hands and turned his head to face Hosteen directly, a puzzled expression on his features as he continued to study the Amerindian.

"Hosteen Storm, Beast Master," Hosteen identified himself and then added, "The war is over, you know."

Najar nodded slowly. "I know. But this is a holdout planet, isn't it? That's why you're here—or is that wrong, too?"

"This is Arzor, a frontier settlement world. We had an Xik holdout pocket, yes, but cleaned it up months ago. And it was only one shipload of Xiks. Most of them blew themselves up when they tried to take off. I'm not here as a soldier—this is my home now."

There were bitter lines about Najar's mouth. "Just some more of Dean's lies. You're Terran, aren't you?"

Hosteen nodded and then added, "Arzoran now. I've taken up land in the plains—"

"And this *is* a Confederacy settlement planet not an Xik world?"

"Yes."

"For how long?"

"Over two hundred Terran years anyway—second and third generations from First Ship families are holding lands now. You came in on the LB?"

"Yes." Najar's bitterness had reached his voice now. "Lafdale was a pilot, and he was a good one—got us down without smashing up. Then we walked out straight into a native attack. They didn't kill us—might have been better if they had—just herded us up the mountainside and put us in a cave. We lost Lafdale in an underground place full of water. He was pulled off a wharf there by something big— something we never really saw. Then"—Najar shook his head slowly from side to side—"it was a kind of nightmare. Roostav—he went missing; we never found him—that was in a cave full of broken walls. Dean kept urging us on. He was excited, said we were on to something big. And Zolti—he'd been a Histtech before the war—he said that this was a settled planet and we could find help if we could get back to the LB com. We never knew if the signals we sent at landing had ever been picked up. But Dean talked him down, said he knew where we were—right in the territory where the Xik had holdouts all over—that the hostile attitude of the natives proved we were in an Xik influence zone."

He paused and rubbed his hand across his face. "The other two of us, Widders and I, we didn't know what to think. Dean and Zolti, they were the big brains. Both of them said we were in a place where there was something big from the old times. And Dean—we were all out of Rehab, you know." He glanced almost furtively at Hosteen.

"For all Terrans there was Rehab—afterwards," the Amerindian replied soberly.

"Well, Dean, he—somehow he didn't want to go back, back to the way he had had it before the war, I mean. He'd been pretty important in the Service, and he liked that. Maybe he was able to cover up in Rehab, but after we landed here he was a different person, excited, alive. Then he just took over, ran us—He kept insisting it was our duty to learn all we could about this place, use it against the Xiks. And he swore Zolti was mistaken, that we had been off course of any settler planet when we dropped here.

"Then we found the place of the path." Again Najar stopped and Hosteen thought he was trying to pick words to explain something he did not understand himself.

"You found this?" The Terran sketched with a finger tip in the dust the spiral and dot.

"Yes. You must have seen it too!"

"And followed it."

"Dean said it was a way out. I don't know how he knew that. He picked information out of the air—or so it seemed. One minute he'd be as puzzled as we were; then all at once he'd explain—and he'd be right! Funny though, he didn't want to try that path first. Zolti did— walked around and around—then he just wasn't there!

"Widders, he was out of his head a little by then. Kept saying over and over that things hid behind rocks to watch us. He threw stones into every shadow. When Zolti went like that, Widders started screaming. He ran around and around the coil, hit the center—and then was gone—

"Dean took the same orbit. And I—well, I wasn't going to stay there alone. So I did it—ended up in a three-cornered box."

"You saw the hall of the machines?" Hosteen asked.

"Yes. Dean was there. And he was crazy-wild, running up and down, patting them and talking to himself about how all this was the place he had been meant to find—that the voices in his head had told him and that now he held the whole world right in his hand. Listening to him was like being back in Rehab in the early days. I hid out and watched him. Then he ended up in a corner where there was a big hoop—got inside that and lay down on the floor, curled up as if he were asleep. There was a light and noise—I couldn't watch— something queer happened to your eyes when you tried to. So I went to hunt Widders and Zolti. Only, if they came that way, they were gone again. I didn't see them—not then."

"But you did later?"

"Maybe—one. Only nobody could be sure—just bones that looked fresh." Najar's eyes closed, and Hosteen felt the shudder that shook his wasted body. "I didn't stay *there* to hunt. Somehow I found this valley outside—"

He looked around, gratitude mirrored in his eyes.

"It was wonderful, after all those other places, to be out in the open with things—real things—growing, almost like home. And there was a way higher up to get out—down to where the natives were. I watched them. Then all at once more and more of them kept coming, and I guessed Dean was up to something. Thunder and lightning—not the normal kind—I tried to find out what was going on, mapped some of the ways in and out—"

"You didn't think of trying to contact Dean again?"

Najar's gaze dropped to his hands. "No—I didn't. You may think that's queer, Storm. But Dean, he'd been changing all the time since we landed here. And when I saw him so wild in that hall—well, I didn't want to have anything to do with him again. He was raving about being picked to rule a world—it was enough to make you think you were crazy, too. I didn't want any part of him."

Hosteen agreed. The man he had fronted at the tunnel mouth had been removed from human kind, unreachable, unless a trained psycho-tech could find a channel to connect Dean again with the world.

"I'm pretty good at trailing"—Najar's ordinary flat tone now held a spark of pride—"being a Recon scout, and I got around so that the natives didn't suspect me. Of course, not many of them ever came far up the mountain, and when they did, they kept to paths. Then I saw a 'copter come over, and it was one of ours! That made Dean's story about an Xik world nonsense, and I thought maybe our boys had moved in and cleaned up.

"So I went down to signal it. There was a flash just after the 'copter set down, and that fire cut around the whole landing area. I couldn't get to it until afterwards—there was a dead man there, and all the rest burned up. And I'd been counting a lot on getting out—" Again he stared at his hands. "I was sick, straight through to my insides, sick enough to get at Dean. So I took to the mountain passages, hoping to meet him. Got to the machine hall twice, only he was never there. You don't have any idea, Storm, about how big this digging really is—passages running through the mountains and under them, all sorts of caverns and rooms. I've seen things—strictly unhealthy." Again shudders ran through him. "Sometimes I wondered if I weren't as crazy as Dean—else I wouldn't be seeing some of those things.

"But I never caught up with Dean—not until the night there was another fire along the mountain. And I saw this native here beating it ahead of the fire with a big cat and a bird swooping along over them. Dean was watching them come upslope, and he was aiming a tube at them. I cut in and signaled the native into a gap, and the cat and bird came along. The gap led in here, then—"

"Then?" Hosteen asked.

"Then," Najar reiterated grimly, his features set, "one of those tame lightning bolts smashed down just as we were almost through it—sealed us in with a landslide and knocked us around some so we weren't much use for days afterwards. Lucky there's water in here and some fruit—The bird tried to get out, but the way it acted made you think there was some kind of lid up there over this whole place. Then one day the cat was gone, and we guessed she'd found a way out. We've been hunting for that ever since. Now you know it all—"

"Yes," Hosteen replied somewhat absently. One piece of Najar's story was enlightening—all of the survivors' party had left the spiral path in the valley at the same time, but apparently not all had landed at the same terminal in the big hall when that beyond-time-and-space journey was completed. Logan—had Logan come out at some other point in the mountain maze? Hosteen turned upon Najar now with a sharpness born of renewed hope.

"There's a way out—do you think you could find your way back to the hall once you were in the tunnels again?"

"I don't know—I honestly don't know."

Hosteen signed to Gorgol across the castaway's hunched shoulders.

"There is no way across the heights?"

"We can look but we cannot go. Come and see for yourself," the Norbie responded.

They went on a rough scramble up the slope in which was the rock crevice of Surra's door. Then they walked a ledge, which ended in a vast pile of debris.

"The mountain fell—" Gorgol indicated the slip. "And from here one can look—"

Another tricky bit of climbing and they could indeed look—a prospect that was enough to leave one giddy. Down—down—a drop no length of rope on Arzor, Hosteen thought, could dangle to touch bottom. And beyond that crack in the earth, well within sight but as far removed from them as if it existed on another world, uplands sere and baked under that sun, which on their side was so abnormally gentle. A window on the outer world but no door.

Swiftly Hosteen signed the facts he had learned in his explorations and what Najar had told him. Gorgol watched the Terran's fingers with a growing expression of resolution.

"If Ukurti says that this is an ill thing," Gorgol's own hands replied, "then will Krotag and those who ride with Krotag listen, for Ukurti is one having wisdom, and always we have hearkened to his drum. To say that one with a twisted mind is using things left by Those-Who-Have-Gone to make him great—that, too, one can believe. And this is true—if he is known to be one who steals from the past to give himself power, then will the tribes turn from him and listen no more to his drumming."

"But how may it be proved that he is such a one? And do we have the time?" Hosteen countered. "Already he drums raids for the plains. And once there is even one such foray, there will be war—war without truce between your people and mine. Always there have been those among my kind who have mistrusted yours."

"That is true." Gorgol's fingers made an emphatic sign of agreement. "And once the war arrow is sped, who can recall it to the quiver? But there is also this—outside this place lies the hand of the Dry. Water secrets we have, but not enough to sustain any large parties through the Peaks. And those who so venture cannot so do in straight lines but must go from one hidden spring to another, using much time. Were men to march today, it would be"— he spread out his fingers, curled them back into his palms, and opened them out again three times—"these many suns before they would reach the plains."

"Would Krotag listen to you?" Hosteen demanded.

"I am a warrior with scars. In the voice of the clan, I have my speech right. He would listen."

"Then if we can get out of here, get you on the other side of the mountain where you can meet with Krotag and Ukurti—?"

Gorgol stared past Hosteen into the brilliance of the parched land beyond. "Krotag would listen—and beyond Krotag stands

Kustig of the Yoris totem, and beyond Kustig, Dankgu of the Xoto standard."

"And if all those listened, the Shosonna would break their peace poles and have no part of this?"

"It might be so. And if the Shosonna marched, then would follow the Warpt of the north and perhaps the Gouskla of the coasts—"

"Splitting Dean's army right down the middle!" Hosteen took fire, but Gorgol's expression was still a sober frown.

"With truce poles broken, there might be another kind of war, for these wild men of the Blue are tied to the medicine here and will fight to uphold it."

"Unless Dean can be proved a false Drummer—"

"Yes. And here are two trails." Gorgol turned away from the "window." "I must find the place of the Zamle totem and you this one who is of your people but a doer of evil."

"And to do those things, we must have a way back through the mountain," Hosteen added.

They held a council of war in the green heart of the valley, Najar, Hosteen, and Gorgol sitting together, Baku and Surra nearby. Storm translated between Gorgol and the off-world veteran as they pooled what knowledge they had of the inner ways. And Najar thought he might be able to guide them to the village side of the heights if he could reach a mid-point within that he had located during his own wanderings. They ate of the fruit from bush and tree, and Hosteen slept, his head pillowed against Surra's furry side, the soft purring of the cat lulling him into a deeper and more restful slumber than any he had known since he left the plains to begin this wild adventure.

It was dark when Gorgol awakened him, and they went to the hole beneath the rock, which was Surra's private exit from the valley. Baku objected with a scream of anger when Hosteen called her to push through with them, and he had to wheedle her into furling wings and taking a footway. Only his firm statement that he and Surra were leaving not to return and that she would remain alone finally brought the eagle to obey, though fierce clicks of her beak made very plain her opinion of the whole maneuver as they crept back through the crack.

Baku settled on Hosteen's shoulder once they reached the

passage, her eyes like harsh sparks in the light of the torch. Surra took the lead, setting a gliding pace that brought the men to a fast walk.

The cat was retracing the way by which she had brought Hosteen in, but long before they reached the place where Dean had vanished into thin air, Najar uttered an exclamation and caught at the Beast Master's arm.

"Here!" He was looking alertly about him with the air of a man who had come across some landmark. "This is the way—"

Hosteen recalled Surra, and the party turned into a side tunnel, Najar was now leading. To Hosteen, one of these unmarked passages was much like another, but he knew that just as he had been trained and conditioned to be the leader of a team, so had the Reconnaissance scouts been selected, trained, and psycho-indoctrinated for their service as pathfinders and "first-in" men.

Najar displayed no hesitation as he threaded from one way to another and crossed several small caverns with the certainty of one treading a well-defined trail. Then they stood in a hollow space and saw near its roof a slit of light. Najar pointed to that.

"Opening made by a landslide. This place is a natural cave and opens on the mountainside."

Hosteen had his hand on the first hold to climb to that door when he heard an odd cry from Najar. He half turned and saw the other's face illuminated in the torch Gorgol held. The scout was glaring at Hosteen, his eyes pure hate as he flung himself at the Beast Master, the momentum of his body jamming Storm against the cave wall.

The Amerindian strove to roll his head and his shoulders to avoid blows he knew were meant to kill. Then the torchlight snapped off, and they were in the dark.

"You dirty Xik liar!" Najar spat almost in Hosteen's face. "Liar—!"

He was choked off in mid-breath, his body jerked away from Hosteen's. Gasping, holding his arm where one of those nerve deadening blows had landed, the Beast Master leaned limply against the rock. A furred body pressed against his leg. He reached down, took the torch from Surra's mouth, and snapped it on.

Gorgol stood, his arm crooked about Najar's throat, the Terran castaway hugged back to the native's chest, his struggles growing weaker as the Norbie exerted pressure on his windpipe.

"Don't kill him!" Hosteen ordered.

Gorgol's grip loosened. He let the off-worlder collapse against him. He transferred his hold to the other's arms, keeping him upright to confront the man he had attacked.

"Why?" Hosteen asked, rubbing feeling back into his arm.

"You said—settler world—no Xik—war over here—" Najar might be helpless in Gorgol's prisoning hand, but his spirit—and his hate—were unbeaten. "There's a recon-broadcaster out there!"

Hosteen stared at him blankly—not that he doubted Najar's word or now wondered at the other's reaction. A Recon scout had an induced sensitivity to certain beamed waves, a homing device that was implanted in him through surgery and hypnotic conditioning. If Najar had caught a recon-beam, he would not be mistaken. But to Hosteen's knowledge the nearest recon-broadcaster was at Galwadi or the Port. Unless—unless Kelson or some other authority was moving into the Blue!

"I told you the truth," he said. "But—maybe—maybe we're already too late. The Patrol could have been called in."

To the west—there—" Najar's right hand was a compass direction, pointing southwest.

Baku—Hosteen thought the command that sent the eagle up and out into the sky. She soared past the point of their sighting, exulting, in the freedom she had not been able to find in the invisibly roofed valley. And from her came the report he wanted.

There was a party of men, encamped in a hollow, doubtless digging in for protection against the heat of the day. Now Hosteen depended upon Gorgol for advice.

"Can we reach them before the sun is too high?"

The Norbie was uncertain. And Hosteen could give him little help as to distance, though Najar insisted from the strength of the recon-beam the camp could not be farther than five miles. Only, five miles in this broken country for men on foot might be equal to half a day's journey in the plains.

"If these others come into the Blue," Gorgol warned, "then will all of my people unite against them, and there will be no hope of breaking truce between tribe and tribe."

"That is so. But if you go to the clans and I and this one who knows much concerning the evil one go to the settlers, then with our talk we may hold them apart until the war arrows can be hidden and wise heads stand up in council."

Gorgol climbed to the top of the rocky pile hiding the cave entrance, studying a southern route. His fingers moved.

"For me the way is not hard; for you it may be impossible. The choice is yours."

"What about it?" Hosteen asked Najar. "They'll have to hole up during the day. But they'll be moving on. And they have scouts out in this territory or you wouldn't have picked up that beam. And once they enter the big valley, there'll be a fight for sure—one that Dean will win under the present circumstances and that will begin his war."

"What will you do?" Najar counterquestioned.

"Try to reach them before night when they'll move on—"

Perhaps that was the wrong decision; perhaps his place was here, pursuing Dean through the interior burrows. But even if some miracle of luck would put the renegade tech into his hands, there would still be war when the off-world force crossed the line into the Blue.

"You'll never find them unless you follow the beam." Najar rubbed the back of his hand across his mouth.

"I have Baku and Surra," Hosteen replied, though in one way Najar was right. With the Recon scout they could take the quickest and easiest route to that camp, following the broadcast.

Najar hitched the cord of a canteen around his bony shoulder. "We'd better blast if we're going." He circled the rocks and started on.

Hosteen waved a hand at Gorgol, and the Norbie slid down the other side of the rock pile, heading into the valley to find the clansmen who might listen to him if they were not provoked by an invasion.

It was still early enough so that the heat was no more than that of midmorning in the milder season. Hosteen, eying the sun's angle, thought they might squeeze in two or two and a half hours of travel before they would have to lay up. Then they might have another hour—if they were lucky—in the early evening. But the best way was to think only of what lay immediately ahead—first of the next ridge or crevice, then, as the sun burnt higher and patches of shade were few, of the next ten steps, five steps, ahead.

Surra, ranging wider than the men, disappeared, only keeping mental contact with Hosteen. The time came when he asked of her the location of a hiding hole, for the time between their rests grew shorter and the land beyond was as barren and sun-seared as that he had seen through the "window" in the sealed valley wall.

Najar took a quick step farther right.

"The beam—it has doubled its strength! We're either practically on top of them or there's an emergency recall." From their careful, slow plod he broke into a trot, topping a small ravine and dropping into it in a cascade of rocks and earth. At the same time Surra's alert came—she had sighted the camp.

The ravine fed them into a larger break, and there they came upon a halt station such as Norbies and hunters used in the Peaks— a collection of stones heaped over a pit in the earth—in which men could rest during the day in a livable atmosphere. Surra prowled about its circumference and raised her voice in a growl of feline exasperation.

Hosteen hurried on and clawed at the frawn-skin robe wet down with seal seam to close the entrance. A moment later the head and shoulders of a man pushed that aside—Kelson!

"Storm! We knew you were on the way—Baku came in a few minutes ago. Come in, man, come in. And you, Logan—" Then the Peace Officer took a closer look at Hosteen's companion.

"That isn't Logan—"

"No." Hosteen shoved Najar ahead of him through the hole as Kelson retreated to give them passage. Then Surra and finally he dropped in. He stood there allowing his eyes to adjust to the gloom.

The quarters had been chosen well, the scooped out pit leading back into a cave of sorts. Only Hosteen had little time to assess his surroundings, for he was facing Brad Quade.

"Logan—?"

The question Hosteen had been asking himself for what seemed now to be days of time was put into words—and by the one he most dreaded hearing it from. All he had beside the bare fact of their parting on that strange transport device of the caves was Najar's story of the other man who had taken that route but had not come to the installation hall. If Logan were still alive, he was lost somewhere in the tunnels.

"I don't know—"

"You were with him?"

"Yes—for a while—"

"Storm"—Kelson's hand on his shoulder brought him partly around to face the other—"we picked up that com cast from in there, the one you sent."

All Hosteen's frustration, fears, and fatigue boiled over into rage.

"Then why in the name of the Dang Devil are you heading in? Take one step into that valley and the rocket goes up for sure!" He was shaking. The anger in him, against this country, against the odds of ever pulling down Dean, against the tricks of the cave passages he could not hope to master, was eating at him until he wanted to scream out as loudly as Surra did upon occasion. And now the cat snarled from the shadows and Baku voiced a cry, both of them sensitive to his loss of control.

Two hands on his shoulders now forced him down, steadily but gently. He tried to twist out of that grip and discovered that his tired body would not obey him. Then there was a cup at his cracked lips, and he drank thirstily until it was removed.

"Listen, boy, no one is trying to run this through blind. We've scouts in the heights, but they have orders not to go into that Valley. Can you give us some idea of what is going on?" Quade spoke quietly as he settled Hosteen on the floor of their sunhide, moistened a cloth in a milky liquid he had poured from a small container, and with it patted Hosteen's face, throat, and chest. The aromatic scent of the stuff brought with it soothing if fleeting memories of relaxing at the day's end back at the holding.

The younger man was as sobered as if in the heat of his anger he had plunged into an icy stream. And in terse sentences he told them what little he knew, then waved Najar forward to add his part of the tale.

"You're right," Kelson commented when they were done. "Dean is the answer. An unstable tech with a genius-level brain turned loose in a Sealed Cave storehouse—Lord, that could finish Arzor just as quickly as a continental Tri-X bomb!"

"You've called the Patrol in?" Hosteen asked.

"Not officially yet. We've borrowed some trained personnel. Maybe now"—he stood up in the dugout, his hands on his hips, his face flushed with more than the heat of their shelter—"the Council will listen to a little common sense. This country should have been adequately patrolled five, ten years ago."

"Intrusion of treaty rights," Quade reminded.

"Treaty rights! Nobody's suggesting we curtail Norbie treaty rights—at least I'm not, though you'd have a different answer from some of those in the Peaks. No! I want—just as I have always wanted—a local force of Norbie-cum-settler to police the outback. That's what we needed from the first—could have had it last year if you taxpayers had pushed for it. Such a corps would have routed out that Xik gang before they dug in—and they could have stopped this before it even started. You say now this Ukurti is against Dean's war talk and he can carry his clan Chief with him. Well, we could get the good will of natives of that type and their backing. That's not breaking any treaty rights I know of—but no, that's too simple for those soft-sitting Galwadi pets. Now it may be too late. If we are forced to call in the Patrol to handle Dean—"

He did not have to continue. They all knew what that would mean—a loss of settler and Norbie independence, a setting up of off-world control for an indefinite period, the end to native growth, which was their hope for the future.

"How long do we have before the authorities will move?" Hosteen asked.

"How long will Dean hold off on his raids?" Kelson barked. "If our scouts report any parties of warriors leaving the Blue and we don't have the power to stop them—"

"Power," repeated Hosteen softly. "Dean's control in there rests on the fact the natives believe it's true medicine. I think there was a residue of some alien knowledge among the Norbies of the Blue— some of those machines must have been left running. There is certainly weather control in the village valley and the smaller one where Najar hid out. Perhaps the Norbies were able to make use of other devices—we saw the village Drummer pull a trick that certainly never originated on Arzor—without understanding them. Then Dean has activated more, so he's a part of the medicine, which makes him taboo and a man of power—"

"And the answer is—remove Dean?" Kelson speculated.

"Not remove him," Quade cut in, and Hosteen nodded agreement. "That would merely add to the medicine—were he to disappear. And if he is removed bodily and that action discovered, it would be a declaration of war. He has to be removed by those who set him up."

"No chance of that that I can see," Kelson exploded.

"Ukurti's attitude is in our favor," Quade pointed out. "And Dean is unstable. We have to get at him on a ground he believes is safe—"

Hosteen stirred. "In the mountain!"

"That's right—in the mountain."

"It's a tangle of passages. To find him in there, when he knows those interdimension transports and we don't—" Hosteen could see the futility of such a chase, and yet that was their only chance. If they could actually capture Dean, hold him prisoner in the taboo mountain where his native allies would not venture, they would have time to work out a method of unmasking him.

"Najar." Quade spoke to the castaway. "You can find that installation hall?"

"I can try. But as Storm says, that's a mighty big mountain or mountains, and there're a lot of passages. It's easy to get lost—"

"We can take off as soon as it cools this evening," Kelson began briskly.

"*We* take off—you stay here and contact the rest of the force," Quade corrected. "No, don't try to finger me down over this, Jon. You're official, and you can swing weight with those rocket boys back in the lowlands. How much do you think they'd listen to me? I'm just another rider scrabbling up a frawn herd as far as they're concerned. Najar," he asked, "are you willing to give us a trail leading back in there?"

The castaway looked down at the ground. As well as if he had said it aloud, Hosteen could guess what the other wanted to reply, that he had finally won free of the nightmare in which he had been encased since the crash landing in the Blue. Najar had a good chance now of completing that interrupted voyage, of getting home. But he was Terran—for him, too, no home world was waiting. Was it that loss that tipped the scales in their favor?

"All right." He wiped his hands across the tatters that served him as a shirt. "Only I make no promises about finding your man."

"That's understood. Anyway—we can fit you out."

Kelson energetically tackled the packs stored at the back of the sunhide, rummaging through supplies meant to equip a scout post. There were arms to be had, stunners, belt knives, fresh clothing, supplies of energy tablets.

Hosteen slept away most of that day. Since his initial inquiry, Quade had not spoken of Logan, but the thought of him was there, and Logan himself walked through Hosteen's troubled dreams. At nightfull he awoke sweating, from a vivid return to the transport wedge in the valley—from which, in that nightmare, he had seen Logan vanish, knowing that he had no way of following after, the reversal of what had actually happened. And now the Amerindian could not understand his earlier action. When he had had that compulsion to walk the spiral, why had he not called Logan, made the other do likewise? Why had he been so buried in concentrated effort that he had ignored his half-brother? He could find no excuse—none at all.

Baku was left with Kelson, with orders to keep liaison between the scout post and the mountainside. The eagle hated the tunnels, and her particular gifts were useless there. But Surra sped with the party, backtracking the route that had brought them there that morning.

Once again within the cave, Hosteen put his arm about the cat. In his hold he could feel the play of her powerful shoulder muscles. Just as she had known his frustrated anger back in the hide-up, so did she now react to the job ahead. They had a mission and one in which time itself was drawing the war arrow against them.

"Find—find!" He projected a mental picture of Dean, urged it upon Surra with all the clarity and force he could muster.

Hosteen felt as well as heard the deep growl that vibrated through her as might the purr of a more contented moment. He did not know whether her feline hunting sense would bring them any nearer their quarry. Luck—or "medicine"—could still play a part in this blind hunt. Over Surra's body he looked to Najar in an appeal that was also part order.

"Can you guide us to any main passage from here?"

"Most of 'em are main passages as far as I know." The other did not sound optimistic, but he took the lead, and they started on into the heart of the mountain.

Here Surra showed no desire to roam ahead; instead, she matched her pace to Hosteen's as well as four feet could match two. He was alert to her always, relying more upon the cat than upon Najar's ability to bring them into a section where they might hope to encounter

Dean, so he knew instantly when the cat paused, even before she swung half across his path to half him.

Quade, knowing of old how Surra operated, stopped, and Najar looked around, puzzled, and then impatient.

"What's the—?" He had out only half the question when Hosteen signaled him to silence.

Surra's actions were the same as the time when Dean had vanished in that other tunnel. And the Amerindian was certain that this must be another of the mysterious transfer points.

The cat's head was cocked slightly to one side, and her whole stance pictured the act of listening—listening to something their dull human ears could not pick up. Without moving more than his hands, Hosteen switched his torch on to full beam, played that bank of light in a careful sweep over the floor under them and the right wall. But there were no spiral markings such as he had more than half hoped to sight. The beam went to his left and again revealed unmarked surface.

Yet Surra was still listening. Then the cat arose on her hind feet, her muzzle pointed up—as if she scented what she had heard.

Overhead! Not under foot as it had been in the valley, but overhead! Hosteen flashed his torch straight up. But how could that pattern he had come to know be followed upside down?

"That it?" Quade asked.

"Yes. Only I don't see—" Hosteen began, and then suddenly he did. Just as he had been pushed by a compulsion he did not understand to walk the spiral in the valley wedge, so here an order outside of his consciousness brought his hand up over his head to touch the open end of the spiral. Only this time he fought that pull, fought it enough to keep his awareness of those with him.

"I think—" It was hard to speak, to be able to keep his mind off the tracing of that pattern with his finger tips. The urgency to do so was like pain, racing from finger tips to flood his whole body. "We must do this," he said at last.

A furred body pressed against his. Surra! Surra who had no hand to trace for her. To go would be deserting Surra. His other hand groped along that furred back after he passed the torch to Quade.

He could no longer turn his eyes away from that pattern, which glowed in his mind as well as on the stone overhead.

Hosteen thought of the pattern and took a grip on the loose skin at the back of the cat's neck, beginning to walk around and around with the fingers of his other hand tracing the roof spiral he had to go on tiptoe to touch. Surra was following his pull without complaint, around—around—Now! His finger tip was on the dot—

Dark—and the terror of that journey through the dark, the red spark that was Surra and a white-yellow one that was Hosteen Storm in company still—

Light around him. Hosteen put out a hand to steady his body and felt the sleek chill of metal. He was back on the dais of the hall platform while Surra pulled free of his hold and faced down the nearest aisle, her mouth wrinkled in a soundless snarl of menace.

CHAPTER EIGHTEEN

osteen drew his stunner. From the cat came knowledge that his less acute human senses could not supply. Down those rows of machines there was a hunt in progress, and the hunted was friend, not enemy. Gorgol—successful in obtaining allies—penetrating to this center of taboo territory? Or—the Terran's grip on the stunner tightened—Logan at last?

Surra leaped from the platform in a distance-covering bound. Then she glided into cover between two installations as Hosteen followed.

Above the hum of the encased machinery Hosteen thought he heard something else—a ticking, more metallic than the drumbeats of the Norbie tambours. He caught up with Surra where she crouched low, intent upon what lay around a corner. The hair along the big cat's spine was roughened; her big ears were folded against her skull. She spat, and one paw arose as if to slash out.

The thing she stalked was unnatural—not alive by her definition of life. Shadow thing—? No! Hosteen caught sound of that scuttle. Something flashed with super speed, very close to the ground, from one machine base to the next! No—no shadows this time.

He edged past the cat and then side-stepped just in time to avoid the headlong rush of someone alive—alive and human.

"Logan!" Housteen caught at the other, and an unkempt head turned. Lips were pressed tight to teeth in a snarl akin to Surra's.

A spark of recognition broke in the depths of those too bright eyes, a hand pawed at Housteen's, and Logan swayed forward, for a moment resting his body against his brother's, his heavy breathing close to a sob. Only for a moment, then his head lifted, his eyes widened, and he gasped:

"Hosteen! Behind you!"

Surra squalled, struck out at the thing whipping across the pavement, and recoiled as if flung back. It was a glittering silver ribbon with an almost intelligent aura of malignancy about it, from which a tapering end rose and pointed at the men.

"Get it—quick!" Logan cried.

Hosteen pressed stunner firing button. An eye-searing burst of light came from the snake thing as the beam caught it full on.

"You did it!" The younger man's voice held the ragged edge of hysteria.

"What?"

"A live machine—one of the crawlers—"

Logan loosed his grip on Hosteen and tottered to the metal ribbon. A thin tendril of smoke arose as it battered its length senselessly against the floor. Logan stamped once, grinding his boot heel into the thing.

"I've wanted to do that for hours," he informed Hosteen. "There's more of 'em, though—we'll have to watch out. And"—his gaze shifted to the weapon in Hosteen's fist—"where in the name of the Seven Suns did you get that?"

"We've reinforcements." For the first time Hosteen wondered about that. Would Najar and Quade be able to follow him, or was this another time when one of the baffling spiral paths would deposit travelers at different destinations?

"Listen." He pulled Logan away from the feebly quivering "snake." "Back there in the valley—did you walk the spiral path the same way I did?"

"Sure. You just vanished into air—I had to follow."

"Where did you land?"

"In a place I wouldn't have believed existed—after seeing the rest of this demon-inspired hole. All the time we were muckin' around there was a place in here with regular livin' quarters. But I ran into someone there—an off-worlder who has the run of this whole holdin'. For days—seems like days anyway—he's been runnin' me!"

Logan was grimly bitter. "Turned those clockwork snakes loose and left me to it. I slowed up one of 'em with rocks in another cavern like the pen one and pushed one into a river. You took out this one, but there's a pack of 'em—"

"Thief!"

The word boomed out of the air right over their heads, freezing both.

"Hide if you wish." There was condescension in that. "You cannot escape, you know. The crawlers will deliver you to me just as I order. Have you not had enough of running?"

Surra had given no warning. Did Dean have some form of video watching them?

"You waste time in skulking. And a rock—if you have one left—is a poor weapon against this which can deal with a mountain if I so will it."

A bolt of fire flashed over their heads well above the level of the machines.

A rock for a weapon! Then Dean did not know Hosteen had joined Logan! He was not watching them; he was only sure Logan had been hunted into the hall and was hiding out there.

"You would be better advised not to keep me waiting. Either you will come to me now or my pets will be given a full charge and turned loose to use it. You will be given to the count of five to consider the disadvantages of being a dead hero, and then you will come to the platform in this hall. One—two—"

Logan's fingers made sign talk. "I'll go and keep him busy."

"Right. Surra will take the left aisle, I the right. We'll flank you in."

"—three—four—"

Logan walked out into full view of the platform. Two fingers of the hand hanging by his side twitched. Dean was up there waiting.

Hosteen started forward at a pace slightly slower than Logan's. All they had to fear for the present was a sudden appearance of another "snake."

Dean stood with his back to the board, over which rainbow lights ran in tubes. He was plainly pleased with himself. And Hosteen did not doubt he was equipped with a stass bulb or some other alien weapon.

"So the thief does not escape."

"As I told you before, I'm no thief!" Logan retorted with genuine heat. "I was lost here, and I don't know how I got into that room where you found me—"

"Maybe not yet a thief in practice, but in intent, yes. Don't you suppose that I know any man would give years of life to master these secrets. Few ever conceive of such power as this hall holds. I am Lord of Thunder, Master of Lightning in the eyes of the natives—and they are right! This world is mine. It took the combined forces of all twenty solar systems in the Confederacy ten years to put down the Xiks. I was one of the techs sent to study and dismantle their headquarters on Raybo. And we thought we had uncovered secrets then. But they had nothing to compare with the knowledge waiting here. I was chosen to use the teaching tapes stored here, the cramming machines—they were waiting for me, *me* alone, not for stupid little men, ignorant thieves. This is all mine—"

Hosteen quickened pace and checked with Surra by mind touch.

"Why didn't you finish me off with your crawlers or your tame lightin'—if that's the way you feel about it?" Logan was keeping Dean talking. The tech, alone so long, must relish an audience of one of his own race.

"There is plenty of time to finish you off, as you say. I wanted you occupied for a space, kept away from places where you might get into mischief. You could not be allowed to interfere with the plan."

"This plan of yours"—Logan was only a few steps from the platform—"is to take over Arzor and then branch out. Beat the Xiks at their old game."

"Those who built this place"—Dean was fingering a small ball, another stass broadcaster Hosteen believed; otherwise, the Terran could not see that the other was armed—"had an empire into which all the Xik worlds and the Confederacy could both have been fitted and forgotten. All their knowledge—it is here. They foresaw some blasting end—made this into a storehouse—" He flung out his hand.

Hosteen fired the stunner. That ray should have clipped Dean alongside the head, a tricky shot, and it failed. A breath of the beam must have cut close enough to confuse him momentarily but not enough to put him out. Logan launched himself at the man who was staggering, only to crash heavily, completely helpless in stass, as Dean thumbed his control globe.

The tech was standing directly before the board, and Hosteen dared not try a second shot. A ray touching those sensitive bulbs might create havoc. The Terran signaled Surra.

Out of hiding the cat made a great arching leap that brought her up on the platform, facing Dean. Then she struck some invisible barrier and screamed aloud in anger and fear, as she was flattened to the floor.

Pressed back against the board, Dean reached for a lever, and Hosteen made his own move. Surra, striving still to reach her quarry, was aiming forepaw blows at nothing, and her raging actions held the tech's attention as Hosteen jumped to the platform in turn. But he did not advance on Dean.

Instead, his own hand went out to a bank of those small bulbs that studded the boards in bands.

"Try that"—his warning crackled as if his words held the voltage born in the installations about them—"and I move too!"

Dean's head whipped about. He stared with feral eyes at the Amerindian. Hosteen knew that his threat could be an empty one; now he must depend upon what some men termed luck and his own breed knew as "medicine."

"You fool! There's death there!"

"I do not doubt it," Hosteen assured him. "Better dead men here than raiders loosed on the plains and a dead world to follow." Bold words—a part of him hoped he would not have to prove them.

"Release the stass!" Hosteen ordered. If he could only keep Dean alarmed for just a few seconds!

But the tech did not obey. Hosteen moved his hand closer to the row of bulbs. He thought he felt warmth there, perhaps a promise of fire to come. Then Dean hurled the ball out into the aisle.

"Fool! Get away from that—you'll have the mountain down upon us!"

Hosteen dropped his hand to the butt of the stunner. Now he could ray the other into unconsciousness, and their job would be over.

A breath of air, a sound came from behind him. He jerked his head. Two figures appeared out of nowhere on the dais. Hosteen heard Logan call out and felt a lash of burning heat about his upper arms and chest so that the stunner dropped from helpless fingers.

Dean was away, running, dodging behind one of the cased machines, Surra a tawny streak at his back. Hosteen swayed, then recovered his balance on the very edge of the platform. He saw Surra drop, roll helplessly—Dean must have picked up the stass.

Quade passed Hosteen, running toward the spot where the cat lay. But before him was Logan, scrambling on hands and knees. The younger man paused, and then he threw—with the practised wrist snap of a veteran knife man. There was a cry from beyond.

Hosteen was only half aware of the struggle there. The pain in his arm and shoulder was like a living thing eating his quivering flesh. He dropped down and watched Logan and his father drag a wildly struggling Dean into view. And in Logan's hand was the weapon that had brought the tech down, the now blood-stained horn he had taken from the skull found in the pens.

As they returned, the tubing on the board came to life. The waving line of lavender, which had always showed steady color from the first time Hosteen had seen the hall, was deepening in hue, its added flow of energy clearly visible.

Dean stopped struggling abruptly. A new kind of concentration molded his features. In an instant he had dropped his frenzied fight for freedom and become an alert tech faced by a problem in his own field.

"What is it?" Brad Quade demanded.

Dean shrugged impatiently, as if to throw off both question and the hold that kept him from the platform. "I don't know—"

Najar was beside Hosteen, giving the Amerindian a hand up. No, he had not been wrong, for Surra had caught it too—the warning that was a part of the brilliance in that band of light, as well as a part of man and beast who shared another kind of awareness.

"We must get out of here." Hosteen lurched toward the dais.

Logan, Quade, Najar—three pairs of eyes were on him. Surra was already by his side.

"What is it?" This time Brad Quade asked his stepson and not the tech.

"I don't know!" Hosteen made the same answer. "But we have to get out of here and fast." His inner tension was swelling into panic—such as had dogged him in the valley of hunting shadows. Logan moved first.

"All right."

"You call it," Brad Quade added. He jerked Dean along and in a second again had a raving, fighting madman in his hold.

Najar struck, a Commando in-fighting blow, and the tech went limp. On the board that pulsing light was now an angry purple. And more bulbs glowed here and there, taking on a winking life. The yellow of the lightning tree was bubbling, frothing.

They crowded together on the dais, the unconscious Dean held upright between Quade and Najar. Hosteen strove to raise his hands to give the signal that would transport them out of there—and found his right arm stiff, pain holding it in a steel band to his side.

The hum of the running machines, which had always formed a purring undercurrent of sound in the hall, was a hum no longer. More of them must be coming alive.

"Your hands—hold them apart over that line of bulbs." Hosteen croaked out instructions to Logan. "Then bring them together in a fast clap—"

Logan's hands, tinted purple in that awesome light, came together. Then they were spinning out and out—

Before them once more was a patch of day. Hosteen was conscious of Logan's arm about him, of stumbling into the light, of the shuffle of feet behind.

Sound—it was not the rising hum of the alien machines but drums, a steady beat—beat of them in chorus. And over all lay the terrible need to be in the open.

They came out on that ledge where Hosteen had lain to watch Dean harangue the Norbie tribesmen. Hosteen pulled ahead, following Surra, for in the cat as well as in him was that bursting need to be away from the cave entrance.

There was no sun, and Hosteen, coming more to himself as he led the way downslope, saw now the clouds gathering in purple-black lines around an irregular space of sky. Had it been five months earlier or later, he would have said one of the terrible cloudbursts of the Wet Time was about to break.

Logan came to a halt. Surra was just a pace or so in advance, crouched belly to earth, her tail swishing, her head pointing at the line of Drummers.

They were there, every one of those who had followed their clan and tribal chieftains into the Blue—strung out in a curving line facing upslope, equidistant from each other, and each pounding out that emphatic beat that was one in a queer way with the billowing clouds. Directly before the party from the cave was Ukurti. And drawn up several yards behind the medicine men were the warriors, serried ranks of them, with here and there a truce pole still showing.

Quade and Najar, with Dean held between them, then Hosteen and Logan—five off-world men facing a thousand or more Norbies. Had the natives come to rescue their Lord of Thunder from the impious? Logan, still propping up Hosteen, brought his other hand before him and moved fingers in the peace sign.

Not an eye blinked nor did a hand lose a fraction of the beat. Seconds became the longest minute Hosteen could remember, while that roll of sound deadened his thinking. Quade and Najar dropped their hold on Dean as if hypnotized. The tech took one stiff step forward, then another. With a set expression on his face, he was heading for Ukurti. Hosteen strove to make some move to stop the other and found that it was impossible.

But Dean had come to a halt once more. He spoke—but the sounds from his lips this time were not the trilling Norbie speech.

"Go—go—" One hand went to his throat, fingers rubbing skin, seeking the band he was not wearing now.

Ukurti's hand on an upswing remained in the air, though his fellows continued to drum. He signed slowly, and Logan, Quade, and Hosteen read his message aloud, though why they did so was beyond their comprehension.

"We-Who-Can-Drum-Thunder under the power have drummed so—and thunder will answer, as will the fire from the sky. Stop this with your own power if you can, Lord of False Lightning."

There was no mistaking the challenge delivered, not as a matter of defiance but as a pronouncement of a judge in court.

The purple-black of the clouds spread, eating up the sky, and now there were flashes of light along the circumference. Dean swayed back and forth, his fingers still rubbing frantically at his throat.

Magic—yes, this was magic of a sort, magic such as the Old Ones of Hosteen's own people had believed in and sought to use. He shook free of Logan, a racing excitement filling him. He forgot the pain of his hurt and could have shouted aloud in a feeling of triumph.

Save for the flashes of true lightning, it was night-dark. And always the drums continued to summon the storm with their power. A weird blue glow crept along rocky outcrops and made candles at the tips of tree and bush branches.

Then—just as Dean had lashed his machine-born lightning about the mountain, using it as a warning and a weapon—so did the real storm-based fire strike square behind them on the very crest of the peak. The answering shock was that of an earthquake, part of the violence young worlds knew before man arose to walk their lands.

Hosteen raised himself from the ground. He was deaf, blind, aware that some giant blow had struck close. And about him was the smell of ozone, the crisp of vegetation changed in an instant into ash.

The black of the storm clouds faded to gray. How long had he lain there? Beside him Logan stirred and sat up. Quade moved toward them on hands and knees. Najar lay where he was, moaning softly.

Downslope lay a form that did not move, and over that loomed a cloaked Drummer—Ukurti. The Norbie's head was lifted. He regarded the four men levelly, and then his hand was raised, his long forefinger pointed up and away behind them. Almost as one they shifted about to see.

Where the ledge of the cave had been was a mass of rock scored and fire-blackened. And the mountain top had an odd, crumpled appearance.

Ukurti's fingers spoke. "The power has decided—Drum power against that of the hidden ancient ones. As the power has wrought, so let it be."

He turned to walk down into the valley, and before him the wave of Norbie clansmen receded. Najar got to his feet and stumbled down to view the body.

"Dean's dead—looks like the lightning got him."

"So be it," Quade said slowly, and he spoke for them all. "As Ukurti says, some power has spoken. The Lord of Thunder is dead. And this is no place for us—"

The mountain was now sealed again. Would the off-world authorities seek to reopen it for its secrets, wondered Hosteen as Quade steered him down the valley. Somehow he thought it would be a long time, if ever, before any man would tempt the retribution of the lightning power again. The "brains" might have some fancy explanation for what had happened—such as that some process inherent in the alien machines had drawn the offseason storm. But he was one in belief with Ukurti—there were powers and powers, and sometimes such met in battle. The power he could understand best had won this time. And out of that victory could come more than one kind of good, perhaps a more permanent truce between warring tribes—even Kelson's dream of the security force of Norbies and humans working together. At least there would be no Lord of Thunder to lay his lash on Arzor—and perhaps to the stars beyond.

ABOUT THE AUTHOR

ANDRE NORTON, named a Grand Master by the Science Fiction Writers of America and awarded a Life Achievement World Fantasy Award, is the author of more than one hundred novels of science fiction and fantasy adventure. Beloved by millions of readers the world over, she has thrilled generations with such series as Beast Master, the Time Traders, the Solar Queen, the Witch World, Central Control, Forerunner, and others. She has also written hundreds of short stories.

Miss Norton's first novel was published in 1934; in the decades since, whether writing as "Andrew North" or Andre Norton, her writing and her gracious willingness to share her experience and knowledge with young writers have inspired countless authors active in the field today.

She lives in Murfreesboro, Tennessee. Visit her Web site at www.andre-norton.org.